Mary Helen Allies

Pius the Seventh

1800-1823

Mary Helen Allies

Pius the Seventh
1800-1823

ISBN/EAN: 9783741157875

Manufactured in Europe, USA, Canada, Australia, Japa

Cover: Foto ©Raphael Reischuk / pixelio.de

Manufactured and distributed by brebook publishing software
(www.brebook.com)

Mary Helen Allies

Pius the Seventh

PIUS THE SEVENTH

Imprimatur.

HERBERTUS CARDINALIS VAUGHAN,

Archiepiscopus Westmonasteriensis.

Die 1 Nov., 1896.

PIUS THE SEVENTH

1800—1823

BY

MARY H. ALLIES

LONDON : BURNS & OATES, Limited
NEW YORK, CINCINNATI, CHICAGO : BENZIGER BROTHERS
1897

CONTENTS

PIUS THE SEVENTH

CHAPTER I

ELECTION OF BARNABA CHIARAMONTI

1800

THE Revolution of 1789, which has been called the French Revolution, but which was in fact a universal revolution, began its operations on the ideas, the customs, laws, and government of nations before it took to itself flesh and blood by outward acts. The causes leading up to it were at work long before the raging torrent swept over society, leaving behind it a vast and dreary waste of doubt and destruction.

The eighteenth century, culminating in that awful crisis, still clamours for its Catholic Gibbon. The philosophy of its history lies hidden to the superficial eye, and the average historian of results rather than of causes, is content to deal with the outcome, which was in reality the logical consequence of events. He points out tottering thrones, and a chaos well-nigh universal, for there was one exception to the general instability; but he does not attempt an explanation.

A

The weakening of the Christian spirit in the world
was typified beforehand in the selfish action of European cabinets.   The great Catholic powers, in particular, had ceased to be Catholic in spirit.   Jansenism
and Gallicanism had sapped the heart out of France,
and carried their destructions far beyond French
boundaries.   They counted as partisans certain ministers of kings: Manuel de Roda in Spain, Pombal in
Portugal, Tanucci at Naples, Kaunitz in Austria, and
everywhere the enemies of the Jesuits.   Catholic
powers had clamoured for the suppression of the
Society, and forced the Pope's hand.   Clement XIV.
had listened to their solicitations in order to prevent
greater evils, the outward apostasy possibly of those
who inwardly were no longer Christian.   The suppression of the Jesuits led to wide secularisation in
the education of youth, and to the predominance of
the secular spirit.   The Holy See, the protector of
all authority, lost its body-guard when the devoted
Society of Jesus was dispersed.   The morality of a
region may not seldom be gauged by the presence or
absence of Jesuits.   Even Rome has had its apostle.
Catholic Europe never needed Jesuits more than
when it called out for their suppression.

After 1773, existing evils were strengthened.
Lawlessness grew apace, and the men who had said
non serviam to the Church now said it to the State.
No party had said it with greater effect than the
Jansenists.   Their bitter dislike of Jesuits had been
founded on a true instinct.   The Society of Jesus

had detected the venom of their heresy and laid it
bare. Their boasted severity ended in fearful laxity,
because if Jansenist saints were " pure as angels, they
were proud as demons." The purity which comes
of pride does not stand. The dynamiters of the eighteenth century may not have worked with absolute
certainty as to the upheaving they were preparing.
They looked for a crowned head whom they might dupe
and lead, and found him in the chief of the Holy
Roman Empire. Joseph II. was all that philosophy
in its alliance with revolt could desire. He tolerated
any form of religion whilst singling the true religion
out for persecution, and making liberty of conscience
his war-cry. It may be surmised that Vienna—as
Rome in the days of St. Philip—needed an apostle,
otherwise Joseph's policy could never have taken
effect. The situation was prepared to his hand. He
found co-operators amongst the clergy and the magistracy ; he had at his side the infidel Kaunitz, the
Pombal of Austria. Josephism was a struggle to
combine Catholicism with Gallican principles, an
attempt on the sovereign's part to unite in his own
person the spiritual and the temporal power. He
aimed at cutting off all appeal to Rome, and at exercising supremacy in the wide arena comprised between
the nomination of bishops and the precise number of
candles required for Benediction. Frederick of Prussia
ironically called him " Mon frère le sacristain ! " But
he did not stay in the sacristy. He attacked Catholic
education, the rights of bishops, religious orders, and

Christian marriage by sanctioning divorce. After publishing, in 1781, an edict of universal tolerance, he soon made it felt that the Pope alone was excluded, and naturally, because there was no room for the Pope in his system. The seminaries which he set up in the great centres of the Empire were imperial rather than ecclesiastical. He carried on and strengthened the worldly traditions of the prince-bishop. In the name of universal tolerance he confiscated the revenues of religious houses, made the reception of novices illegal, forbade his bishops to have any intercourse with Rome. Yet Joseph II. lived to have his own arms used against himself, and to accuse Belgium of his premature death. Catholic Belgium, then a part of his hereditary states, broke out in insurrection on the suppression of Louvain University, and on the appointment of a Jansenist, Stoegger, as director of theology at the new General Seminary. Joseph II. appealed to Pius VI. to recall his subjects to loyalty, and he did not appeal in vain. It was the year 1790: the days were evil, and the reigning Pontiff, reigning by his spiritual power, too poor himself to help his afflicted children, raised his voice willingly to remind the Belgians of their allegiance. Joseph II. founded his tradition and finally unmade Catholic Germany. A few years later the generosity of Pius VI. was forgotten, and ill requited by Austria to Pius VII., whilst the climax of ignominy was reached when the proud house of Hapsburg consented to give a daughter to Napoleon.

Pius VI. expired at Valence on August 29th, 1799; and if ever the darkness of Calvary could be seen and felt, it was in that hour. The Pontiff who had gone to his rest was worn out with the strife. Men and events had conspired against him, and made his pontificate a weariness and an anguish. He had contemplated the different phases of the French Revolution, its hideous deeds, followed by universal insecurity. The thrones which it left standing expected to fall: they existed, as it were, in fear of the shock that would wrench them from their foundations. The despotism of *Liberté, Egalité*, and *Fraternité* had fallen with grip of iron on the Holy See, despoiled it of its patrimony, and banished the Pope to die in penury and exile at Valence. Amongst its feats of destruction, the Revolution now flattered itself that it had annihilated the Papacy. The Temporal Power was gone, and the Chair of Peter, if it had not been founded on the Rock, would have been swept away. At no time was authority more needed than when the storm of human passions, let loose over the world, burst asunder every social breakwater. The sagacity of Pitt saw not only the evil, but also the remedy. The Bishop of Arras, a French emigrant, had an interview, in 1794, with the English Premier, and wrote an account of it to Cardinal de Bernis. "Mr. Pitt," he says, "expressed a deep and sincere admiration for the vigour of the Court of Rome"—a purely spiritual vigour, be it noted, in 1794. The revolutionary torrent was only to be stemmed by Europe armed for the combat. A coalition of its sovereigns would serve as a dyke, and the Pope alone would furnish a common bond. He alone could speak with an impartial voice. In fact, Pitt suggested no more nor less than that a Papal Bull should be despatched to Catholic courts by legates *a latere*, announcing war to anarchy. "If," he said, "the Pope consented to the Bull, and what he called this 'holy war,' an English fleet should be sent to protect the Roman States."[1]

Pitt's scheme was carried out, though not in the way which he contemplated. Bonaparte, the most brilliant son of the Revolution, stemmed anarchy by the exaltation of himself. His was no "impartial voice," to speak peace to nations, neither did his "holy war"—the restoration of religion—cover all his plan of campaign. When his own fortunes had reached a giddy pinnacle, his fall contributed to the lost European equilibrium, and replaced the Pope in his natural place.

The Popes who suffer most reign longest. Pius VI. had nearly reached the years of Peter when the end came at Valence. Successive acts of hostility on the part of the French marked the last years of his pontificate. Forced to submit to the violation and confiscation of his territory, Pius VI. signed, in February 1797, a treaty with the French Republic, to the following effect. He revoked all treaties contrary to the French alliance, acknowledged the Republic, and declared himself to be at peace, and on a peaceful footing

---

[1] Crétineau Joly: *L'Église Romaine en face de la Révolution*, t. I. p. 189.

with it. He ceded to it all his rights to the Comtat
Venaissin; abandoned to the Cispadane Republic the
Legations of Bologna and Ferrara and the province of
Romagna. The city and important fortress of Ancona
remained in the power of France till the general
peace. The two provinces of the duchy of Urbino
and Macerata, invaded by a French army, were restored to the Pope on payment of fifteen million
francs. The same sum was to be paid according to
the armistice of Bologna, which was still unexecuted.
The thirty millions were payable, two-thirds in money
and one-third in diamonds or other precious stones.
The Pope was called upon besides to provide eight
hundred cavalry horses and eight hundred draught
horses, buffaloes, and other productions of Church
territory. He was to disclaim the assassination of
Basseville, and cause three hundred thousand francs
to be paid to the heirs of the victim and to those
who had been injured by his violent death. All
works of art and manuscripts ceded to France by
the armistice of Bologna were to be immediately
transferred to Paris.[1]

Another assassination served as a pretext for open
war against the Temporal Sovereignty. Duphot, a
hot-headed republican, who stirred up the Romans
to revolt and revolution, fell in a popular riot, and
this was the signal for the consummation, the French
invasion and occupation of the Eternal City, under
General Berthier, in February 1798. The Papal

[1] Thiers: *Histoire de la Révolution*, t. iv. p. 76.

Government was declared at an end, and the Roman
Republic proclaimed in its stead. A French guard
replaced the Swiss round the person of the Pope, who
was directed to retire into Tuscany. He answered the
commands in fearless words. "I am prepared," he said,
"for every species of disgrace. As Supreme Pontiff, I
am resolved to die in the exercise of all my powers."

The scene of dispossession which followed was the
Revolution in action. The person of the Pope was
not spared. He was "dragged from the altar in his
palace, his repositories all ransacked and plundered,
the rings even torn from his fingers, the whole effects
in the Vatican and Quirinal inventoried and seized,"
and he himself conducted, by scoffing and sacrilegious French dragoons, into exile. The French
Government would not suffer him to remain in Tuscany. They feared the influence which he exercised,
and ordered him across the Alps. Multitudes flocked
to see him as he passed, so that in the midst of his
sorrows tears of emotion were frequently in his eyes.
"Verily I say unto you, I have not seen such faith,
no, not in Israel," he would say, in the words of our
Lord.[1]

Pain, fatigue, and brutal treatment shortened the
life which was too long for the impatience of the
French Directory. With great difficulty, Pius VI.
reached Valence—to die.

The last months of 1799 passed in vacancy of the
Apostolic See. Human wickedness seems to frus-

[1] Alison: "History of Europe," iii. 653.

trate Divine goodness, and, with the experiences of the decade 1790—1800 before their minds, it is conceivable that temptation to faithful Catholics may have come in the form of the perplexing doubt, "Where now is God to find a man after His own heart, and how?"

. The Directory had not long survived its treatment of the Holy Father. Bonaparte founded the tradition of *coups d'état*, and in November 1799 (18th brumaire) he became First Consul of the Republic.[1] Slowly and surely he was embodying the huge and unwieldy impersonality called the French Revolution. The events of brumaire 1799 were all-sufficing to those concerned, and France had no part in repairing the breach which it had helped to make by hurrying the Pope to exile and death.

It was a characteristic sign of the times that Russia, England, and Turkey, in conjunction with Austria, facilitated the Conclave which opened on November 30th, 1799, in the Benedictine monastery of the little island of St. George at Venice. It was composed of thirty-five Cardinals out of the whole number, forty-six; and the Roman prelate, Consalvi, who had received the dying wishes of Pius VI., was naturally designated as secretary. The German Emperor defrayed the expenses of the Conclave. For a long time the votes were divided between Cardinals Bellisoni and Mattei. Austria opposed Bellisoni, being specially anxious to secure a Pope who would favour its continued possession of the

―――――――――
[1] Capefigue: *L'Europe sous Napoléon*, ii. 268.

three Legations.   However, Austria's interested foresight, which represented rather the tendencies of the German Cabinet than the personal sentiments of the Emperor Francis, was baffled in the ultimate result of the Conclave.   On the 14th March 1800, the new Pontiff was proclaimed to the world.   He was emphatically not the man suggested by human wisdom, unless simplicity, guilelessness, and holiness of life can best cope with the forces of this world.

Barnaba Chiaramonti was born at Cesena, in 1742, of an illustrious family.   His mother was a Ghini, and a woman of remarkable sanctity.   In 1763 she became a Carmelite at Fano, where her memory was long cherished, and it was there that she foretold to Barnaba both his election and the suffering he would have to undergo.   It seems that only the opposition of the son, who dreaded nepotism, prevented the beatification of the mother.   At the age of sixteen Barnaba entered the Benedictine monastery of Sta. Maria del Monte, near Cesena, as a novice, and took the name of Gregory.   On the accession of Clement XIV. in 1769, the young man, who was anxious to witness the Benediction from the *loggia*, leapt up behind an empty carriage.   The coachman, far from resenting the intrusion, greeted him with the singular words : "My dear little monk, why are you so anxious to see a function which one day will fall to your lot ?"[1]

When Pius VI. became Pope, Dom Chiaramonti

[1] Wiseman: "Recollections of the Four Last Popes."

held the office of Professor of Theology in the Benedictine convent of San Calisto. As a kind of compensation to him for some shabby treatment from his fellow-monks, Gregorio received the title of *abbate*, which signified that he had a right to certain privileges, the ring and mitre amongst others, without, however, power of jurisdiction. From *abbate*, the future Pope rose to the dignity of bishop, and finally, in 1785, to that of cardinal. He governed successively the dioceses of Tivoli and Imola. It was at Imola, in 1798, in the midst of the trouble and alarm caused by the French invasion of Rome and the Papal States, that Cardinal Chiaramonti published a homily which was remembered at the moment of his election to the See of Peter. The object of this homily was possibly to prevent a popular insurrection in favour of Pius VI., whose cause it would have injured.

The triple crown was set upon the brow of Cardinal Chiaramonti in the church of the monastery of St. George, and not at St. Mark's, the faithful Venetians incurring all the expenses of the coronation. He took with it the name of Pius, out of gratitude to the memory of Pius VI. The tiara unites temporal to spiritual sovereignty. It was, however, in absolute destitution that the new Pontiff entered on his inheritance and confronted the power in possession—the Revolution—which was soon to be personified and crowned in one man. The conduct and policy of Austria became palpable after the event. Though dead, Joseph II. was still speaking in the ignoble

tradition which he had founded in Catholic Austria.
Before the result of the Conclave became known, fear
and hope lurked in the German Cabinet.   It had left
no means untried to secure the election of a Pope
willing to further its views upon the three Legations
(Romagna, Bologna, and Ferrara), and the states in Lombardy ceded by the French Republic.   Now that the
Conclave had been ruled by a higher power, and had
freely chosen as Pope Cardinal Chiaramonti, Austria
would at least abstain from compromising itself by
sanctioning publicly the Temporal Power.   Bonaparte's
arms were achieving fresh victories every day and
destroying old boundaries.   Who could say whether
he would not blot out the Papal States from the map
of Europe ?   This being far from an impossible hypothesis, it was absolutely necessary to give no official
recognition of the new Pope as a temporal sovereign.
At the time that Austria was acting this selfish part,
the troops of the King of Naples occupied Rome;
the administration was carried on in the name of
Ferdinand, and remodelled after that of Naples. Fully
acquainted with Austria's designs upon the Eternal
City, the Neapolitans professed to be guarding Rome
for its true sovereign.   In the face of present difficulties, Austria resorted to compromises. Cardinal Chiaramonti had been no politician ; for many years he had
lived as a simple Benedictine monk, yet a character
naturally upright and straightforward is sometimes no
bad match for the wiliest diplomatist. A pressing
invitation to go to Vienna was sent to Pius VII., to-

gether with a demand that he would choose a certain
Cardinal Flangini as his Secretary of State. This
Cardinal was a Venetian, consequently a subject of
his Imperial Majesty. In vain Cardinal Herzan, who
had been Austria's envoy in the Conclave, urged
upon Pius VII. the importance of this journey, and
the good that might follow for the Church. The
Pontiff refused with that gentle firmness which formed
the principal trait in his character, and constituted
his peculiar charm. Time pressed, and he yearned
for his Roman people. Every Pope has the instinct
of Rome in his heart: it is his true home, even
when fickle Romans make it a thorny one, or when
crowned Revolution forces him to become a prisoner
in his own palace. As to a Secretary of State, the
request was strange, since, as Pius VII. remarked, he
owned no State. But to avoid taking a creature of the
Emperor's, he continued to employ as Pro-Secretary the
secretary of the Conclavi, Hercules Consalvi, who is to
play so great a part in this pontificate. Only at Rome,
free from all undue influence, would the Pope nominate
his chief officers. Austria could gain nothing.

As a last resource, Vienna bethought itself of an
extraordinary ambassador, who should go to the Pope
duly primed by de Thugut, the successor to some
extent at the Austrian Court of the policy and work
of Kaunitz. The Marquis Ghislieri was the chosen
man. He communicated his orders to Consalvi, as
Pro-Secretary of State. The German Emperor would
magnanimously cede to the Pope the territory in

Lombardy recently won by the Imperial arms, but he would keep the three Legations. He required, moreover, that the Pope should agree to the spoliation of his own territory. Consalvi, although he guessed instinctively the intentions of Austria, was astonished beyond measure at the shameless way in which they were specified. He answered that he would act conformably to the orders of His Holiness, though persuaded that Pius VII. would never consent to the transaction.[1] Surely enough the answer was as negative as Consalvi had expected it to be. Then it was that Ghislieri somewhat relented. The Emperor, his master, would keep only two Legations, and would cede the third, that of Romagna, to the Pope. This was positively Austria's last word, and Ghislieri, not content with his high-flown conditions, passed to threats. Pope Pius took no account of them, but caused an official letter to be written from the Pro-Secretary to Baron de Thugut, and himself penned two letters, one to the Emperor, the other to his minister, in which he set forth his rights to the invaded provinces. Neither ever received an answer, for reasons which may be shrewdly guessed. Consalvi supposes that Thugut intercepted the Papal letter, and that he made all applications to the Emperor in this question an impossibility. However this may be, it seems pretty certain that the spoliation of the Pope was to be attributed rather to the manœuvring of the minister than to the will of the

[1] d'Haussonville : *L'Église Romaine et le Premier Empire*, t. l. pp. 39, 40.

master.[1]   The Pope continued to demand justice from
Ghislieri ; and one day, wearied with the ambassador's
importunity, he made this prophetic speech : " Since
the Emperor obstinately refused a restitution which
both religion and justice required, he (the Pope)
knew not what more he could allege, as he had
exhausted the most pressing arguments.   Nevertheless, let his Majesty look to himself, and be careful
not to place in his wardrobe clothes not belonging
to him, but to the Church.   He would not enjoy
them.   On the contrary, they might introduce rust,
and thus spoil his own clothes, that is, his hereditary
states."   Ghislieri could hardly contain his anger,
but he vented his feelings to Consalvi.   " The new
Pontiff," he said, " is young in the trade ; he proves
that he knows nothing of the power of Austria.   Very
great events would be requisite before the hereditary
states could be touched."

These *very great events* were nearer than could have
been supposed.   It was then the end of May, and on
the 14th of June 1800, the battle of Marengo was
fought, which decided the fate of Italy, and, we may
add, of Austria.

In the meantime, Pius VII. expressed his wish and
determination to go to Rome.   Austria felt that the
desire carried out would not further its interests.
Following the natural overland route, the Pope would
have to traverse two at least of the three Legations ;
but they were disputed territory.   The Catholic feel-

1 *Mémoires de Consalvi*, t. i. p. 282.

ings of the population were apprehended; yet how forbid demonstrations of loyalty towards the Successor of Peter ?   There was only one course open to Austria, and Austria did not scruple to follow it.   The Vicar of Christ was embarked in the *Bellona*, a wretched frigate, lacking in the most ordinary comfort, with a crew too few to manage a vessel, even if they had been skilful, whereas they were quite incapable. The *Bellona* landed at Pesaro, a place with no port, but with the advantage of not being situated in the Legations.   Here, with four cardinals, Consalvi, and a few other prelates, Pius VII. passed twelve days, instead of twenty-four hours, in very close quarters with Ghislieri, who, by way of doing the honours of the *Bellona*, was in reality his gaoler.   At Ancona, news of the battle of Marengo, with its tremendous consequences for Austria, startled them both.   In truth, the "rust" had lost no time in working havoc in the Emperor's wardrobe.   In one day Austria was doomed to lose, not only the stolen goods, but even part of its hereditary states, by the cession to France of Liguria, Lombardy, and the country as far as the Adige.   Yet more.   A few years later, in 1804, when Bonaparte's victorious arms enabled him to crown himself Emperor of the French, the chief of the Hapsburgs ceased to be Emperor of Germany.[1]   Emperor of Austria was henceforth his title, and the Holy Roman Empire, with the glories of a thousand years, was at an end.

[1] Cantù: *Storia Universale*, 19, p. 62.

Under these circumstances, Ghislieri could no longer
have any objection to the lawful restitution of the
Papal territory, and at Foligno he notified his forced
agreement to the Holy Father.   Naples, through interested policy, was moving in the same direction.
All things considered, the Pope was a pleasanter
neighbour than Austria, whose close vicinity might
become dangerous.   Until the Peace of Florence,
which was concluded some months after the return
to Rome of Pius VII., Neapolitan troops continued
to occupy Rome and Terracina.   The Sovereign Pontiff entered Rome on the 3rd of July 1800, in the
midst of universal joy, and his first act in his own
city was to visit the shrine of St. Peter.   Nominally,
he was a temporal sovereign.   The rising star of
France had taken away from Austria the power mis-
used against the Church, and, as a more striking
humiliation, the power had gone whilst the will to
harm remained.   Naples, with a keen eye to its own
interests, had preferred the neighbourhood of the Pope
as a lesser evil.   It did not, therefore, seem likely
that, in the trials and struggles of his temporal sovereignty, Pius VII. would find auxiliaries in the Catholic
powers.   Self-seeking blinded them, whilst the states-
manship of Pitt made him desirous of coalition under
the auspices of the Pope.   Tacitly he recognised the
axiom that the entire independence of the Holy Father
is only to be attained by the possession of a territory
" large enough for liberty, too small for domination." [1]

[1] Lacordaire : *Quatrième Conférence de Notre Dame de Paris*, t. l.

CHAPTER II

Now that Pius VII. was in Rome, his natural home, his most obvious duty was to strengthen his Government by the choice of an able minister. None appeared to unite greater qualifications for the post of Secretary of State than Hercules Consalvi, the Secretary of the Conclave, who had had a great share in the election of Cardinal Chiaramonti. This prelate, hitherto, to use his own expression, only a "pro," was confirmed in his appointment on the Pope's coming to Rome, and created a cardinal deacon. The very fact of his being a "pro" at all had been a middle course adopted by Pius VII. to avoid, in a matter of extreme importance, obeying the imperious dictates of Austria.

Many things might be said of Consalvi, and it would be hard to speak too favourably of one who, in times so perilous and critical, was so completely the man of the situation. Indeed, to know Pius VII. fully, we must also study his Secretary of State, for the sympathy which existed between the Pope and his minister constituted one of those very rare friendships that traverse the vicissitudes of time entirely uninfluenced by external causes of temporary discord or misunderstanding. They had, as a German proverb says, "one soul in two bodies." What was the bond of union between them? Mutual attraction, and love of the Church, no doubt, but more than this—the one completed the other. By nature and by his early vocation the Pope tended to disbelieve in the proverbial degeneracy of the human race. He would have liked to think men better than they are. Consalvi, on the contrary, was a man of the world in the sense that he had a very considerable knowledge of men and of things. A few words as to the antecedents of the "great Cardinal" will not be out of place in this history. He was born in 1757. Brunacci, not Consalvi, had been the name of his family, and this was not unimportant. Good birth makes life easier, even for geniuses, and the Consalvis, though enjoying a certain position, did not belong to the Roman nobility. His grandfather, a Brunacci, had changed his name on inheriting the fortune of a Consalvi, to whom he was related. Cardinal Consalvi did not tell the world at large that he came of an old stock. It was popularly supposed that he was of new blood. Educated at Frascati, he turned his thoughts to the prelature and made it his career, without, however, taking Orders. He occupied several posts in the household of Pius VI., until, in 1792, he became Auditor of the Rota. This last appointment led on of itself in due time to the Cardinalate. Pius VI., who had laughingly promised Consalvi that he should be employed rather in diplomacy than in material administration,[1] could not, in the face of the Revolution, act up to his assurance. The Auditor of the Rota suddenly became Minister of War at the disastrous period of the French Revolution. In his official capacity he was unfortunately implicated in Duphot's assassination, or rather was punished for an event in which he had had no part, by a temporary imprisonment in the citadel of Sant' Angelo. His strong sympathies as a Roman and a Catholic made him an object of jealousy to the French Government, who transferred him from place to place. His one desire was to soothe the anxious moments of the Holy Father, his sovereign, then a prisoner at the Florence Certosa. He did, indeed, as we have said, contrive to see Pius VI. and obtain his instructions for the Sacred College, which, with his last blessing, constituted all the testamentary riches of the Pontiff. Truly, Consalvi seems to have gloried in honouring fallen causes with a disinterestedness as noble as it is rare. The last of the Stuarts, the Cardinal of York, acted as his patron; but only on one condition would Consalvi become his executor. He required that he should receive no benefit from the Cardinal's will. In his Memoirs he particularly insists on his conduct in refusing gifts. A ring, he says, presented by a friend, is all that he would consent to accept.[2] But the man so jealous of his reputation, so averse to currying favour for himself, possessed a magic charm of attraction which few could withstand, and employed

---

[1] "*Al tavolino e non in bottega.*"   [2] *Mémoires*, t. ii. p. 112.

it, be it said to his glory, in the service of the Catholic Church. The attraction which he exercised was allied to true independence and nobility of character, and thus a rare union of strength and sweetness. He has been called the " Roman charmer," and his gift of stealing into the caskets and strong boxes of human hearts compared to a fragrant and all-pervading perfume. His natural characteristics adapted him admirably for the task of throwing oil on the troubled waters.

The first few months of Consalvi's administration were, as he tells us himself, full of anxieties, arising from the reformatory measures which he set on foot. Two departments claimed his special attention—the state of trade and the state of the coinage. His introduction of free trade into the Papal States was far from acceptable to Cardinal Camerlingo Braschi, who was a loser by the new system. Justice and economy made it a necessity. The Papal treasury was exhausted with contributions levied upon it, the loss of provinces, and the abolition of paper money (cedole); while the common and pressing actual needs absorbed the small state revenue. All these causes prevented the sale of provisions under cost price. Free trade would put a stop to certain privileges, prerogatives, rights, and consequently abuses, for the rights of the few are wont to be the wrongs of the many. Cardinal Braschi, who presided over the old system and superintended the transmission of licences for purchase of grain for exportation, and even for circulation in the state, did not submit with a very good grace to the new order. By his tact and kindness Consalvi ultimately succeeded in winning back the affection of one whose alienation, as the nephew of Pius VI., would have been keenly felt.

The second administrative reform was directed to the suppression of bad money, which had become current in the Papal States. Six Roman scudi had fallen to the value of three in good coin. It cost the Government of Pius VII. fifteen hundred thousand scudi to restore the currency, and the measure, as affecting the prosperity of his subjects, met with the Holy Father's warm approval.[1]

At Rome the sovereign and the minister were employing their energies for the public weal, whilst the eyes of Europe were fixed upon one man, in whose policy a notable change was displayed after the battle of Marengo. Victorious over Austria, Bonaparte set himself to win public opinion by making advances to the representatives of religion. At this stage of his career his one aim was to impose his own cause on the multitude as that of the Church, therefore he posed before the French people as its patron and defender. He concentrated in himself the wayward energies of revolution. To the long-sightedness of genius he added a will of iron. He saw the distant bourne of universal empire, and set out for it without a moment's hesitation. Highwaymen, thieves, murderers on the road would not have daunted him; neither did the Church. He would

---

[1] Artaud de Montor : *Histoire de Pie VII.*, t. l. p. 114.

not·"lose the kingdom of France for the sake of a Mass." Reorganising public worship was a necessary part of his scheme, and he accepted it in this spirit as means to an end. To the mass of the Catholic French people, spiritually famished as they had been, he meant to be the great man who would take away the interdict of revolution and reopen the sanctuary.

Bonaparte was leading his victorious troops across the Alps in May 1800, as Pius VII. announced his accession to all the bishops of the universal Church. In Egypt he had flattered Mussulman vanity by speaking of our Lord and Mahomet in pretty nearly the same terms;[1] at Milan he ordered a *Te Deum* in thanksgiving for the deliverance of Italy from heretics and infidels. This was an allusion to the assistance which the subjects of the Great Turk and those of his Britannic Majesty had lent to Austria. We find in an address to the clergy of Milan a sketch of the future Concordat. "My intention," Bonaparte says, "is that the Christian, Catholic, and Roman religion be maintained in all its purity, practised publicly, and that it may enjoy this freedom with the same extensive, entire, and inviolable liberty as at the time of my first visit to these smiling countries. . . . France, having acquired experience through its misfortunes, has awakened to a true knowledge of the state of the case, and now sees in the Catholic religion an unfailing support, which alone can tranquillise internal

---

[1] *Mémoires de Napoléon*, part concerning Egyptian Campaign, dictated to General Bertrand.

struggles, and save her from being swept away. . . .
When I am able to confer with the Pope, I shall, I
hope, succeed in levelling all obstacles in the way of
an entire reconciliation between France and the Head
of the Church." [1]

Bonaparte, craving a blessing for his victorious
arms in the Ambrosian Cathedral, presented a striking spectacle to Italians. He had still more at heart
the edification, through report, of the French. He
sent his good deeds before him; the fame of his
doings for religion in Italy crossed the Alps, and
prepared the way for the great Concordat. Shortly
after the Milan address, the First Consul charged
Cardinal Martiniani to inform Pius VII. of his wish
to open preliminary negotiations for the arrangement
of religious matters, and to ask that Spina, Archbishop of Corinth *in partibus*, might be sent to him
as an envoy from the Court of Rome.

In all his dealings with the Church, Bonaparte
kept his purpose of personal empire steadily in view.
For the first time on this occasion Consalvi became
aware of something artificial in Bonaparte's behaviour.

Spina, who had had orders to confer with the First
Consul at Turin, suddenly received a summons to
Paris. A Papal envoy soliciting an audience amongst
the crowd of petitioners at the Tuileries would produce a magical effect, as Bonaparte reasoned in his
worldly wisdom. Spina, arming himself with the
presence and assistance of a consummate theologian,

---

[1] *L'Église Romaine et le Premier Empire*, t. i. pp. 65, 66.

Father Caselli, General of the Servites, reached Paris about the middle of July 1800. The Revolution, in the person of the First Consul, was nearly ripe for crowning, and this is how he proceeded. He was surrounded by men whom he used; for although he made a pretence of consulting them, he was his own counsellor throughout, and he fully intended to dominate the pending negotiations with the Holy See. The Minister of Foreign Affairs, M. de Talleyrand, ex-Bishop of Autun, was frequently consulted in questions touching upon the conciliation of the old with the new *régime*. But in this matter de Talleyrand might have shown one of two dispositions—either great hostility to the Church which he had publicly left, or excessive servility, in order to obtain a formal secularisation. Bonaparte was quite shrewd enough to feel the force of this, and even the ex-bishop half guessed it, and restricted himself quietly to the official exercise of his charge, asking no questions. But the presence of other persons was absolutely necessary for the form of the thing, however little for the substance ; and Bonaparte consequently selected the best Gallicans he could find in his Council of State, Bigot de Préameneu, Portalis, and Cretet. M. Bigot, especially, possessed a conscience which Gallicanism had endowed with elasticity for all future dealings with the Holy See. He is a very fair specimen of the autocrat French magistrate, who, in the seventeenth and eighteenth centuries, legislated, if he could, for both Church and State. La Bruyère said a *dévot* was "*celui qui sous un roi athée serait athée,*" and the words might be applied to the Gallican, only the individual was far better than his religion.   In all, however, Erastianism was strong, and M. Bigot gave undoubted proofs of Gallican vigour during his official career.

To Bigot, Portalis, and Cretet, the First Consul adjoined the Abbé Bernier, who was to represent the ecclesiastical element.   A man of shifting views, he was one of those who could be easily led if allowed the pleasant delusion that he himself was leading others.   The antecedents of the future Bishop of Orleans did not bear witness to an excess of loyalty. Bonaparte had made his acquaintance in Brittany before the last Italian campaign.   Bernier was then a curé, with immense popular influence, desiring nothing so much as notoriety.   The fusion of the Republican generals with the Catholic clergy of La Vendée seemed to open out the way to the goal he coveted.   He betrayed his secret soul when he said, in a letter of December 1799, "Talk of me and get others to talk, that my name may become known."

In the eyes of the Republican Government he was a priest belonging to the old *régime* by birth and education, but to the new order of things by his sympathies.   However this may be, he was playing into the hands of both parties, making a pretence on the one side of leaving the Royalists, and on the other seeking to ingratiate himself with the emigrant princes, from whom he asked and received confidence.   In 1800 he seems to have gone over entirely to Bonaparte, and to have found grace with the First Consul. It was less a question of pleasing than of suiting, and it was Bonaparte's way to make use of men, and to choose only those whom he could lead. It must be acknowledged that if he had honestly consented to be counselled in the matter of the Concordat, Bernier was not the priest Catholic instincts would have chosen.

In the meantime, Spina, whose mission in going to Paris had been to hear and to report (*con ordine di sentire e di riferire*), found himself engaged in a very difficult matter. He complained that everything was changed in France. One particular form of religion had become a thing and notion of the past. Either the drafts of a Concordat proposed to him by the First Consul were impossible, and totally contrary to the most fundamental principles of religion, or those which he himself found less objectionable were rejected by the Court of Rome. At this moment of wearisome uncertainty, M. Cacault, an envoy from the First Consul, without, however, the character or title of ambassador, arrived in Rome to treat with the Holy See. Consalvi laconically says of him, "that he had an admirable knowledge of customs, men, and things in the Court of Rome." He was a frank, honest, large-minded Breton, a "corrected Republican," and he soon won for himself the esteem and affection of Pius VII. and the Sacred College. With Cacault for negotiator, Consalvi hoped Rome and Paris might soon come to an understanding, but Bonaparte intended to finish the matter by a stroke of his own policy and an abrupt conclusion, which nobody expected. He now required the acceptance of the last projected Concordat, which Pope and Cardinals had judged contrary to the principles and honour of the Holy See. If it was not signed without alteration five days after this intimation, he would withdraw Cacault, and declare all negotiations at an end. Under these trying circumstances the French envoy suggested a middle course, which was that Consalvi should start immediately for Paris and treat personally with Bonaparte. The Roman charmer, in his capacity of Prime Minister to Pius VII., would be irresistible. What food for the vanity of the First Consul! Cacault seized the thing at once in all its bearings. The Pope hesitated. . "Most Holy Father," urged Cacault, " Consalvi must start at once : he must be the bearer of your reply. He will negotiate in Paris with the power you give him here. I am fifty-nine years old, and have seen many things since the *États de Bretagne*, which were beyond a doubt the most unmanageable of *États*. Take my word, something stronger than cold-blooded reason, an instinct, prompts me to speak—a foolish instinct, if you will, but a sure one. In sending Consalvi, you appear as it were yourself. People wish for a religious Concordat. Here it is."

The opposition of Pius VII. was conquered. It had become a question of clearing himself in the eyes of the First Consul from a charge of obstinacy and personal ill-will, whereas duty alone had prompted his conduct, and his constant refusal to bend to terms injurious and dishonourable to the Holy See.

Cacault's orders to leave Rome were peremptory, though his absence was a temporary one. As far as Florence he and Consalvi travelled together. The Cardinal knew what he was doing, and where he was going. He expressed his secret conviction to the King of Naples: "The good of religion requires a victim. I am going to see the First Consul. I am walking to martyrdom. The will of God be done." [1]

It will be seen how far the Cardinal's presentiment was verified.

[1] *L'Église Romaine et le Premier Empire,* t. i. p. 90.

CHAPTER III

TWO CARDINALS

1801–2

THE object of Consalvi's journey to Paris in the summer of 1801 was to bring his personal influence to bear upon the First Consul, and to make a Concordat possible. Bonaparte required the support of the Church, and for this reason was prepared to lend his strong arm to the cause of religion. He was guided by no motive of charity to souls, and his Christian faith, if he ever had any, was swamped by his ambition. He meant to reign, and the undoubted power he possessed had fostered the notion, fed by both men and circumstances, that it was his call. Not even Bonaparte could have two masters: the dream of power and empire inebriated him to the total extinction of the Christian life or the Christian virtues. A kindred spirit[1] speaks with some enthusiasm of Bonaparte's scanty religious creed. Under the starry firmament in the park at La Malmaison, he who believed in no outward form of religion professed his conviction in the

---

[1] It may be interesting to relate M. Thiers' admission, it cannot be called a confession of faith, to the late Cardinal Manning. The Cardinal put him the question, "Etes-vous croyant, Monsieur?" "Oui, je crois en Dieu," was Thiers' reply.

existence of God. If M. Thiers was right, Bonaparte
had thrown away the precious inheritance of the
Catholic faith, after tasting the pure joy of a good
First Communion, and he now satisfied himself with
groping after an "unknown God." Certainly his conduct during his brilliant years of fortune does not
suggest a Christian basis or mode of thought. It was
only when adversity covered him with a premature
shroud at St. Helena, that he remembered the faith
of his First Communion. It will be seen, therefore,
what little importance Bonaparte attached to the due
restoration of the Catholic religion in all its purity.
To him the Concordat was merely a stepping-stone to
empire. It was far otherwise with Pius VII., who,
as the Chief of Christians, cherished as the apple of
his eye, at once integrity of dogma and the interests
of living souls. The different attitude of the Pope and
the First Consul is apparent throughout: Pius VII.
was prepared to make all possible concessions con-
sistent with his conscience, and even, if necessary,
to sacrifice individuals. Bonaparte, on the contrary,
trading on the Holy Father's absolute sincerity,
wrenched from him all that he could, fairly or
unfairly, and sacrificed the good of religion and of
souls to himself, and what he considered his own
interests.

In a few words the Concordat may be said to have
represented to the Holy Father the restoration of
religion, the total extinction of schism, and the deposition of the constitutional clergy. After declaring

the Catholic religion to be that of the great majority
of the French people, it re-established the Hierarchy
in France on a new footing. The Holy Father was
called upon to depose the emigrant bishops who had
borne the burden and heat of the day, and perhaps in
their estimation to pass for a Pontiff more anxious to
ingratiate himself with the First Consul than to reward the well-tried fidelity of sons. Pius VII. was
the single Pope who used this prerogative of the Holy
See, and invited a whole hierarchy to retire from the
Episcopate. The admirable men who listened to his
voice never gave a greater proof of pastoral spirit;
they spoke victory in their obedience. A very small
minority declined to resign, and saddened the Holy
Father by the schism of the *Petite Église.*

The twenty-three metropolitan churches were reduced to ten, and the one hundred and twenty-five
episcopal sees to fifty.[1] The French Hierarchy, drawn,
as it had been, almost exclusively from the higher
classes, had stood with noble fortitude the fiery trial
of the Revolution. Six pastors had died violent
deaths, whilst the rest had gone into exile, had
known want, and every kind of suffering. Some in
their poverty had been obliged to appeal to Pius VI,
who in his own distress never turned a deaf ear to
their sorrows.[2] The Concordat placed the nomination
of bishops in the hands of the First Consul, and their

[1] Le P. Armand Jean : *Les Archévêques et Évêques de France,* t. i. ;
Avant Propos, viii.
[2] Theiner : *Affaires Religieuses de la France,* i. p. 425, &c.

confirmation as usual in those of the Pope. It required a promise of submission from them to the established Government. The clergy were to be supported by the State, and the Church to renounce all alienated possessions. This was the substance of the convention now under consideration, and to carry it out, Consalvi needed other requirements than personal charm. The very first article, which concerned the public exercise of the Catholic religion, gave rise to a hot dispute, and Bonaparte was loath to part with the Constitutional bishops. Outwardly he appeared to have yielded the point that they should not be appointed to the new dioceses, but it was with the secret resolution to take back, at whatever price it might be, that which he had granted. Submission always bore for him the semblance of weakness. During Consalvi's sojourn in Paris, the First Consul affected indifference as to the ultimate success of the Concordat, when in point of fact it was a matter of the very greatest consequence to him, and he knew it, to act as the restorer of religion in France.

After a fatiguing journey of fifteen days, Cardinal Consalvi arrived in Paris, and joined Spina and the theologian, Caselli. At that time the Revolution still displayed its ensigns abroad, and held possession of the places once sacred to God's worship. Catholic churches were dedicated to Friendship, Commerce, Fraternity, Liberty, as the case might be ; whilst every one, even Consalvi himself, was addressed as *citoyen*. The Abbé Bernier, Bonaparte's man of business in the

affair of the Concordat, hastened to visit the Cardinal,
and told him when and how he would be admitted to
see the First Consul. "I was to go at two o'clock
that very afternoon," Consalvi says, "*le plus en Cardinal que je pourrais.*" Having arrived on the previous
night only, he was thus hurried to the Tuileries, with
the dust and fatigue of travel about him. He reflected, however, that a cardinal appears before the
Pope alone in full dress, and contented himself with
scarlet stockings, biretta, and collar, as adequate
indications of his rank. At the appointed time the
Master of Ceremonies came to take the Cardinal to
the Tuileries, and he was ushered into a room on the
ground floor called the ambassadors' 'room, a silent
nook of the palace, where he waited several minutes
quite alone. There was a design in this. The bustle
and turmoil of a brilliant Court were to break suddenly
as a bewildering vision upon eyes unprepared for
grandeur. He was directed by the Master of Ceremonies to open a little door leading to the great stair-
case of the palace, on doing which he likens his
surprise to the astonishment produced at a theatre by
the sudden transformation of the scene "from a
cottage, a wood, or a prison, to the most splendid
and dazzling royal pomp."[1] Through a bevy of states-
men, senators, dignitaries of the household, ministers,
generals, and an immense crowd of troops and idle
spectators, the astonished Cardinal passed to an interview with the man who judged others by himself. He

[1] *Mémoires,* t. i. p. 329.

hoped to overawe the Roman plenipotentiary. Consalvi could hardly believe that his first audience was to be a public one. He imagined, therefore, in his ignorance, that the crowd had been attracted to witness his presentation, whereas it was *jour de parade*, a formality renewed every fortnight at the Tuileries. Conducted at length by M. de Talleyrand to the culminating point of display, he innocently hoped that he was going to be alone with the First Consul. Not at all. A room filled with an immense number of people, arranged as if for effect, opened before him. There were the Senate, the Tribunate, the Legislative body, and the higher magistracy, surrounded by generals, officers of all kinds, and dignitaries of every degree; and, lastly, three persons standing by themselves in a marked position—the three Consuls of the French Republic.

Bonaparte, who held the place of honour in the middle, left the Cardinal no time to speak, but began immediately in a tone neither affable nor the reverse, "I know what brings you to France. I wish the negotiations to begin at once. I give you five days, and I warn you that, if at the end of the fifth day matters are not arranged, you must return to Rome. In that case, I have already determined on my own course."

Bonaparte wished before all things to convey that he had no need of Rome. However, both his pomp and his threat were lost upon the Cardinal, and, quick to perceive it, he was inclined to be favourably

impressed by Consalvi, with whom he conversed for
more than half-an-hour on matters connected with
the Concordat.   An abrupt nod from the First Consul
brought the interview to a close, and Consalvi to the
hard work urged upon him, without a moment's delay,
by Bonaparte's imperious commands.   The Cardinal
sacrificed his time and rest in order that he might not
sacrifice the honour of the Church, should it be at
stake, as he too plainly foresaw.

He spent one whole night over a memoir which
was to justify the Holy Father's refusal of the former
scheme submitted by the French Government. Points
of minor importance might be conceded, but principles, he urged, were sacred.   He did not convince,
and M. de Talleyrand's report of the memoir only
served to foster Bonaparte's notion that Consalvi bore
personal ill-will to the French Government.   ·

The conferences took place at the Cardinal's hotel.
Instead of five, they lasted twenty-five days, during
which he worked in common with Spina and Caselli,
and received a daily visit from Bernier. They were
laborious days, full, too, of intense anxiety. In the
difficulties that arose, Bernier would decide nothing
without having recourse to the First Consul, but
when Consalvi would have wished for the same
liberty on his side, he was told that a plenipotentiary was capable of acting upon his own responsibility. The orders of Pius VII. sustained his minister
through this delicate negotiation, and carried him
over the shoals and quicksands of Bonaparte's diplo-

macy. Other influences, too, were at work with the prince of the Church. The Austrian and Spanish ministers entreated him to conclude the Concordat almost at any price. "Their pressure," Consalvi says, "only served to confirm me in the determination which the Pope's orders imposed upon me, namely, that I should neither break off negotiations nor refuse the Concordat, because the latter is not as favourable as it might have been, but that I should not conclude it by going further than my instructions."

When the First Consul called upon the Pope to depose from eighty to a hundred bishops, he was asking for a great and most unusual sacrifice, yet all that he would concede was that the Pope should word the Brief of Deposition. Consalvi's herculean labours could obtain no more, though he had been absolutely firm in matters involving principle. Bonaparte knew it well, and was determined to regain by stratagem the ground which the firmness of Hercules had won. He bided his time.

At length, on the 13th of July 1801, the Abbé Bernier reported that the First Consul accepted all the points under discussion, and was prepared to ratify the Concordat. Three persons were to sign for Pius VII.—Consalvi, Spina, and Caselli—and three for the French Government—the *citoyen* Joseph Bonaparte, brother of the First Consul, Bernier, and Cretet. At the suggestion of Bernier they adjourned to Joseph's house, as a more fitting place to witness

so important a consummation. Bernier arrived at
four o'clock with a roll of paper in his hand, which,
he said, was the Concordat, but did not unfold. When
the Cardinal claimed the right of signing first, this
roll of paper was produced, and Bernier seemed
anxious that Consalvi should sign it at once, and
without examination. The glance which he cast
over the very first lines revealed the stratagem. This
was not only the plan rejected by the Holy Father,
but it also contained other points which Rome had
condemned absolutely. "The proceeding speaks for
itself,"[1] is Consalvi's comment. It was Bonaparte's
reply to Consalvi's unflinching fidelity to principles.
The Cardinal was painfully surprised. His signature
to the document would have been a calamity, which
his prudence had averted. Between the storm of
anger which was to be expected from the First
Consul, and Consalvi's inflexibility, only one course
remained. It was necessary to reopen discussions
without losing a moment, for on the following day,
July 14th, Bonaparte intended to proclaim the signing of the Concordat at a grand patriotic dinner of
over three hundred guests. This meeting, imposed
by Bonaparte's fraud, lasted from 4 P.M. till four the
following afternoon, that is, twenty-four hours con-
secutively. The servants and carriages waited at the
door through the summer night, and then through
the day. The hours ran on, and only at four o'clock
was the new document ready. One point, however,

[1] *Mémoires*, t. i. p. 355.

surpassed the plenipotential powers of Consalvi. In order not to disappoint the First Consul, he would sign all the rest, and refer that point to the Holy Father.

In the meantime, five o'clock was the hour fixed for the dinner, and Consalvi, with Spina and Caselli, were bound to appear. The Cardinal was greeted by a burst of anger from the First Consul.

"As soon as he saw me," writes Consalvi, he called out in a mocking tone: "'So you wish to break with me, Monsieur le Cardinal! Well, be it so! I have no need of Rome. I can act by myself. I have no need of the Pope! If Henry VIII., without the twentieth part of my power, was able successfully to change the religion of his country, how much more have not I the same power and will? Rome shall feel the losses she has caused; she shall mourn over them, but it will be too late. You may go; indeed, it is the best thing you can do. By your own will you have broken off negotiations with me. Well, be it so, since you wish it! When will you go?'"[1]

Consalvi met this angry outburst with perfect calmness and self-possession. Principle was at stake, he replied, therefore why urge an impossible concession? why treat honourable and conscientious resistance as obstinacy? At last Bonaparte agreed to a new discussion, only he insisted that the article under dispute should stand as it was. It was Con-

[1] *Mémoires*, t. i. pp. 365, 366.

salvi's aim to make the Catholic Faith as independent
as possible of the secular power, and to protect the
Church from being tied hand and foot by the State.
Rome looked upon the liberty and publicity of Catholic
worship as the two pivots of the Concordat. Against
this point the Government set the objections of the
non-Catholic—it should have said, the irreligious,
population.   The liberty and publicity in question,
it argued, would be contrary to the universal equality
proclaimed by the Constitution. Consalvi knew what
to expect of tolerance. Joseph II. had been a liberal
sovereign, tolerating every form of religious opinion
except the true religion. The proposed article ran :
" Worship shall be public, but conformable to the
regulations of the police." This phrase, in which
religion was handed over to the police, justly appeared
to Consalvi inadmissible in the Concordat. Spina
and Caselli were weary of resisting, and agreed to
sign the article. Consalvi, who preferred an open
rupture to unlawful conditions, pursued the fight
alone and unaided. Once more the discussion opened
at Joseph Bonaparte's hotel, and the sitting this time
lasted twelve hours, from midday to midnight. The
article was finally settled by defining the terms of
the restriction. In the phrase " conformable to the
regulations of the police," the Government intimated
that it had only public order and security in view,
and no design upon the free action of the Church.
Joseph proposed to carry the Concordat signed to
the First Consul. The negotiators hoped to obtain

his consent when he found the great step had been already taken, and his brother seemed the most fitting person to bear the brunt of his possible wrath. Bonaparte greeted Joseph's information by tearing the minute of the treaty into a hundred pieces, and declaring that he could not accept it at any price. However, this was his ordinary manner of meeting another's initiative. He yielded at last, or seemed to yield, and Joseph was able to bear the good tidings to the Cardinal. The publication of the Concordat would legalise the practice of the Catholic Faith, and so far Bonaparte was an instrument for great things. His arm restored the fallen altars and removed the ban of outlawry. The general public, who at best only suspected his "stepping-stone to fame," were overjoyed at the happy termination of negotiations.

Consalvi had accomplished the object of his mission, and was eager to return to Rome, where his duties as Prime Minister could ill afford to wait for him. Before leaving Paris he had two significant audiences with Bonaparte. To the first, a private one, he was called unexpectedly, and did not at once perceive the drift of the First Consul. Many points foreign to the Concordat were discussed, and at length, as if by accident, Bonaparte revealed his secret mind. He was much embarrassed, he said, at having to choose the new bishops from the Constitutional as well as the non-Constitutional clergy. This was a blow to Consalvi. The principal aim of the Holy See in conceding so much had been to secure the total extinction of schism. Bonaparte had far more regard for his own policy than for religion. These nominations, Consalvi urged, would be a scandal, and no Constitutional priest could be accepted without retracting his errors. The First Consul wished before all things to conciliate the body, who represented a strong party, and it was a matter of very small importance to him whether they were perfectly orthodox or not. He considered it an indignity that they should be called upon publicly to acknowledge the Holy See's decision with regard to the Civil Constitution. In vain Consalvi suggested that they should not be nominated at all. Bonaparte, after promising again and again to give them up, now manifestly intended to do nothing of the kind.

The second audience was a diplomatic reception at which Consalvi held the first rank. Bonaparte, however, wished to show the public that he made no account of either the Cardinal or the Holy See when once they had served his purpose, and therefore he did not once speak to Consalvi. Purposely, as it seemed to the Cardinal, he avoided any display of the most ordinary courtesy, and purposely, too, engaged in a long conversation upon indifferent topics with Cobentzel, the Austrian ambassador, who was standing near. He only looked at Consalvi.[1]

Just as the Cardinal was getting into the carriage which was to take him away, Bonaparte played his last stroke. Bernier appeared, saying that the First

---

[1] *Mémoires*, t. i. p. 394.

Consul wished positively to know what the Bull would contain, which, according to custom, would be published with the Concordat. A Bull is not the mechanical work of a few hours, nor was he authorised to compose it. Neither was the time seasonable for propounding the gravest questions. "The First Consul hoped to surprise me in the hurry of leave-taking," says the Cardinal in his memoirs; "he hoped in this way to prevent the insertion in the Bull of certain things he did not quite like." [1]

With the understanding that the Concordat was now ready for the Pope's ratification, Consalvi used the greatest speed on his journey, stopping only three times on the road—at Lyons, Milan, and Parma. Pius VII. had a warm welcome for his minister, and the Cardinals met immediately in Consistory to discuss the Concordat. Two points alone raised some difficulty—the publicity of worship, and the promise of the Church not to claim alienated possessions. The Holy Father, after listening attentively to the Sacred College, spoke last. The liberty of the Church, he said, was not respected as much as he could wish, still, under the circumstances, it was useless to hope for better terms. He therefore ratified what had been done. The proverbial slowness of Rome was not apparent on this occasion. Thirty-five days after the signing of the Concordat a special courier took to Paris the official approval of the Holy See.

After the signing in Paris of the Concordat, and

[1] *Mémoires*, t. i. p. 95.

before its publication, Bonaparte was anxious to have the presence of a legate who should countenance him in his scheme for modifying certain points laid down by Consalvi. He and his shadow, the Abbé Bernier, considered them quite too exacting. The man he singled out was Cardinal Caprara, and the choice proved his keen observation of character. Caprara had been Papal Nuncio at Vienna under Joseph II. and Kaunitz, and had managed to remain on good terms with both Emperor and Minister—a fact which in itself excited the suspicions of Rome. His line with the secular power had been one of weak concession and compromise, nevertheless he had remained perfectly orthodox in his convictions. He was wanting in courage, not in faith, and did not perceive that courage was just what was necessary in dealing with Bonaparte. "We must," he said, "at all costs, keep on our legs : if there is a fall we shall never get up again." The method of "keeping on his legs" that he adopted was sanctioning many things which Rome would have wished him never to sanction. With good intentions, he often acted without consulting the Pope, sometimes, indeed, against the orders he had received from Rome. That which he thus effected could not be undone, and the Holy Father's remonstrances were of no avail.[1] Caprara was evidently far from being the right man in the right place. The First Consul charmed and awed him at the same time, and the Cardinal took the kindness of his wel-

---

[1] *Mémoires*, t. i. p. 405.

come as a personal compliment. He had not Consalvi's penetration, and failed to see that no one could be more charming than Bonaparte when he had something to gain. On this occasion, the nomination of Constitutional bishops was the object which made him gracious to the Papal Legate. The Pope, whose rule of conduct it was to gratify Bonaparte in all things lawful, could easily foresee what he had to expect from Caprara.

Before leaving Rome, Caprara was charged by Pius VII. to bear two points specially in mind. The Cardinal was to throw all the weight of his authority against the Constitutional bishops—a matter the Holy Father took most seriously to heart. In the second place, he was to prepare the way for the restoration of the three Legations. Bonaparte had made up his mind on both subjects. It pleased him, however, to lock it up until he could enforce it with authority, and to flatter the hopes of the Holy Father, neither granting nor refusing what he asked. Caprara's entry into Paris is a revelation in itself of Bonaparte's tactics. It took place by night in a sort of incognito, which was an expedient of the First Consul's to prevent any noisy demonstrations.

Caprara arrived in Paris on October 4th, 1801. It was with the Cardinal Legate as it had been with Consalvi. The iron will, which had so soon and naturally learnt to carry all before it, had recourse to the same devices—stormy interviews at unwonted hours, and compulsory measures for disarming conscience. The threat, "If you refuse me what I ask, I will do without your consent, and break with Rome," filled with terror the legate who wished above all things, as he said, " to keep on his legs." Men were not wanting to predict a kind of universal deluge if he should really come to a rupture with Bonaparte, so that to his somewhat feeble mind the choice may have often seemed to lie between two evils, and his only course to be in taking the lesser. In a word, it may sometimes happen that the situation is more vicious than the individual.

Caprara's official correspondence to Consalvi may be summed up in a few words. The Cardinal and the First Consul were badly matched : the Church was weak, and the State was a man of surpassing genius. Bonaparte charmed and awed whilst ·he wrung unlawful concessions from the legate. Principle and moral obstacle were mere words to the First Consul, and he treated those who urged them as obstinate, or bearing personal ill-will towards himself. In the petty war carried on against a weak Papal legate, Portalis, Councillor of State, and Bernier, the intriguing Abbé, played an important part. Portalis was a conscientious Catholic in many respects, but Gallicanism had given him a religious twist, that is, a tendency to see in the State something more than it is. Early education and prejudices were, perhaps, to blame, that his mind did not embrace the prerogatives of the Holy See in all their plenitude. Caprara wrote to Consalvi on March 13th, 1802, -that not a single Constitutional priest was on the list for nomination. A few days later he began to entertain doubts on the subject, for the First Consul required a formal declaration from him as to whether or not the Constitutional clergy could be nominated. At this stage of the question, the Peace of Amiens was signed, and Bonaparte determined that the legate's scruples should not long stand in the way of the solemn *Te Deum* at Notre Dame, which, thus connected with great national events, would more surely appeal to the general public.

A single interview between Caprara, Portalis, and Bernier will illustrate Bonaparte's immutable fidelity to his violent tactics. At five o'clock one afternoon, the Councillor of State and the *ci-devant* Vendéen curé waited upon the legate. Portalis opened the conversation by declaring that at the approaching *Te Deum* the First Consul would make use of both Constitutional and non-Constitutional clergy. The Cardinal remonstrated vehemently against the announcement. But, represented Portalis, a refusal on his part would undo all the good accomplished, and serve to prolong the schism. Caprara thought that non-compliance with an impossible order ought to produce nothing of the kind. "Ah!" exclaimed the minister, "you don't know him (Bonaparte), or you pretend not to know him. He wishes to have a large gathering of clergy at the *Te Deum*, iu order that the ceremony may be a great success."

Portalis had no time to lose, as the answer was required before seven o'clock. The legate replied with firmness, "that if he could once be sure that principles

would be respected, he would willingly listen to reason-
able proposals, but that nobody could wish to force
him to do what was against his conscience, and
directly opposed to his duty." So far, so good. But,
now, it was Bernier's turn to step forward. He had
foreseen the Cardinal's resistance, and, to shorten
matters, had concerted with Portalis a proper answer
to the First Consul. Thereupon, he drew a paper
from his pocket, which contained, he said, "nothing
offensive to the legate's feelings or his duty." This
memorandum propounded in substance five propositions which Caprara had already refused to sign when
submitted to him by Portalis on a former occasion. Now
he was wearied by the talk, which was just what the
others had expected and counted upon, and he followed
his usual reasoning that it was gain all or lose all.
He therefore replied to Bernier: " You have had time
to examine the memorandum. If you can give me
your word in conscience that it contains nothing contrary to our just demands, I see no reason why I should
not sign it, and return it to you signed, simply to avoid
a greater evil, which you both say is at hand."

So it was that Caprara gave his name to the deed
which Bonaparte needed as a preliminary to the
nomination of the Constitutional clergy. They now
possessed in it an official attestation that Rome did
not deny their fitness for the episcopal dignity.[1]

Very superficial knowledge must Caprara have had

---

[1] Weiss : *Lehrbuch der Weltgeschichte*, ix. 1030 ; *L'Église Romaine et
le Premier Empire*, t. i. pp. 185-191.

of the First Consul, if he imagined that he could with impunity in their mutual dealings sign a deed in the dark. Three days after this preconcerted interview, the Cardinal legate learned from Bonaparte that ten bishops, two of the number being archbishops, were to be nominated from the Constitutional clergy. It was "this or nothing." Caprara, whose remonstrances were vain, would at least, he said, submit the Constitutional priests elected to a severe examination. But in point of fact he took upon himself to acquiesce in their nomination. The Holy Father's instructions had been positive, limiting his powers to admitting the schismatic clergy to lay communion. The Pope had never consented that the Constitutional bishops should be re-established in their episcopal functions; the extent of indulgence, as far as they were concerned, was to consist in reconciling them with the Church.

With Bonaparte, more than any other man, the line of concession was fatal. Firmness got the better of him, difficult as he made it; and in his heart he respected only those who resisted his demands, when unlawful. Caprara then agreed, though with impotent tears, to confirm the new Constitutional bishops, but he stipulated that they should first make an act of submission to the Holy See. When they met at the legate's house, they positively and unanimously refused to subscribe the formula drawn up by him to that effect. Instead of it they chose to sign a letter composed by Bonaparte, Portalis, and Bernier. On Palm Sunday, Caprara had installed Monseigneur Belloy,

the new Archbishop of Paris, at Notre Dame, and consecrated Monseigneur Cambacérès for Rouen, Bernier
for Orleans, and Pancemont for Vannes.   The following Friday, that is, Good Friday, the new Bishop of
Orleans paid him an important visit.   The preparations for the *Te Deum* on Easter Sunday were all
suspended, and the only course open to the legate, if
he wished to see them reopened, was to accept the
letter to Rome proposed by the Constitutional bishops.
Caprara's trouble and perplexity were extreme.   He
hoped each concession was the last, instead of which
one led to another.   Now he humbled himself, and
his office of legate, so far as to go the length urged by
Bernier, though he made a condition.   He required
that the submission to Rome of the Constitutional
bishops should be published through the press, and that
the bishops-elect should, in presence of Monseigneur
Bernier and Monseigneur de Pancemont, explicitly con-
fess their participation in schism, and renounce their
former errors.   The newly consecrated bishops deceived
the Cardinal, and gave him to understand that the Constitutional bishops had made their submission to Rome
with tears in their eyes, and had sincerely retracted
their errors in their own presence.   The truth really
was that a few days later the Constitutional bishops
were boasting not only that they had persisted in their
opinion, but also that they had indignantly torn up the
schedule of the proposed letter to Rome.[1]   Napoleon's

---

[1] *Correspondance de Napoléon I.*, t. vii. p. 269 ; t. viii. p. 99 ; and
L'Église Romaine et le Premier Empire, tom. i. p. 205.

correspondence has a light to throw on the unworthy behaviour of Bernier and Pancemont. It contains an order to Talleyrand to pay 30,000 francs to Monseigneur Bernier "as a subsidy for the entertainment of the legate," and 50,000 francs to Monseigneur Pancemont, as secretly as possible. All obstacles to the proclamation of the Concordat were thus ignobly swept away.

The morning of Easter Sunday, April 18th, 1802, dawned brightly with its double promise of resurrection for France. Splendid preparations were on foot at the Tuileries. The gala carriages of the old Court were in requisition, and when filled with ladies in full dress, and with brilliant uniforms, the scene may well have taken the bystanders back some twelve or fifteen years. The Bonaparte family played a semi-royal part in the pageant, and Madame Bonaparte's circle already formed the nucleus of the future imperial court. From eight o'clock in the morning M. Réal, Prefect of Police, accompanied by his civil officers, was on parade, proclaiming the articles of the Concordat through the city. At eleven o'clock the Cardinal legate in his scarlet robes, followed by the new archbishops and bishops, entered the Cathedral of Notre Dame. Bonaparte's victorious sword had stemmed democracy, and he now lent it to the outward exaltation of religion, more with a view to what that restored religion would profit him than what he could profit it. His generals alone showed disaffection to his proceedings, and could scarcely be induced to attend the solemn function. A device of Berthier,

Minister of the War Department, was successful. He invited them to breakfast, and they all went from his house to the Tuileries, which they reached just as the cortège was setting out. Bonaparte had commanded their attendance, but he could not command their piety. Their behaviour in the great cathedral was that of protesting heathens. Bonaparte was stern and self-contained. His attitude expressed neither recollection nor piety, and the announcement conveyed to Rome by Caprara, and too easily believed, that he meant to perform his Easter duties, was a pure fable.[1] During the banquet which followed the ceremony, Bonaparte was amiability itself to Caprara. " You see Rome is safe now," he said. " The solemnity of to-day is inspiring. More could not have been done in favour of a creed which we wish to proclaim as dominant." Yet it was Bonaparte, not the Church, who was dominant.[2]

Soon after the festivities of the Concordat another concession was wrung from the Cardinal Legate. It concerned the reconciliation of Constitutional priests. The First Consul urged that no further retractation should be required from them than submission to their bishop. As usual, a vivid picture was drawn of the evils which would follow opposition, and once more Caprara was moved to sanction the step. He felt, however, that he was not successful, and earnestly asked for his recall. He put the finishing stroke to

---

[1] *L'Église Romaine et le Premier Empire*, tom. i. p. 216 ; Weiss : *Lehrbuch der Weltgeschichte*, ix. 1032.   [2] Weiss, ix. 1038.

his false position by accepting the rich Archbishopric of Milan from the First Consul, as head of the Italian Republic. The title of benefactor gave a certain weight to Bonaparte's exactions. When, now, the Cardinal objected his want of power, the reply was, " Bah, this is one of your usual tricks." [1] It dawned upon Caprara at times that he had been duped by Bonaparte. In a great measure, he had lost ground with Pius VII. and Consalvi, and gained, on the other hand, no influence over the First Consul.

Bonaparte, not the Church, was dominant, and this was proved by the publication with the Concordat of certain Organic Articles, as if they formed part of it, and were sanctioned by the Pope. They were, on the contrary, " constitutional laws," which went far to undo the good effected by the Concordat. The truth of this assertion will be best proved by giving an abstract of those important points in which the Organic Articles went outside and beyond the solemn compact publicly entered into by the First Consul and the Holy Father. First, as to the Concordat, the text runs as follows :—

" Convention between the French Government and His Holiness Pius VII.

" The Government of the Republic recognises that the Catholic Apostolic and Roman religion is the religion of the great majority of French citizens.

---

[1] *Correspondance du Card. Caprara avec le Cardinal Consalvi,* 3 juillet, 1802.

" His Holiness likewise recognises that the said religion has received, and further at this time expects the greatest good and the greatest honour from the establishment of the Catholic worship in France, and from the particular profession of it made by the Consuls of the Republic.

" Consequently, after this mutual recognition, they have agreed upon what follows as well for the good of religion as for the maintenance of internal tranquillity.

" Art. 1. The Catholic, Apostolic, and Roman religion shall be freely exercised in France. Its worship shall be public, but in conformity with the rules of police which the Government shall judge necessary for public tranquillity.

" 2. A new circumscription of French dioceses shall be made by the Holy See in concert with the Government.

" 3. His Holiness shall declare to the titularies of the French sees, that he expects of them with a firm confidence every sort of sacrifice, even that of their sees, for the good of peace and unity.

" After this exhortation, should they refuse this sacrifice required by the good of the Church, a refusal nevertheless which His Holiness does not expect, provision shall be made by new titularies for the government of the bishoprics of the new circumscription, as follows :—

" 4. The First Consul of the Republic shall name, within the three months following the publication of

the Bull of His Holiness, archbishops and bishops of
the new circumscription. His Holiness will confer
canonical institution according to the forms established in respect of France before the change of
Government.

" 5. Nominations to bishoprics, which afterwards become vacant, shall also be made by the First Consul,
and canonical institution shall be given by the Holy
See, in conformity with the preceding Article.

" 6. The bishops, before entering upon their office,
shall make direct to the First Consul the oath of
fidelity which was in use before the change of Government, as follows :—

" 'I swear and promise to God, upon the holy
Gospels, to maintain obedience and fidelity to the
Government established by the Constitution of the
French Republic. I promise likewise not to hold
any communication, not to be present at any design,
nor to enter into any engagement, whether within
or without, which is contrary to the public tranquillity : and if in my diocese or elsewhere I learn
of any design to the prejudice of the State, I will
make it known to the Government.'

" 7. Ecclesiastics of the second order shall make
the same oath to the civil authorities designated by
the Government.

" 8. The following prayer shall be recited at the end of
the Divine Office in all the Catholic churches of France :

" ' Domine, salvam fac rempublicam ; Domine, salvos
fac consules.'

"9. The bishops shall make a new circumscription of the parishes of their dioceses, which shall not take effect until it has received the consent of the Government.

"10. The bishops shall appoint the curés. Their choice can only fall on persons accepted by the Government.

"11. The bishops may have a Chapter for their cathedral, and a seminary for their diocese, without obligation on the part of the Government to endow them.

"12. All metropolitan, cathedral, parochial, and other churches not alienated, which are necessary for worship, shall be put at the disposition of the bishops.

"13. His Holiness, for the good of peace and the happy re-establishment of the Catholic religion, declares that neither he nor his successors shall in any way trouble those who have acquired alienated ecclesiastical goods, and that in consequence the property of these goods, the rights and revenues attached to them, shall remain unchanged in their hands and in those of their representatives.

"14. The Government will assure a suitable support to the bishops and the curés whose dioceses and cures shall be comprised in the new circumscription.

"15. The Government will likewise take measures in order that French Catholics may, if they choose, make endowments in favour of the churches.

"16. His Holiness recognises in the First Consul of the French Republic the same rights and prerogatives as the old Government enjoyed in regard to the Holy See.

" 17. It is agreed between the contracting parties that in case any one of the successors of the actual First Consul should not be Catholic, the rights and prerogatives mentioned in the article above and the appointment of bishops shall be regulated in respect to him by a new convention.

" Ratifications shall be exchanged at Paris within forty days.

" Done at Paris, the 26th messidor of the ninth year of the French Republic, 15th July, 1801." [1]

The Organic Articles, seventy-six in number, were presented for acceptance to the French Legislature at the same time as the Concordat, being called " the Organic Articles of the said Convention," and were promulgated with it as a " law of the Republic."

As to the liberty of the Church in the important point of intercourse between the Head and the members, the Organic Articles laid down that no Bull, Brief, or other communication from the Holy See, even if it concerned only individuals, should be received, published, printed, or put into execution without the authorisation of the Government. Further, that no nuncio, legate, or any other officer, should, without the same authorisation, exercise, on French soil or elsewhere, any function connected with the affairs of the Gallican Church. With regard to the

____

[1] Weiss, ix. 1032.

Church as the one divine kingdom of God upon earth, the Organic Articles laid down that no decrees of foreign synods, not even of general councils, could be published in France before the Government had examined their form, their conformity with the laws, rights, and franchises of the French Republic, and all that which in their publication could affect public tranquillity. That no national or metropolitan council, no diocesan synod, no deliberative assembly, should take place without express permission of the Government. The Articles created an appeal to the Council of State in all cases of abuse on the part of ecclesiastical superiors or other persons. And cases of abuse were defined to be usurpation, or excess of power; contravention of the laws and regulations of the Republic; infraction of rules established by the canons received in France; infringement of the liberties, practices, and customs of the Gallican Church; and every attempt or procedure in the exercise of worship which may affect the honour of citizens, arbitrarily trouble their conscience, degenerate into oppression of them, or into public scandal. As to the ministry of the Church, three articles of very pregnant meaning ran thus: "The Catholic worship shall be exercised under the direction of archbishops and bishops in their dioceses, and under that of curés in their parishes. Every privilege carrying with it either exemption from episcopal jurisdiction, or possession of it, is abolished. Archbishops and bishops shall be able, upon authorisation of the Government, to establish in their dioceses cathedral chapters and seminaries. All other ecclesiastical establishments are suppressed."

The bishops were to name and institute the curés, but were not to declare their nomination, nor to give them canonical institution, before that nomination had been accepted by the First Consul. They were bound to reside in their dioceses, nor could they leave them without the First Consul's permission. They were charged with the organisation of their seminaries, the rules of such organisation being submitted to the approval of the First Consul.

Those who were selected to teach in the seminaries were bound to subscribe the declaration made by the clergy of France in 1682, and to consent to teach the doctrine therein contained; and the bishops were called upon to notify a formal statement of this consent to the Minister of Public Worship. "The bishops shall send every year to this councillor the names of the persons studying in the seminaries and intended for the ecclesiastical state." "The bishops shall hold no ordination before the number of the persons to be ordained has been submitted to the Government and approved by it." "No foreigner can be employed in the functions of the ecclesiastical ministry without permission of the Government."

It is especially to be noted that the Organic Articles, in requiring that all teachers in seminaries should profess their adherence to the four articles of the declaration of 1682, and promise to teach the doctrine

contained in them, required as a law of the French
State, that those teachers should profess and teach
two doctrines which lay under the censure of the
Holy See. The one doctrine concerned the power
of the Holy See in respect to a general council;
the other the due relation between the spiritual and
the.temporal powers.[1]

At the moment, therefore, that Bonaparte was
entering with the Holy Father into a Concordat,
every article, and even every word of which had
been carefully examined by the Cardinal Plenipotentiary, lest the liberty of the Church should receive
any injury, he was imposing on the Catholics of his
empire, as a law of the State, articles against their
religious conscience. Not only did those Articles
inflict a complete captivity on the Church, but the
educators of the clergy were enjoined to teach what
is false. To this Bonaparte added the falsehood of
representing these Articles as "Organic Articles of
the Convention made with Pius VII." For three
years after the publication of the Concordat, Pius
VII. spared neither labour, trouble, nor fatigue to
bring about either the revocation or the revision of
the Organic Articles, and the retractation of the Constitutional bishops. The Pope may have credited
Bonaparte with some zeal for religion, whereas he
was toiling for an imperial crown, and soon to put
out his hand to set it on his own head.

[1] Weiss, ix. 1046, and *Portalis sur le Concordat de* 1801, pp. 58-77.

CHAPTER IV

FIRST-FRUITS OF ORGANIC ARTICLES

1802–1804

IN the time which intervened between Easter 1802 and the great event of December 1804, Bonaparte was steadily carrying out his policy of domination. Already, in January 1802, as a preliminary in his vast Italian scheme, he had been proclaimed President of the Italian Republic. To keep, outwardly at least, on friendly terms with the Pope, he made the Holy Father well-timed presents. For instance, he presented Pius VII. now with Pesaro, now with Ancona, and again with two fully equipped men-of-war for the protection of the Papal States, whilst he was deliberately planning the complete overthrow of the Papal power in Italy. An Italian Concordat followed upon the Italian Republic, and it was a fairly good copy of its French forerunner. Pius VII. gave his consent, with the stipulation that nothing should be altered without his permission. Nevertheless, Organic Articles, which remained in practice, though outwardly rejected, were attached to it. They undid the good effected by the Concordat, and in France, as it will be seen, things were much the same.

The Holy Father received Bonaparte's gifts with gracious kindness, and was always inclined to put a favourable interpretation even upon doubtful benefits, yet his mild language was firm. As early as June 1802, he wrote to the First Consul: " We are glad to meet your wishes, but it is often impossible ; and yet, dear son, this is just what you require us to do. Perhaps you are unacquainted with the laws of the Church, which bind us, or you apply them erroneously, owing to a faulty interpretation. We can understand that through great pressure of business you scarcely have time to take in our letters. It would therefore give us pleasure to see you and speak with you." He expressed the same firmness to Cacault: " I should be very glad to give satisfaction to the First Consul, but let him not ask what a Pope cannot grant. I have done what I could for France, and God will reward me for it. But the Pope is the keeper and defender of the laws and customs of the Catholic religion, and I would not be the first Pope to act against the dictates of conscience." [1]

The Organic Articles, which represented a direct attack upon the free action of the Church, and partially undid the Concordat both in France and Italy, filled the Holy Father with anguish, and prompted his sorrowful words to Cacault : " We find true peace and repose only in those governments where Catholics are subject to infidels and heretics. The Catholics of Russia, England, Prussia, and the Levant give us

[1] Weiss, ix. 1042.

no trouble. They ask for Bulls and for necessary counsels, and then they go their way peaceably in perfect conformity to the laws of the Church. You know what our predecessor suffered from the changes which the Emperors Joseph and Leopold brought about. You can see for yourself the daily assaults of the Spanish and Neapolitan Courts. At this present moment no man is so unhappy as the Sovereign Pontiff, who is the guardian and supreme chief of religion and its divine ordinances. Men pretend to want us in order that they may destroy religion, and they do not reflect that all these changes are against our honour and our conscience. Our representations are ever rejected with temper or anger, and our wishes cast back in our face with threats." [1]

The tradition of the Organic Articles is still powerful in Europe, and our own country is the single government which allows the Church a free action. Bonaparte skilfully engrafted it upon the old tree of Gallican liberties. His genius for organisation was a fatal gift, as he used it without spiritual control. Under the direction of the Holy See he might have renovated the educational system, and the resources of his wonderful brain might have lent singular energy to his every scheme. Instead of subordination to the Church, however, he chose to be Cæsar in the sanctuary as well as out of it. In July 1802, a nomination of cardinals occurred, and Bonaparte demanded imperiously that the five vacant hats should be given to

---

[1] *Histoire de Pie VII.*, t. i. pp. 319, 320 ; Weiss, ix. 1043.

France. The tone of his despatch on the subject to M. de Talleyrand is that of a monarch, crowned by hereditary right and the will of his people. " You will inform the *citoyen* Cacault that I claim these places for France. If my just request is uncomplied with, I renounce from this moment all nomination of cardinals, preferring that France should have nothing to do with the Sacred College, than that it should be treated with less distinction than other powers." [1]

He created a minister who became at his master's bidding Controller-General of the French bishops. Portalis, the Councillor of State, did not then bear the title which afterwards distinguished him. Still he was practically *Ministre des Cultes* from the publication of the Concordat, although not called so. Under his supervision the bishops were required to submit their pastorals, letters, and other official documents to secular censure. They were also forbidden to publish anything that was not printed at their respective prefectures. The results produced by this system were so ludicrous that M. Portalis was constrained at last to transfer the various provincial courts of censure to one central bureau in Paris, thus securing Bonaparte's attention for it. Prelates specially zealous in his cause could obtain from this office ready-made bulletins and pastorals, only needing a little ecclesiastical colouring to be fit for use. Bulletins from the army were then read in church. Political questions in the pulpit were forbidden.

[1] *Correspondance de Napoléon I.*, 8 juillet 1802.

In a circular issued in June 1802, M. Portalis announced "that the civil law tolerates divorce, and that consequently it would be unjust as well as imprudent to refuse the nuptial benediction to those who wish to contract a second marriage after divorce."[1] The tone of the First Consul's correspondence at this time is inimitable. "I send you, *citoyen* Councillor of State," he writes to Portalis, "a memorandum concerning the Bishop of Rennes, which I have received from the Inspector of Police. Write and tell the bishop that it is time he stopped this behaviour of his, that he is wrong to have displaced a Constitutional priest without my leave, for an emigrant priest. . . . If Gospel morality is not a sufficient check upon his passions, policy, or fear of the Government, which might be down upon him as a disturber of the public peace, ought to be. Write less harshly to the Bishop of Clermont. His diocese is filled with Constitutional priests, the friends of order, who enjoy the popular confidence. It is both impolitic and immoral to banish these useful men from State and Church. . . . Write to the Bishop of Bayeux, that in the commune of Balleroy he has illegally displaced a curé, a step which is contrary to my orders. . . . Impress upon all the bishops as a permanent order, *that I wish for Constitutional priests as curés, vicars-general, and canons.*"

At another time he wanted to punish some priests who had corresponded with the "infamous" Bishop of Arras. "I wish to know" (to M. Portalis), "what

---

[1] *Circulaire de M. Portalis*, 19 prairial an x. (juin 1802).

E

the canonical form of degradation for them would be, in order that they may be delivered over to justice, for I think the clergy require a forcible example. I am no longer pleased with the *vicaire* of St. Sulpice. He also should be degraded." Then follows an arrest warrant, and Bonaparte proceeds to ask what is the proper punishment for a priest who withdraws from his bishop. " God," he remarks, " will certainly punish him (the refractory priest) in the next world, but Cæsar must punish him in this." [1]

Bonaparte's fortunes were reflected on his family, and one member of it, in particular, came before the public as early as 1802. This was Joseph Fesch, maternal uncle of Bonaparte, called later on the *Cardinal Oncle*. The First Consul nominated him, in January 1802, to the archiepiscopal see of Lyons, and in 1803 he became Cardinal. [2] He was a singular personage : good and sincere, obstinate and tactless. At a time when the First Consul's nearer relations were kept in ignorance of his grand design on an imperial crown, Cardinal Fesch alone was let into the secret. In July 1803 he was sent to Rome to replace Cacault, who had said with truth : " How men have spoilt my General and my First Consul for me. He listens to me no longer. He has made me a senator and silenced me." [3] Bonaparte's choice of Fesch as ambassador was unfortunate. From the

---

[1] *Correspondance de Napoléon I.*, t. vii. p. 28 ; t. ix. pp. 4, 74, 310.
[2] *Kirchen Lexicon*, Artikel "*Joseph Fesch.*"
[3] *Vie de Pie VII.*, t. i. p. 483.

first instant that he appeared in Rome, Fesch made
an unfavourable impression. Bonaparte rarely mis-
took his man, so it may be supposed that he intended,
through his haughty and unconciliating ambassador,
to solicit the special and crowning favour he had in
view. The Holy Father had protected a certain
Comte de Vernègues, a Russian, whom the French
Embassy accused of plotting and intriguing against
their Government. Bonaparte, in an imperious and
threatening letter to M. de Talleyrand, urged him to
require absolutely that the unfortunate count should
be delivered over to France. Consalvi, after a long
and brave resistance, suddenly consented to a step
which was only a prelude to still greater concessions.

On the 16th May 1804, the Senate voted and
determined that Napoleon should take the title of
Emperor. The hideous murder of March 21st, when,
by his orders, the last of the Condés perished at
Vincennes, should have precluded him from mounting
a throne, and stigmatised him as an object of horror
to universal suffrage itself. The Bourbon sovereigns
were slowest to express their feelings. The Czar,
Alexander I., distinguished himself by the severity
of his attitude.[1] He and his Court wore mourning
for the last of the Condés. Pius VII. wept aloud

---

[1] The following inscription, published at St. Petersburg, to the
Prince's memory, does honour to Russian feeling :—

"Inclyto principi Ludovico Antonio Henrico Borbonio-Condæo,
duci d'Enghien, non minus propria et avita virtute quam sorte funesta
claro, quem devoravit bellua Corsica, Europæ terror et totius humani
generis lues.—*Mémoires Secrets sur Napoléon Buonaparte avec un Précis
Historique*, 215.

when the news was broken to him by Fesch, as much,
he said, for the deed as for the victim.[1] The young Duc
d'Enghien, although not allowed the privileges which
are offered even to criminals, died as a Christian and
a hero. It has been said with truth that every heresy
has a political reason, and the same remark applies
to all the deeds of blood perpetrated by Napoleon.
This assassination was not a mere act of violence,
committed in a momentary fit of anger, but a design
meditated in cold blood, as an act of useful policy.[2]

Repudiating, as he did, the murder of Vincennes,
the Holy Father would have wished not to crown the
murderer. Stress of circumstances, which forced him
to be either for or against Napoleon, finally moved
him to an act that was against his inclination and
his judgment. After what had happened, he could
not choose to be Napoleon's enemy, and his neutrality would have been accounted as hostility. The
language of Cardinal Caprara, exaggerated as it was,
shows the difficulties of the position. On May 10th,
1804, he wrote to Consalvi: "It has become question of crowning a monarch who would take it very
ill if His Holiness sought an excuse for not crowning him. He would take it as a personal insult
if His Holiness raised difficulties in any way. The
Emperor's resentment would be stronger from the
fact that the Holy Father, as Head of the Church,
can do more than any one else to fix the succession in

---

[1] Weiss: *Lehrbuch der Weltgeschichte*, ix. 1229.
[2] *L'Église Romaine et le Premier Empire*, t. i. p. 308.

the family of a man who has just re-established and re-organised religious and Catholic worship.   No excuse would be accepted as valid, were it even confirmed by the testimony of Cardinal Fesch.   It would be looked upon as a mere pretext.   I limit myself, then, to beseech your Eminence, not even to hint in your answer at any difficulty, be it of age, of health, or anything whatever."   The enthusiasm of Caprara was not shared by Rome any more than by the Holy Father himself.   The public recognition of a new dynasty involved in the act of coronation should present some very deep and weighty religious grounds. Already Pius VII. had to count with the umbrage of other European cabinets, who nicknamed him the Emperor's chaplain.   The state of the case was in reality this : by not condescending to Napoleon's wish, the Pope feared to lose his support in religion, which might have led to schism and heresy in Christendom. Napoleon would not suffer the Sovereign Pontiff to remain neutral, and Rome must consent either to take up his cause, or to wound his pride by an open and flat refusal—a middle course was no longer possible.

To justify so grave a step on the part of the Holy Father, Consalvi required as a condition the retractation of the Constitutional bishops and the repeal of the Organic Articles.   Furthermore, in the ceremony itself, due and customary respect was to be paid to the Vicar of Christ.   The sincere fulfilment of these conditions could alone justify a condescension so unwonted from a Sovereign Pontiff.   The substance of

the oath which the First Consul purposed taking at
his coronation was also rejected at Rome. Caprara
was dismayed. Again, to his consternation, Consalvi
wrote that "the essence of the Catholic Church is to
be intolerant."[1] The one true religion proclaims
itself infallible, and teaches with authority. At this
juncture Cardinal Fesch intervened to try and conciliate matters between Rome and Napoleon. He was
not distinguished for the qualities which make a good
negotiator. One day after a stormy interview with
Consalvi about the Coronation, he had so far lost his
head as to order his coachman to drive *alla casa del
diavolo.*[2] His one thought was that the Holy Father
should make the opportunity serve for the restoration
of the three Legations. As in the Concordat, however, so in this circumstance, Pius VII. put aside the
question of temporal interests. He would not allow
any material consideration to affect his decision.[3] It
is curious that the French ambassador, and not the
Holy Father, should have been thus urgent for the
Temporal Power.

It would be well for Napoleon's honour if he had
given no formal written statement that he would concede the disputed points. Cardinal Consalvi knew
very well the force of *littera scripta manet*, little as
Napoleon allowed himself to be bound. He writes :
"We at length wrested an official note from M. de

---

[1] *Consalvi à Caprara,* 6 juin 1804.
[2] *Histoire de Pie VII.,* t. i. p. 489.
[3] *Mémoires de Consalvi,* t. ii. p. 392.

Talleyrand to the Cardinal legate, for transmission to Rome. It contained the most positive assurances that the Pope should receive full satisfaction as to the Organic Articles. . . . M. de Talleyrand's note promised a great deal about the Constitutional bishops. But it seemed to us that the purport and also the vagueness of these latter promises did not offer the Holy Father that assurance of redress which he desired." Consalvi was determined to put the Constitutional bishops on the same footing as the Organic Articles, and he therefore pursued negotiations with Fesch. "At last," he says, "Cardinal Fesch gave us in writing, in the Emperor's name, a promise that the Constitutional Bishops should place their retractation in the Pope's hands, according to the form prescribed by him, and that His Holiness's presence in Paris would give them a good opportunity of doing this. In the event of a Constitutional bishop's refusing to retract, which was unlikely, he should be deposed from his see by the Government." This statement was confirmed by M. de Talleyrand; but, remarks Consalvi, "All the efforts made by the French Government tended solely to obtain the Pope's presence in Paris, for it had not the smallest intention of keeping one of its promises." [1] These words were written long after the event.

Napoleon had now gained his end, and proceeded in his usual manner to carry out details. He entrusted his official invitation, not to the highest

---

[1] *Mémoires de Consalvi*, t. ii. pp. 394, 398.

Church dignitary of his empire, but to a general of brigade, Caffarelli. The letter itself was so shabby in every respect that the Pope was on the point of breaking off all negotiations. He had required that two bishops should present the letter of invitation. If Napoleon proved so soon faithless to his word, what might he not be later on, when he had no interested motive for keeping it ? The Sacred College, after consultation, urged that, as the journey to Paris was undertaken purely for the good of the Church, every other consideration should be sacrificed.[1]

[1] *Mémoires de Consalvi*, t. ii. p. 402.

CHAPTER V

1804–1805

Pius VII. left Rome on November 2nd, 1804, accompanied by six cardinals. The French Government would gladly have welcomed a larger number to swell the brilliant cortège in Napoleon's triumph. The faithful Secretary of State remained at the helm in Rome. The Holy Father was not suffered to travel at his leisure. Couriers were constantly despatched to goad him on, and he was allowed only two stoppages—one at Florence, and one at Turin. No consideration was shown for his weak health, nor was he consulted as to the day of the ceremony, which would have seemed the most ordinary courtesy. In fact, he was summoned to Paris as if he had been in very truth the " Emperor's chaplain." [1]

The Pope and the Emperor met for the first time in the open country between Fontainebleau and Nemours. This was a trick of Napoleon. As a sovereign-elect, it would have been a terrible trial to his pride to meet another crowned head half-way.

---

[1] *Mémoires de Consalvi*, t. ii. p. 402.

In the case of the Pope, he, as an outward Catholic
at least, must have given that sort of homage which
is hallowed by a reverential and lively faith. He
must have fallen on his knees in homage, not to the
man indeed, but to the Divine Person whom that
man represented, and so have proclaimed before his
Court that he owned a superior on earth. To avoid
this act of humility, Napoleon arranged the scene,
which, to all appearances, was a spontaneous encounter. There he stood, a sportsman for the time
being, booted, spurred, and surrounded by a pack of
hounds. The Holy Father's carriage stopped as soon
as he saw the Emperor. Napoleon did not approach,
because he had settled in his own mind that the
Sovereign Pontiff was to meet him half-way. So,
although it was a wet November day, he allowed the
Pope to encounter the muddy road. When both
Pope and Emperor had taken a certain number of
steps towards each other, they met and embraced.
The imperial carriage was to convey Pius VII. to the
palace of Fontainebleau, and by every law of supe-
riority and good breeding he should have taken precedence of his host. Here, too, scheming had been at
work to spare the parvenu's feelings. The carriage
drew up so as to separate Pope and Emperor. Two
footmen on each side opened the respective doors
simultaneously. The Emperor took the right, and
his august visitor the left, as they entered together.
Napoleon began as he intended to proceed : he made
the Pope throughout a secondary personage. Once,

and once only, the Sovereign Pontiff was allowed the place of honour—on the occasion of his entry into Paris. As in the case of the Cardinal legate, it was contrived to take place by night, so that the people might not witness what Napoleon evidently considered degrading to himself.

At the Tuileries, the Holy Father occupied the Pavillon de Flore, the abode of "another saint," as he expressed it to the biographer of Madame Louise. The aunt had left the Court for Carmel, and the niece had stayed at Court and found more than Carmel at the Temple. Pius VII. recognised the heroic virtues of Madame Elizabeth in speaking of her as "*une autre sainte.*"[1] He won the respect and regard of all during his sojourn in Paris. Gallicanism had not spoilt the French people, neither had the guillotine blunted their faith. It burst out enthusiastically as they contemplated the Vicar of Christ, who added personal charm to the highest of earthly dignities. Every morning, in the Galerie du Louvre, the Pope could be seen and approached by the multitude. On one occasion a man held himself aloof from the crowd as if he feared contact with the Pope. The Holy Father saw it, and accosted him. "Why do you run away from me?" he asked. "Can the blessing of an old man do you any harm?"[2]

These friendly demonstrations did not suit Napoleon. He was jealous of the Pope's popularity, and

---

[1] de Ravignan: *Clément XIII. et Clément XIV.*, p. 562.

[2] Madame de Rémusat: *Mémoires*, ii. p. 66.

did his utmost to keep the Holy Father in the shade.[1]
The Pope reached Paris on November 28th. On the
30th he was asked to accept what proved to be an
insincere retractation from the Constitutional Bishop
of Besançon, Lecoy. Napoleon hurriedly read the
document aloud to the Holy Father, and left it in his
hands. The next day Pius VII. thought it necessary
to write as follows to the Emperor :—

"Last night, as soon as we had a spare minute, we
considered the declaration of the Bishop Lecoy, which
your Majesty had the goodness to bring to us yourself.
Looking over it, we perceived a point which had
escaped our notice in the very rapid reading of your
Majesty. The said bishop has altered the original
words of the formula minuted by Cardinal Fesch and ·
M. Portalis, *submission to his decisions in the ecclesiastical affairs of France*, to, *in the canonical affairs of
France*. We can appreciate the meaning of the
change, and do not admit it. We have considered
ourself bound to tell your Majesty this without
delay, because we are pressed for time, nothing
having as yet been obtained from a small number
of obstinate refractories. We have a sufficient knowledge of the piety and discerning wisdom of your
Majesty to feel sure you will deign to take the
necessary measures, that we may not find ourselves
compromised, and that nothing may disturb or mar
the solemn function of to-morrow morning. We

[1] Weiss, ix. 1247.

pray God to pour His choicest blessings on your Imperial Majesty, to whom we heartily give the Apostolical benediction.

" From our house, the 1st of December of the year 1804, and the fifth of our Pontificate.

" Pius, P.P. VII." [1]

Time pressed, and yet another burning question had to be settled before the Coronation. One person at the Tuileries was unfeignedly glad of the Holy Father's presence, and that was the Empress Josephine. Her position weighed heavily upon her, and the jealousy of the Bonapartes profited by its insecurity to make all sorts of insinuations. The Holy Father treated her with great kindness, called her " Daughter," and brought her handsome vases as a present. Before leaving Rome, he had made inquiries as to whether Josephine was Napoleon's legitimate wife, because in that case, he said, he should crown her also. So little had transpired about Napoleon's domestic affairs that the Holy Father's inquiries were answered in the affirmative.[2]

The marriage of Bonaparte and Josephine de Beauharnais, in 1796, had been a purely civil contract, though at that time, and in Bonaparte's position, the blessing of the Church might have been obtained. The worst days of revolutionary fury were over, and the requirements of Trent were no longer impossible to carry out. The matter never troubled Bonaparte,

---

[1] *Histoire de Pie VII.*, t. i. p. 517.
[2] *Zeitschrift für Katholische Theologie*, 1888, iv. 604.

and possibly Josephine's conscience would have slumbered tranquilly had it not been for her insecurity. At any moment she felt that her enemies might bring forward the civil contract of 1796, and separate her for ever from Napoleon and her dreams of earthly glory. Josephine, therefore, urged the necessity of a religious marriage before the Coronation. Napoleon would not hear of it, except on condition that there should be no witnesses. The Sovereign Pontiff alone could dispense with the formalities of matrimony as ordered by the Council of Trent, and give validity to a clandestine marriage rite, performed at midnight without witnesses. Cardinal Fesch went to Pius VII. and laid the case, shrouded in mysterious words, before the Head of the Church. As Grand Almoner, he might find himself in an extremely difficult position, and be unable to confide in the Archbishop of Paris without betraying secret matters of the greatest importance. The Pope, guessing what the "secret matters" were, replied—

"I give you every faculty which I have it in my power to give you."

Cardinal Fesch rightly concluded that the Papal faculties dispensed with clandestinity, the presence of the parish priest and witnesses, and the publication of banns. In the night preceding the Coronation, therefore, an altar was secretly erected in the Emperor's room, and Cardinal Fesch, in strictest privacy and without witnesses, made Napoleon and Josephine man and wife before God. Josephine, in the joy of her heart, obtained a marriage certificate from the Cardinal, which caused an outburst of auger from Napoleon. He had not given, and could not give, a true consent to the marriage, he told the Cardinal.[1]

Two incidents connected with the Coronation are striking. First of all, the imperial party kept the Holy Father waiting for an hour and a half, if not, according to an eye-witness, for hours, at Notre Dame. During the ceremony, Pius VII. wore an air of sadness and resignation.[2] The solemn moment came when the Holy Father asked the Emperor-elect, in the words of the Ritual, "Dost thou promise to maintain peace in the Church of God?" and Napoleon firmly answered, "*Polliceor*."

The Emperor and Empress knelt together as Pius VII. proceeded to anoint Napoleon. The sword and the sceptre, each typical, and each the subject of a special prayer, had been given. The crown alone remained, and the Pope was about to set it on Napoleon's head, when the Emperor rose hastily, snatched it from the altar, and crowned himself. Every one understood the force of his action. Then he took the second crown and put it on Josephine's head. At the public banquet following the ceremony, the Pope occupied a third rank after both Emperor and

---

[1] Pater Duhr : *Ehescheidung u. zweite Heirat Napoleons*, i. 603. This account tallies with M. Thiers' *Histoire de l'Empire*, t. i. p. 76, and ii. 368 ; and with Cardinal Fesch's own testimony, in 1809, on the *Comité Ecclésiastique*.

[2] Madame de Rémusat : *Mémoires*, ii.

[3] Weiss, ix. 1248.

Empress. Again, contrary to Consalvi's stipulation, there was a second coronation in the Champ de Mars. Napoleon had given his word that there should be only one coronation, but he allowed no obstacle of any kind to interfere with his will. The Holy Father's meekness under personal insult did not make him weak. The ceremonial had not been carried out according to previous agreement, and he declared that if the press published anything derogatory to his office, he would protest that he had not been a free agent. Thus it happened that whilst foreign newspapers were full of the Coronation, the *Moniteur* maintained a dead silence on the subject. Napoleon would not brook even a semblance of submission.

In return for his sovereign act of condescension, the Pope gained little if anything. He was captivated by Napoleon, in spite of faults and disloyal treatment; and as to the Emperor, he thought he knew Pius VII., and that he should find him pliable as the courtier bishops, whom he could twist in his fingers. "I know Pius VII.," he confided to one of his generals. "I took his measure during the Concordat. . . . The father of the faithful does not alarm me. I know how to shape him according to my fancy."[1]

For once Napoleon's diagnosis was at fault, and the Father of the Faithful, whom he thought to control, was "narrow-minded and obstinate." M. Portalis was at hand to prepare the Emperor for his confer-

---

[1] "Je sais le pétrir à mon gré." (*Mémoires Secrets sur Napoléon Buonaparte*, 217).

ences with the Pope ; but history is not learnt in a
day.   On one occasion, Napoleon angrily exclaimed,
"Does your Holiness take me for *a Charles IV. ?*"[1]
The first memoir which Pius VII. drew up and presented to the Government met with little or no result.   The   second concerned the Temporal Power,
or, rather, comparing Napoleon to Charlemagne, he
demanded a restitution of his patrimony.[2]

M. de Talleyrand was charged to reply to this
appeal, and his answer reveals the diplomatist.   It
is full of courtesy and vague politeness, speaking in
flattering terms of the Pope's personal qualities, but
conceding nothing to his *office*.   If Napoleon had ever
been touched by the Pope's confidence in himself,
which is doubtful, he had long ago determined not to
restore the Temporal Power.   M. de Talleyrand ad-
roitly introduced this sentence into his reply : "Power
and riches are impotent against the attacks of this
enemy of ours " (the Revolution).   The Holy Father
did not ask for "power and riches," only for the rights
of his See.   Finally, Napoleon clothed his selfish intentions in big words, and assured the Pope that if
God gave him the ordinary years of man, he hoped
"to consolidate and extend the domain of the Holy
See"; to make it his glory and his happiness, to support it with unsurpassed constancy.[3]   His plan of
campaign was distinctly marked out in his own mind,

---

[1] *L'Église Romaine et le Premier Empire,* t. ii. p. 360.
[2] Ibid., t. i. p. 370.
[3] *Histoire de Pie VII.,* ii. p. 34.

F

and the first move towards "consolidating the domain
of the Holy See" was the proclamation in the Senate
of the new Kingdom of Italy. The Papal Keys together with the Venetian Lion would grace the new
escutcheon. Shortly after Easter 1805, Pius VII.
was invited to honour by his presence the Emperor's
coronation at Milan as King of Italy. He remained,
however, absolutely deaf to the proposal.[1]

On Christmas Day the Holy Father said Mass in
an obscure parish church, because the splendid ceremonial at Notre Dame would not have suited Napoleon. For the same reason the Easter solemnities
were to be avoided, and the Pope was constrained to
leave Paris before they began. The man who thus
grudged small triumphs to Pius VII. had yet contemplated the advantages of keeping the Pope in
France, as Popes were once kept at Avignon. One
day an important member of the Imperial Court introduced the topic in the Pope's presence. It was
Napoleon's way to air his schemes beforehand, in
order to ascertain how far they would be popular. In
the event of the Pope's residence in France, he
would choose between Paris and Avignon. Alarmed
at the bare notion, Pius VII. hastened to put
a stop to any thought of acquiescence. "It is
rumoured," he exclaimed, "that we are willing to
remain in France. Well, then, all possibilities have
been met. Before leaving Rome we signed a formal
abdication, which would come into force in case of

1 *Mémoires de Consalvi*, t. ii. pp. 410, 412.

our imprisonment. The document is beyond the reach of the French. Cardinal Pignatelli is in possession of it at Palermo, and when your plan is signified to us, he who is now in your power will be nothing more than a poor simple monk, called Barnaba Chiaramonti."[1] Napoleon's design, therefore, aimed at obliterating the name and mission of Catholic Rome.

The only real advantage reaped by Pius VII. in France was the work, not of the Government, but the effect of his own personal influence. The venerable presence, full of sweetness and dignity; the benign countenance, which had a smile for all—irresistibly attracted those whose instincts and hearts were profoundly Catholic. The Constitutional Bishops, one and all, retracted their errors; and perhaps the Holy Father saw, in this joyful result, a compensation for the numerous deceptions of his journey to Paris.

The return to Rome was marked by the same disregard of the Holy Father. The Pope and the Emperor were both leaving the capital about the same time, but Napoleon, with what may be called his usual want of courtesy, started the first. The Holy Father was forced to follow him, and to wait at each relay for the horses which had already served the Emperor. On the other hand, the Catholic population of France poured out to welcome the Sovereign Pontiff as he passed. The Holy Father

---

[1] *Histoire de Pie VII.*, t. ii. p. 45.

thus described in his own words to M. Artaud, Secretary of the French Legation in Rome, some of the emotions he had experienced on his return through France : "At Châlons-sur-Sâone, we were on the point of leaving a house we had inhabited for a few days; we were bound for Lyons. We could not pass for the crowd. More than two thousand women and children, old men and young men, separated us from the carriage, which could not pull up. Two dragoons" (the Pope called our mounted police dragoons, because his own were so called) "charged to escort us, conducted us on foot to the carriage. At their suggestion we just managed to walk between their horses. These dragoons seemed proud of their invention and of outdoing the crowd. Having gained the carriage in an almost stifled condition, we were just about to jump in as quickly and cleverly as possible, for it really was a work of skill, when a young girl, who had livelier wits than we and the two dragoons put together, had got between the horses, took hold of our foot to kiss it, and held it until she could pass it to her mother, who reached us in the same way. Almost losing our equilibrium, we leant on one of the dragoons—him who appeared the least pious of the two, to judge by his face— begging of him to hold us up. We said to him, 'Take pity on us, Signor Dragone.' Thereupon the good soldier (see whether we are to judge by faces !), instead of helping us in our embarrassment, seized our hands more than once to kiss them. So between the young girl and your soldier, we remained suspended in the air, asking to be restored to equilibrium."[1]

The Holy Father was thus able to distinguish between the people and the sovereign.

[1] *Histoire de Pie VII.*

CHAPTER VI

NAPOLEON'S hurried journey from Paris had another crown in view. On May 26th, 1805, the scene at Notre Dame was repeated at Milan. He stretched out his hand to the altar, and set the Iron Crown of Italy upon his head, with the words, "*Il cielo me l'ha data, guai a chi la toccherà.*" [1] A kingdom of Italy without the Pope should have dispelled any remaining illusions of Pius VII., but it is probable there were none to dispel. Napoleon had disappointed the Holy Father's confidence, whilst what Consalvi calls his "serenity" remained undisturbed.

The Pope had scarcely regained Rome when a domestic incident in the Bonaparte family became the immediate cause of that struggle between Pope and Emperor which ended only with Napoleon's downfall. This apple of discord was a Protestant girl, whose rights as a wife crossed Napoleon's ambitious schemes, and were, therefore, sacrificed by him, whilst they were upheld by the Holy Father.

Napoleon did not tolerate neutrality in his family

---

[1] Weiss, ix. 1261.

any more than in his official intercourse with other powers. Hostility was imposed where allegiance was not spontaneous. Having crowned himself, he meant to crown his brothers and sisters, who were to be as the satellites of his solar system. Lucien alone of his brothers refused a crown. Joseph, his eldest brother, and Louis, consented to be kings at his bidding, but gave him trouble. It had been Napoleon's wish to establish the succession in the family of his brother Louis, conferring upon the father the crown of Italy till the majority of his son. This plan, not unnaturally, appeared derogatory to his own dignity; and although Napoleon had deep reasons for not over-favouring Josephine's family, he ended by making Eugène de Beauharnais Viceroy of Italy. On his side, Joseph would not relinquish his claims to the imperial throne, and his pertinacity produced an ill feeling between himself and Napoleon, who became all the more anxious to rule the destiny of his younger brother, Jerome. Before putting on the harness of an imperial prince, Jerome, as a simple sailor, had crossed the Atlantic in an admiral's squadron, and found himself a wife at Baltimore. This was Miss Patterson, a Protestant, the daughter of a rich and well-known citizen of the United States. With the ardour of youth, Jerome had not waited for his mother's consent, a formality laid down by the Code Napoléon. Neither this omission nor the difference of religion appeared to the Bishop of Baltimore to offer an effective obstacle. He therefore married the young couple, and thus

threatened one at least of Napoleon's schemes.   Miss
Patterson was not to be recognised in France as
Jerome's wife.   Orders were given, that should she
succeed in landing on French territory, she was to be
sent immediately to Amsterdam, and from thence to
the United States, by the first opportunity.[1]

Napoleon could, and did, annul the civil marriage
by imperial decree, but the Catholic marriage still
remained, and what God had put together the Church
could not part.   There was only one course open to
the Emperor if he wished to keep up appearances with
Catholics—recourse to Rome.   He forgot, or did not
wish to remember, that the power of binding and loos-
ing is applicable to the law of the Church alone, not
to the law of God, and that the dissolution of legitimate
marriage surpasses even the supreme powers of the
Keys.   On May 24th, 1808, he addressed a letter to
the Holy Father.   According to his usual mode of attack,
he introduced the question of the marriage casually, as
if a sentence of dissolution was the most ordinary
thing in the world.   After other matters, he said—

" I have spoken several times to your Holiness
of a young brother of nineteen, whom I sent to
America in a frigate, and who, although a minor,
has married a Protestant, the daughter of a merchant
of the United States, after a month's sojourn at Baltimore.   He has just come back.   He is aware of his
fault.   I have sent back Miss Patterson, his so-called

[1] *Lettre de Napoléon I. à M. Decrès*, 23 avril 1805.

wife, to America. According to our laws, the marriage is invalid. A Spanish priest was so far forgetful of his duty as to give the nuptial benediction. I wish for a Bull from your Holiness annulling the marriage. I send your Holiness several memorandums, one by Cardinal Caselli, which will enlighten your Holiness. It would be easy for me to have the marriage annulled, as the Gallican Church recognises (declares) the non-validity of such marriages. But it would be better effected at Rome, were it only to serve as an example to members of reigning houses who contract marriage with Protestants. I would urge great secrecy in this proceeding on your Holiness. Only when I learn that you consent to this step will I cause the marriage to be civilly annulled. It is important, even in France, that no Protestant girl should be so nearly related to me. It is dangerous that a minor of nineteen years of age, of prominent position, should be exposed to so great a temptation, contrary to civil laws, and every sort of propriety.

"With this, I pray that God may preserve you many years, most Holy Father, to the government of our Mother, Holy Church. Your devoted Son,

"NAPOLEON."[1]

Pius VII., the simple but learned Benedictine monk of former years, had no need to consult the Sacred College, nor even his faithful friend, Consalvi, on a

[1] *Histoire de Pie VII.*, t. ii. p. 57.

point so strictly within the range of his own theological science. Four obstacles had been submitted to the Holy Father's consideration in the different memorandums: disparity of religion, absence of the maternal consent, undue pressure, the absence of the parish priest—involving the non-fulfilment of a necessary formality, and rendering the marriage clandestine. In all countries where the decree of Trent, known as *de Reformatione Matrimonii*, had been published, the latter point was binding. This alone, then, of all the four gave some colour to the alleged non-validity. The Holy Father, consequently, directed particular attention to the question whether or not the decree had been published at Baltimore. The result of his diligent inquiries showed that the publication had not been made, and the dissolution of the marriage was therefore an impossibility. In his reply to Napoleon, he entered fully into his reasons, wishing to convince the Emperor that he could not put aside the moral obstacle. The letter ends with these noble words:—

"If we usurped an authority which we do not possess, we should be guilty before the tribunal of God, and before the whole Church, of most grievously abusing our sacred ministry. For this reason we earnestly hope your Majesty will feel assured that our ardent desire of gratifying you in whatever touches your Majesty's sacred person and your family is in this case simply powerless. We therefore pray you to accept this our declaration as a proof of our paternal affection. We most heartily give you the Apostolical blessing. Pius, P.P. VII." [1]

This letter was lost upon Napoleon. He saw in it not a reply suggested by the conscience of the Sovereign Pontiff, but a revenge on the Pope's part for the lost three Legations. Was it not preposterous to thwart the Emperor merely because a decree of Trent had not been published at Baltimore? It was astonishing, too, that the Sovereign Pontiff should lend a hand towards legitimatising the position of a Protestant as sister-in-law to the man who had restored the Catholic religion. This was Napoleon's reasoning. He forgot all his scruples when it became a question of marrying his brother Jerome to the Protestant daughter of the King of Wurtemburg.

The immediate effect of the Papal decision was to produce a painful state of things in the new kingdom of Italy. The Italian Concordat had proclaimed the Catholic religion to be the religion of the State, but now, in direct contradiction to Catholic teaching as to the sanctity of marriage, divorce was recognised by the Code Napoléon. The Emperor had been legislating for the Italian clergy somewhat after the fashion of Joseph II. He excused his proceedings to the Holy Father by alleging " that the Court of Rome was too slow, that it followed a policy which might have been wise in other days, but was no

[1] *Histoire de Pie VII.*, t. ii. p. 65.

longer adapted to the times. He had committed
no other fault than acting 'without the co-operation
of the Holy See.' He knew by experience that
Rome would have spent three or four years in
settling Italian affairs, and that they might have
collapsed altogether, had he not lent a speedy suc-
cour." This letter, despite the imperious character
of these remarks, was the last cordial one penned
by Napoleon to Pius VII. It pleased the Pope by
entering fully into ecclesiastical matters. A direct
answer to a question was a favour the Emperor too
rarely conferred upon the Head of the Church.
Napoleon spoke of "possible modification," yet did
not revise his Code, and bring it into harmony with
the law of the Church.

During his sojourn in Italy for his coronation at
Milan, Napoleon, besides legislating for the clergy,
made new allotments of Italian territory. Genoa was
united to the French Empire, Lucca was given to
his sister, Eliza Bacciocchi, and the State of Parma
organised as a dependence of the French crown.
Austria saw these changes with jealousy, for they
lessened its own hope of reconquering the Lombard
States. The Cabinet of St. James profited by this
discontent to draw Austria into a long-desired alliance, hitherto rejected by Austrian reserve. Russia,
Austria, and England, united in the common interest
of dislike and dread of France, constituted allies whom
Napoleon could not disregard. Prussia, as the fourth
great power, wished for nothing better than a favour-

able opportunity for declaring itself against the murderer of the Duc d'Enghien. Yet England, and England's minister, Pitt, were the heart and soul of the anti-Napoleonic movement in Europe. Pitt not only watched and directed it with keen interest, he also supported it with English gold. England then should suffer; England, Napoleon's mortal enemy, who had her own "strip of silver sea" to thank that she was not swallowed up in the great French Empire, and used as a convenient prey for a new Bonaparte sovereign. Napoleon had prepared a fleet to carry across the Channel that invincible army, fired with ardour at the mere name of England. His design was frustrated. Germany claimed his attention, and he possessed in a most singular degree the faculty of directing and concentrating his energies at a moment's notice. The campaign was thrown off almost in a breath, and presented a wonderful compendium of military genius.

The sum and substance of this project was to humble the "odious house of Austria," and to make Bavaria an interposing State between Austria and France. The crowning point was the peace which he aimed at signing in the palace of the Austrian Emperor. On the Italian side of the Alps the French troops were commanded by Massena. Facing the Austrian army on the Adige, they were to preserve a merely defensive attitude. On the other hand, some twenty thousand French soldiers, under General Gouvion-Saint-Cyr, were garrisoned in Otranto. In order to

ensure the object of the campaign, viz., to bring two
armies to bear upon the enemy's city, Vienna, General
Gouvion-Saint-Cyr's troops required to take up a position in Lombardy.   To do this they were obliged to
traverse the States of the Church, and then it was that
Napoleon commanded the violent occupation of Ancona,
which he had had the generosity to restore uncondi-
tionally to the Pope.   He now regretted his liberality:
The occupation of Ancona was the first aggressive
step taken against the Temporal Power, for the case of
the Legations did not present the same character of
violence.   The Holy Father's conscientious refusal to
dissolve Jerome's marriage had probably much to do
with this beginning of open hostility.

It is strange that at this very time Pius VII.
should have incurred the universal reproach of partiality for Napoleon.   In vain the Sovereign Pontiff
protested that a strict neutrality, whenever it could
be maintained, was the result of his position.   European cabinets were absorbed by petty intrigues, and
burning to further their own interests.   The Pope's
utterances were received with outward respect, but
not credited.   The occupation of Ancona effected this
good.   Inasmuch as it was an act of violence, it served
to justify the Holy Father's assertions, and also to
dispel whatever illusions he still retained as to Napoleon's friendliness.   On November 13th, 1805, he
placed a sealed letter for the Emperor in the hands
of Fesch.   He expostulated gently, yet firmly, with
Napoleon for not corresponding to the marks of con-

fidence heaped upon him by the Holy See. Then
as to the occupation of Ancona, the Pope intimated
that unless it was evacuated by the French troops he
could not continue official relations with France.
Not until January 7th, 1806, could Napoleon find
time to answer his injured correspondent. During
those two months he had gone from glory to glory.
He had conquered two Emperors, and dictated his own
terms to them. He could now afford to bestow crowns
on those whose bravery he desired to reward, as well
as on his near relations. Magnificent in his conquests, he could dispose of what had once constituted
the hereditary possessions of his enemies. Thus
Caroline of Naples received the announcement that
" the Bourbons of Naples had ceased to reign."

The Elector of Bavaria exchanged his title for
that of King; Stéphanie de Beauharnais deemed
that she was honouring the Grand Duke of Baden
by marrying him;[1] Joseph Bonaparte was given to
Naples as king, Louis to Holland. It became a case
of providing a prince or princess of royal blood for
all unmarried members of the Bonaparte family, and
the claims of Miss Patterson to be Jerome's wife
were peremptorily set aside for " State reasons." A
marriage was concluded between Eugène de Beauharnais and Augusta, Princess of Bavaria; and it was
proposed that Jerome, the legitimate husband of Protestant Miss Patterson, should espouse the Protestant
daughter of Wurtemburg. No discordant element had

---

[1] Madame de Rémusat : *Mémoires*, ii.

marred this triumph of Napoleon till he opened the Papal letter, and discovered that, in the universal hymn of flattery, one still remained who dared to speak unpalatable truth to him. He wrote from Munich the following angry reply to the Holy Father :—

"Most Holy Father,—I am in receipt of a letter from your Holiness, dated November 13th. I could not avoid feeling deeply that, at a time when the Powers of Europe were united against me in a coalition supported by English money, your Holiness should have listened to bad advice, and written me this blunt letter. Your Holiness is perfectly free to keep or to send away my minister from Rome. The occupation of Ancona is an immediate and necessary consequence of the Holy See's defective military organisation. It was to the true interest of your Holiness that I should hold this fortress rather than the Turks or the English. Your Holiness complains that, since your return to Rome, you have had only painful experiences. That is because all those who feared my power, or expressed friendship for me, have changed their opinion, thanks to the material power of the coalition, and also because, during that time, I myself have ever been thwarted, even on points of first-class importance in religious matters, as, for instance, in the question of checking Protestantism in France. I have looked upon myself as the protector of the Holy See, and on this ground have

occupied Ancona. As my predecessors of the second
and third race, I have looked upon myself as the
eldest son of the Church, and considered that I alone
possessed a sword powerful enough to protect her
from the insults of Greeks and Mussulmen. I shall
always protect the Holy See, in spite of disloyal
steps, ingratitude, and badly disposed men, who have
appeared in their true colours during the last three
months. They thought all was over with me. God
has manifestly shown, by the success with which He
has favoured my arms, the protection He gives to my
cause. I shall be the friend of your Holiness as
often as you consult only your own heart and the
true friends of religion. I repeat, if your Holiness
wishes to send away my minister, you are free to
give the preference to the English and the Caliph·
of Constantinople. Not wishing to expose Cardinal
Fesch to similar insults, I shall replace him by a
secular. The enmity, too, of Cardinal Consalvi is so
persistent that he (Cardinal Fesch) has never had
a hearing, and my enemies have been preferred to
me. God knows who has done the most for religion
amongst reigning princes.

"With this, I pray that God, most Holy Father,
may give you many more years to govern our Mother,
Holy Church.—The Emperor of the French, King of
Italy,   NAPOLEON.

"MUNICH, 7th *January* 1806."[1]

---

[1] *Histoire de Pie VII.*, t. ii. p. 160.

The self-constituted protector of the Holy See claimed the right to occupy Ancona with French troops. In his touching reply, the Holy Father used for the first time the expression "dolorous" in connection with his pontificate.

On the same day, January 7th, Napoleon wrote to Cardinal Fesch, recommending his ambassador to make no secret of the discourteous remarks the letter contained. He said—

"The Pope has written me a most ridiculous, a most foolish letter. These people thought I was dead. I had Ancona occupied because, in spite of your remonstrances, no steps had been taken to fortify it; and besides, it is so miserably organised that it could not have held out against attack. Make it well understood that I will no longer endure this child's play, and that I do not wish representatives of Russia and Sardinia to be received in Rome. My intention is to recall you and to replace you by a secular. Since these idiots do not object to the possibility of a Protestant occupying the throne of France, I will send them a Protestant ambassador. . . . I am a Christian, but I am not sanctimonious. Constantine separated the civil from the military power, and I also can name a senator who shall command at Rome in my name. It is a fine thing indeed for those who have admitted Russians, rejected Malta, and who wish now to send away my minister, to talk about religion. It is they who defame religion. . . . Tell Consalvi, tell the Pope, that as he wishes to send away my minister from Rome, I am quite capable of going there myself to re-establish him. Nothing is to be done with such men. . . . They are becoming the laughing-stock of courts and of nations. I gave them advice, which they would never take. They imagined that Russians, English, and Neapolitans would respect the Pope's neutrality. To the Pope I represent Charlemagne, because, as Charlemagne did, I unite the French and Lombard crowns, and my empire stretches to the East. It must be understood, then, that we come to an understanding on these points. I will change nothing outwardly, if people treat me properly; but otherwise, I shall reduce the Pope to be Bishop of Rome. . . . Really, nothing is so wanting in sense as the Court of Rome." [1]

The States of the Church, serving as they did to separate the two French armies camped in Italy—the one under Eugène de Beauharnais, and the other under Joseph Bonaparte—were an easy prey to the man who did not recognise moral obstacles. Bent on securing Italy for himself, Napoleon was concerned, he said, to relieve the Chief of Christians from the burden of material cares—in other words, from the independence of his States. Wherever this anxiety has existed, it has been a symptom of personal ambition. It revealed itself in the tone of command Napoleon now adopted to the Holy Father. On February 13th, 1806, he wrote to Pius VII. as follows :—

---

[1] *L'Église Romaine et le Premier Empire*, t. ii. p. 77.

"Most Holy Father,—I have received the letter of your Holiness, dated January 29th. I share all your troubles, and can imagine that you have your difficulties. You can avoid both by walking straight on, by holding aloof from politics and disregarding powers who in religion are heretical or outside the Church, and in politics are far removed from your States, incapable of protecting you, and only powerful for evil. All Italy shall acknowledge my government. I shall not touch the independence of the Holy See. I will even bear the expenses of my army in your territory.

"But these must be our conditions. Your Holiness must profess the same regard for me in the temporal order as I profess for you in the spiritual order. You must discontinue a profitless regard for heretics who are enemies of the Church, and for European powers who are incapable of benefiting your cause. Your Holiness is the Sovereign, but I am the Emperor, of Rome. All my enemies must be your enemies. That an Englishman, a Russian, a Swede, or a minister of the Sardinian King should henceforth reside in Rome, or in any part of your States, is entirely unfitting. No vessel belonging to any of these nations should enter your ports. As hitherto, I shall always manifest a filial respect for your Holiness as Head of our faith. But I am answerable before God for religion, which He has willed to restore through my means. How can I then, without deep lamentation, see it compromised by the tardy proceedings of the Court of

Rome, where nothing is completed, where the true basis of religion—souls—are allowed to perish, all through certain worldly interests, or foolish disputes founded on the prerogatives of the tiara ? They who leave Germany in anarchy, who so zealously protect Protestant marriages, and wish to oblige me to unite my family with Protestant princes, who keep back the Bulls of my bishops, and deliver up my dioceses to anarchy, will be accountable to God for such conduct. Six months are necessary to supply a bishop with working powers, when it might be done in eight days. As to Italian affairs, I have done everything for the bishops. I have consolidated the interests of the Church, and not meddled in spiritual matters. What I have done for Milan, I will do for Naples, and for every other place within my dominion. I do not refuse the assistance of men who are inspired with true zeal for religion, nor to come to an understanding with them. But since God has chosen me to watch over religion after such tremendous catastrophes, and if at Rome time is wasted in a guilty indifference, I can neither become nor remain heedless as to what might endanger the prosperity and the good of my subjects. I know, most Holy Father, that your Holiness wishes to do right, but you are surrounded by men who have no such wish, who have erroneous principles, and who aggravate present evils instead of endeavouring to remedy them. If your Holiness would be mindful of what I told you in Paris, religion in Germany would be organised, and not remain in its present miserable condition. . . . But I cannot let a thing which might be done in a fortnight last a whole year. It is not by sleeping away the time that I have raised the state of the clergy and the publicity of worship to its high actual level, that I have reorganised religion in France on such a footing that no country exists where it works so much good, is more respected, or enjoys greater consideration. Those who speak a different language to your Holiness deceive you, and are your enemies; they will bring down misfortunes which will end by proving fatal to themselves.

"With this, I pray that God, most Holy Father, may give you many years to govern our mother, Holy Church.—Your devoted son,   NAPOLEON.[1]

"PARIS, 13*th February* 1806."

In the Parliamentary discussions raised in 1805 in England, on the subject of Catholic Emancipation, a member of the House of Lords gave utterance to a view of the reigning Sovereign Pontiff which it may be well to mention. " I think," he said, " indeed, I am certain, that the Pope is nothing but a miserable puppet in the hands of the French usurper; that he does not dare to take the simplest step without Napoleon's orders, and that if the Emperor asked for a Bull to stir up the priests of Ireland against the Government, the Pope would not refuse the tyrant.[2]

[1] *Histoire de Pie VII.*, t. ii. p. 113.
[2] See *Du Pape*, J. de Maistre, t. i. p. 267.

Summoned by Napoleon to accede to the Continental blockade, which was to weaken England's maritime power, the "miserable puppet" answered in these strong and noble terms :—

"As Vicar of that Eternal Word Who is not the God of dissension, but the God of peace—Who came to blot out our iniquities, and to preach peace to those who are near, and to those who are far off (these are the Apostle's expressions), how can we deviate from the teachings of our Divine Founder? How can we act in contradiction with our mission? It is not our will, but God's, whose place we occupy on earth, which lays down the duty of peace towards all men, whether Catholics or heretics, near or remote, whether or no we have to expect good or evil from them. We cannot betray the office entrusted to us by Almighty God, and we should betray it if, for the motives alleged by your Majesty, as, for instance, in the case of heretical powers who can work us no good (these are your Majesty's own words), we consented to demands which would force us to take active part in a war against them. Some of our predecessors may have departed from neutrality when aggression made it necessary, or the good of religion was at stake. If any one among them, through human frailty, ever departed from these principles, we do not hestitate to say that his conduct could never serve as an example to us. You say, further, that your enemies must be our enemies. This is opposed to the character of our Divine mission, which owns no enmities, not even with those who have broken from the centre of our unity."[1]

The Holy Father had called a Congregation (not a Consistory) of the Sacred College, to discuss the two points officially communicated to him by Fesch :—

1. The expulsion of Russians, English, Swedes, and Sardinians from Rome and the Papal States.

2. The closing of the Papal ports to English, Russian, and Swedish vessels.

Napoleon, who recommended the Pope to hold aloof from politics, would have drawn him into a partiality ill becoming his dignity, by inducing him to favour, not the cause of France, but Napoleon Bonaparte, to the exclusion of four European powers. Fesch, in his capacity of French ambassador, consented to remain away from the Congregation, for, as Consalvi urged, his presence would have fettered the liberty of the cardinals. Only one, a French cardinal, gave his vote for the Emperor's demands. After the event Fesch bitterly complained that he had been kept at a distance. He had been unable to use that personal influence from which the Emperor pretended to expect so much. He was irritated and distressed at the result of the Congregation, and he seemed determined to find a personal grievance in the matter. With an ill-will for Consalvi, which he had never attempted to master, he did his utmost to bring down Napoleon's displeasure on the devoted minister. The conduct of Fesch at this time was out of harmony with Catholic

---

[1] *Histoire de Pie VII.*, t. ii. pp. 122, 123, 128.

instincts, because he was trying to play an impossible game. "No man can serve God and Mammon," but this is precisely what Fesch was striving after at Rome. He had a conscience, and he was a prince of the Church. It is probable, then, that he secretly thought things were going a great deal too far, and his own part was distasteful to him. On the other hand, he was uncle to the man who was convulsing Europe, crowning and uncrowning its kings as if more than Emperor of the West. He had not the moral courage to shut his eyes to the pomp of empire, to proclaim himself boldly one of two things: a zealous cardinal or a devoted courtier. Because he tried to conciliate God and the world, he failed to please either.

> "Incontanente intesi e certo fui
> Che quest'era la setta dei cattivi,
> A Dio spiacenti, ed ai nemici sui!" [1]

Thus his position was full of thorns. His conscience was uncomfortable, and he showed it by extreme sensitiveness, a great faculty for taking offence, and no less for giving it by his restless meddling and his want of tact. Later on in his career he redeemed the period of his ambassadorship, because he allowed his ecclesiastical character to predominate. In the beginning of 1806 he was recalled and replaced by M. Alquier, who was rather an ex-Republican than a "corrected" one. The parting words of Pius VII. to Fesch were, that "although the Emperor behaved

---

[1] Dante: *Inferno*, canto iii. 61.

so badly, he remained firmly attached to the imperial person and to the French nation."

Napoleon, however, attributed to Consalvi the Pope's firm resistance to his wishes, and for this reason he determined to overthrow the Secretary of State. "Tell him" (Consalvi), Napoleon wrote to Fesch, "that only two courses remain open to him—always to do what I wish, or to quit the ministry." Later on, Alquier was charged to signify to the Cardinal that none of his movements escaped the Emperor, and that for the first compromising act he should answer with his head. Napoleon would have him arrested in the streets of Rome.[1]

For a long time Pius VII. opposed Consalvi's wish to leave the ministry. Consent on his part seemed to give a colouring to the slanderous accusations of Consalvi's enemies. There was just one advantage about the resignation. It would prove to France—to Europe —that Pius VII. was acting freely, and that he was not ruled by the Prime Minister, when, instead of what would have been weak acquiescence, he accepted the combat. The Holy Father was wont to say sometimes, "Will those people" (the French Ministry) "persist in believing that I am a mere puppet (*fantoccino*)? I shall show them that they are quite wrong."[2]

Cardinal Consalvi retired from the ministry at a critical moment, June 1806. Napoleon's hand was

---

[1] *Correspondance de Napoléon I.*, t. xii. p. 402.

[2] *L'Église Romaine et le Premier Empire*, t. ii. p. 202.

more clearly shown day by day. Not satisfied with the violent occupation of Ancona, he alienated the Pope's possessions in favour of his particular friends. Benevento was bestowed upon the ex-Bishop of Autun, Talleyrand, and Ponte-Corvo on General Bernadotte. Yet the accomplishment of his dream of glory brought no satisfaction to Napoleon. He coveted spiritual as well as temporal sovereignty, and angrily said of priests : " They keep the soul for themselves, and throw me the carcass."

By a singular disposition of Providence, the Head of the Catholic Church had estranged the Emperor of French Democracy, because he had fearlessly defended the honour of a Protestant girl, the daughter of a simple American citizen, against the attacks of pretensions marked with the extremest pride of the old *régime.* And now he was destined to witness the gradual deprivation of the remaining fragments of his temporal power, because at a time of peace he refused to close his ports against England.[1]

[1] *L'Église Romaine et le Premier Empire*, t. ii. p. 44.

CHAPTER VII

NAPOLEON, as he showed himself in 1806, was, after
all, a natural development of the First Consul, who in
1800 had approached the Church, not as a mother
having claim to his reverence, but as an unquestion-
able power in human society, which he needed. Hence,
while the men about him were almost all involved in
that gross disregard of the Church which the times
had generated, the First Consul, of his own accord,
approached the Sovereign Pontiff, and proposed a visible
re-establishment of religion. He not only treated the
Pope as the sole and absolute representative of the
Church, but even called upon him for an exercise of spiritual authority which the preceding eighteen centuries
could scarcely show. The First Consul, himself still a
Republican officer, invited the Pope to extinguish the
jurisdiction of all remaining among the one hundred
and forty-eight legitimate bishops, confessors for the
Faith ; to erect sixty new sees, and to fill those sees
with new occupants. No proceeding can be conceived
which would cut away more completely from its root
the whole growth of so-called Gallician liberties.

Yet that proceeding was the basis of the Concordat which he made with the Holy Father. The Pope considered the agreement a great gain, though it exposed him to some painful refusals from the bishops in question. Thirty-six declined to resign, and the schism of the *Petite Église* was the consequence. In the abstract, the First Consul had recognised the Pope as head of Christendom; in the concrete, he had endeavoured to unmake the Concordat, first by a counterfeit document, then by Organic Articles, which he introduced as part of the compact. The First Consul ripened in the Emperor, who became for the Church and the State what he had been in his family —a tyrant. From the Concordat till 1814 the French clergy endured a system of secular intrusion which was the price paid by France for crowned Revolution, in Napoleon's person.

After the Holy Father had given the highest religious sanction to Napoleon's crown, the Emperor's policy with regard to the nomination of bishops visibly changed. He gradually discarded the Constitutional clergy, who as a body were favourable to 1789. As the founder of a new dynasty, he now sought out those who were Royalists by birth and education. After his coronation he began openly to patronise the followers of the old Royal House. He looked to those who had frequented Trianon and Versailles to introduce tone and etiquette into the new Court; and, as before the Concordat, so much more now, he sought to make the Catholic faith his handmaid.   After each great victory he wrote in pressing terms to the archbishops and bishops of his empire, to order a *Te Deum* in thanksgiving to God for his victorious arms.

These *Te Deums* were generally accompanied by an episcopal exhortation or a pastoral, furnished by M. Portalis, or even by the Emperor himself, and were worded according to the occasion.   Whilst Prussians were under attack, great lamentations were poured forth on their state of heresy and schism.   The bishops were specially recommended to foster the national hatred against England, on the ground of England's perfidious heresy.

"Monsieur Portalis," the Emperor wrote on April 21st, 1807, "it would be well, especially in Britanny and La Vendée, if some bishop would undertake a pastoral on the persecutions inflicted on Irish Catholics.   He might recommend the duty of prayer that our brethren, the persecuted Catholics of Ireland, may enjoy freedom in religion.   For this it would be necessary to read up the subject, and you might write a telling article in the *Moniteur*, which would furnish matter for a pastoral."

But it was not enough to preach a passive crusade against the Emperor's enemies.   It was furthermore required to give him personal praise, with no half-and-half measure.   "You must praise the Emperor more in your pastorals," said M. Réal one day to Mgr. de Broglie.   The prelate had just been reproducing Bossuet's expressions of joy to honour the

King of Rome's birth. "Give me the measure of praise that is expected from me," he answered. "I do not know it," was the reply.

The custom of reading army bulletins from the altar had been gradually adopted. The reader often added his own comments, which was not difficult as long as Napoleon continued to be a magnificent conqueror. The task, however, was delicate when doubtful issues became the order of the day. Napoleon gradually suppressed the custom, on the ground that priests should not be allowed to feel their political importance. At the same time, he saw no harm in taking upon himself spiritual importance. He not only supervised pastorals—the sermons of provincial *curés* affected his peace of mind. He writes: "Inform M. Robert, a priest of Bourges, of my displeasure. He preached a very foolish sermon on the 15th of August. L'Abbé de Coucy is a great worry to me. He keeps up too large a correspondence. I wish him to be arrested and put into a monastery. . . . It is most urgent that you should keep your eye on the diocese of Poitiers. It is really shameful that you have not yet arrested M. Stevens. People are too sleepy, else how could a wretched priest have escaped? . . . I see from your letter that you have had a La Vendée *curé* arrested. You have acted very wisely. Keep him in prison."[1]

The press was severely kept in check. The Emperor suppressed all newspapers of a religious

---

[1] *Corespondance de Napoléon I.*, 1805-1807.

tone, save one, the *Journal des Curés*, which he overhauled. "No priest," he observed, "should bother his head about the Church, except in his sermons."[1] Certainly the Emperor did "bother his head" a good deal. He ruled the number and quality of the feasts which he wished his people to solemnise. In the year 1638, Louis XIII., upon the birth of a son, afterwards Louis XIV., chose the 15th of August, the feast of the Assumption, to place his person, his crown, and France under the special protection of Our Lady, and ordered that every year a solemn procession should take place throughout the kingdom in memory of that consecration. Now, however, the 15th of August was allotted to St. Napoleon, in token of the Emperor's birthday; it was to recall Napoleon's birth, as well as the new order of things signified by the Concordat. The distinguishing feature of the day was to be not Our Lady's honour, but thanksgiving for the prosperity of the Empire—in other words, for the Emperor himself. Besides St. Napoleon, the first Sunday following the 11th Frimaire (December) was to be kept in memory of the Coronation and the successes of the *Grande Armée*. These were the only feasts specially marked in Napoleon's calendar. The others he considered vain and extravagant. St. Napoleon was entirely unknown. M. Portalis was obliged to own as much to Mgr. d'Osmond, Bishop of Nancy, who could find no facts as a basis of popular devo-

---

[1] *Lettre de l'Empereur à M. Portalis*, 14 août 1807.

tion. At length some information was provided in the discovery that amongst those who had suffered martyrdom at Alexandria in Egypt, under Diocletian and Maximian, was a certain *Neopolis* or *Neopolas*. The name was Greek, and became gradually *Napoleo*, and later the Italian, *Napoleone*.[1]

Napoleon had the instincts of a military genius, and knew that obedience is possible only in perfect unity. A paragraph in the Organic Articles had spoken of one catechism for all France. In itself this unity could present nothing displeasing to the Holy Father, as long as the catechism was drawn up by ecclesiastical authority and duly authorised. In the autumn of 1805, Caprara sent a draught of the proposed compendium to Rome, asking for a decision. Rome's answer may have been purposely delayed. Pressed by the legate, Consalvi, who evidently expected no good from the business, at length declared that were the Government to choose or to compose a catechism, His Holiness would look upon the act as an insult offered to the French Episcopate. To the Apostles, and to their successors alone, had the power of teaching been given.[2] This explicit answer was as if it had never been for the weak legate. In direct disobedience to his instructions, he not only contributed to the catechism, but he also kept the whole proceeding a secret from Pius VII. and from Consalvi, so

---

[1] *L'Église Romaine et le Premier Empire*, t. ii. p. 252.
[2] Ibid., t. ii. p. 278.

H

that they first heard of its publication through a newspaper.

In April 1806 an imperial decree was passed, ordering the use of one catechism for the whole of France. M. Portalis, the lay *Ministre des Cultes*, was charged to draw it up. He in his turn gave it to his nephew, M. d'Astros, the vicar-general of the aged Monseigneur de Belloy, Archbishop of Paris. M. d'Astros had already given proof of heroic fortitude and devotedness, and he was preparing by a most holy life for a true confessorship. His part in the imperial catechism must be qualified as an error of judgment. He could not receive from M. Portalis the order to do and to preach. The position of M. Portalis himself was an anomaly in a government calling itself Catholic. The catechism was largely taken from that of Bossuet for the diocese of Meaux, but neither Bossuet nor M. d'Astros contributed the article on the Fourth Commandment. This reveals another hand, which was no other than that of Caprara.[1] Napoleon's point of view with regard to the catechism was the amount of submission and obedience he could claim from the French nation. Caprara humoured his bent in the following questions and answers :—

" *Q.* What are the duties of Christians with regard to reigning princes, and what are our duties in particular towards Napoleon, our Emperor ?

[1] Caussette : *Vie de Monseigneur d'Astros, Archévêque de Toulouse,* p. 110.

" *A*. Christians are bound to give their princes love, respect, obedience, fidelity, and military service, and we in particular are bound to give the same, together with the taxes which are ordered for the preservation and defence of the Empire and of the throne, to Napoleon, our Emperor. We are bound, moreover, to give him our fervent prayers for the spiritual and temporal prosperity of the State.

" *Q*. Why are we so bound towards our Emperor ?

" *A*. In the first place, because God, Who creates and distributes empires according to His pleasure, has, in loading our Emperor with talents, both for war and peace, established him as our sovereign, and has made him the minister of Almighty power, as well as the divine image on earth. The honour, then, and the service of our Emperor is one and the same thing as the honour and service of God.

" Secondly, because our Lord Jesus Christ has Himself taught us, by His doctrine and His example, what we owe to our Sovereign. In His birth, He was obedient to the edict of Cæsar Augustus. He did not refuse the lawful tribute ; and just as He commanded us to render to God those things which are God's, so He desired that we should render to Cæsar that which is Cæsar's.

" *Q*. Are there not particular reasons which should attach us to the person of Napoleon I., our Emperor ?

" *A*. Yes, for he is the man raised by God in difficult circumstances to re-establish public worship, and the holy religion of our fathers, and to be its protector.   He has consolidated public tranquillity by his consummate and active wisdom ; he preserves the State with his mighty arm ; he has become the Lord's Anointed by the consecration of the Supreme Pontiff and Head of the Universal Church.

" *Q.* What opinion is to be entertained of those who are wanting in their duty towards our Emperor ?

" *A.* According to the Apostle St. Paul, they resist the order of things established by God Himself, and render themselves worthy of eternal damnation.

" *Q.* Will our duty towards our Emperor bind us equally in the case of his legitimate successors, as stipulated by the constitutions of the Empire ?

" *A.* Yes, certainly ; for we read in Holy Scripture, that God, Who is the Lord of heaven and earth, gives empires by a disposition of His supreme will and providence, not merely to an individual but to a family.

" *Q.* What are our obligations towards our magistrates ?

" *A.* We must honour, respect, and obey them, as depositaries of the authority of our Emperor.

" *Q.* What is forbidden by the Fourth Commandment ?

" *A.* It forbids disobedience to our superiors, conduct prejudicial to them, or evil speaking of them." [1]

Napoleon appreciated Caprara's devotion to his cause.   " I will willingly purchase Caprara's palace at Bologna for him," he wrote to Prince Eugène ; " even should it cost me a few thousand francs more, I

---

[1] *L'Église Romaine et le Premier Empire*, t. ii. p. 268.

will make the sacrifice in order to get him out of his difficulties. Entrust this purchase to my steward. I will have the money paid by instalments, giving securities for the loan. I know Caprara's faults, and I recommend him to you. He is one of the first and the truest friends I have had in Italy."[1]

One day Napoleon was showing Fontanes a ring. It represented Augustus, with the inscription, *Summus Pontifex*. "How do you like it?" inquired Napoleon of Fontanes. Fontanes turned it over, but missed the inscription, which was the point of Napoleon's query. "Augustus possessed a dignity which does not belong to me," was Napoleon's comment.[2]

[1] *Lettre de l'Empereur au Prince Eugène*, 23 mars 1806.
[2] *Vie de Monseigneur d'Astros*, p. 163.

CHAPTER VIII

ON the resignation of Consalvi, Pius VII. purposely chose a man who would not have been naturally pointed out as a Pope's Prime Minister. Cardinal Casoni was a mild and gentle old man, without strong views, and certainly no diplomatist. His first act as Secretary of State was to address a circular to the various Papal Nuncios of Europe, informing them that Benevento and Ponte Corvo had been spoliated. The Pope's design in publishing this officially was not so much to obtain redress as to prove how little Consalvi had coerced him. He had no expectations from European Cabinets, for the man who was persecuting him was humbling them, and diminishing their political importance day by day. The Pope was called upon to belong to the French Federation, and as a temporal sovereign to bind himself to a league, offensive and defensive, against all the enemies of the Empire, or to submit to the loss of his States. The Holy Father had thwarted Napoleon's ambitious designs, and hitherto all similar obstacles had been swept away. The Emperor, therefore, was determined to bring the

Court of Rome to reason by fair means or by foul. He would have preferred to do it quietly (*sans secousse*), but, if impossible, he should not hesitate to use violence. This was the state of affairs between Pius VII. and Napoleon in the summer of 1806. He made, as usual, considerable use of Caprara, and many were the scenes, half-spontaneous, half-preconcerted, which he inflicted on the bewildered legate. He was well aware that they would be communicated to Pius VII., and perhaps induce the Holy Father's entire adhesion to his extravagant demands. Caprara was in the habit of frequenting, nearly every evening, Josephine's small and chosen circle. One day the Empress was slightly indisposed, and the legate, as it happened, was taken to the Emperor's reception, at which his own household, that of the Empress, and the principal members of the Court were present. Hardly had Napoleon perceived the legate when he began speaking about Roman matters in a loud voice, and inveighing against the evil councillors of the Holy Father. These rages were Napoleonic, but very undignified.

"My demands," he said, "were entirely of a temporal and political nature. But the world shall judge between the Pope and me. It shall see that I also am bound in conscience to ensure my subjects their rights. St. Louis was tenacious of them, yet he was beatified by Rome."

Caprara ventured on some inoffensive remark, but Napoleon, with the impetuosity of a torrent, would

not let him finish his sentence. " Write to Rome," he
pursued vehemently, " that I am resolved to prevent
the English from effecting a diversion, and from cutting
the communication between my troops of the kingdom
of Italy and those of the kingdom of Naples.   Write
that I demand of His Holiness an unreserved and
frank declaration to the effect that during the present
war, and all future wars, all the ports of the Pontifical
States shall be closed to all English men-of-war and
merchant ships.   Write this to the Pope, write it at
once, because if within the shortest possible delay I
do not receive the declaration which I demand, I shall
cause the rest of the Pontifical territory to be occupied.
I shall have the French eagles posted on the gates of
all his cities and of all his domains, and I shall divide
the Papal provinces into duchies and principalities,
which I shall confer upon whom I please, as I have
already done with Benevento and Ponte-Corvo.   If the
Pope persists in his refusal, I shall establish a Senate at
Rome ; and when once Rome and the Pontifical States
are in my hands, they will stay there.[1]   Write this explicitly ; conceal nothing : I shall see, from the Pope's
answer, whether you have been a faithful reporter.[2]
The time had come when Napoleon could reveal a long-
meditated design without shame.   No more was to be
obtained from that Pope, who in too sanguine a moment of confidence had consented to recognise his crown

---

[1] We are reminded here of a later power which has said, "Ci siamo
e ci staremo."

[2] *L'Église Romaine et le Premier Empire*, t. ii. p. 307.

before the throne of God, in sight of all the people. He was to be sacrificed because the Emperor willed it. Napoleon's determination was fixed, and, what is more, he had committed himself to it before his Court. He rarely acted from impulse; but when a plan had grown and worked in his mind to full maturity, it poured forth with the impetuosity of a mountain torrent, *seemingly* the birth of mere hastiness or anger. As an immediate effect of the scene inflicted on Caprara, which had lasted a whole hour, Alquier wrote an ultimatum to the Holy Father. It told Pius VII., in rude and offensive language, that he was on the way to lose his remaining provinces through his own fault, and that no letters written "in the style of Boniface VIII. to Philippe le Bel" would avail to save his temporal power.[1] Secret instructions were given to the French troops stationed at Ancona and Cività Vecchia, to seize the Papal revenues, and to incorporate the Pontifical troops with their army. Dues on the salt tax and all available money likewise passed into the hands of the French. These violent acts of aggression, and the occupation of the Pope's territory, produced a penury in the Papal treasury which rejoiced Napoleon. He shrunk at nothing to bring the Holy Father to terms. Power wrongfully used is a true inebriation.

"By what right do you act in this way?" asked a Papal officer one day of the official thief who came to rob the Pope's treasury.

---

[1] *Note de M. Alquier*, 8 juillet 1807.

" You serve a small prince, I a mighty sovereign : that is all my right," replied the aggressor.

If we may believe Cardinal Casoni, the mental and physical anxiety of this downright persecution threatened to prove fatal to the Holy Father. But at a time when an active system of State usurpation thus disturbed the rest of Pius VII., there were not wanting those amongst his children who were disposed to complain of what they termed an imprudent resistance. Caprara represented in his despatches that his own sentiments, favourable to the Emperor's demands, were shared by the most prominent Catholics of France, and Spina besought the Holy Father not to persevere in a line of conduct which must draw down irreparable evils upon the Church.[1] At our actual distance from the events in question, it seems almost incredible that such advice could ever have been given. In weighing, therefore, all the difficulties which beset his path as Sovereign Pontiff, praise and heartfelt gratitude are due to the memory of Pius VII. Resistance was prompted by his conscience, and by no worldly motive of interest, and this is so true that, after writing with his own hand the following letter to Caprara, he expected, with perfect serenity and resignation, what afterwards really came to pass, the occupation of Rome.[2]

" We have earnestly commended ourself to God, whose unworthy Vicar we are upon earth, and to the Apostle St. Peter, whose successor we are, in order to

---

[1] *Lettre du Cardinal Spina au Saint-Père,* 1806.
[2] Pacca : *Memorie Storiche,* t. i. p. 68.

obtain the necessary light wherewith to answer your
question.   Here is this answer, which we write with
our own hand, to give you a new proof of the importance which we attribute to questions so weighty, and
to impress upon you still more the earnest and solemn
character of the convictions which we feel bound to
communicate to you.   The reasons for which we have
refused to make the desired declaration are too weighty
and too just to allow us to change our opinion.   They
are founded, not upon human motives, which is generally supposed, but upon the very basis of those duties
which are ours as the common Father of the Faithful
and the minister of peace.   It may be true, as His
Majesty has told you, that the English will never
believe that Rome has risked everything, for them,
and that they will never bear, in consequence, the
least gratitude to the Holy See: this is not what we
have to take into consideration.   We have only consulted our duty, which imposes upon us the obligation
to cause no injury to religion by the interruption of
communication between the Head and members of
the Church in all places where Catholics exist.   We
should ourself provoke this interruption by the exercise of hostile acts against any nation whatever, and
by taking part in a war against that nation.   If the
evil caused to religion proceeded from the conduct
of another, such for instance as that which might
result from any measures His Majesty might set on
foot owing to our refusal, we should deplore it in
the bitterness of our heart, and we should adore the

judgments of God, Who permits such evil for the
accomplishment of the inscrutable workings of His
Providence.   But if, betraying our character and the
nature of our office, we consented to aggressive measures which proved the source of evil for the Church,
we ourself should be the cause of such evil, and in
this precisely consists the point of our refusal.   We
cannot, in the face of an evil which threatens us,
cause the Church to suffer in the way we have specified.   But these very calamities with which we are
threatened are not necessary calamities.   They depend
entirely on the will of His Majesty, who is free either
to put them into execution or not.   We still venture
to hope that his regard for religion, his equity, and
his magnanimity, and the remembrance of all we have
done for him, will speak to his heart, and will not
allow him to come before the world and posterity as
the persecutor of the Church, rather than her protector and benefactor.   Whatever happens, we put
our cause in God's hands.   He is far above us and
the most powerful monarchs, and we rely upon His
Divine help, which will not fail us at the moment
foreseen by His wisdom.   His Majesty has told you
that when once Rome and the States of the Church
are in his hands, they will stay in them.   His Majesty
is free to believe this.   We, however, frankly reply
that if His Majesty rightly supposes he can command
material power, we look beyond all kings to God, the
Avenger and Protector of Justice, Who controls all
human power.   You inform us that the Emperor has

told you that the public nature of the question makes it impossible for him to relent. We must remind His Majesty that he cannot lose in real greatness or true magnanimity, when, instead of earthly potentate or rival, he listens to his father and friend, the priest of Jesus Christ. If this consideration fails to move him, we are bound to tell him in Apostolical liberty, that if His Majesty's honour is involved before men, our conscience is pledged before God, never, as Head of the Church, to take part in war. Certainly, we have no intention of being the first to set the Church and the world an example which no one of our predecessors has given during the course of eighteen centuries. We could not adopt a hostile attitude, indefinitely or permanently, against any nation whatever. We cannot accede to the Federal System of the French Empire. The territory transmitted to us, independent of federal bond, must remain independent by the nature of our Apostolical liberty. If this independence were attacked, or if the threats were carried out which are constantly urged, in spite of our dignity and our friendship for His Majesty, we should see in the step the signal of open persecution, and we should refer to the judgment of God. Our determination is fixed. Nothing can change it—neither threats, nor their realisation. . . . These are the feelings which you may look upon as our last will and testament, and we are ready, if need be, to sign it with our blood. If persecution falls upon us, the words of our Divine

Lord are our strength : '*Blessed are they who suffer persecution for justice' sake.*' Make our state of mind fully known to His Majesty; we expressly command it. The ocean of pain and anguish in which we are plunged makes us cry to God every day, that He would shorten this bitter life. It is time to emerge from it. Meanwhile be sure to tell the Emperor that we still cherish him, that we are disposed to give him all possible proofs of affection, and to continue being his best friend; but do not let him ask for what it is not in our power to bestow." [1]

This letter exhibits the Pontiff and the man. The Pope says, "I simply cannot do what you ask," and the man, who was so full of tenderness, cannot resist adding, *but* "I am still your friend." The voice of friendship produced small echo in Napoleon's heart. The Emperor, affronted because Pius VII. had communicated one of his letters to the Sacred College, refused to correspond personally with Rome, hence the Holy Father's reason for writing to Caprara. The weak legate failed even to secure an audience for the Papal document. Instead of listening, Napoleon exclaimed, "*Monsieur le Cardinal, que vous sentez les clubs de Rome,*" and turned his back upon the Cardinal.[2]

In September 1806, Napoleon's thoughts were running on new conquests. They would lead him,

---

[1] *L'Église Romaine et le Premier Empire*, t. ii. p. 321 ; *Letter de Pius VII. au Cardinal Caprara*, 31 juillet 1806.

[2] *L'Église Romaine et le Premier Empire*, t. ii. p. 325.

as he reasoned, to carry all before him. France was on the eve of war with Prussia, then, as now, a great military power, and to Prussian affairs Napoleon devoted all his energies and the resources of his genius. The annihilation of Frederick's wonderful troops, and the temporary fall of the Prussian Monarchy, were events which added fuel to the fire of Napoleon's ambition. From Frederick's palace at Berlin he once more dictated his terms to the Holy Father. Monseigneur d'Arezzo, Bishop of Seleucia, was deputed to "signify peremptorily" to Pius VII. that he must accede to the confederation of the French Empire. Either the Pope would consent, in which case he should lose nothing, or he would refuse, and be subjected to the deprivation of his States! "Let the Pope do as I wish," were Napoleon's last words to Monseigneur d'Arezzo, "and he will be repaid for the past and for the future." [1]

The Emperor pressed to have a new legate at Paris, or rather he would have been too glad to keep Caprara, if the Holy Father consented to invest the weak Cardinal with the necessary power for transacting the business in question. He said to Monseigneur d'Arezzo, "Let the Holy Father entrust the affair to his legate in Paris, who is a good man, or to Spina, with full powers, or to anybody else." This "anybody else" sounded ambiguous, but it was not, for Napoleon had settled that Cardinal de Bayane, and only he, should come to Paris. As

---

[1] *L'Église Romaine et le Premier Empire*, t. ii. p. 341.

a Frenchman, he alone of the Sacred College had voted in favour of the Emperor's extravagant demands, and it was therefore clear that something might be done with him. Before, however, the Prussian campaign produced the brilliant results, which may even have astonished Napoleon himself, the Battle of Friedland and the Peace of Tilsit, Pius VII. had been asserting his spiritual rights in Italy. He refused to confirm certain bishops nominated by the French Government to the vacant sees in the duchy of Milan, and the Venetian provinces annexed to the Empire in 1806. The Italian Concordat had not been carried out, and the French troops during the Prussian War were grossly wanting to the Holy Father as a temporal sovereign.[1] In refusing, therefore, to confirm the new Italian bishops, Pius VII. was discharging a duty. Napoleon had broken his contract, and so made the treaty void. He now affected to view the Pope's refusal as a grievance. "The Pope wishes me then no longer to have bishops in Italy," he wrote to Prince Eugène. "All the better! If that is benefiting religion, how must they act who wish *to destroy it?*"[2] Pius VII. afterwards consented to nominate *motu proprio* the bishops already proposed, but condescension was entirely useless where the will to be conciliated was so utterly wanting. Napoleon had beaten all his enemies. Save England, Europe was at his

---

[1] Pacca: *Memorie Storiche*, t. i. p. 74.
[2] *Lettre de l'Empereur au Prince Eugène*, 12 avril 1807.

feet. Now was the moment to conquer the obstinacy or the weakness of the Holy Father, for that he alone should hold aloof from the European league, or continue to defend the interests of a Protestant country against the might of a second Charlemagne, was an impossible hypothesis. It was against Napoleon's dignity, as he judged, to renew a direct correspondence with the Head of the Church, so that in order to speak his mind to Pius VII., he had recourse to artifice. He wrote a short letter from Dresden to Prince Eugène, on the 22nd July 1807, containing two enclosures : (1) a letter that the Viceroy of Italy was to write to the Holy Father, as if coming from himself ; (2) a letter which was to have all the appearance of having been written by Napoleon to Eugène, and spontaneously communicated by the latter to the Holy Father.[1]   The first was the following :—

"MOST HOLY FATHER,—I communicated the letter of your Holiness to my most honoured father and sovereign, who has sent me a detailed reply from Dresden, of which I make an extract. . . . Let your Holiness allow me to say that all the discussions raised by the Court of Rome tend to aggravate a great sovereign, who, penetrated with pious feelings, is conscious of the invaluable aid he has been to religion in France, Italy, Germany, Poland, or Saxony, as the case may be.   He knows that the world looks

---

[1] *L'Église Romaine et le Premier Empire*, t. ii. p. 355.

upon him as the pillar of the Christian Faith, and the enemies of religion as a prince who has restored the lost supremacy of Catholicity in Europe. Is the Court of Rome actuated by love of religion, when on frivolous pretences and in things which could be settled with a little moderation it makes use of threats derogatory to the rights of the throne, which are no less sacred than those of the tiara? If your Holiness is really moved by devotion to duty and love of religion, send plenipotential faculties to the Cardinal Legate in Paris, and in eight days all will be settled. If you do not agree to this step, your pontificate will be more fatal to the Court of Rome than that under which Germany and England broke off from its jurisdiction."

Here the Emperor's letter (the second enclosure) began :—

"My Son,—I see in a letter from His Holiness, which certainly he never wrote, that he threatens me. Does he think, then, that the rights of the throne are less sacred than those of the tiara? There were kings before there were Popes. They say that they want to publish all the evil that I have committed against religion. The idiots! They ignore, then, that there does not exist a spot in Italy, Germany, or Poland, where I have not done more for religion than the Pope has done evil, not with a bad intention, but owing to the irascible counsels of a few narrow-minded

men that surround him. They wish to denounce me
to Christendom! So monstrous a notion can proceed
only from a dense ignorance of our century. It belongs to a thousand years ago. A Pope who could
lend himself to the step would cease to be Pope in
my eyes. To me he would be Antichrist, sent to
disturb the world and to injure men, and I should
thank God for his helplessness. If this happened,
I should cut off my people from all communication
with Rome, and establish a civil guard there. . . .
What does Pius VII. mean by denouncing me to
Christendom? Would he put my throne under an
interdict, or excommunicate me? Does he imagine
that their arms will fall from the hands of my
soldiers,[1] or does he think to give my people a dagger
with which they can assassinate me? Some infuriated
Popes have preached this doctrine. All that the
Holy Father would have to do would be to cut off
my hair, and to shut me up in a monastery. Does
he take me for Louis le Débonnaire? . . . The
present Pope is too powerful. Priests are not made
to reign. Let them imitate St. Peter, St. Paul, and

[1] M. le Comte de Ségur, in his book, *Histoire de Napoléon et de la
Grande Armée*, remarks, *à propos* of the Russian campaign: "Their
very arms (those of the French soldiers) turned against them. They
seemed an insupportable weight to their numbed limbs. The men
frequently stumbled down, and then the *arms fell from their hands*, or
got broken or lost in the snow. If they managed to regain their legs,
it was without arms. *They did not throw down* their weapons; hunger
and cold caused them to drop. The fingers of many other soldiers
froze on their gun which they still held, and so made movement
impossible, which would have produced a little warmth and life"
(t. i. c. xi.).

the holy Apostles, who are certainly worth a Julius, a Boniface, a Gregory, or a Leo. . . . It is disorder in the Church, not the good of religion, which necessitates a Court of Rome. Rome is interested in promoting discord, whereby an arbitrary power is assumed, and the limits of temporal and spiritual dominion are confused. Really, I am beginning to blush, and to feel humbled at the foolish conduct which Rome has inflicted on me; and perhaps the time is not far off when, if this meddling in my affairs does not stop, I shall see in the Pope nothing more than the Bishop of Rome, with a rank entirely similar to my bishops. I shall unite without fear the Gallican, Italian, German, and Polish Churches in a Council, despatch my business without the Pope, and deliver my people from the pretensions of Roman priests. . . . In two words, this is the last time that I consent to treat with these wretched priests of Rome. It is possible to despise and to disown them without deviating from the right path, and in point of fact what is capable of saving in one country is capable of saving in another. . . . I hold my crown from God, and from the will of my people. I shall always remain Charlemagne, not Louis le Débonnaire, for the Court of Rome. I have never wished for anything but to come to an understanding with Rome. If Rome does not wish it, let it not name any bishops. My people will dispense with bishops, and my churches with direction, until the interest of religion points to a course which is imperatively necessary for their good and that of my crown."

Here Prince Eugène was to say, as if coming from himself : "Most Holy Father, this letter was not written for the eyes of your Holiness. I beseech you to put an end to these disputes, not to listen to the perfidious counsels of irascible men, who, blind to circumstances and to the true interests of religion, are animated by unworthy passions. . . . These wish to equal in power, I make bold to say in haughtiness, a sovereign whom we can compare only to Cyrus or to Charlemagne. Did the Patriarch of Jerusalem so comport himself towards Cyrus, or the contemporary Pontiffs towards Charlemagne ? Flies ought not to worry a lion. They cannot harm him, but they irritate him. . . . The Romans are in an unhappy plight, for which they have to thank the councillors of your Holiness. The Church is suffering, because the Sovereign Pontiff will not confirm bishops, through a foolish regard for prerogatives. . . . For that matter this is the last time that I am authorised to write to your Holiness. You will hear no more either of my sovereign or of me. You are free to confirm bishops or not. If after this any one shows insubordination or insurrection, he will be punished by the justice of the law, which is a power likewise emanating from the Divinity."

"Send this letter to the Pope," was the final injunction of the enclosure from Dresden, "and tell me when M. Alquier delivers it." [1]

About this time M. de Champagny succeeded M. de Talleyrand as Minister of the Exterior. As a man

---

[1] *L'Église Romaine et le Premier Empire*, t. ii. p. 375.

intellectually inferior to the Prince of Benevento, he exactly suited Napoleon at the height of his social and military glory. As the Emperor would have wished to despatch spiritual affairs without the Pope, so in the material administration of his empire he meant henceforth to deal only with men willing to be led and governed in the minutest details. Napoleon looked with suspicion on the very capacity of the ex-bishop. Talleyrand had ingenuously imagined that he would in some measure direct the pen of the new minister, but he discovered that the Emperor intended to rule the Empire without his assistance. He wisely retired behind his dignity of Grand Elector and Arch-Chancellor of State. This change of minister aggravated, if possible, or, in any case, did not tend to smooth, matters between Pope and Emperor. M. de Champagny's first note was only an echo of the letter from Dresden. Pius VII. would have disarmed any other than Napoleon, whose threats he answered by a cordial letter of invitation. How press insult and violence upon the Sovereign Pontiff who would " cede to no one the honour of receiving the Emperor ? " The diplomacy of a humble and sincere heart is at times the most telling.

" Although your Majesty has left several of our letters unanswered," the Pope wrote to Napoleon, on the 11th of September 1807, "we nevertheless venture to address you once more. Not without pain have we learnt from our Cardinal Legate that your Majesty believes we are estranged from you, and that we

oppose you simply for the sake of opposing you.
Your Majesty, God is our witness : He knows that we
speak truth. It is not the wish to contradict you,
but the voice of duty which has obliged us to refuse
several of your demands. Nothing can be more agreeable to us than to second your desires with all our
power, and to prove this we shall manifest our condescension by sending Cardinal de Bayane to Paris,
according to your wish. . . . It has been rumoured
that your Majesty purposed visiting this country.
Thus, the satisfaction of so desirable an arrangement
would be enhanced by the pleasure of seeing your
Majesty. In this case, we shall cede to no one the
honour of receiving so illustrious a guest : our right
to the preference is indisputable. The Vatican Palace,
which we will have set in order to the best of our
power, will be at your disposal. After all the business
has been despatched in Paris, we, in Rome, shall be at
liberty to promote the Catholic religion, by obtaining
for it those blessings which your Majesty, as its protector, has promised to grant. In the meantime, may
your Majesty feel confidence in our regard. As an
earnest of it, we give you the Apostolical blessing." [1]

At this stage of his career it was no part of
Napoleon's plan to be "an illustrious guest" at the
Vatican. The Temporal Power of the Holy See
thwarted his schemes in Italy. Sooner or later he
meant to possess the Papal States, which were incon-
veniently situated between the French Empire and the

---

[1] *L'Église Romaine et le Premier Empire*, t. ii. p. 367.

kingdom of the Two Sicilies. Apart from the terri-
torial question, a Sovereign Pontiff who held aloof from
the confederal league of any particular nation, and
defended an injured people in virtue of his spiritual
position, was an offender, a stumbling-block that
called for removal. The answer, therefore, to Pius the
Seventh's invitation was an order to Prince Eugène
to let General Lemarrois proceed to occupy the Duchy
of Urbino, and the provinces of Macerata, Fermo, and
Spoleto. Napoleon was provoked rather than pleased
at the prospect of having Cardinal de Bayane at Paris,
and determined to stultify his mission by haughty
and arrogant terms. The Pope was told that his
intervention in the spiritual affairs of France was not
required, that the Gallican Church was enjoying its
privileges in a peace due to the Emperor; that monks
were no longer wanted, but soldiers to fight infidels
and heretics.[1] If ecclesiastical difficulties required it,
the Emperor would call together a General Council,
the " only organ of the Infallible Church, and sovereign
arbitrator of all religious controversy." His object
was to make Cardinal de Bayane draw back, and so to
enable him to complain of the Pope's intractability.

When the news of what had befallen his fairest
provinces reached Pius VII., Cardinal de Bayane had
already started. Early in October, M. Alquier induced the Pope to believe "that what the Emperor
said to the legate in a momentary fit of impatience,

---

[1] *Note de M. de Champagny à Son Eminence le Cardinal Caprara,*
27 septembre, 1807.

was not to be taken too seriously; that in his (M. Alquier's) official instructions, there was no talk of obliging His Holiness to league against all the enemies of the Empire, but only against heretics and the English." The Holy Father then agreed to a final act of condescension. Casoni, in an official despatch to Cardinal de Bayane, intimates its precise nature. "The latest requests of his Imperial Majesty with regard to the English have been confined to the closing of the ports. The Holy Father has every reason to believe that this is all that is involved by his adhesion. But if anything more were asked of him, he would consent, *provided that it did not oblige him to present war, nor touch the independence of his pontifical sovereignty.*"[1]

As a matter of fact, the closing of ports to the English was by no means all that Napoleon required of Pius VII. Napoleon's exactions would have involved a total sacrifice of Papal independence, and to this the Sovereign Pontiff never consented. What he said was, that, firmly resolved to bring about peace, he would concede all that could be conceded. Hardly, however, had he adopted this tone, when the Emperor renewed, through M. de Champagny, his former claims. In a most discourteous memorandum the Minister of the Exterior signified to Pius VII. the *ultimatum* of the French Emperor. It was in reality a project for submitting the Sovereign Pontiff, as supreme arbitrator of Catholic doctrine, to the good pleasure of

---

[1] *Lettre du Cardinal Casoni au Cardinal de Bayane,* 14 octobre 1807.

secular power; or, in other words, for making the spiritual power entirely subordinate to the State. The position of the Chief Pastor must be, to some extent, in accordance with his teaching and his pastoral charge; he must be free and independent of nations and empires. In lending himself, therefore, to similar demands, Pius VII. would have ceased to be Head of the Universal Church. If he had consented to the closing of the ports, he had never intended to join a federal league, as he wrote to Cardinal de Bayane. His words are most clear: "As the treaty in contemplation is not restricted to the closing of the ports, but as we should be compelled to adopt a league which would involve us in a state of perpetual war, utterly incompatible with our character and our ministry of peace, our adhesion is impossible. Upon what grounds are we to risk the danger, or rather the certainty of seeing all spiritual communications with English Catholics cut off, which we now freely carry on? This restriction would surely follow immediately, if we consented to a permanent system of enmity against a power for a cause wholly foreign to us."

These are points of special interest for the English. Other demands were equally derogatory to the Holy Father's dignity. Napoleon would have forced him to guarantee that French cardinals should occupy a third of the Sacred College. Lastly, the memorandum did not mention really spiritual matters at all, and the Holy Father closed his letter in sadness: "We feel that we are treated as an enemy. This is the fruit of our journey to Paris, of our patience, of the long-suffering which has prompted us to undergo so many sacrifices and so many humiliations." If Napoleon did not withdraw his claims, Cardinal de Bayane was recalled and Caprara was to hold himself in readiness to leave Paris.[1]

A month after this letter, Napoleon wrote minute directions to the King of Naples and to the Viceroy of Italy for the French occupation of Rome under General Miollis. The troops of Miollis and Lemarrois, numbering 6000 men, were to enter Rome—General Miollis the first, under pretext of joining the army at Naples. Joseph was to wait for news of Miollis' arrival in Rome, in case the troops under his command had to serve as a reserve, keeping at a distance of four or five leagues from the Eternal City. Orders were issued to General Miollis, when in Rome, to occupy the citadel of Sant' Angelo, to arrest the Neapolitan and English consuls, and even the English residents in Rome. All operations were to be carried out with the greatest secrecy, and seemed to spring from a mind ashamed of its proceedings. The Emperor, in his directions to M. de Champagny, speaks as if Miollis were merely making Rome a stepping-stone to Naples. M. Alquier was to represent to the Holy Father that the General came to Rome in order to cover the rear of the Neapolitan army. Whilst there he was to clear the city of

---

[1] *L'Église Romaine et le Premier Empire*, t. ii. p. 393 (Lettre du 2 décembre 1807).

brigands and the enemies of France. The unoffending English residents were classed under the latter category with disturbers of public security. The same imperial memorandum contains the following words in cipher :—

"The Emperor's intention in writing this memorandum and taking these steps is to accustom the people of Rome and the French troops to live together, so that if the Court of Rome continues to act as foolishly as hitherto, it may cease so gradually to exist that the disappearance will cause no surprise. The smallest insurrection must be put down by material force, if necessary, and by telling examples." [1]

Napoleon thought to incorporate thus simply the Eternal City with his Empire, and by one and the same stroke to become in reality Emperor of Rome, and to efface the temporal action of the Sovereign Pontiff. He had not weighed his arms in a just balance, and they were to fall back upon himself to his own destruction.

Under Napoleon's aggressive and victorious action anxiety and a troubled agitation reigned in Rome. No man knew what the morrow might bring, and for one moment the Holy Father manifested his intention of retiring to Sant' Angelo. The Sacred College dissuaded him from the step. Napoleon wanted only the merest pretext for asserting that he took possession of Rome as a right of conquest.

---

[1] *Lettre de l'Empereur à M. de Champagny et au Prince Eugène*, 1808.

On the 2nd of February 1808, the French troops passed through the open gates of Rome, disarming the Pontifical guards stationed at them. A compact body of cavalry and infantry surrounded the Quirinal Palace, then inhabited by the Holy Father, whilst a huge battery was pointed at the window of his apartments. The peaceful sovereign, whose city was thus ruthlessly invaded by armed force, was celebrating in the Quirinal Chapel the Feast of the Purification. Surrounded by the Sacred College, he was offering to God on the altar of which the Temple was only the figure, the Child who had been set up for the ruin and for the salvation of many in Israel. "The old man held the Child in his arms, but the Child was the old man's Lord."[1] There was the serenity of holy Simeon about the Pope's reception of the French. He pushed condescension so far as to receive Miollis with his ordinary affability, and to say with a smile on his lips, that he still loved France, and "could not complain of the French nation."

On the 3rd of February, M. de Champagny peremptorily signified that the French troops would remain in Rome until the Pope consented to enter the Italian Federation, and to make common cause with those who belonged to it, that is, with Napoleon. The Holy Father answered by a protest, in his own name and in that of his successors, against all usurpation of his domains. It was printed secretly at

[1] Vesper Office of the Purification.

the Quirinal during the night, and pasted myste-
riously on the walls of Rome. It enjoined the Romans
to keep the peace, and to abstain from acts injurious
to the French. They were to be mindful of the
welcome and of the affection shown to Pius VII. by
that nation in other and happier days.[1]

The Holy Father was a prisoner in his own capital,
and unable, through the French monopoly of the post
and the press, to appeal to Catholic Europe. It was
of primary importance in Napoleon's eyes that France
should be kept in ignorance of what was passing in
Rome. During the same month of February all the
Neapolitan cardinals received orders to leave Rome
in twenty-four hours; and as Pius VII., warned of
Napoleon's intentions, had forbidden them to obey,
they were carried off by force. The treatment inflicted on the cardinals was extended to some other
diplomatic personages, to the utter disregard of common justice.[2] Yet a further measure at length roused
the anger of the Sovereign Pontiff, for it was a direct
infringement of his spiritual authority. Early in
March Prince Eugène was ordered to require the
dismissal of all cardinals who were not native subjects
of the Pope. The whole number was fourteen, and
amongst them was the Pro-Secretary of State, Doria,
who had succeeded Casoni. The Neapolitan cardinals
had numbered seven, so that in all twenty-one members
of the Sacred College, occupying important posts in

---

[1] Pacca: *Memorie*, t. i. p. 107.
[2] *L'Église Romaine et le Premier Empire*, t. iii. p. 14.

Rome, had been taken away in one month, and by
sheer force, from the scene of their labours.   Three
days were given to each cardinal as the utmost term
of delay.   This order put an end to Caprara's legatine
faculties.   Submission to it without protest on the
Pope's part would have been, not Christian meekness,
but weak pusillanimity.

"We feel," he said, "that a great persecution is
coming upon us.   Nevertheless we are prepared, for-
tified by our divine Lord's words, 'Blessed are they
who suffer persecution for justice.'"

It was not enough for Napoleon to overthrow the
Papal Government.   He was at the same time organis-
ing a revolution against Charles IV. of Spain, whose
crown he placed on his brother Joseph's head.   He
uncrowned as easily as he crowned, but his crowns
partook of his own fortunes, and, if they were magnificent they were also insecure.   Joseph had been a
short-lived King of Naples, and now he was sent to a
people of whom he knew absolutely nothing.

The Pontifical States were incorporated officially
with the French Empire by a decree of April 2nd,
1808.   They were declared irrevocably united to the
kingdom of Italy, in the form of three departments,
and the Code Napoléon was published at the same
time.   Armed force pushed its way by fraud into the
very palace of the Pope, in order to disarm those who
kept up a certain semblance of a court.   Miollis likewise caused the Governor of Rome, Mgr. Cavalchini,
a personal friend of Pius VII., to be arrested.   The

Holy Father sent a circular to the bishops of the annexed provinces. It enjoined them to withhold submission to their new government. The Pro-Secretary of State, Cardinal Gabrielli, justly suspected by Miollis of signing this document, was arrested, and relegated to his see of Sinigaglia. It was thus that the ministry of Cardinal Pacca was inaugurated in June 1808. No wiser choice could have been made for the hour of misfortune and exile, for though Pacca drew back from the heavy responsibilities of office at so critical a time, he was eminently suited to be both councillor and comforter. He belonged to the party who had opposed from the beginning concessions to France, yet now his first endeavour was to speak peace "where there was no peace." Pius VII., "the meekest of men on the face of the earth," according to Pacca, said to him one day, knowing now the fruitlessness of conciliation, "My Lord Cardinal, they say in Rome that we have been sleeping. We must show them that we are awake, and make a vigorous protest to General Miollis against recent acts of violence!"[1]

For instance, civil volunteers, taken from the refuse of the people, were organised in the heart of the Papal States. They fomented discord, and constituted beyond a doubt all that is commonly understood by brigands. In one of Pacca's remonstrances with Miollis, the General ventured to express Napoleon's orders to shoot or to hang all persons in the

---

[1] *Memorie Storiche*, t. i. pp. 119, 124, 126, &c.

Papal States who were rash enough to oppose the imperial commands.

"General," answered Pacca quietly, "during your stay in Rome you must have seen that the ministers of His Holiness are not to be cowed by threats. For my part, I shall faithfully execute the orders of my sovereign, whatever may be the results." "I soon learned," remarks the Cardinal, "the uselessness of conciliation, and should have reproached myself with prevarication in the discharge of my office, had I not strengthened the Holy Father's resolution to give a public disapproval of the civil volunteers."[1] This proclamation, issued on the 24th of August, under the Pontifical seal, produced the determination on the part of Miollis to send Pacca into exile in his turn, a measure, however, which was thwarted by the courageous resistance of the Cardinal. A few days afterwards, on the 6th of September 1808, whilst the Pro-Secretary was discussing affairs with a Roman prelate, two officers in the service of France entered his apartment, and signified an order from General Miollis, that Pacca should leave Rome in twenty-four hours. At the Porta di San Giovanni the Pope's Minister would find an escort of dragoons, with the commission to take him back to his country, Benevento. Without the least perturbation, Pacca replied that in Rome he took orders of no other but the Pope; that if His Holiness forbade him to go, he should not think of doing so; and he declared his intention of consulting the

[1] *Memorie*, t. i. pp. 140, 142.

K

Holy Father. This was, however, entirely prohibited, for the officers were not to let the Cardinal out of their sight. Pacca petitioned to send a note to Pius VII., and to this they consented. A few minutes afterwards the door was hastily opened. It was the Holy Father who had come to his minister, since his minister could not go to him. For the first time in his life, Pacca saw a startling effect of great anger. The Holy Father, beside himself, did not recognise the Cardinal, and his hair was literally standing on end.

"Who is it, who is it?" he asked in a loud tone.

"I am the Cardinal," replied Pacca, kissing his hand.

"Where is the official?" And turning to him, the Holy Father said, "Go and tell your General that I am weary of suffering so many insults and outrages from a man who still has the effrontery to call himself a Catholic. I am aware what is aimed at by these violent measures. They wish, in separating me gradually from all my councillors, to make the exercise of my ministry, and the defence of my temporal sovereignty, impossible. I command my minister not to obey the injunctions of illegitimate authority. Let your General know that if force must be used to separate the Cardinal from me, he will be obliged first to break open all the doors, and will have besides the responsibility of a shameful proceeding."[1]

When Pacca had explained the Pope's words to the officer (who did not understand Italian), the Holy Father took his minister's hand, saying, "*Signor Car-*

[1] *Memorie,* t. i. p. 143.

dinale, andiamo," and led him through a crowd of applauding servants and friends to the Papal apartment, where three rooms in close proximity to Pius VII. were immediately assigned to the faithful Cardinal. " Here," remarks Pacca, " I had the consolation and the special honour to live for ten whole months, until the fatal 6th of July 1809."

Gabrielli had planned a scheme for flight, but the Holy Father resolutely refused to leave Rome, unless it were by force. To England alone, or to a country in alliance with England, could he have turned, yet a Sovereign Pontiff could hardly have had recourse to a heretical power. Pius VII. had been reproached with partiality for Napoleon, and also by a strange inconsistency with an excessive regard for English interests. It would then have been compromising to his dignity had he accepted the offer of escape which, it seems, was really made by the Cabinet of St. James. One evening, before he had taken refuge in the Pope's apartment, Pacca received a visit from a Franciscan friar, who had avowedly come from Sicily in an English frigate to contrive the flight of the Holy Father. The Cardinal answered the friar's advances very coldly, fearing him to be a spy ; but many years afterwards he learned that the Franciscan had spoken truth, that the frigate belonged to the English navy, and that it was sent by the connivance of the English Cabinet. It had been magnificently fitted up for the accommodation of the Pope and of an accompanying Cardinal.[1]

[1] *Memorie.* See Note, t. i. p. 160.

At that time, thrones seemed to follow the precarious fortunes of the Holy See. The crown of Naples had been given to Joachim Murat, and the new Neapolitan king proved a docile instrument in carrying out Napoleon's designs upon Rome. From Spain, whose affairs he had undertaken to unsettle, the Emperor wrote to Murat in November 1808: "The Code Napoléon is adopted in all the kingdom of Italy. Florence has it; Rome will soon have it; and priests will be obliged to stop pandering to prejudices, and will be forced to mind their own business." In a circular addressed in December to the bishops, he invited them "to sing a *Te Deum* in their holy churches, with their accustomed prayers, in order to obtain from God, Who possesses all things, that He would continue to bless the French arms, and that He would preserve the Continent from the malignant influence of the English, the enemies of all religion, as they are of the peace and tranquillity of nations."[1]

On January 1st, 1809, a needlessly insulting letter was sent by Napoleon to M. de Champagny, with regard to the approaching feast of Candlemas.

"Monsieur de Champagny, the Pope is accustomed to give candles to the different powers; write to my agent in Rome that I do not wish for any. Neither does the King of Spain. Write to Naples and to Holland, that they may be refused there too. None

---

[1] *Circulaire aux Évêques d'Italie*, 1808.

must be received, because last year they were insolent enough not to offer any. This is how I understand the business. My *chargé d'affaires* will make it known that on the Purification I receive blessed candles from my curé; that it is neither the purple nor power which give these things their value; there may be Popes in hell as well as curés, so that the candle blessed by my curé can very well be as holy a thing as that blessed by the Pope. I will not receive those which the Pope gives, and all the princes of my family must act in like manner.

"With this, I pray that God may have you in His holy keeping. NAPOLEON."[1]

M. Alquier had already left Rome. Miollis represented France only too much as superintendent of both military and civil proceedings.

The decree of April 1808, announcing the incorporation of the Papal States with the French Empire, had not materially altered the situation in Rome. Two more specific decrees appeared in May 1809. The first declared that "the temporal pretensions of the Pope were irreconcilable with the safety, tranquillity, and prosperity of the Empire." The second named a council to ensure the peaceful introduction in Rome of the new measures, on the 1st of January 1810. The whole plan of attack was placed under the direction of Joachim Murat. The decree which dethroned the sovereign, who was already a prisoner

---

[1] *Histoire de Pie VII.*, ii. p. 200.

in his palace, was proclaimed in Rome on the 10th of
June 1809. The Papal arms disappeared from the
summit of Sant' Angelo, and were replaced by the
victorious Tricolour, which was hoisted with a military
salute. All was over with the Temporal Power as
far as short-sighted human prudence could predict.
As Pacca hurried into the Holy Father's apartment,
the same words fell from their lips, *consummatum est*.
The Cardinal strove to read aloud the imperial decree :
emotion almost checked his utterances, and outside
the cannon was thundering. Having listened in
silence, the Holy Father calmly affixed his signature
to an Italian protest, which appeared the same night
on the walls of the basilicas. Then Pacca spoke
about the Bull of Excommunication. After the event
of the 6th September, it had been prepared against
two possible eventualities : one, the storming of the
Papal palace and the exile of the Holy Father; the
other, his deposition as a sovereign. Both documents
had been signed by Pius VII. in the event of either
emergency. Now, therefore, it would become necessary only to issue the latter formula. In reading
the Bull over again, the Holy Father hesitated at
certain expressions against the French Government.
They were not too severe, Pacca remarked, but if the
Pope still doubted, let him " lift up his heart to God
in prayer," and he would be enlightened.

" Well," he exclaimed at length, " issue the Bull
(*Ebbene, le dia corso*), but let those who execute your
orders look to themselves. Above all, let them avoid

discovery, for they would be shot, and we should be inconsolable."

Despite the vigilance of the French, and at the risk of life itself,[1] the Bull *Quum memoranda illa die* was effectively placarded on the usual places, that is, on the walls of St. Peter, St. Mary Major, and St. John Lateran. After enumerating the indignities which had been for so long inflicted on the Church—the violation of the Concordat, the usurpation of authority, the tyranny exercised towards cardinals, bishops, and priests, and finally the destruction of the Holy See's temporal authority—Pius VII. passed to the actual excommunication. The paragraph in the Bull which offers the most interest was prompted out of regard for those whose duty or office would throw them into unavoidable contact with Napoleon.

" Notwithstanding the necessity imposed upon us of using the spiritual arms of anathema, we may not forget that we, though unworthy, occupy on earth the place of Him Who, even in His acts of justice, is mindful of His mercy. For this reason we desire and command our own subjects, in the first place, and in the next, all Christian people, in virtue of holy obedience, not to make these presents an excuse for inflicting injury, bad treatment, or damage, on the person, property, or good name of those who fall under our censure. For in chastising them with the kind of punishment which God has put in our power,

---

[1] This has been amply proved in the case of Mencacci, the memory of whose noble deed is treasured as an heirloom in his family, represented at present by Commendatore Mencacci.

and in repaying thus great and crying injuries against God and against His church, we seek only one thing, to draw back to ourself those who afflict us, to make them share our sorrows, if God gives them the grace of repentance, so as to enable them to see truth." [1]

Although the Bull was seen only for a moment, and although it did not mention Napoleon by name, it decided, in all probability, the fate of the Holy Father. At St. Helena, Napoleon denied having ever commanded the Pope's arrest. His correspondence, however, tells another tale. In a letter to Joachim Murat, dated June 19th, 1809 (nine days after the Bull of Excommunication had appeared), he said, "I have already told you it is my intention that Roman affairs should be vigorously prosecuted, and that no sort of resistance should be tolerated. If my decrees are not met by submission, no place is to be respected, and under no circumstances whatever is resistance to be suffered. If the Pope, contrary to the spirit of his ministry and of the Gospel, preaches revolt, and makes use of his position for printing circulars, *let him be arrested.* The days for these things are long past and over. Philippe le Bel had Boniface arrested, and Charles V. kept Clement VII. in a long imprisonment, and they (Boniface and Clement) had been less disagreeable (than Pius VII.). A priest who preaches discord and war to temporal powers, instead of peace, sins against his office." [2]

---

[1] Laurentie : *Histoire de France*, vii. p. 268.
[2] *L'Église Romaine et le Premier Empire*, t. iii. p. 102.

CHAPTER IX

DURING the night of July 5th, 1809, Cardinal Pacca's suspicions had been aroused by hearing that the streets of Rome were full of troops. There was a feeling of insecurity abroad, which induced Pacca to remain up till dawn. Then, deceived by the silence and hush of the quarter immediately surrounding the Quirinal, he thought the danger past once more, and went to seek a few hours' rest. But General Baron Radet, who was charged with the ignominious business of expelling the Pope from his own palace, had been watching for the disappearance of the last sentinel at the Quirinal. A little after half-past two he gave the signal of attack, thus setting in motion three separate detachments of troops, who, by dividing for the invasion, wished to ensure greater success. Radet himself was to confront the Holy Father in the midst of his private apartments. He was escorted by a wretched man who had lately been discharged by the Pope for theft. The noise of armed force entering in, the breaking open of doors, and the cries of the French soldiers, awakened those in the palace who had ventured to seek repose. Pacca had scarcely retired before he was apprised of the invasion, and his first thought was to send his nephew, Tiberius Pacca, to call the Holy Father. Pius VII. was already up when the Cardinal entered his room. He had on the mozetta and stole, and was perfectly calm.

"Now, I have my true friends round me," he exclaimed, alluding to the presence of Cardinals Pacca and Despuig, a Spaniard, who was pro-vicar of Rome. The noise of approaching troops grew louder each moment, as they forced successive doors in order to penetrate to the very chamber of the Pope. Pius VII. would not listen to Cardinal Despuig's suggestion that he should retire to his domestic chapel. He wished to meet his enemies, not to fly from them. He seated himself on a sofa behind a table, and here, with the Cardinals at his side, surrounded by the chief members of his household, received Radet. The French formed a semicircle round the General. About eighteen officers had been introduced into the apartment, and now they stood with bared heads and naked swords in a respectful attitude of attention. Both parties observed each other in silence for more than five minutes. In this curious scene it was not the Holy Father but Radet who lost courage, so that with great difficulty and evident embarrassment he at length managed to broach the object of his unseasonable visit to the Quirinal. He had "a painful commission to fulfil, which, however, was imposed by the obligations of his position."

The Holy Father rose and said with dignity, "What do you want of me? And why do you come at this untimely hour to trouble my rest and my abode?"

"Most Holy Father, I come in the name of my Government to ask your Holiness once more formally to renounce the Temporal Power. If your Holiness consents, I do not doubt that all may still be arranged, and the Emperor will treat your Holiness with the greatest consideration."

"If you think yourself obliged to execute these orders of the Emperor because of your oath of fidelity and obedience to him, consider how much more we ought to defend the rights of the Holy See, to which so many oaths bind us. We cannot give up what is not ours. The Temporal Power, of which we are only the administrator, belongs to the Church. The Emperor may tear us to pieces, but he will not succeed. After all that we have done for him, is this what we might have expected?"

"I know that the Emperor is greatly indebted to you," replied Radet, much embarrassed.

"He is indeed, and more than you can know. But what are your orders?"

"Most Holy Father, I regret my instructions, but I have orders to take you away with me."

Pius VII. turned to Radet with his irresistible tenderness, and said gently—

"Truly, my son, this order will not bring you God's blessing. This is then the gratitude shown to me for

all that I have done for your Emperor. This is the
reward for my great condescension to him and to the
Church in France. But perhaps I have been guilty
in this respect before God, and He wishes to punish
me. I resign myself in all humility."

In the meantime the further orders of General
Miollis had been ascertained : the Holy Father and
Cardinal Pacca were to be immediately arrested, and
taken away from Rome. Pius VII. would have
wished for at least two hours to make his preparations for the journey, but they were refused. He and
Pacca were to start at once, and other members of his
household were to follow. General Radet here relates
that he helped the Holy Father, who was weak and
ill, to reach his bedroom, and took the opportunity of
assuring the Pope that his things would not be
touched. "He who attaches no importance to his
life cares still less for his possessions," was the reply
of Pope Pius. Taking only his breviary and his
crucifix, he walked down the grand .staircase of the
Quirinal, followed by Pacca. It was four o'clock in
the morning, and the only sign of life in the streets
was the armed force of France. A carriage, with
blinds fast closed, was in waiting. Radet had both
doors locked on his prisoners, after which, seating
himself by the driver's side, he ordered the postillions
to leave Rome by the Porta Pia. A detachment of
police accompanied the carriage. The Holy Father
left his blessing and a touching farewell for the
Romans. "He was comforted," he told them, "to

see the fulfilment in our person of that which was foretold by our Redeemer to the Prince of the Apostles, St. Peter, of whom, though unworthy, we are the successor, ' When thou shalt be old, thou shalt stretch forth thy hand and another shall gird thee, and lead thee whither thou wouldst not.' " [1]

The Holy Father sat in that fast-closed carriage as " the man of most rich poverty." [2]   The Pope and the Cardinal lost no time in comparing their stock of possessions.   The Holy Father's purse contained one *papetto* (about fivepence), and Pacca's three *grossi* (one shilling of our money).   It cast a little mirth over the anguish of the hour.   The Pope showed his *papetto* to Radet, saying, "See, of all my States, this is all I possess."   An anxiety of another kind secretly troubled Pacca.   He feared that the Pope might now regret having issued the Bull of Excommunication, as likely to produce still greater severity, and he was therefore relieved when the Holy Father said, with a smile on his lips, "Cardinal, we acted wisely in publishing the Bull of Excommunication on the 10th of June. Otherwise, what should we do now ? " [3]

The journey was pursued to Florence as quickly as Radet could manage it.   *His* business was to ensure speed, and to prevent the recognition of the Holy Father, so that Pius VII. might be already far away before his arrest became generally known.   The

[1] Written proclamation of the Holy Father, July 6th, 1809.
[2] *Vir ditissimæ paupertatis* (St. Jerome).
[3] *Memorie*, t. i. p. 219.

prisoner, thus hurried on, was suffering very much
from an infirmity which travelling greatly aggravated.
Once he was so ill that he declared he would wait
for the arrival of his household, and Radet was obliged
to consent.   When the populations between Poggi-
bonzi and Florence, having guessed the occupants of
the dark and well-guarded carriage, turned out to try
and obtain a glimpse of the Holy Father, Radet
resorted to the expedient of telling them to kneel
down on each side for the Papal Benediction.   "They
were still on their knees," he remarks, "whilst we had
galloped on." [1]

The Certosa at Florence was reached at midnight
on the 8th of July.   The Pope was so ill and over-
come by fatigue that rest seemed an absolute necessity.
The same room was prepared for him which Pius VI.
had formerly occupied.   It recalled painful memories,
in addition to the illness and dejection of his successor.
The Grand Duchess of Tuscany, Elisa Bacciocchi
(Bonaparte), sent a chamberlain to compliment the
Holy Father, who, prostrated by fatigue and sickness,
answered, in a scarcely audible tone, without raising
his head.   After partaking of the splendid supper
which had been prepared for them, they retired to
rest with the prospect of an undisturbed night.   But
at 3 A.M. another envoy from Elisa urged the immediate departure of the Holy Father, for he was a
dangerous guest.   She feared her brother's anger far .
more than the suffering of the Sovereign Pontiff, and

---

[1] *Le Général Radet au Ministre de la Guerre,* 1809.

her only aim was to rid herself, at the earliest opportunity, of a weighty responsibility. Therefore she had decided that Pius VII., no matter in what state, should proceed at once on his journey, in spite, too, of the day being Sunday, which involved the impossibility of his saying, or even hearing, Mass, as he earnestly petitioned to do. Pacca went to warn him of the cruel order, and found him much distressed, and in great pain. "I see too well," he said, "that they want to cause my death by bad treatment, and indeed I feel that at this rate they will soon gain their object."[1]

It was important that Florence should not be traversed in broad daylight, as a hearty reception from the Florentines would have compromised the Grand Duchess. The Holy Father was deprived for the time of Pacca's company, a foretaste of what was to come, and reached Genoa after three more weary days of incessant travelling. Catholic feeling there made another departure by night necessary. The Holy Father, with Mgr. Doria, his high steward, were hurried off at dusk on litters to Alexandria, and from thence proceeded to Turin. Prince Borghese,[2] who reigned at the Piedmontese capital, showed the same heartlessness as his sister-in-law at Florence. The sooner the Pope could be conveyed out of his dominions, the better it appeared to him. Extreme fatigue and the lack of ordinary care might easily have proved fatal to one in the Pope's suffering condition. At Mondovi he experienced a real ovation. Clergy, religious orders

---

[1] *Memorie*, t. i. p. 41.   [2] Married to Pauline Bonaparte.

with their banners, went out to meet him, whilst bells
pealed joyfully; women and children offered him
rosaries and flowers to bless. As the Holy Father
approached France, the enthusiasm became greater.
Whole villages poured out to await his passage, eager
to have his blessing. Many ran after the carriage,
whilst in motion, to risk kissing the Pope's hand.
At Grenoble, where Pacca was restored to him, the
popular reception was equally hearty, in spite of un-
gracious authorities. The Holy Father might have
been taken, not for a prisoner conducted to an appointed place of confinement, but for a "loved father
returning after a long absence to his devoted family."[1]
It is none the less true that the Sovereign Pontiff
was strictly guarded at Grenoble. He occupied the
Prefecture, and Pacca a separate house, for all intercourse between Pope and Cardinal was forbidden.
The officials treated the Holy Father with perfect
respect, and offered him carriages, of which he never
consented to avail himself, to visit the surrounding
country. He restricted his exercise to the garden of
the Prefecture, and here the people, who soon learned
his hours, showed great enthusiasm about seeing him
and receiving his blessing. It never failed during his
ten days' stay.

As for Napoleon, who had just gained the battle of
Wagram, he was somewhat vexed that Murat and
Miollis had so punctually obeyed his injunctions.
Elisa Bacciochi and Prince Borghese had been over

---

[1] *Memorie*, t. ii. p. 51.

anxious, as it now appeared, to rid their States of
the Holy Father. The Emperor's policy aimed rather
at destroying the moral influence of the Pope than at
inflicting violence on the person of Pius VII. What
could be more opposed to the end in view than hurrying the Sovereign Pontiff from one French town to
another? The effect had been exactly the opposite to
Napoleon's wishes. The Emperor was greatly annoyed
that Pius VII. should have been brought into close contact with the French people, and on the 18th of July,
forgetting his own words, he wrote to Fouché that the
Pope's arrest had been an act of "great folly." If he
(the Pope) would now listen to reason, Napoleon had
no objection in allowing him to return to Rome, but
in the meantime Savona would be the right place for
him. Fouché was to read the Pope's correspondence,
and to have Pacca imprisoned at Fenestrello. "Should
a single Frenchman perish through the Cardinal, he
will pay for it with his head."[1]

One effect of despotism is to make men unreal.
The South, which had set eyes on the Pope as he
passed, broke for the moment into spontaneous greeting. It threw off the bondage never equalled under
a Bourbon king, and men became themselves. Whole
populations poured out to strew flowers before the
Holy Father; bands of Italian peasants serenaded
at his windows; towns were festooned with garlands,
and illuminated as if to honour the triumphal march
of a sovereign; whilst in the North servility made

---

[1] *Lettre de l'Empereur à Fouché (Ministre de la Police)*, 18 juillet 1809.

people shrink from asking themselves or others the question, "Where is the Pope?" Despotism ruled the press. Not a word had transpired concerning the assault at the Quirinal, the arrest of the Pope, or his journey through the South.

The *Moniteur* could not entirely ignore Napoleon's proceeding in expelling the Sovereign Pontiff from his palace, because he would not adopt the Emperor's personal quarrels. Public curiosity on the subject was fed by a miserable parody of the truth, because the press itself was a wretched instrument in the hands of Fouché, Inspector of Police. A letter, dated August 1st, 1809, appeared a few days later in the *Moniteur*: "The public here is very much preoccupied by the passage in the commune of Bornin" (the Pope had passed through this commune on his way to Grenoble) "of an unknown animal. Judging by the traces which it has left behind, we may conclude that it is a reptile of extraordinary dimensions." Half a page followed, full of details as to the course pursued by the animal, which, "after having so much engrossed public attention, ended," said the paper, "by losing itself in a torrent."

Peaceful Savona, washed by the calm waters of the Mediterranean, was the solitude in which it was hoped to bury the Pope. Pius VII. became a monk once more in the cenobitical life, which was imposed upon him by Napoleon's will and policy. The Holy Father occupied a small suite of apartments in the Episcopal Palace, where isolation, not confinement, was his trial.

His food consisted almost entirely of vegetables and a little fish. Air and exercise he had none, beyond an occasional walk in the garden, which was very small, and surrounded by high walls. He was often pressed by his guardians to sing High Mass at the Cathedral of Savona, but did not consider the step in keeping with his state of captivity. The domestic chapel was his sole consolation. In it he said his daily Mass, and poured out his soul in prayer, both for the persecuted Church and the persecutor. He was entirely cut off from councillors and theological books, and cast wholly upon God and divine inspirations. Thus Napoleon hoped to shape the Sovereign Pontiff's will to his schemes. However, if Pius VII. had no human councillor, he had gaolers. Foremost amongst them was the Prefect of Montenotte, the Comte Chabrol de Volvic, a man of science and capacity, who consented to lay his intelligence at Napoleon's feet. The Comte de Salmatoris arrived from Paris to carry out his branch of the undertaking. He was charged to organise the Papal household on the footing of a reigning prince. Expense, indeed, would have been a mere detail to Napoleon, could he have succeeded in making the Vicar of Christ his vassal. His offer of carriages, liveries, horses, and a monthly pension of a hundred thousand francs, proffered through Comte de Salmatoris, was consequently rejected. The Holy Father's household likewise were tempted by the promise of a salary equal to what they had received in Rome.

Comte César Berthier's mission at Savona was to spend money lavishly before the Holy Father's eyes. He was to keep open house, to show great hospitality to those connected with the Papal household, and to prove to the public, as far as he could, that the Pope was no prisoner at all. At the same time he was to exercise a minute inspection over the Episcopal Palace. He was to be at once an entertainer and a sort of private detective.

The article in the Concordat relating to the confirmation in Rome of bishops nominated by the First Consul was rendered null and void by the Holy Father's captivity. Pius VII. refused to confirm the bishops named by Napoleon, and thus brought the government of the Church to a stand-still, as far as the French Empire was concerned. In other days the First Consul had said of Pius VII., "*Je sais le pétrir*," and now in burying the Pope at Savona, he found he had put away the key, without which the spiritual doors remained fast closed. As an expedient for coming to terms with the Pope, he ordered the highest dignitaries of the French Church to write to him, *as if from themselves*, and to represent the grievous results of his refusal to confirm bishops. Fesch, Caprara, Maury, and several other bishops promptly obeyed, their several letters being characterised by their individual convictions. Fesch expressed great sympathy with the trials of the Holy Father, and Maury alluded to them in becoming terms; but others, afraid of committing themselves, passed over in silence the indignities offered to Pius VII., and expatiated upon

the evils he fostered by his resistance.[1] Caprara was
one of those who were thus dead to loyalty and justice.
The Holy Father's reply to his former legate was a
complete answer to unjustifiable demands.

"However little, my Lord Cardinal, you reflect
upon this proposition, you are bound to understand
that we cannot acquiesce in it without acknowledging
that the Emperor has both the right of nominating and
of confirming bishops. You say that our Bulls would
be conceded, not to him, but to the Council and to the
Minister of Worship. In the first place, the Catholic
Church does not recognise any minister of worship
who derives his authority from the secular power; then,
are not this Council and this Minister one and the same
thing as the Emperor himself ? The Emperor has
introduced many innovations fatal to religion, against
which we have long protested in vain. Many priests in
our States have suffered vexations. Bishops, and the
majority of our cardinals, have been exiled. Cardinal
Pacca has been imprisoned at Fenestrello, St. Peter's
Patrimony usurped. We have been violently arrested
iu our own palace. During our peregrinations from
city to city, we were so closely watched that the
neighbouring bishops could not approach us nor speak
to us without witnesses. After all these and numerous
other sacrilegious attempts, which it would take too
long to enumerate, anathematised, as they are, by
General Councils and the Apostolic Constitutions,
have we done more than obey these Constitutions,

[1] *L'Église Romaine et le Premier Empire*, t. iii. p. 401.

as indeed our duty compelled us?   How then could
we now recognise in the author of these violent
measures the right in question?   How consent to
his exercising it?   Could we do this without being
guilty of prevarication, or making our conduct absolutely inconsistent?   Should we not disedify the
faithful, and give them cause to believe that, broken
down by so much suffering, and dreading still greater
anguish, we were weak enough to betray our conscience, and to approve what it compels us to forbid?
Weigh all these reasons, my Lord Cardinal, not indeed
in the measure of human wisdom, but in the measure
of the sanctuary, and you will feel their force.   In
spite of existing evils, God knows how much we desire
to fill the vacant sees of that Church, which we have
always so specially cherished, and to discover an expedient for doing it in a fitting manner.   But are we
to act in so grave a matter without consulting our
natural councillors, the Sacred College?   And how
can we consult them, when all communication between
us has been stopped by violence, and we are forbidden
every facility for despatching business?   Hitherto we
have been denied even a secretary."[1]

The Pope's absolute and unqualified refusal made the
Emperor joyfully accede to a proposal of his courtier
friends.   They affected to study French history in search
of precedent, and came upon a convenient incident.
Louis XIV., in flat contradiction of Canon Law, had
required that the chapter should confer the jurisdiction

[1] *Bref du Pape au Cardinal Caprara,* 25 août 1809.

of vicar-capitular on the bishop-elect. Thus, a bishop became a permanent vicar-capitular, and the prince could dispense with the Pope and his Bulls. Louis XIV. had so acted in an emergency, but he had not, as was alleged, been supported by Bossuet.[1] Napoleon did all he could to adopt the plan of vicar-capitular. It was not his fault that he met with serious opposition, nor that he failed to put down that opposition with his usual measures, the police and imprisonment. He now had two supposed grievances against the Sovereign Pontiff—the excommunication, and the refusal to confirm bishops. The Bull *Quum Memoranda* had made a deep impression upon him, and is proved by his acts, which were in direct contradiction to his language. In the first place, at the time of the Holy Father's arrest, July 1809, he issued strict orders that the Bull was to be kept a profound secret, under pain of the severest punishment. One of the Pope's valets, who was asked at Avignon whether Napoleon had really been excommunicated, replied, that it was as much as his life was worth to answer. The Comte Bigot de Préameneu had succeeded M. Portalis as Minister of Worship. This new functionary was charged to examine the Bull, and see how far it practically affected the Emperor. He replied, as a good Gallican, that because the Pope had not mentioned Napoleon, his intention had not been to excommunicate him personally; therefore, the wiser plan would be to bury the whole matter in oblivion. "The Bull

[1] Caussette : *Vie du Cardinal d'Astros*, 133.

of Excommunication was too ridiculous a document
to deserve the smallest attention," wrote Napoleon to
M. Bigot,[1] whilst his conduct paid it the utmost
attention. Missionary priests, who were found to
elude the police, and thus were more likely to divulge
the secret, were suppressed in France. Spiritual conferences at St. Sulpice were, on similar grounds, pronounced dangerous, and prohibited. It was impossible
for priests to meet without falling immediately under
the suspicion of " plotting," which was a general term
used by the Emperor to signify anything he did not
like.[2] His resentment, however, fell the most heavily
on Rome, the headquarters of all the mischief. In
September 1809, he ordered the departure, within
twenty-four hours, of the cardinals still there, specially
mentioning Cardinal di Pietro (who had been concerned with the Bull), and those prelates actively
engaged in spiritual administration, " which is no longer
to be carried out in Rome."[3]

After the Peace of Vienna, in October 1809, all the
cardinals, except a very small number, whose age or
ill-health rendered the journey impossible, were summoned to Paris, to grace the Imperial, instead of the
Papal, Court. Consalvi censures a certain number of
them, afterwards known as the Red Cardinals, who
accepted worldly dissipation too readily at a time
when their chief was suffering a dreary imprisonment.[4]

---

[1] 3 juillet 1809.

[2] *Lettre de l'Empereur à M. Fouché*, 15 septembre 1809.

[3] *Lettre de l'Empereur au Comte Bigot*, 18 septembre 1809. *Not* inserted in his Correspondence.   [4] *Mémoires*, t. ii. p. 167.

A few months later, February 1810, the Penitentiary and Dataria Tribunals were transferred to the French capital.[1] The Roman Court lives and breathes through its Head, and removing the mutilated body to Paris answered no purpose. It was as the kingdom of France without the French king, or the empire of Russia without the Czar, a direct consequence of managing spiritual matters as "if no Pope existed." On August 13th, 1809, Napoleon wrote to M. Bigot: "I will by no means tolerate payment for Bulls, dispensations, &c. . . . It is a profanation of sacred things."[2]   And later, he inquired of his Council "whether the Minister of Worship has sent a circular to the bishops, ordering them to suppress prayers to St. Gregory the Seventh, and to substitute another feast for that of this saint, whom the Gallican Church cannot recognise."[3] Napoleon, with his alleged horror for the *profanation of holy things*, showed no scruples of conscience about diminishing the number of Italian bishoprics, confiscating their revenues, and those of all religious houses.

[1] *Lettre de Napoléon à M. Bigot*, 4 février 1810.

[2] Whatever is paid at Rome for this kind of dispensation, is a very small and legitimate indemnity for the cost of sending them, and the salary of those employed in the work. Simple common-sense, and a natural feeling of justice, have introduced emoluments into every court in the world. If Protestants maintain the contrary, they on their side have no right to enjoy any living, or to receive any fee for baptisms, marriages, or funerals. The same principle would render *any* salary or indemnity unlawful, for every man being capable of doing service to his neighbour without money, he is bound to do it without money (*Histoire de la Révolution Religieuse en Suisse.*—Haller).

[3] *Note dictée par l'Empereur au Conseil des Ministres*, le 18 janvier 1810. *Not* inserted in his Correspondence.

The *Sénatus Consulte* of February 1810 made Rome the second city of the Empire, imposed upon the Sovereign Pontiff at his accession an oath of fidelity to the Four Propositions of the Gallican Church, with two million francs for revenue, and a palace wherever he might choose to reside. The Holy Father absolutely ignored it, and the Italian clergy in the mass refused alike the oath and the gold of the new Government. The Pope would not confirm bishops-elect, and the clergy in their turn refused the oath of fidelity to Gallican propositions. Napoleon reproached Pius VII. with the widowed condition of so many dioceses and the poverty of numerous priests, cast upon the world, when not thrown into imprisonment, because they would not take an oath against their conscience. In February 1811, a year after the promulgation of the *Sénatus Consulte*, these were the results obtained by Napoleon's legislation. Thirteen cardinals had been degraded, and were confined in various provincial towns, under strict supervision. Nineteen bishops of the Roman States had been sent to France, to live also by grace of the Imperial police. A multitude of canons and vicar-generals, whose number it is impossible to fix, had fallen victims to similar measures, and more than two hundred priests had been banished to Corsica.[1] There were worse fates than Corsica, and the dreaded gates of Vincennes could close on others besides the Duc d'Enghien.

---

[1] *L'Église Romaine et le Premier Empire*, t. iii. p. 375.

CHAPTER X

THE time was now at hand when Napoleon could mature the design which had formed part of his plan from his early days in power. In 1804 his position was not sufficiently secure for disclosure. The marriage rite, which took place a few hours before the Coronation, was a secondary consideration, and he had disregarded it as far as he could by refusing his consent. Pius VII. and Napoleon were at cross purposes. The Pope had before him the ideal of Christian marriage: the Emperor his ambition of founding a dynasty; and this had been in his mind when he protested, in his selfishness, that he did not consent to the indissoluble marriage-tie with Josephine. He wished to be free to cast her off whenever his policy required it. Napoleon stood outside or above his Code, which prohibited divorce to the Imperial Family, whilst tolerating it for the rest of the world. When once he had fully made up his mind, he did not delay to broach the subject to Josephine. Her consent was tearfully given. She loved Napoleon as much as she loved anybody, and quite enough not to stand in the

way of his worldly glory.   Of his true glory as a
Christian she seems never to have thought.   Napoleon
expressed his regrets in characteristic words, "*Avouez
que cette femme là fait regretter de n'être pas sultan.*"[1]

A grand reception took place at the Tuileries on
the evening of Josephine's departure, and she sustained
her part with perfect grace.   The Emperor's choice
lay between a grand-duchess and an archduchess.   The
marriage of crowned heads, and his in particular, is
not a matter of inclination.   In securing an heir, he
wished also to strengthen his influence at home and
abroad.   The Arch-Chancellor Cambacérès, alone of
all the Court, remained favourable to the Russian
alliance.   When asked why, he replied, "I am
morally certain that before two years are over we
shall have war with that sovereign of the two whose
daughter the Emperor has not married.   War with
Austria does not in the least alarm me, but war
with Russia makes me tremble : the consequences are
incalculable.   I know that the Emperor can find his
way to Vienna, but I am not so sure of Petersburg."[2]

Cambacérès spoke as a politician, not as a Catholic.
At the end of 1809 the Austrian alliance was finally
chosen, and, as usual, Napoleon affected not to see the
moral obstacles.   He could not sweep them away;
he therefore treated them as *non avenu*.   In the first
place, only one person was qualified to deal with the
case, and that was the Sovereign Pontiff.   No other

---

[1] *Mémoires Secrets sur Napoléon Bonaparte, avec un Précis Historique,*
p. 264.

[2] *L'Église Romaine et le Premier Empire,* t. iii. p. 223.

authority, Cardinal Fesch declared, would be better than "uncertain or dangerous." Nevertheless, Napoleon did not choose to have recourse to the Pope, and, as in the bishop question, he resorted to a paltry device. Three officialities were created for the circumstance, a diocesan, a metropolitan, and a third tribunal, under the immediate presidency of Cardinal Fesch, Primate of France. These three officialities were allowed no liberty of action. The Emperor set them to consider three points, and ordered their answer for a certain day. The three points were (1) clandestinity; (2) the absence of witnesses; (3) Napoleon's want of consent, of which he had protested at the time. Clandestinity, and the absence of witnesses, were over-ruled by the Papal faculties, which Cardinal Fesch had received for any and every emergency. Although the Pope was not told its nature in so many words, he could hardly fail to guess what it signified. When he heard that the validity of the marriage was disputed, he remarked—

"How can the Emperor think of dissolving his marriage after I had given all necessary dispensations to Cardinal Fesch?"[1]

The *Officialités* had been set up to do the Emperor's bidding, and they answered their purpose, in spite of the extraordinary position thus thrust upon Fesch. He had performed the first marriage secretly, on the night of December 1st, 1804, and he would be required to marry Napoleon to his Austrian bride. The

[1] Duhr: *Ehescheidung und zweite Heirat Napoleons I. Zeitschrift für Katholische Theologie*, iv. 1888.

sentence of civil dissolution was given on December 16th, 1809.

Worldly considerations weighed with Austria and with Kaiser Franz. One person alone raised serious objections on the score of Napoleon's first marriage in 1796, which he declared binding. The Archbishop of Vienna really showed conscience in the matter, and required positive proof from the French ambassador that there had been no true marriage between Napoleon and Josephine. In his reply, the ambassador grounded his statement of nullity on the *Officialités*, who in reality constituted no authority whatever.[1] Whether it entered into the Archbishop's province to know this is a further point. His resistance was genuine and disinterested, and he professed himself satisfied with the ambassador's explanation. No one, not even the Archbishop of Vienna, hinted at the indignity of marrying an archduchess to a man under the ban of excommunication. The religious ceremony was carried out by proxy at Vienna on March 11th, 1810, the Archbishop himself officiating.

The servile French *Officialités*, who represented Napoleon, and Austria, ground down by fear and worldly considerations, do not compare favourably with the faithful portion of the Sacred College. It was a matter of great moment to Napoleon to secure for his Austrian alliance the approval and the sympathy of the Cardinals. Cardinals di Pietro and Consalvi

---

[1] Duhr: *Ehescheidung und zweite Heirat Napoleons I, Zeitschrift für Katholische Theologie,* iv. p. 626.

yielded only to absolute necessity in coming to Paris. They arrived in February 1810. Consalvi was a marked man, and could not be suffered to remain in peaceful incognito. Most of all, he dreaded Napoleon's advances. How could he accept the kindness of a man who was actively persecuting the Holy Father? " With the Divine assistance,"[1] he mortified his natural bent, and responded coldly to courtesy and civility. The other cardinals, who had preceded him to Paris, had made no difficulty in accepting the Government pension of thirty thousand francs. Some took it as a compensation for their Italian benefices, and later on, better informed of the Holy Father's wish, refused it.[2] Consalvi, however, at once rejected it, as did Cardinals di Pietro, Saluzzo, and Pignatelli, who arrived at about the same time. Di Pietro, Saluzzo, and Pignatelli, who were unknown in Paris, could easily adopt the retired life, which was in accordance with the Holy Father's instructions. For Consalvi, the negotiator of the Concordat, it was far more difficult. If he explained his real motive in holding aloof from the world, he incriminated the conduct of those cardinals who not only took the Government allowance, but freely accepted official invitations. Six days after his arrival, Consalvi presented himself at the Tuileries, in company with four other cardinals. Fesch introduced each by name to the Emperor in order of precedence. Napoleon passed over Consalvi's companions with slight comment. The Primate had

---

[1] *Mémoires*, t. ii. p. 169.   [2] Pacca : *Memorie*, t. ii. p. 129.

not named Consalvi before he exclaimed, in a kind tone—

"Oh, Cardinal Consalvi, how thin you have got! I should hardly have known you."

As a comment on the Emperor's words, the Cardinal replied: "Sire, years pass so quickly. It is nearly nine since I have had the honour of speaking to your Majesty."

" Yes, it will soon be nine years since you came for the Concordat, which took place in this very room. But of what use has it been ? It has ended in smoke. Rome has lost everything. I own I made a mistake in leading to your resignation. If you had continued at your post, things would never have come to this pass."

This was just what Consalvi feared, only conveyed in stronger terms than he had expected. Consulting " his honour and the truth," he replied : " Sire, if I had remained Secretary of State, I should have been faithful to my duty."

Napoleon gave him a look. Then, as he went round the room, he poured out complaints against the Pope and Rome, and finished once more by stopping before Consalvi, and repeating : "No, if you had remained at your post, things would never have come to this pass."

And once more Consalvi answered : "Let your Majesty be persuaded that I should have done my duty."

Napoleon wished to give emphasis to the matter.

A second time he went round the audience-chamber, uttering the same complaints against Rome. Then, addressing di Pietro, so as to be heard by Consalvi, he said, for the third time: "If Cardinal Consalvi had remained Secretary of State, things would not have gone so far."

"Sire," exclaimed Consalvi, laying his hand on the Emperor's arm, "I have already assured your Majesty that, if I had remained at my post, I should most certainly have done my duty."

"I repeat it—your duty would not have allowed you to sacrifice spiritual to temporal interests."[1]

This is a specimen of Napoleon's courtesy, and he wished on this occasion to conciliate Consalvi, so as to obtain the Cardinal's presence at the approaching marriage ceremony. Consalvi was the soul of the party amongst the Cardinals who declared that the question belonged and should be submitted to the Holy See. It became necessary for them to determine at once what their course of action should be. They could not be present at the marriage, and would have to take the consequences, even at the risk of life itself. The party numbered thirteen: Cardinals Mattei, Pignatelli, della Somaglia, di Pietro, Litta, Saluzzo, Ruffo Scilla, Brancadoro, Galeffi, Scotti, Gabrielli, Opizzoni, and Consalvi. The Dean of the Thirteen, Mattei, formally communicated the decision to the majority of the Fourteen. The Thirteen did not wish to make themselves conspicuous by their absence, or

[1] *Mémoires*, t. ii. p. 177.

M

to raise a commotion. Want of space might cover it. Cardinal Consalvi's great tact was at work. To use his expression, it was a question of wounding Napoleon " in the apple of his eye," and nothing short of conscience could have suggested the step. Fourteen cardinals, without including Fesch, and Caprara, who was feeble in mind and dying, gave it as their opinion that the dissolution of the marriage was valid. Consalvi had proposed to Fesch that the Thirteen should not be invited, but the bare thought of their opposition threw Napoleon into a terrible fit of anger. " Bah! they will not dare," he had exclaimed to his uncle.

Consalvi speaks of a fourth audience at the Tuileries a week before the marriage. He might well call them ordeals. Napoleon, apprised of Consalvi's intentions, sought to strike terror into him by the dreadful looks of which his eyes possessed the secret. " He came up to me on purpose," the Cardinal says ; " without saying a single civil word to me, he stopped in front of me, and gave me a thundering look. Then to make me clearly understand that I was the person in fault, he turned immediately with a smiling face to Cardinal Doria (one of the Fourteen) by my side, and talked most amiably with him. Then he walked about, and made himself pleasant to other cardinals. Suddenly he came back, stood straight in front of me, and once more looked at me most ferociously." [1]

The imperial marriage gave rise to four invitations.

[1] *Mémoires*, t. ii. p. 195.

The thirteen cardinals accepted only two.   First there was to be a reception at St. Cloud, when the chief officers of State were to be presented to Marie Louise.   The second and third had to do directly with the marriage.   The fourth, the most splendid of all, was a full Court reception, at which the sovereigns would be seated on their thrones.   The Cardinals resolved to go to the first and to the last.   Whilst waiting at St. Cloud for the Emperor and Empress, Consalvi was taken aside by Fouché, Minister of Police, and compelled to listen to the advice of worldly wisdom.   Fouché could hardly believe that a man of Consalvi's good sense should refuse to be present at the marriage.   He was tempted to fetch the Cardinal in his own carriage.   His absence would produce terrible consequences, and for what good ? The imperial marriage had 'already taken place by proxy at Vienna : the rest was pure formality.   This logic failed to convince Consalvi, though the agitation of it produced "a heavy sweat."[1]   The Emperor appeared, leading Marie Louise by the hand.   He was all smiles and affability, and introduced Consalvi as the cardinal " who had negotiated the Concordat."

On Monday, April 2nd, the religious ceremony took place at the Louvre, in the grand reception-room, temporarily and magnificently arranged as a chapel. As they passed slowly through the picture-gallery preceding the grand *salon*, the imperial pair riveted all eyes. Napoleon wore an air of extraordinary

---

[1] *Mémoires*, t. ii. p. 198.

triumph, which became visibly overcast when he reached the chapel. His quick eyes noted the deficiency amongst the cardinals, and quickly counted only fourteen.

"Where are the cardinals?" he asked the Master of Ceremonies.

"A great number are here," was the guarded reply. "Many of them, besides, are infirm and old, and the weather is so bad."

"Ah, the fools! but they are not here," said Napoleon, with another glance at the empty seats. "The fools! the fools!"

The Emperor managed to contain his anger during the ceremony, and to put off till the next day the explosion of his wrath, when he intended to inflict summary and public chastisement on the refractory cardinals. In the meantime, the Thirteen kept closely to the house, awaiting the consequences of their fidelity to the Sovereign Pontiff. On Tuesday, April 3rd, the day fixed for the grand State reception, Consalvi and his companions went to the Tuileries. After three hours of ante-chamber, the Emperor suddenly sent orders that the thirteen cardinals should leave the palace at once, as he would not see them. Not content with ordering bishops to act in defiance of the Pope, he now degraded cardinals, or, to speak more correctly, he forbade the Thirteen to wear their scarlet. They were called Black Cardinals, in contradistinction to the fourteen Red Cardinals, who had degraded their scarlet robes in very truth. Chastisement did not stop with dress. The property, both ecclesiastical and private, of the Black Cardinals was seized and confiscated by the French Government. They were obliged to live on the alms which charitable persons never failed to bestow, and were exiled to different provincial towns, care being taken to throw together those who were least sympathetic to each other.[1]

Napoleon resented a mere counsel given against his Austrian alliance. Cardinal della Somaglia consulted M. Emery as to whether he could attend the marriage. " I myself should have no objection to attend if my rank obliged me," was Emery's reply, " because I think the dissolution of the marriage valid. But if, in the sanctuary of your conscience, you have a contrary opinion, you will perhaps do better not to go, because conscience binds us."

Napoleon vented his anger against M. Emery on the congregation to which he belonged. The Sulpicians were declared to be " people who made a great deal out of nothing,"[2] and suppressed.

The years 1810 and 1811 were the most tranquil of the Empire, on account of the two events so flattering to the Emperor's ambition, which they witnessed : his marriage with the daughter of the Hapsburgs, and the birth of the King of Rome. The outward tranquillity was, however, far removed from true peace. Prosperity only widened the breach with the Church, and straitened the Holy Father's captivity. Napoleon

<hr>

[1] *Mémoires*, t. ii. p. 215.
[2] *L'Église Romaine et le Premier Empire*, t. iii. p. 298.

found it easier to degrade cardinals than to dispense
with the confirmation of bishops. Spiritual government came to a standstill, and could not be moved
or galvanised into a semblance of life by his marching orders. Napoleon, therefore, insisted on fighting
out the confirmation question with the Pope. The
sovereign of sixty million subjects matched himself
against the despoiled prisoner of Savona.

CHAPTER XI

WHATEVER indiscreet and unlawful punishment was heaped by the Emperor on those who in anything acknowledged the Pope's authority, he could not absolutely create bishops. The expedient suggested by his courtier historians was only a temporary *modus vivendi.* A General Council *without the Pope* had for a moment been contemplated. Then it seemed simpler to approach Pius VII, if it could be done indirectly by a third person. In May 1810, Prince Metternich, who had shown great zeal for the Austrian alliance, wanted to settle some ecclesiastical matters which required the Pope. He sought Napoleon's leave to send an agent to Savona, and the Emperor saw in the Austrian envoy's visit the desired opportunity for taking counsel of the Pope on French affairs without appearing to do so. M. de Lebzeltern, the chosen deputy, had been formerly Austrian ambassador at the Quirinal. Pius VII. was pleased and touched to see him again. The sight of a friendly face was an event at Savona. He spoke kindly of Napoleon. Painful circumstances had not effaced the Holy Father's partiality, even if they had weakened it. Lebzeltern spoke of the dangers which threatened the Church—dangers, indeed, of Napoleon's creation ; and he inquired if the Pope would do nothing to get out of his dependent and effaced state. "We had foreseen this state of things," was Pius the Seventh's reply, "and it is the only matter which preoccupies us. This interruption of all intercourse with the clergy of various nationalities, the difficulty of communicating with the French bishops, cause us the deepest grief. We are confined here without liberty of correspondence, without news, except the very vague statements contained in a loose page or two of the *Moniteur*, supplied to us by the General (le Cte. César Berthier, Napoleon's gaoler); yet we can form some notion of what the bishops have to contend with, and we continually complain to him (Berthier) of our position with regard to them. It is a real schism for all practical purposes. Personally, we ask the Emperor for nothing. We have nothing more to lose: we have sacrificed all to duty. We are old, and have no personal requirements. What interested consideration, then, could induce us not to follow our conscience ? Personally, we have absolutely no wishes. We desire neither pension nor honours. The alms of the faithful are enough for us. There have been Popes poorer than we are, and we do not soar beyond the narrow limits where you find us. Our great desire is that our intercourse with the bishops and the faithful be re-established."[1]

Pius VII. then told M. de Lebzeltern that Mgr. Menochio, his confessor, and the Secretary of Briefs,

---

[1] *Lettre de M. de Lebzeltern au Cte. de Metternich*, 16 mai 1810.

Mgr. Torsa, were kept away from him. He was obliged, in consequence, to use one of his servants, whose writing was legible, and had thus been able to despatch five hundred dispensations required by the French bishops. Upon the suggestion of the Austrian envoy, that the Pope would do well to break the silence, and to inform the Emperor of his wishes with regard to spiritual matters, Pius VII. replied—

"He (Napoleon) is well aware of our complete isolation. We have protested and remonstrated with the Prefect and the General over and over again, and he must certainly know it."

The Holy Father alluded only indirectly to his temporal sovereignty, in striking words. "That which is founded on the dictates of conscience and of duty is lasting," he said; "and be assured that, in the long run, *no material force in the world can combat a moral force of this nature.* What we said concerning the sad events which have befallen the Apostolic See was prompted by this conviction, and consequently we can never express ourself otherwise on the subject."[1]

M. de Lebzeltern's account of the Holy Father, which was drawn up as much for Napoleon as for the Austrian Emperor, resulted in the secret and non-official visit to Savona of Cardinals Spina and Caselli. The Emperor still hoped to over-rule the Pope, and in the meantime two cardinals, who had become French in tone and feeling, could open the way to the necessary negotiations. Their mission was to offer

---

[1] *Dépêche de M. de Lebzeltern au Cte. de Metternich,* 10 mai 1810.

every appearance of a casual encounter, for Spina, as Archbishop of Genoa, naturally took Savona on the way to his diocese. That Caselli should accompany him, and that they both should stop to see the Holy Father, was also quite intelligible. Pius VII. was not slow in guessing the object of their visit. He felt they had come to sound him, and to report to Napoleon. This produced diffidence in his mind, and he showed no desire to open negotiations. Spina and Caselli spent two days at Savona before they were admitted to an audience; and when at last the Holy Father saw them, he gave them perfectly to understand that before ecclesiastical matters could be settled, he expected to have the choice of two cardinals as councillors. He expressed himself strongly against a residence at Avignon. If he left Savona at all, it must be for Rome. Under any other circumstances he preferred to remain where he was. He would be very much grieved to be taken to Paris, but would always seek to check popular indignation on his own account. Perhaps, however, if forced to pontificate in public, he might not be able to control his feelings, and thus scandal would be produced.[1] The cardinals erroneously concluded, from the conversation of the Holy Father, that he might be induced to confirm bishops if he were allowed impartial councillors.

After this visit to Savona, Napoleon's course of action became still more decided. He now summoned

---

[1] *Lettre de M. le Cte. de Chabrol à M. le Cte. Bigot de Préameneu,* 11 juillet 1810.

the French clergy, with Fesch at their head, to give an open preference to his claims. The time for compromises and half-measures was past. They were called upon to join with him in setting the Holy Father's authority at defiance, or else to accept the terrible consequences of a resistance which became heroic. The French clergy seemed more compliant than they really were, through Napoleon's summary measures. The voice of confessorship was promptly silenced in prisons or dungeons. More than ever now Napoleon counted upon the zealous co-operation of the Primate, who was nominated to the Archbishopric of Paris, in succession to Cardinal de Belloy. At first Cardinal Fesch accepted the election, though contrary to the Canons; but when it came to taking possession of a second see without Papal confirmation, he preferred to retire. His resistance on this occasion was a really courageous act, whilst Napoleon's play upon his words was no less flippant.

"I can force you to obey me," said Napoleon to his uncle.

"Sire, *potius mori.*"

"Ah, ah, *potius mori*, rather Maury. Be it so. You shall have Maury."[1]

Cardinal Maury, who accepted the position, although already wedded to the church of Montefiascone, manifested a strange joy at the choice, which convicted him of being the Emperor's creature. Napoleon was anxious to provide for the vacant archdiocese of

[1] Lyonnet: *Vie du Cardinal Fesch*, t. ii. p. 174.

Florence also. His design in selecting for the post the Bishop of Nancy, Mgr. d'Osmond, was the same as in Maury's case. Two important dioceses of his Empire would thus be governed in open defiance of the Holy Father. To gain his end, he deceived Mgr. d'Osmond, who demurred to take possession of a new diocese without Papal confirmation. The departure of the prelate was pressed forward with the promise that he should receive his Bulls at Lyons. Too confident in the Emperor's word, he stopped three times on the way to Florence: his hope proved an utter fallacy. What he found on arrival was a Chapter quite unprepared to receive Napoleon's nominee in opposition to the Holy See. The Archdeacon applied to the Holy Father, who forbade the intrusion of Mgr. d'Osmond. Episcopal matters in Paris and Florence gave rise to three Briefs at the end of 1810. The first was addressed to Cardinal Maury, who had informed the Pope of his nomination to Paris in quite a casual way. Pius VII. adjured the Cardinal in the strongest terms to give up the see, which he had accepted in flagrant disregard of ecclesiastical law. "We shall not cease to pray most earnestly to Almighty God that He would deign to calm the wind and storm which are raging against Peter's bark," are the Holy Father's closing words, and to restore us to the desired harbour, where we may freely carry out the duties of our charge.[1]

[1] "Interea non cessabimus Deum optimum maximum enixis precibus exorare," &c. (*Bref du Pape au Cardinal Maury*, Nov. 1810; *Vie du Cardinal d'Astros*, Appendice xx.)

The second Brief was despatched to Evrard Corboli, Archdeacon of Florence. The case being exactly similar as to Napoleon's part in the business, the Pope reiterated what he had said to Cardinal Maury. Resistance to the imperial nominee was not only lawful, it was a positive duty. The Chapter of Florence preferred to obey the Sovereign Pontiff, whilst the Chapter of Paris protested in a single man, the Vicar-General, M. d'Astros, who suffered confessorship for his fidelity to the Pope.

Once at an ordination, as the Cardinal exacted the promise of obedience to himself from the priest before him, the Abbé d'Astros exclaimed in an audible tone: " My Lord, let me remind you, for the instruction of this young priest, that you have no right to require this promise."

On another occasion, the Vicar-General ordered the cross-bearer, who was about to precede Maury, to go back to the sacristy. Both Maury and d'Astros were in a false position. The Vicar-General could not stand by and allow the Cardinal to assume a dignity he did not possess canonically, without, as he thought, being a party to the intrusion. He decided at length to ask counsel of the Pope, who sent him, in December 1810, the third Brief on the subject, and the strongest of the three. It was discovered by the Government, and made a matter of grave accusation against M. d'Astros. Intercourse with the Pope at Savona was a penal act in Napoleon's code. M. d'Astros learnt what it was to cost him at the

official reception on January 1st, 1811, at the Tuileries.
Cardinal Maury went to pay the customary visit to
the sovereigns, his Chapter accompanying him, vested
in rochet, according to Napoleon's wish.   The Vicar-
General was greeted in these words, which are, in fact,
a high testimony to M. d'Astros: "I have cause to
suspect you more than any other man in my Empire.
We should be French before everything, and hold to
the Gallican liberties.   There is as much difference
between the religion of Bossuet and of Gregory VII.
as between heaven and hell.   Well, 1 have my sword.
Look to yourself."

After this speech, Napoleon sought out the man
who represented "the sword," viz., the Inspector of
Police, and ordered him to arrest M. d'Astros.   Cardinal Maury himself delivered the Vicar-General into
M. Savary's hands.   Before leaving the Tuileries, he
proposed that they should both go to the Inspector
of Police.   M. Savary, he said, had some questions
to put to M. d'Astros, but there was nothing to fear.
An explicit statement of attachment to Gallican
liberties would be required—that was all.   The inter-
rogatory of M. Savary was short and to the point.

"Are you not carrying on a correspondence with
the Pope at Savona?" he asked the Vicar-General.
"Have you seen a Brief from the Pope to Cardinal
Maury?   Resign, and there will be an end of it."

"I cannot."

"Resign, I say, or you are my prisoner."

"I *am* your prisoner, then."

" You would like to be a martyr, but you shall be nothing of the kind."

Every inducement was then brought forward to make him name his accomplices. His refusal, he was told, would be visited by the most serious consequences. He might never see his family, perhaps even the light of day, again. M. Savary and M. Réal helped him to prolong his life by the cross-questionings which facilitated an uncouscious confession. He named in this way three persons who had seen the Brief: his cousin, M. Portalis, and two priests. "You showed the Brief to your cousin, because he told me so," were words which might have deceived any man.

On January 4th, 1811, M. d'Astros was taken to Vincennes, aud there he remained till the fall of the Empire. At that time the Duc d'Enghien's blood was scarcely dry, and a prisoner in the gloomy dungeon knew only too well that at any hour of the day or night he might be called out to suffer the same fate. For a year the Vicar-General was subjected to absolute solitude and inactivity. He was deprived of Mass and Sacraments, and restricted to his own thoughts. At last, he proffered a modest request, which was not refused. He asked for the companionship of his canary. The little bird cheered and relieved the sense of loneliness, till one day it drooped and died, leaving a true mourner in the faithful priest.[1] Cardinals di Pietro and Gabrielli were confined at Vincennes about the same time. Gabrielli

---

[1] *Vie du Cardinal d'Astros*, 188, and chap. xiii.

had experienced something worse even than Vincennes, a fortnight's imprisonment at *La Force* with two public criminals who were afterwards executed.

Whilst those at a distance could not pay the smallest homage to the Holy Father without incurring these severe penalties, Savona itself was subjected to the strictest inspection.   Pius VII. was never suffered to give private audiences, and in order to approach him at all the Emperor's permission was necessary. Some priests from Marseilles had been thrown into a filthy dungeon for simply disregarding Napoleon's injunctions on this score.   On the other hand, there was a natural reaction against his tyranny.   Secret committees were organised, both in France and in Italy, to facilitate spiritual intercourse with the Holy Father.   He could count upon a certain number of devoted persons, young men especially, who held themselves in readiness at all hours of the day and night to carry out the Papal service.   The Pope's official correspondence passed through their hands, when they could succeed in snatching documents from the gaolers around him, who neither slumbered nor slept.   The Black Cardinals were subsidised by alms on a large scale from the noblest in France, and, curiously enough, the Cardinal Primate was amongst the contributors.[1]   Napoleon followed in the train of persecutors, recognising every effort made on behalf of his prisoner by increased severity.   Restrict as he would, he could not efface the Pope or his action, and in

---

[1] *L'Église Romaine et le Premier Empire*, t. iii. p. 448.

the simple matter of episcopal confirmation, he found himself entirely defeated. Hence his orders to M. Bigot. "Write to inform the Prefect of Montenotte of the letter which the Pope has written to the Vicar-General in Paris (M. d'Astros). Enlighten him as to the duplicity of the Pope, who, pretexting conciliation and charity, secretly stirs up discord and rebellion. Order him to prevent couriers from being received or sent, with letters for the Pope or his household. He must neither receive nor send out letters. The Prefect should therefore have free hand with the director of the post. Tell him that I am having the Bishop of Savona removed to Paris, as he might have kept up a secret understanding with the Pope. Order the Bishop to come to Paris, where I wish to see him. Impress upon M. de Chabrol that he must take a firmer tone in speaking to the Pope, and should let His Holiness know the harm he is doing to religion. He is trying to sow trouble and discord, disregarding conciliation and moderation, which might have succeeded with me. He will obtain nothing by the means he is using, and the Church will, in the end, lose the remains of the Temporal Power. Those who are ignorant and foolish enough to listen to him will forfeit their place, and it will be his fault. This must be strongly put to him. It is useless for the Pope to write ; the less he does, the better it will be. Let the Prefect describe the persons who surround the Pope, pointing out the most actively inclined amongst them, so that I may send them away, and thus prohibit the

N

Pope from writing or circulating what is poisonous. Then tell him he is to send no more letters from the Pope to the kingdoms of Italy or Naples, to Tuscany, Piedmont, or France, neither is he to give the Pope any letters. They are to be sent here. Have all letters which the Pope may write or have written to him sent to you. As a general rule, the less of what he writes reaches its destination, the better it will be. Inform the Prefect and Prince Borghese that I wish the Papal household to feel the effect of my displeasure. Henceforth a sum of from twelve to fifteen thousand francs only will be allotted for its expenses. The carriages which were put at his disposal (the Pope had never used them) are to be sent back to Turin. Tell M. de Chabrol not to give the Pope the slightest ground for thinking that I want to come to terms with him. . . . I trouble myself very little about what he does. We are too enlightened not to distinguish between the doctrine of Jesus Christ and that of Gregory VII. The Prefect must let the Pope know that all the canons and theologians in France and Italy are indignant at the letters he has written to the chapters, and that he was to blame for the arrest of three canons at Florence, and the confiscation of their benefices. The same may be said of similar treatment exercised towards the Chapter of Asti, the arrest of Cardinal di Pietro, Canon d'Astros, the priests Fontana and Gregori, who have all been sent to a distance, to keep them out of mischief. He must tell the Pope that this sly behaviour is unworthy of him, and that he will bring misfortune on those with whom he corresponds. Since he is a declared enemy of the Emperor, and says himself that he is a *prisoner*, he must act as a prisoner, and give up corresponding either with his agents or those who have found means of establishing intercourse with him. Let him be told that it is a misfortune for Christendom to have a Pope so ignorant of what is due to sovereigns, but that government will proceed, and good be effected without him." [1]

On the 8th of January 1811, therefore, a strict search was instituted at the Episcopal Palace of the Holy Father's correspondence and papers. Some experts at the trade of forcing open doors and drawers came expressly from Paris to ransack the premises at the dead of night, when all the Papal household had retired. They stopped at nothing to carry out their orders. Clothes were unsewn, even those of the Pope himself, in this unscrupulous search after suspicious documents. A little later in the day, whilst the Holy Father was taking a walk in the garden, his desk was forced open, and all that it contained was confiscated, amongst other things his Breviary, and an Office of Our Lady. Some money, the alms of a secret committee, was discovered in Mgr. Doria's apartment.

"Let them take the purse," said the Pope, when he heard of the proceeding, "but what will they do with my Breviary, and the Office of Our Lady?"

---

[1] *Lettres de l'Empereur au Cte. Bigot de Préamencu, du* 31 decembre 1810, *et du* 17 janvier 1811.

As far as possible, Pius VII. was parted from familiar faces and objects. Those of his household whom he most affected were sent off to Fenestrello.[1]

Napoleon's object in reducing the Pope to powerlessness was to make the Papacy a dependency of his crown. One order of his at this time seemed to overshoot the mark, and to go beyond even his transgression of all justice and propriety. He required the Holy Father to surrender the Ring of the Fisherman. Pius VII., deeply moved, broke the ring in two, and handed it in this state to Napoleon's officer. The sufferings of Peter must be shared by all the Church, and the broken ring was typical of a great anguish. In the religious world of Paris it took the form of terror. Napoleon would not be crossed. His revenge pursued even charitable ladies who had interested themselves in the Black Cardinals. Napoleon was absolute master of the Senate, and of the Notre Dame Chapter. Cardinal Maury strove to allay the fears of his canons. No man could witness the fate of M. d'Astros without a feeling of insecurity as to his own fortunes. Maury drew up an address from the Chapter, in which he maintained its right to institute bishops without Papal confirmation. A single sentence will show its worth. "According to the principles of the French clergy, there being in the Church no power *independent of the canons*, none exists which by measures contrary to the canons has the right of opposing this prerogative, or rather this duty

[1] *L'Église Romaine et le Premier Empire*, t. iii. p. 479.

of the Chapter "[1] (the exclusive nomination of bishops). When this was read in Notre Dame, M. Emery alone conscientiously remonstrated with Maury. Bossuet's example had, as usual, been quoted in the matter against the Holy Father, and Emery, who knew his ground well, challenged the Cardinal to prove that Bossuet had really counselled Louis XIV. to dispense with Papal confirmation from 1682 to 1693. Maury replied that "since Bossuet had been consulted by the King on all ecclesiastical matters of the day, he must necessarily have counselled *this* step."

In spite of the plainly trifling character of this and other assertions in the address, Maury was particularly anxious to gratify the Emperor by having it read at a Court reception in January 1811. The second Vicar-General, M. Jalabert, received a copy of what he was to read only when already on the spot. He was agitated and impressed by the presence of the Imperial Court, and neglected to restore to the text the Chapter's commendation of M. d'Astros and M. Emery's corrections. Napoleon cared very little in reality about the Chapter of Notre Dame. All that he wanted was that the address should appear as the spontaneous opinion of the Canons, and it was therefore inserted in the *Moniteur* of January 7th to deceive the unwary. In his answer, Napoleon told the Chapter that the unity of Italy had been a necessity, in order to ensure success against *heretical England*. To this end he had required to be absolute

---

[1] *L'Église Romaine et le Premier Empire*, t. iv. p. 18.

master of the Adriatic. These powerful considerations, he said, had not moved the Pope, who, as the common Father of all Christians, had declined to league himself against any nation. The Sovereign Pontiff had, in fact, preferred the destruction of his temporal sovereignty. In spiritual affairs it had been the same. Bishoprics had become vacant, and the Pope had obstinately refused canonical confirmation.[1]

Capitular addresses were not allowed to drop. Napoleon encouraged them from all parts, and had them published in the *Moniteur*, in order that they might fall under the Pope's eye, and induce him to believe that his children were playing him false. For several months the *Moniteur* was full of these addresses, great preference being shown for the Italian chapters. This paper constituted the whole reading of the Holy Father. However much of painful doubt it suggested, he was certainly not blind to the fact that all the addresses were drawn up after one model. The same tone ran through them all. Savona achieved a disgraceful notoriety in the competition, and the Bishop received in consequence a reward of six thousand francs from imperial gratitude.[2]

But chapters might be as eloquent as they would, they could not institute bishops to the satisfaction of Christendom.

---

[1] *L'Église Romaine et le Premier Empire*, t. iv. p. 18.
[2] *Lettre de l'Empereur au Cte. Bigot de Préameneu*, 10 mars 1811.

In 1809 Napoleon had created an Ecclesiastical Commission, which he called together again in 1811. As a tribunal to carry out his will, not to legislate, it was eminently successful. Imaginary difficulties were laid before the Commission, which could be solved in one way alone—reconciliation with the Pope. M. Emery, a member of the Commission, had, with his sound good sense, put his finger on the real evil : "Let the Emperor leave the Church in peace," he wrote to a friend; "let him restore the Pope, the cardinals, and the bishops, to their functions; let him give up his extravagant pretensions: the rest will soon take care of itself."[1]   M. Emery was Superior of St. Sulpice, and one of the very few who ventured to speak the truth to the Emperor. Napoleon treated him with respect, and honoured him for his strength of conviction. On a former occasion, at Fontainebleau, M. Emery had remonstrated with Napoleon, both for his treatment of the Holy Father and of the Temporal Power. The Emperor told M. Emery that he respected the Pope's spiritual power, but that his temporal power came from Charlemagne, not from our Lord.   He was anxious, as many other ambitious sovereigns have been, to relieve the Sovereign Pontiff from the burden of material cares.   To this M. Emery replied that the Pope's territory was already considerable in the fifth century, long before Charlemagne. Let the Emperor, then, at least respect that which

---

[1] *L'Église Romaine et le Premier Empire*, t. iv. p. 69.

had not entered into Charlemagne's gift.   M. Emery
offered Napoleon his book on Fleury, in the hope of
indoctrinating the Emperor in Church History.   Its
testimony was strong enough for the usual agent to
be called in.   The police seized and condemned it.

The Commission had originally been composed of
Cardinals Fesch and Maury, Mgr. de Barral, Archbishop of Tours, Mgr. Duvoisin, Bishop of Nantes,
the Bishops of Trèves, Verceil, and Evreux, M. Emery,
and Fr. Fontana, General of the Barnabites.   Of
these ecclesiastics, Pius VII. could thoroughly count
only on two, M. Emery and Fr. Fontana, and their
practical withdrawal from all doings of the first
Commission is the best proof of it.   Fesch was
blamed for his Roman sentiments, and they were
scarcely more than sentiments.   He was still faithful
to his character of playing two parts, breaking neither
with Pope nor with Emperor, yet not pleasing either,
and spoiling the good he might have done by his
want of tact.   Maury's influence was small.   Napoleon ruled him, and at the bottom despised him for
being ruled.   Mgr. de Barral and Mgr. Duvoisin
were courtier bishops with great theological science,
which it seemed they could not or would not apply
to the case in point.   Of the two, Mgr. Duvoisin
was the Emperor's favourite.   Sometimes in the
course of his angry outbursts, Napoleon would ex-
claim, "Do not imagine, Monsieur l'Évêque, that
what I say applies to you."   If Mgr. Duvoisin had
been an Emery, he might have done great things

with the Emperor, who described him in these words:
" M. Duvoisin is one of those bishops who could make me do all he wished, and perhaps more than I ought."

The questions submitted to this committee in 1809 urgently required an answer. The Church is a kingdom vast as the world, and cannot be governed without a head, yet this was the impossible problem put before a few French ecclesiastics. The worst enemies of the Papacy have sought rather to transfer the office of Pope than to abolish it. So now Napoleon's mind had given sentence before his Committee pronounced it. He was firmly resolved to take the reins of spiritual government into his own hands, and the Commission was his mouthpiece. He could not call an Œcumenical Council for the best of reasons, but a National Council would, as he imagined, answer his purpose, and the Commission was to prepare the way thereunto in all docility. In January 1811, it declared the National Council competent to deal with the question of episcopal confirmation conferred temporarily by the Metropolitan without the customary Papal Bulls. As for the Bull *Quum Memoranda*, the Commission declared that it was null and void, and binding on no man's conscience, because called forth by the invasion of the Papal States. The Faith is not essentially committed to the Temporal Power. It is certainly proved by the whole course of events in this long conflict that the Holy Father's spiritual jurisdiction rested for its practical exercise upon the liberty which he enjoyed

as a temporal sovereign. Napoleon had a system, and
insisted on drawing the Pope into and under it. At
the height of his glory he could devise nothing wiser
to solve the spiritual difficulties which he had created,
than to call an assembly whose very reason for existing was a fallacy.

The Commission was not allowed more liberty
of action and speech than any other human tool of
which Napoleon made use. Fr. Fontana had been
sent to Vincennes, and was replaced by Cardinal
Caselli, and the Bishop of Verceil, who had died,
by M. de Pradt, Archbishop-Elect of Malines. The
cause of Pius VII. gained in no particular by these
changes.

Two burning questions were to be laid before the
National Council: (1.) All intercourse between the Pope
and the Emperor's subjects being for the present suspended, who is to furnish the dispensations which were
formerly accorded by the Holy See? (2.) How are
bishops-elect to receive canonical confirmation when the
Pope refuses to confer it?[1] These points raised some
discussion, and M. Emery, who was forced to take a part
in the second Commission, left the Council-room with
a sorrowful consciousness of all that they involved.
He energetically represented to Fesch that Napoleon
was asking an impossibility of the bishops, and
declared to the Cardinal that, as Primate of France,
it was his personal duty to resist even unto blood.
Martyrs were made by such measures as these, but

---

[1] *L'Église Romaine et le Premier Empire*, t. iv. pp. 74, 75.

they were not sitting on this Commission. No martyr spirit was apparent in its timid, halting answers. To the first inquiry it replied that "if unfortunate circumstances temporarily prevented recourse to the Pope for dispensations, the bishops could temporarily bestow them." To the second, that "as the Pope refused the Bulls without alleging any canonical reason for his refusal, the wisest plan would be to add a clause to the Concordat, stipulating that the Pope should be bound to confirm in a given time. If he refused, the right of confirming should devolve upon the Provincial Synod, and then the best course of action would be to re-establish, as far as the bishops were concerned, the regulations of the *Pragmatique Sanction.*"[1] The Commission resolved upon a deputation to Savona. Under the circumstances, they could have nothing to say to the Pope, still they wished to save appearances.[2] It mattered little to them whether they approached him fairly or not, and they would not raise a finger to put a stop to one of his grievances.

The convocation of the National Council was still pending when, in March 1811, Napoleon summoned the grand dignitaries of the Empire to a conference at the Tuileries. M. Emery, whose learning and courage made the day memorable, was taken almost by force to the palace. Just as he was setting out

---

[1] The *Pragmatique Sanction* was the work of a King of France (Charles VII.). Its aim was to replace the Papal power by civil legislation, and its spirit was jealousy of the Holy See's supreme jurisdiction.

[2] *L'Église Romaine et le Premier Empire*, t. iv. p. 79.

for the country, two bishops arrived with an urgent
message from Fesch that they were to bring the
Sulpician back with them in the Primate's carriage.
Emery had no wish to go to the Tuileries. He had
never, he said, had a deliberative voice in the Commission, and had nothing to do with its sittings.
After fervent prayer in his oratory, however, he submitted with calm resignation to be taken to the
Tuileries. Napoleon kept the assembly waiting for
two hours, and then declared those who waited were
wanting in common-sense. He opened proceedings
by one of his violent diatribes against the Pope.
The conference received it in a frightened silence,
and then, to create a diversion, as it seemed, Napoleon
addressed M. Emery, and asked what he thought
upon the subject. Not a single bishop present had
ventured to contradict the Emperor's untruthful
assertions. This was a perilous glory reserved for
M. Emery. "Sire," he answered, "I cannot on this
point own a different opinion to that which is contained in the catechism taught by your orders in
every church of the Empire. I read in this catechism
that *the Pope is the visible Head of the Church.* Now,
can a Body exist without its Head, without him to
whom it owes obedience by Divine right? We are
obliged in France to uphold the Four Articles contained in the Declaration of 1682, but we must
accept the doctrine in its entirety. In the introduction to this Declaration we read that the supremacy of St. Peter and of the Roman Pontiffs was

instituted by Jesus Christ, and that all Christians owe obedience to this supremacy. Nay, more. The Four Articles, it is added, were judged necessary in order to prevent, that, under pretext of the liberties of the Gallican Church, this supremacy might suffer infringement." The logical conclusion of M. Emery's speech, which, as a deeply felt conviction, should have been in the mouth of every prelate assembled at the Tuileries, was, that, "a Council convoked without the Pope would be utterly powerless."

"Well," replied the Emperor, displaying no sign of anger at being thus thwarted by a simple ecclesiastic, "I do not contest the spiritual power of the Pope, because he received it from Jesus Christ. But Jesus Christ did not give him the Temporal Power. It was Charlemagne who gave it to him, and I, as successor of Charlemagne, mean to take it away, because it is an obstacle in the way of his spiritual functions."

"Sire," replied M. Emery, "here again I can have no other opinion but that of Bossuet, whose great authority your Majesty respects, and whom you are pleased often to quote. This great prelate, in his 'Defence of the Declaration of the Clergy,' expressly states that the independence and the entire liberty of the Sovereign Pontiff *are* necessary for the free exercise of his spiritual authority in all the universe, and in such a multiplicity of kingdoms and of empires." Here M. Emery, whose memory where Bossuet was concerned was particularly keen, quoted verbally the testimony of the Eagle of Meaux in favour of the Temporal Power: "We congratulate not only the Apostolic See on account of the temporal sovereignty, but the universal Church; and we desire with all our heart that this sacred dominion may retain its independent character in every particular."

Nothing could be more irrefutable than this argument. Napoleon listened patiently. He maintained on his own side a totally different state of things in Europe. "I do not question Bossuet's authority," he said. "All that was true in his time, when Europe owned several masters. It was not fitting *then* that the Pope should be under the thraldom of any particular sovereign. Why should the Pope not acknowledge my authority, now that all Europe owns it?"

M. Emery passed over the personal part of the remark, and objected the instability of human fortune. What had happened once might happen again, and in any case why subvert a wise and established order of things?[1]

Napoleon went on to the clause which the bishops had proposed to add to the Concordat: *that His Holiness should confer canonical confirmation in a given time, failing which the right of confirming would devolve upon the Provincial Synod.* Was this a concession to which the Pope would be likely to yield, the Emperor asked? M. Emery at once answered that it was most highly improbable, as it would annihilate the Sove-

---

[1] *L'Église Romaine et le Premier Empire,* t. iv. p. 85.

reign Pontiff's right of confirmation. So the proposed step was founded on the pusillanimity of the bishops, and Napoleon resented it. "*Vous vouliez me faire faire un pas de clerc,*" he angrily exclaimed to them.

The noble words and reasoning of M. Emery produced, if not a lasting effect, a certain impression on Napoleon. His esteem for the Sulpician was undoubted. On leaving the room of the debate, he bowed most graciously in passing M. Emery, and pretty well ignored the other members of the Commission, who had so perfectly drilled themselves to silence. A few days afterwards, when Cardinal Fesch was entertaining him with theology, he exclaimed, without ceremony, " Be quiet. You are an ignoramus. Where did you learn theology ? It is with M. Emery, who knows it, that I wish to discuss these matters !"[1]

How would it have been if there had been ten M. Emery's ? Would they have stayed Napoleon's hand ? It is a secret of God's Providence; but ten just men would have saved even Sodom and Gomorrha.

M. Emery had borne a courageous testimony to the Holy See as his last words on earth. He expired on April 28th, 1811, rather more than a month after uttering them. The legacy he bequeathed was disregarded, but for himself it may be said—his works do follow him.

[1] *Vie de M. Emery.*

CHAPTER XII

A GALLICAN COUNCIL

1811

THE Council convoked in June 1811 was more truly a Gallican, than a National, Council, since not half the sees recently united to the French Empire were represented at it. The will of Napoleon called it into being to meet a difficulty of his own creation. He complained that the Pope had broken the Concordat by his refusal to confer episcopal confirmation, whereas he himself had first been faithless to the compact. He had driven Pius VII. from the Quirinal, forced the Holy Father to fly from place to place at the risk of his life, and at last imprisoned him strictly at Savona, without the resources of books or councillors. Napoleon's evil will was the sole obstacle in the matter, which no council could touch. He wished his assembly to proclaim one fact loudly to the Head of the Church: Pius VII. was to draw the conclusion that the French Episcopate would side with the Emperor rather than with himself. Then, possibly, he would do more than confirm bishops. He would accept the cherished programme of a residence at Avignon or Paris, a revenue of two million francs, and the position of first subject to the French Emperor. The French bishops themselves for the most part obeyed the summons to Paris, in ignorance as to the exact state of the case between Pope and Emperor. In the meantime four prelates were chosen to form a deputation to Savona before the opening of the Council. They were Mgr. de Barral, Archbishop of Tours, Mgr. Duvoisin, Bishop of Nantes, Mgr. de Trèves, and the Patriarch-Elect of Venice, and they, at least, had no excuse of ignorance for the unworthy part they played at the Emperor's bidding. The deputation, thus inspired by Napoleon alone, and receiving instructions from M. Bigot, his Minister of Worship, was to act as if a free and spontaneous representative of ecclesiastical France. M. Bigot composed a letter from the deputation in the name of all the bishops, in which Pius VII. was assured that the whole Gallican Church was speaking by its mouthpiece. Napoleon required the principal prelates in his Empire to support the deputation by a letter as spontaneous as the rest of the proceedings. Cardinal Fesch thus submitted to write confidentially to Pius VII., urging him to that prompt settlement "which the state of the Church justified." Nineteen bishops were weak enough to comply. Vincennes and other state prisons stifled the voice of resistance. "If the Holy Father left their petition unanswered," as the bishops expressed it in the letter written to order, "the very nature of things would compel them to grant dispensations by their private authority. The

Sovereign Pontiff would surely not prolong an impossible resistance." [1]

The members of the deputation were authorised to negotiate separately with the Holy Father, that is, to urge upon him the affair of episcopal confirmation, and the general state of ecclesiastical matters, in which hopeless confusion had reigned for two years, at least since the free action of the Pope had been stopped.

Two distinct batteries were plied against the Holy Father's conscience; the one was set in motion by the deputation on religious grounds, the other by M. de Chabrol on a secular score. Napoleon was the real mover of both springs : he directed the unworthy Churchmen as well as the gaoler-in-chief. The health of Pope Pius was in a very precarious state, and Porta, his doctor, was bribed to make his very weakness serve the Emperor's will. "The Pope's doctor, M. Porta, does us admirable service," wrote M. de Chabrol in May 1811. The kind of treatment implied in these words, joined to complete isolation, had had its effect on the Holy Father. It was now four months since he had been deprived of his papers, books, and writing materials, and of the familiar and cherished servants who had somewhat softened his imprisonment. When on the 9th of May he was officially told the bishops deputed by the French clergy had arrived, he thought they came to take down his depositions for the council which was to try and judge him. Napoleon had done

<hr>

[1] *Fragments Historiques*, 316.

all he could to strengthen the preposterous notion. The Pope's real attitude with regard to the deputation is therefore a matter of importance, trifling and cringing as was the deputation itself. During the first few days of the bishops' stay, from the 9th to the 16th of May, the Holy Father invariably replied to their remonstrances that "he could and would do nothing without councillors." Once they suggested that they should take the place of the much-desired cardinals, but the Pope courteously dismissed the suggestion. He did not consider them sufficiently disinterested, he said. It was less than the truth, since they were actually ruled by the secret instructions of Napoleon, communicated through M. Bigot. One day, when the bishops were as usual expatiating with the Holy Father on the troubles caused by his resistance, Pius VII. raised his eyes to heaven, exclaiming, "Pazienza! I am without counsel, and the Head of the Church is in prison. *Plus vident oculi quam oculus.*"[1]

The bishops were already discouraged, and thought of returning to Paris, *re infecta*. But if they showed signs of weariness, not so M. de Chabrol. On the 13th of May he had a long interview with the Holy Father, and did ample justice to the full confidence reposed in him by the Emperor. He feigned immense astonishment at the refusal of Pius VII. to meet the demands of the bishops. The council, he said, was

---

[1] *Troisième Lettre des Évêques Députés au Ministre des Cultes,* 13 mai 1811.

prepared to pronounce sentence against the Sovereign
Pontiff, and to deprive him of his rights.   Pius VII.
gently answered M. de Chabrol, that in matters of
conscience he referred to the judgment of God.   This
"incomprehensible obstinacy" baffled the time-serving
prefect.   Meantime he learnt from Porta that the
Holy Father was suffering cruelly in health from the
fatigue and anxiety caused by perpetual discussions.
He could hardly sleep or eat, he was sad and down-
cast, and troubled at the sense of responsibility from
which his restricted life gave him no escape.   Anything solacing or recreative was purposely withheld.
His brain and nerves gave way, and for some days his
state amounted to temporary insanity.   M. de Chabrol
took advantage of these symptoms to pay the Holy
Father another of his overbearing visits.   "Dr. Porta
has been of great service to us," in warning us when
to approach the august prisoner, he might have added.
Wearied out of his mind, the Pope expressed to M.
de Chabrol on this occasion a desire to see the bishops
immediately for a final consideration of their sugges-
tions.   On the 17th May they had submitted a memorandum to the Holy Father, which he read and kept,
but in their letters they gave little hopes of being
ultimately successful.   On the 18th, owing to the
visit so well timed through Dr. Porta's connivance,
the deputation found the Holy Father more disposed
to concession.   It was "well timed," because of the
Pope's extreme physical weakness.   The bishops drew
up in the Pope's room a rough draft of that which

they were directed to request of him. After Pius VII. had suggested a few not very material corrections, the deputation left the draft which he had accepted on the mantelpiece, and 'the next day set off early in the morning for Paris. This was the full extent of their boasted victory, one seized with the point of the sword over a Pope worn out with anxiety, privations, sickness, and a cruel imprisonment. During the night following the interview, a valet who slept near the Pope heard him accusing himself audibly in the most contrite terms for what he called his prevarication. The next morning, in a state of extreme agitation, he sent first for M. la Gorse, to know if the bishops had already gone, and then for M. de Chabrol. The Holy Father told the Prefect he had been surprised into unlawful concession the previous day, and that he withdrew it altogether. The last words of the draft were heretical in their tendency, and he would rather die a thousand times than accept them. However, the document had been no more than a preliminary draft, to which the Holy Father had not put his signature. This consoled him. It is not quite clear how he could have protested had Napoleon used it against him; but this is what he threatened to do.[1]

For some days those who surrounded the Holy Father were able to detect all the symptoms of madness. At the end of May, M. de Chabrol wrote to M. Bigot: "You will have seen by my last letters

---

[1] *Lettres de M. de Chabrol au Ministre des Cultes, du 22 et du 23 mai 1811.*

that the Pope's hesitation, when left to himself, is so great as to *affect his reason and his health*. At present the *mental alienation has passed off*, and the physical indisposition is less grave, but everything warns us that the support of counsel is indispensable to a mind that is weakened, and to a sensitive conscience."[1] Napoleon's gratitude to Dr. Porta was expressed in the most significant way. "Dr. Porta has only to name his terms," he wrote to Bigot some months later, "and his allowance will be paid to him as when the Pope was in Rome. A sum of twelve thousand francs yearly shall be paid to him, and shall be continued as long as he remains with the Pope."[2]

The deputation had no cause to be proud of its results. If a rough draft, suggestive of concession, had been torn from Pius VII., it possessed no official value without a signature, and was openly protested against by the Holy Father, who declared what was only plain truth, that he had been surprised into yielding, not to say forced, and that if the document were produced against him he would use those spiritual arms which were beyond the reach of violence. Napoleon was too ready to take advantage of the slightest faltering in the Holy Father, not to have speedily published a triumph effected at any price over his weakest yet his strongest opponent. The Emperor, on the contrary,

---

[1] *Lettre de M. de Chabrol au Ministre des Cultes*, 30 mai 1811.

[2] *Lettre de l'Empereur au Cte. Bigot de Préameneu*, 1 novembre 1811.

ordered the bishops to maintain absolute secrecy concerning the deputation. They obeyed so effectively that during the conferences preliminary to the Council, no single bishop present clearly understood what they had really done. Napoleon was virtual president of an assembly whose every member was placed under his control. Fesch assumed the title by courtesy, for in truth the Primate was nothing more than presiding prelate, still wavering between conscience and regard for his imperial nephew. It was noticed that Napoleon sat on the throne as one not to the manner born. The same unpractised hand was noticeable when he surreptitiously wielded the keys of Peter. On the eve of the Council, the Bishop of Séez, and M. le Gallois, a Vicar-General, had fallen under his displeasure, the Bishop, for recommending his *curés* to keep certain feasts suppressed by the Emperor, and for neglecting to be present at the marriages of the *rosières*. A month before the Council, Napoleon happened to be in Normandy. He did not forget that he had a bishop to punish, and sent for Mgr. de Séez. The following conversation took place :—

"Are you the Bishop of Séez ?"

"Yes, Sire."

"I am very displeased with you. You are the only bishop of whom I have heard complaints. You keep up party spirit here. Instead of uniting different parties, you still make a distinction between Constitutional clergy and non-Constitutional priests.

You are the only person in France who so acts.
You wish for civil war. You have already caused
it; you have stained your hands in French blood.
Your diocese stands by itself for unruliness."

"Sire, everything is in the best order."

"You wrote a very mischievous circular."

"I changed it."

"I sent for you to Paris to show you my displeasure, and nothing does you any good. You are
utterly good for nothing; resign at once."

"Sire!"

"Let his papers be seized!" exclaimed the Emperor to M. Rœderer, who was in the room. The
Chapter of Séez, who came to the formidable audience-
chamber after the Bishop had retired, had their
share in the explosion of wrath. The brunt of it,
however, fell on M. le Gallois, a Vicar-General, and
much-respected priest. The canons had hardly
appeared before Napoleon shouted out rudely—

"Which of you is it who leads that simpleton of
a bishop?"

M. le Gallois' name was mentioned.

"So it is you, is it?" continued the Emperor.
"Why did you advise him not to be present at the
marriages of the *rosières?*"

"Sire, I was absent at the time of those
marriages."

"Why did you counsel your bishop to write that
circular about the suppressed feasts?"

"Sire, I was absent then too, and, to speak truth,

as soon as I knew about it, I came to Séez expressly to advise an entirely different circular."

"Where were you, then ?"

"With my family."

"How could you go away so often when your bishop is the simpleton he is? Who governed the diocese, and how did you become Vicar-General ?"

"Sire, I obeyed my superiors—every priest owes them obedience."

"Are you a good Gallican ?"

"Yes, Sire, and perhaps one of the heartiest in your Empire."

Forty-eight hours later M. le Gallois was arrested in the Episcopal Palace, taken between two policemen to prison at Alençon, from thence to *La Force*, to the cell just vacated by a criminal condemned to capital punishment. After eleven days at *La Force* he was sent to Vincennes. He was too intelligent not to be "dangerous," and his intelligence was his only crime. He fell ill at Vincennes, and on this account he was removed to a place of milder confinement, and kept in it till the fall of the Empire.[1]

Napoleon expressly chose the 16th of June 1811, the eve of the Council, for the opening of the Legislative Session. He did not wish the Council, which, after all, was an ecclesiastical business, to absorb too much attention. For the same reason the *Moniteur* gave meagre details of the splendid scene presented by ninety-five bishops, in cope and mitre,

---

[1] *L'Église Romaine et le Premier Empire*, t. iv. pp. 177-183.

at Notre Dame. The *Moniteur* was the *official news-paper of the French Empire*, and in this capacity shared the fortune of all other public organs devoted to the new dynasty, that of having neither will nor voice of its own. The simple people of those days (if they existed), who founded all their hopes of the day's news on the *Moniteur*, were defrauded of their rights as far as the doings of the Council were concerned. The nature of the proceedings imposed absolute silence later on. The prelates who specially distinguished themselves as Catholic bishops were Mgr. d'Aviau, Archbishop of Bordeaux, Mgr. de Broglie, Bishop of Ghent, Mgr. de Boulogne (Troyes), and Mgr. Hirn (Tournai). Opened on the 17th of June, the Council was prematurely dissolved on July 12th, by the will that ruled all its proceedings. The attempt to reopen it again was a feeble effort productive of no consequences. The first and only session of the Council denied more powerfully than mere words can ever do the statement which Napoleon had tried to impose on the Pope's good faith. Pius VII. had been told that the French bishops were ready to side with Napoleon should matters come to a crisis, but here in the midst of Notre Dame the orator of the day, Mgr. de Boulogne, alluded in eloquent and burning terms " to the supreme Head of the Episcopate, without whom it could only resemble a withered branch severed from the trunk, or a ship without rudder or steersman, tossed by the waves. Whatever vicissitudes the See of Peter may

experience, whatever the state and condition of his
successor may be, we shall always be united to him
by ties of filial respect and veneration. This See
may be removed, it cannot be destroyed. Its magnificence may be taken away, never its strength.
Wherever it is established, it will draw all others
round it. Be it where it may, all Catholics will
follow it, because everywhere it must continue to be
the representative of the succession, the centre of
government, and the sacred deposit of Apostolical
traditions." [1]

Napoleon had foreseen what might be made of
the opening discourse, and both Fesch and Mgr. de
Boulogne had promised that no words liable to misinterpretation should fall from the pulpit. In the
ardour of his oratory the Bishop of Troyes allowed
himself to be carried away : his words fell as burning
coals in the midst of the learned assembly, and produced strong emotion. The effect had not died away
when the Bishop of Nantes rose to fulfil a necessary
formality in asking each prelate individually whether
it pleased him that the Council should be opened.
Mgr. d'Aviau answered conditionally : "Yes, saving
the obedience due to the Sovereign Pontiff, to whom
I bind myself, and to whom I swear obedience." Then
Cardinal Fesch, with the singular inconsistency which
distinguished him, prepared to ascend a raised platform placed in the middle of the choir, from whence
he read in a loud tone of voice the oath prescribed

---

[1] *Œuvres Complètes de Mgr. de Boulogne, Évêque de Troyes.*

by a Bull of Pius IV. As officiating prelate, he represented the Assembly when he said: "I acknowledge the Holy, Catholic, Apostolic, and Roman Church to be the mother and mistress of all other churches; I promise and swear perfect obedience to the Roman Pontiff, the Successor of St. Peter, Prince of the Apostles, and Vicar of Jesus Christ on earth." This oath was repeated by every bishop in the cathedral, placing his hands in those of Cardinal Fesch. One by one they bound themselves irrevocably to the cause of Pius VII. If the formula was uttered feebly, the Primate required a repetition; and he directed particular atteution to those who had been Constitutional bishops, or were suspected of unorthodox views.[1]

An eloquent sermon, containing expressions of inviolable attachment to Pius VII. and an oath of fidelity to him, imposed upon each prelate present, certainly did not find favour with Napoleon. If the bishops imagined they had been summoned to Paris to proclaim the supremacy of St. Peter's See, they were woefully mistaken. Napoleon lost no time in letting them know it. Angry as he was with Fesch for "making one of his scenes," he was determined to tell the Council his mind in terms clear enough to cause "foolish attempts" at opposition to fall to the ground. As an expedient for controlling every breath of the Council, he resolved upon the presence at it of two functionaries whose office he had created—the respective Ministers of Worship for France and Italy,

---

[1] *Vie du Cardinal Fesch*, par l'Abbé Lyonnet, ii. p. 329.

M. Bigot de Préameneu and M. de Marescalchi.   At
the first General Congregation, which was held at the
Archiepiscopal Palace, these State ministers appeared
in official costume, one on the right, the other on the
left, of Fesch.   It was the beginning of disenchant-
ment for those bishops who were not in the secret.
They were further enlightened by an imperial decree
ordering the Council to be submitted to a State Committee on which the Ministers of Worship would sit.
One of them remarked that this was rather influencing
the decisions of the Council than protecting its delibera-
tions.   All that the bishops could obtain was to nominate to the Committee, which was to sit with State
officers.   The imperial message was a violent tissue
of abuse against Pius VII., who had listened to " evil
counsels" and meditated "dark designs."   Of his
sufferings, his imprisonment, his illness, or the miserable means which the Emperor had used to alienate
the members of his household, there was naturally
not a word.   The whole programme was preconcerted
and carried out by Napoleon through M. Bigot.   " Be
careful," he wrote to his officer, " that nothing is
printed without my knowledge.   See that no reporter
or foreigner be admitted into the Assembly.   The
attendance is limited to bishops alone.   As for the
presence of priests, I will admit a dozen ecclesiastics,
if it is absolutely necessary, whose names and qualifications you must give me beforehand.   They must
be virtuous priests, not reactionists.   The report,
which you are to draw up at the Council, is not to

be printed. You must simply read it and hand it over to the Committee of the Council. The Committee is not authorised to publish its report till I have approved it."[1]

The real President here paints himself in his true colours. Cardinal Fesch, on the other hand, hovered between courtier prelates and the majority, more frightened than potent, whose conscience refused to accept the Emperor's will without a struggle. Still the frightened majority resisted as a body where they might have yielded as individuals.

The Bishop of Nantes, Mgr. Duvoisin, achieved a melancholy notoriety as the Emperor's man. He produced an address to Napoleon which he had drawn up, speaking in strong and disrespectful terms of the Bull *Quum Memoranda*. His work, he said ingenuously, "had been laid before the Emperor, and had received his entire approval." A stormy discussion followed, but the effect of the address, when read at a general congregation of the Council, was something more. It called forth a spontaneous and irresistible movement in favour of the Pope. The cry, "the liberty of the Pope," was raised, and the Bishop of Chambéry put into eloquent words the feeling which was in the Assembly almost in spite of itself.

"How is it, my Lords, that there is no question of the Pope's liberty in the address which has just been read to us? What are we doing here, we Catholic bishops, assembled in Council, without the power of

---

[1] *Note de l'Empereur au Cte. Bigot de Préameneu*, 20 juin 1811.

holding intercourse with our Head? How can we do otherwise than request the Emperor to set the Pope at liberty? It is our right, and it is also our duty. We owe it to the Catholics of Europe and of the whole world. Let us not hesitate to fall at the Emperor's feet in order to obtain this deliverance."[1]

This speech produced indescribable enthusiasm, hardly checked by the observation of a courtier prelate, who, wishing to divert the public attention, objected that a Council should not kneel to a prince.

"I can truly appreciate the episcopal dignity, whose rights I respect and could defend as well as any man," replied Mgr. de Chambéry; "but, believe me, bishops should be able to fall on their knees before their sovereign to obtain the liberty of their spiritual Head. Is it not the time, in so great a cause, to follow the Apostle's advice, *Be instant in season and out of season, correct, supplicate, threaten?* How shall it be said that the Chapter of Paris could solicit M. d'Astros' pardon, whilst we dare not ask for the liberty of the Pope! Why should the Emperor be angry, my Lords? Even Almighty God consents to be entreated and importuned by our prayers. Sovereigns are the images of God upon earth. Why should they complain if we treat them as we treat our Father in heaven?"

"Alas, I had foreseen we should come to this," remarked one of Napoleon's prelates in an undertone,

[1] *Journal de Mgr. de Broglie, Évêque de Gand.*

whilst M. Bigot was gesticulating with despairing energy for the Primate's benefit, during Mgr. de Chambéry's speech. He had received particular injunctions from Napoleon that the Council was never to come to a resolution on its own authority.

At this stage Cardinal Fesch might have turned the scale irrevocably in favour of the Holy Father. He might have prevented the arbitrary acts and imprisonment which were visited on the protesting bishops. He preferred the arguments of worldly tact. He shared, he said, the sentiments of Mgr. de Chambéry, but they were inopportune, and could not be carried out. Fesch replunged the Assembly into confusion, and the discussion of impossible questions; as, for instance, whether the Pope possessed or not authority to change established discipline; whether he could revoke what his predecessors had granted; if his censures with regard to temporal matters were not, *ipso facto*, null and void. The censures in question pointed to the Bull. Cardinal Maury ventured to declare that the Holy Father had exceeded his powers in publishing *Quum Memoranda*. He was peremptorily silenced by Mgr. d'Aviau, who laid the Decrees of Trent on the Council table, and confronted all present with its decision respecting the Pope's right of excommunicating sovereigns.

Mgr. Duvoisin had claimed for his address the Emperor's knowledge and approval of it. Nevertheless it was not adopted. A compromise was effected which failed to satisfy either conscience or the Emperor.

This was signed by the presiding prelate and the secretaries. Compromise as it was, it did not find favour with Napoleon. The Council was to understand once for all that its proceedings were to be submitted to the head of the State, and that nothing was to be done without his authorisation. He summoned the Assembly now to put an end to its "idle debates," and to find an answer to the Imperial Message—that was to discover an expedient for providing bishops. Eight days were allowed for the invention. In the meantime Napoleon declined to receive the Council officially at the Tuileries. Several bishops nevertheless went to the palace, and met with a studied indifference or a forced courtesy. One of them spoke with emotion of Pius VII. and his sufferings. "Yes, he is a simple man," said Napoleon. "He is a saintly man," answered the Bishop of Como. Some Italian prelates loudly complained to the Emperor that the addresses from their chapters had been falsified in the *Moniteur*. False or genuine, they had produced their effect, and that was the Emperor's point. Seeing a group of bishops in one of the reception rooms, he went up to them and said—

"My will has made you princes of the Church. Take heed that you are not mere beadles. The Pope refuses to execute the Concordat. Be it so: I care nothing for the Concordat." [1]

The Council then was required to find in eight days an expedient for conferring canonical confirmation without the Pope. It was a task for which it was

<hr>

[1] *Vie de Monseigneur d'Osmond*, p. 587.

wholly incompetent. After three sittings devoted to
the question, the Commission of the Message (as it
was called) acknowledged its own impotence, and
suggested a deputation to the Pope, with full facilities
for conferring with His Holiness. On the 5th of July
Fesch carried this declaration, signed by himself and
the members of the Commission, to his imperial
nephew. He was received with an angry outburst,
and as for the bishops, they should soon be shown
their place. When the Primate urged canonical
reasons in their defence, the Emperor rudely answered,
" What! theology again! Where did you learn it?
Be quiet: you are an ignoramus. In six months I
should beat you."

In this interview he for the first time threatened
to dissolve the Council, and Fesch to withstand him.
The Prefects should henceforth nominate to bishoprics,
and organise a system of State religion, which is the
proper development of Gallicanism. Fesch is said to
have answered Napoleon's intimation by the words:
" If you wish to make martyrs, begin with your own
family. I am ready to give my life to seal my faith.
You may be quite sure that, as long as the Pope has
not consented to this measure, I, as Metropolitan, shall
refuse to confirm my suffragans. I go further. If
one of them in my default were to confirm a bishop
of my province, I would excommunicate him on the
spot." [1]

After two hours of angry words between the Em-

----

[1] *Vie du Cardinal Fesch*, par l'Abbé Lyonnet.

peror and his uncle, Mgr. Duvoisin was announced. Napoleon saw him privately, and it is probable that the Bishop of Nantes suggested what followed. The Emperor called a secretary, and dictated a decree for the Council to pass, saying first to Fesch, " *Vous n'êtes tous que des nigauds. Ce sera moi qui vous tirerai d'affaire.*" The secretary wrote at Napoleon's bidding:

" The Council decrees: (1.) That bishoprics cannot remain vacant for more than a year, during which time the nomination, consecration, and confirmation shall take place.

"(2.) That according to the Concordat the Emperor shall name to the vacant sees.

"(3.) That six months at most after the Emperor's nomination the Pope shall confer canonical confirmation.

"(4.) That the term of six months having expired, the Metropolitan shall, in virtue of the Pope's refusal, be invested with power to consecrate, and shall proceed to canonical consecration and confirmation.

"(5.) That this decree shall, with the Emperor's approval, be published as a law of the State.

"(6.) That the Council shall crave the Emperor's leave to send a deputation of bishops to the Pope, in order to thank him for putting an end, by this concession, to the troubles of the Church."

" Now," exclaimed Napoleon, when he had finished dictating, " everything is settled." [1]

The accounts from Savona in no way authorised the statement contained in this decree of Napoleonic

---

[1] *L'Église Romaine et le Premier Empire*, t. iv. p. 328.

manufacture. M. de Chabrol wrote word that the mental symptoms in the Holy Father had passed off, that he was now much cast down, though perfectly calm, and constantly protesting against the concession the deputation had nearly wrung from him. There was no likelihood that he would yield, and to assert the contrary was to practise a gross deception on the bishops. Cardinal Fesch knew all that had taken place, yet he never enlightened his brethren. He not only allowed Napoleon's false statement to pass, but he professed admiration for the Emperor's sagacity. The bishops on the Commission of the Message were ignorant of the case. With the exception of Mgr. d'Aviau and Mgr. de Broglie, they voted in favour of the imperial decree. A few hours' reflection, however, brought the right conclusion forcibly before the fairest amongst them. If Pius VII. had really made so great a concession, why were they apprised of the fact so late in the day? It was an awakening for Spina, Caselli, the Bishops of Tournai, Troyes and Ivrea. Fesch consented to put the decree a second time to the vote, and then to be the bearer of the new decision to Napoleon. The Bishops of Tours, Trèves, and Nantes refused to accompany the presiding prelate to St. Cloud, in fear of imperial wrath. Possibly the Council might sanction what the Commission rejected, so the Emperor made no difficulty about authorising a General Congregation for July 10th. He wished everything to be settled by the 14th. As soon, however, as the bishops had decided to accept the struggle, on the ground that the Council was incompetent, they were silenced by dissolution. On the morning of July 11th, 1811, the Council was declared at an end. On the 12th, at 3 o'clock in the morning, Mgr. de Broglie (Ghent), Mgr. de Boulogne (Troyes), and Mgr. Hirn (Tournai), were arrested in their beds, and then conveyed to Vincennes, where the lot of the Holy Father, severe solitary confinement, became their portion. Mgr. d'Aviau escaped the same punishment, because he was a saint, and all the world would have been up in arms if violence had been used against him. For once under the First Empire it was good, even in a material sense, to be holy. The same Minister of Police who spared Mgr. d'Aviau, perfectly understood the damage which the imprisonment of bishops would do the Imperial cause. So with an utter disregard of truth, he told all the world that the arrest of the three prelates was in nowise connected with the Council. The Emperor did not patronise *this* lie, for Vincennes was his great resource, and he counted upon it for bringing the remaining bishops to reason.

A few months earlier, the Chapter of Notre Dame had ventured to intercede for M. d'Astros, but the Bishops of Ghent, Tournai, and Troyes found no champions. Cardinal Fesch and Mgr. Duvoisin were entreated by the relations of Mgr. de Broglie to use their influence with Napoleon on his behalf. They proved inadequate to a task which should have been joyfully undertaken in the midst of so much ignominy.

M. de Chabrol persisted in telling M. Bigot that
the Holy Father might still be brought to adopt the
Emperor's views.   The only ground he seems to have
had for the assertion was the Pope's equanimity.   He
possessed his soul in patience, and so could deceive
his gaoler.   Napoleon had hastily dissolved a Council
he could not bend to his will.   He had some thoughts
of calling it together again.   Three of the most tire-
some opponents were lodged at Vincennes, and nine
of the least obliging out of the remaining ninety-one
bishops, without counting Mgr. d'Aviau, had left Paris.
M. Bigot contributed practical assistance.   He had
been present at the Council, and seen for himself
what prelates would be likely to surrender to pressure.
He brought it to bear upon them accordingly.   The
bishop was called to a private conference, then asked
to sign the imperial decree.   In most cases, consent
was given, but there were some noble exceptions.
Mgr. Carletti had replied that the Pope alone could
confirm bishops, and that he could not accept the
decree in his diocese without scandalising his flock.

"*But nobody will know it*," urged M. Bigot.

"My conscience will know it, and that is enough."

"Do you think then that his Majesty is to depend
upon the Pope for the confirmation of bishops?   It
is quite impossible."

Then the minister said His Holiness had given
way, and that he held the proof of it in his hand.

"No," answered the Italian bishop.   "What you
hold is not drawn up in the authentic manner."

"You will be in a very small minority. The greater number have signed."

"In that case you do not require my signature."[1]

The success of M. Bigot's operations fully supported Napoleon's determination to reopen the Council, and Cardinal Fesch consented to preside over its last and feeble attempt at a congregation. It took place on August 5th, and, for the first time, the negotiations at Savona in the previous May were officially made known. The Archbishop of Tours read a memorandum on the draft then left by the deputation with the Holy Father, Napoleon having first expunged what displeased him. Cowardly submission was the order of the day. The decree, signed by Fesch and the secretaries, which miserably closed the Gallican Council of 1811, ran thus :—

"ART. I. Conformably with the holy canons, Archbishoprics and Bishoprics cannot remain vacant longer than a year. During this time the nomination, consecration, and confirmation should be accomplished.

"ART. II. The Emperor shall be entreated still to nominate to vacant sees according to the Concordat and bishops nominated by the Emperor shall seek confirmation of our Holy Father the Pope.

"ART. III. Within the six months following the notice given to the Pope in the customary manner, he shall confer canonical confirmation according to the Concordat.

"ART. IV. If Papal confirmation has not been

[1] *L'Église Romaine et le Premier Empire*, t. iv. p. 360.

conferred at the end of the six months, the Metropolitan, or, in his default, the oldest bishop of the province, shall proceed to confirm the bishop-elect. In the case of the Metropolitan himself, the oldest bishop shall confer confirmation.

"ART. V. The present decree shall be submitted to the approval of our Holy Father the Pope, and to this effect his Majesty shall be entreated to allow a deputation of six bishops to visit His Holiness, in order to obtain his sanction to this decree. Only in this way can an end be put to the troubles of the Church in France and Italy."[1]

[1] *L'Église Romaine et le Premier Empire*, t. iv. p. 368.

CHAPTER XIII

THE Gallican Council was immediately followed by
the deputation to Savona, which one of its articles
had entreated Napoleon to allow. The Holy Father
had often complained that he needed the advice of
cardinals to help him in the grave responsibilities
which his charge, and his position as prisoner, ac-
cumulated upon his head. Napoleon was prepared
to grant this demand in the letter, it is true, but not
in the spirit. The Council furnished him with
ground for proceeding by submitting its decision to
the Papal approval. Napoleon now charged eight
bishops and five cardinals to convey this information
to Savona.   In the case of the first deputation, in
May 1811, Napoleon noted a tendency to soft-
heartedness in the bishops. They had been involun-
tarily touched. This time he elicited a written
promise from the cardinals that they would make
it their one object to gain the Pope's acceptance of
the so-called decree. The members of the Sacred
College who consented to do this ignominious work

were Red Cardinals, viz., Roverella, Dugnami, Ruffo, Doria, and de Bayane, and their assistants were the Archbishops of Tours (Mgr. de Barral) and Malines, the Patriarch of Venice, the Bishops of Feltro, Piacenza, Pavia, Trèves, and Evreux. The Archbishop of Edessa, *in partibus*, Mgr. Bertazzoli, was ordered to Savona as a personal friend of Pius VII. Much was expected from his influence, and his part was to appeal constantly to the feelings of the Holy Father. So firmly resolved was Napoleon to reduce the Pope to an instrument in his system, that no religion, rather than the one which owned Pius VII. as its spiritual head, appeared to him preferable for France and Italy.[1]

The conscience and feelings of Pius VII. were to be unceasingly worked upon for a period of five months, from September 1811 to February 1812. If he resisted evil influence, it was surely through superhuman strength. Naturally, he must have succumbed, either physically, or, worse, mentally. No familiar servant had been left to refresh his drooping hours but the bribed doctor, whose presence had become indispensable in Napoleon's scheme.[2] His only visitor was M. de Chabrol, the zealous imperialist, who talked theology after the fashion of his master, and stepped in when the Pope, or his tormentors, were exhausted. The Prefect of Montenotte was indefatigable. At times he reproached Pius VII.

---

[1] *Lettre de l'Empereur à M. Bigot de Préameneu*, 16 août 1811.
[2] *L'Église Romaine et le Premier Empire*, t. v. p. 21.

with dulness of conception for not rising to the
Emperor's magnificent scheme of a Sovereign Pontiff
at the Imperial Court. It was not his vocation, the
Holy Father would gently reply. Rome had been
chosen by the Popes in preference to the Holy Land;
and when in a vision St. Peter had met his Master,
and had asked Him whither He was going, our Lord
had answered, "To Rome, where I am to be crucified
again."[1] The Cross and Rome were closely connected
in the mind of Pius VII. Rome, indeed, without the
Cross was possible, but the Cross without Rome was
almost unbearable.

The cardinals and bishops left Paris at the end of
August 1811. They avoided travelling together, or
taking the same route, in order to give the deputation
an appearance of spontaneity, which would carry
weight with Pius VII. Mgr. Bertazzoli shed tears
on seeing the Pope. "He can certainly do a great
deal by lamentations and tears," commented de Chabrol.
"The Pope's doctor shall see him (Bertazzoli), and I
myself will cultivate him assiduously." The Prefect
was a gaoler, and he never forgot his office. Mgr.
Bertazzoli was so lodged that he could not visit the
Holy Father without the knowledge of La Gorse.
However, he proved so useful that he was summoned
whenever his presence "was required." Cardinals
Dugnami and Ruffo noticed, perhaps for the first
time, the Sovereign Pontiff's imprisonment. M. de
Chabrol affected surprise. The Pope, he told M.

---

[1] *Lettre de M. de Chabrol à M. Bigot*, 15 juillet 1811.

Bigot, had kept in the house for a year and a half, although he had been urged to go out. All who wished to see him were free to approach him![1]

Cardinal Roverella was credited as the best theologian of the deputation, and up to that time had been thoroughly orthodox in his sentiments. For one moment the whole truth flashed across the Holy Father: the deputation was blindly doing Napoleon's bidding without any regard to religion or justice. He confided his suspicion to M. de Chabrol, who summarily dismissed it. The attitude of the cardinals themselves dispelled further suspicion. They maintained a reserve which had every appearance of modesty, and affected great diffidence about conferring officially with the bishops *sent by his Majesty*. In answer to the Holy Father's arguments, they produced replies made to order, and then M. de Chabrol would suggest that they should retire and leave their sophistry to take root; the Pope followed the "slow fashion of the Court of Rome."

To force the decree of the Council upon the Sovereign Pontiff was their one object. Pius VII. was never told that it had been wrung from some seventy bishops with the prospect of Vincennes looming before them. He signed the Brief of Adhesion on September 20th, 1811, and wrote an autograph letter to the Emperor at the same time. "His son, though rebellious, was still his son."[2] The Holy Father

---

[1] *Lettre de M. de Chabrol à M. Bigot*, 1 septembre 1811.
[2] *L'Archévêque de Tours au Ministre des Cultes*, 15 septembre 1811.

expressed gratitude for the counsel obtained. He had been completely duped, and he thanked his deceiver with a guileless heart.

On the other hand, no one ever satisfied Napoleon. His ambition found neither repose nor boundary in the world of time and space. In the autumn of 1811 his thoughts were not fixed on the negotiating prelates and his menials at Savona. He was meditating the conquest of Russia, and already, in imagination, he had returned victorious to behold the accomplishment of his dream. An old man, weakened by imprisonment and suffering, could no longer object to become the universal Pontiff of Europe's conqueror. Napoleon was what his heated imagination pointed him out, a king amongst sovereigns, therefore no terms were good enough for him. He was affronted at the Brief, partly because it had been addressed to *his* bishops, and the Pope had thus ignored his pretensions to be an Erastian *Summus Pontifex;* and as for the Holy Father's affectionate letter, he decided that no answer would be the course best in keeping with his dignity. The Brief had been unlawfully obtained. That was a detail which did not trouble the courtier bishops. As it stood, it went beyond their most sanguine expectations; yet Napoleon dictated conditions to the Sovereign Pontiff before he would consent to receive it.

" Inform the bishops of the deputation," he wrote once more to M. Bigot, "that I shall answer no letter, nor come to any determination, as long as my bishops

are without their Bulls."   His lawless ambition
goaded him on to the region where Cambacérès had
almost foreseen his destruction, and where the arms
would literally fall from the hands of his soldiers.
On the eve of his departure for Russia he was not
altogether sorry that his new requirements should
leave the question between the Pope and himself still
an open one.   Far-seeing ambition overleaps itself,
and Napoleon, whose victory over the Emperor of all
the Russias was already a fact in his imagination,
dwelt in an Elysium of earthly glory, when he should
in very truth reign over Europe.   The Pope would be
at his side to reproduce a perfect example of those
bishops and *curés* who accepted the pastorals and
discourses furnished by the Ministry of Worship,
praised the Emperor's allies, and execrated his enemies.
Where would the Catholic Church have been after ten
years of Napoleon's system ?   She would simply have
ceased to exist, or, in other words, contrary to the
Divine promise, the gates of hell *would* have prevailed.

Napoleon had ordered the deputation to give
prominence with the Holy Father to the vacant
bishoprics in the States of the Church.   Even they
had demurred at first to the indignity of the insistence,
but now it seemed they could not urge the Holy
Father strongly enough in this sense.   The confirmation of a few bishops in the Roman States was not to
be compared to the misery of protracted misunderstanding.   What would be the consternation of the
faithful, said these unworthy bishops, if they learned

that the Pope had rejected the only course by which the troubles of the Church could be remedied?[1] But the limits of concession had been reached, and the Holy Father declared that in doing more he should "dishonour his character in the eyes of all Catholics."[2] His mind full of the Russian campaign, Napoleon refused to accept the Brief of September, or even to correspond with the Pope. "His Majesty," M. Bigot wrote to the deputation, in December, "awaits the simple acceptance of the Council's decree before he can believe that the first step has been taken towards an agreement."[3]

Gradually the Holy Father was arriving at the truth in all its crudity. By degrees he discovered that those who had been sent to counsel him in his hour of mental anguish, when a long imprisonment and its accompanying hardships had impaired his bodily and mental faculties, were nothing better than imperial emissaries. Princes of the Church had strewn his path with falsehoods and misrepresentations; they had grossly deceived him as to the real demeanour of the Council, and they had suffered him to issue a Brief which rested on false statements. In an audience held in December 1811, the deputation urged the Holy Father to compose a new Brief, "in the spirit of perfect conformity to the Emperor's wishes." The Sovereign Pontiff now knew the worth

---

[1] *Note adressée par MM. les Cardinaux,* 16 novembre 1811.
[2] *L'Église Romaine et le Premier Empire,* t. v. p. 94.
[3] *Note pour les Évêques Députés à Savone,* 3 décembre 1811.

of their advice, and resolved to trust entirely to God
and his own conscience. He drew a fountain of
peace and strength from the decision, receiving kindly
the members of the deputation and M. de Chabrol,
whilst he showed them plainly that concession was
at an end. The deputation had only "one bit of
artillery left in their arsenal," as Mgr. de Barral
expressed it. This was a farewell letter to the Holy
Father, which caused him indeed some emotion, but
no indecision. The Prefect of Montenotte, who visited
him whilst still under the impression it had produced, took occasion once more to tell him that
he was making his "cause odious by a resistance which appealed to nobody."[1] The Pope
appeared pensive, and the enlightened M. de Chabrol
concluded that he was lost in uncertainty. In reality
the Holy Father was contemplating a humble appeal
to Napoleon's feelings: humility is sometimes more
powerful than diplomacy. On the 24th of January
1812 he again wrote to Napoleon in the simple and
affectionate style which was his own. Let the Emperor allow him disinterested councillors and free
intercourse with the faithful, and he might then recon-
sider the Brief. As usual, Napoleon treated the Pope's
letter with contumely. M. Bigot was charged to
write an answer full of arrogance and abuse, directed,
not to Pius VII., but to the false deputation. "His
Majesty deems that it is beneath his dignity to answer
the Pope's letter," wrote M. Bigot. . . . "The Pope

[1] *Lettre de M. de Chabrol au Ministre des Cultes*, 16 janvier 1812.

asks for free intercourse with the faithful. How has he lost it? By violating every duty of peace and charity. He cursed the Emperor and civil authority by a Bull of Excommunication, which was seized in Rome. Was it to curse sovereigns that Jesus Christ was crucified? . . . Now, the Emperor has allowed the Pope at Savona to have intercourse with the faithful, and what use has he made of his ministry? He has sent Briefs which have been as remarkable for ignorance of the canons as for their spiteful attempt to stir up rebellion in chapters. . . . The only counsels he asks for are those of the Black Cardinals, and these he shall never have. If the Pope imagines that he can decide nothing without them, it is his fault. If, in consequence, he *loses his right of confirming bishops*, it is also his fault. Religion will get on without him, and every day it is clearly proved that he is not wanted, as in default of bishops vicar-capitulars administer the dioceses. . . . Within three days after receiving this letter secure a simple consent to confirm bishops-elect of all sees except Rome, or else leave Savona. . . . If the Pope cannot make a distinction simple enough to be grasped by the merest seminarist, why does he not voluntarily resign, and leave the Papal Chair to a man of less feeble mind and higher principles, who may repair at last the misfortunes he has caused in Germany and all other countries of Christendom?"[1]

[1] *Lettre à MM. les Députés, dictée par sa Majesté l'Empereur à M. Bigot de Préameneu,* 9 février 1812. *Not* inserted in Napoleon's Correspondence.

The deputation had already left Savona, and M. de Chabrol undertook the task of communicating this insulting document to Pius VII. The Holy Father showed deep emotion at the suggestion that he should resign. His gaoler noted it.

"I saw," he says, "that he (the Pope) was quite disheartened, and so agitated that his hand shook a good deal. . . . He was very much moved, but I do not think that he was shaken."[1] It was not enough to wound the Pope's deepest feelings. Orders were given that his books and writing materials were to be taken away, and that since nothing had been gained from their use, his former state of destitution was to be once more imposed. The days at Savona ended, as they had begun, in sorrow and privation. A few months later, Napoleon, alleging the presence at Savona of English cruisers, who meant to convey the Pope either to Sicily or to Spain, sent orders that Pius VII. should be removed to Fontainebleau. The English cruisers were a pretext for covering a political reason.[2] Napoleon wished to have the Pope at hand when he returned from the Russian campaign, which was to be, as he supposed, his crowning glory. Pius VII. should contemplate his triumph, and grant him everything. The Holy Father's journey, which would take him nearly right through France, was placed under the management of Prince Borghese, who had to provide two carriages for the Pope and his suite.

[1] *Lettre de M. de Chabrol à M. Bigot,* 19 février 1812.
[2] *L'Église Romaine et le Premier Empire,* t. v. p. 153.

Porta was considered indispensable, and was to travel with the Pope. The travellers were to use the greatest possible speed, and to stop only once, at the Mont Cenis. They were to avoid large towns by daylight, and at all costs the Pope's incognito was to be preserved. The imperial summons reached the Episcopal Palace at Savona on the 9th of June 1812, and found the Holy Father taking his siesta. MM. Chabrol and La Gorse immediately roused him, telling him that in a few hours he would have to start for France. Pius VII. showed no surprise; and when the Emperor's officers pointed out the inconvenience of travelling in the Papal dress, he submitted to have the embroidered cross taken off his white shoes, and the shoes smeared with ink. Quietly and patiently he put them on again, still damp from the operation.[1] The gold pectoral cross was also removed. He wore the hat of an ordinary priest, and a grey overcoat of his own. In this strange accoutrement for a Sovereign Pontiff, and still accompanied by his two gaolers, he was obliged to walk through Savona to reach the carriage which awaited him beyond its walls. For a week after the Pope had left the palace, no change was made in its internal arrangements. The Pope's dinner was regularly served at the usual hours, and the candles were lighted for his Mass. M. de Chabrol endeavoured to keep up the popular delusion by

[1] *Rilazione della traslazione di Pio VII. nel Castello di Fontainebleau.* MS. at British Museum, No. 8, 390: quoted by M. d'Haussonville.

continuing to visit the Papal apartments in his official costume.[1] For a few days the Holy Father's journey progressed favourably, but just before reaching the Mont Cenis, he fell dangerously ill. He was subject to an infirmity which rapid travelling seriously aggravated. This time his suffering was fearful, and evidently dangerous. He seemed to reach the Monastery of the Mont Cenis only to die, and the monks might well have thought that they were to have the privilege of solacing his last hours. General la Gorse's embarrassment was extreme, between the Pope's serious condition and the peremptory orders he received to proceed at all costs. In breathless haste he sent for a surgeon, who was summoned to use his healing art without an instant's delay.

"You are going to see a sick man whose sufferings you must alleviate at any price," were La Gorse's words. "You will certainly know him, but if you publish the fact of his presence here, it is as much as your liberty, perhaps your life, is worth."[2]

The surgeon managed to give the Holy Father some ease, and by the help of a couch in the carriage, he was able to proceed on his journey. Sometimes, out of compassion for his suffering state, La Gorse consented to a few hours' repose at postal relays. When at length, on June the 19th, 1812, Pius VII. reached Fontainebleau, he was worn out

[1] *Rilazione della traslazione di Pio VII. nel Castello di Fontainebleau.* MS. at British Muesum, No. 8, 390: quoted by M. d'Haussonville.

[2] *Lettre du Docteur Claraz.*

with fatigue and pain. He found closed gates, and a *concierge* wholly unprepared for his arrival. The worthy man was more humane than the sovereign whose orders he dared not disregard. Until further instructions, he offered the Holy Father a small house he owned near the palace. The Sovereign Pontiff was thankful to find rest, and spent his first night at Fontainebleau in the humble cottage. Three weeks of pain and illness followed. Napoleon, who feared no army stretched in battle array, was jealous of the Pope's prestige; therefore he chose to risk the Holy Father's life by a rapid and dangerous journey, and then to keep the Apostolic Wanderer waiting at the imperial door. The reception was typical of what followed. Napoleon's ministers and agents hastened to the palace, M. Bigot de Préameneu first of the number. The Holy Father was too ill to see them, but they were anxious to show him that they had no part in the treatment inflicted upon him. If Prince Borghese and La Gorse had brought the Pope to death's door it was no business of theirs. What concerned them personally was the same fervour and zeal in Napoleon's service which characterised Prince Borghese and La Gorse. The journey episode effected no radical alteration of conduct.

A new phase in the chequered life of Pius VII. opened at Fontainebleau. It was a trial of ease and magnificence, of deep heart-loneliness in the midst of a worldly crowd. The Holy Father occupied the same rooms, furnished now with great magnificence, as at the time of the Coronation. Mgr. Bertazzoli, Dr. Porta, and his household were lodged close by, and other apartments belonging to the same wing were destined for Church dignitaries who should come to visit the Sovereign Pontiff. Visitors who could act as tempters, and offer the Pope bad advice, were encouraged. Cardinal Maury had orders to prepare his episcopal palace in Paris for the Papal residence, and alterations were being organised on a large scale. A little book, the "Guide of Travellers in Paris," was published about this time, less probably to direct wanderers in the great city than to apprize Parisians that they possessed a "Papal Palace," instead of, as formerly, an archiepiscopal residence.[1] The Holy Father baffled all these grandiloquous designs. Fontainebleau was no less a prison than Savona had been, and he never forgot the fact. In the midst of a luxurious opulence, he chose to practise poverty, as a kind of protest against becoming the Emperor's vassal. Carriages and horses were vainly put at his disposal. He declared that he would never use them, nor did he even consent to walk in the gardens of the palace. He said Mass in a room close to his bedroom, instead of using the chapel of the château, into which the element of ceremony must have entered. He refused no visit, hearing and seeing patiently all who came to Fontainebleau, with the exception of Cardinal Maury. Even for Pius VII.

---

[1] *L'Église Romaine et le Premier Empire*, t. v. p. 171.

he was an ungrateful deserter. The Holy Father's demeanour was most significant and full of dignity. The bishops of the deputation were received with perfect courtesy indeed, but a marked reserve, and they found that they could make no further impression on the Pope's mind. He invariably asked for liberty and counsel, thus indirectly telling them what he thought about themselves. Some people spoke contemptuously of the Holy Father, because he was seen to mend his clothes, and never "to open a book."[1] The memories of Diane de Poitiers and Gabrielle d'Estrées hung over the library at Fontainebleau, prohibiting its shelves to a Sovereign Pontiff. From St. Sulpice Pius VII. obtained the works of St. Cyprian, a course of Canon Law, and other volumes.[2]

The September Brief had been kept secret from the French bishops, and from Cardinal Fesch himself. None knew how to practise concealment and repression better than Napoleon. The Russian campaign gave special prominence to the Conscription, and he now used it as an expedient for punishing bishops and faithful who were even suspected of sympathising with the Holy Father. Uncompliant pastors might be brought to reason by losing their young seminarists, who should be torn from their quiet seminaries and marched to useless battle-fields,

---

[1] *Mémoires du Duc de Rovigo*, vi. p. 73.
[2] *L'Église Romaine et le Premier Empire*, t. v. p. 175.

" In your last memorandum," he wrote to M. Bigot, on October 22nd, 1811, "I found requests for exemption from the military service for two hundred and thirty-nine students destined for ecclesiastical orders, and for the nomination of one hundred and forty-nine bourses in the seminaries. I have struck off from the list all demands relating to the bishoprics of Saint-Brieuc, Bordeaux, Gand, Tournai, Troyes, and the Alpes-Maritimes, because I am not satisfied with the principles manifested by the bishops of these dioceses. It is my will that you do *not* propose for these dioceses any exemption from service for the conscripts, nor any nomination for bourses, *curés*, or canons. Draw up a memorandum of the dioceses which ought to fall under this interdict. This mode of proceeding must be followed with the greatest secrecy. When bishops insist upon their nominations, tell them that I have refused my consent. Henceforth you will be responsible if you ask either for a bourse, or for exemption for a conscript, in a seminary where the principles of the Gallican Church are not carefully taught. Mind that you get at the truth, and begin by finding out what passes at your door in the diocese of Paris."[1]

In March 1812, the Sisters of Charity fell under the ban of Napoleon's displeasure, or rather the

[1] *Lettre de l'Empereur au Cte. Bigot de Préameneu*, 22 octobre 1811.

clouds, which had been long gathering, burst into a storm. M. Hanon, General of the Lazarists, refused to accept as Superioress for his spiritual daughters Napoleon's nominee. He was sent to Fenestrello for his pains, and the Sisters of Charity, who would have preferred suppression to state servility, were severely persecuted for M. Hanon's independent action. Again, Napoleon wrote to the Minister of Worship, " We must put an end to this scandal—Sisters of Charity in rebellion against their superiors. I wish to suppress all their houses which, twenty-four hours after your warning, show symptoms of unruliness. You must fill the suppressed houses not with Sisters of Charity, but with another active order." [1]

The Church in France reflected the imprisonment of the Sovereign Pontiff, and every day that passed increased the gravity of the situation. The Emperor persisted in refusing the Brief of September, and the expedient of vicar-capitulars was proved to be a mere expedient. It could not meet the most elementary spiritual requirements. In some dioceses the Chapters were divided, and the canons refused to admit the jurisdiction of the administrator so nominated. Strife, division, and famine were the necessary consequences to the Body of the Head's affliction. The dioceses of Tournai, Ghent, and Troyes were in the most singular position of all. The imprisonment of their respective bishops at Vincennes had at first been of the strictest

---

[1] *Lettre de l'Empereur au Cte. Bigot de Préameneu,* 3 mars 1812.

kind. They were in solitary confinement, and for a long time knew nothing of Cardinals di Pietro and Gabrielli, who were detained in close vicinity to themselves. At length, imperial favour allowed them to meet other human beings, and to take exercise in a sort of public corridor. A resignation, which they had not the option of refusing, was drawn from them by the Minister of Worship, and M. Bigot lost no time in writing to their respective chapters that the "episcopal see being now vacant, they must proceed to nominate a vicar-capitular and vicar-generals." The Bishops of Tournai and Troyes had provided for the emergency, but the Chapter of Ghent answered the Minister of Worship by a true and canonical statement of facts. "It was not the resignation of a bishop which made his see vacant," ran the answer, "but the acceptance of his resignation by the Sovereign Pontiff. If the canons took unlawful faculties upon themselves, the faithful would be greatly disquieted. The clergy of the country, attached, as they were, to the principles and customs of the Church, would not submit to measures taken by vicar-generals thus nominated. Disobedience would undermine the new administrator's authority, and division between pastor and flock would infallibly follow."[1]

The chapter raised a difficulty which could be solved only by Mgr. de Broglie himself. The three

---

[1] *Lettre de MM. les Membres du Chapitre de Gand à Monsieur le Cte. Bigot*, 27 octobre 1811.

Bishops were no longer at Vincennes, but imprisoned in different towns at forty leagues from Paris. Beaune was assigned to the Bishop of Ghent. Before leaving Vincennes, the prisoners were told that they must sign a written promise not to hold any correspondence whatever with their diocesans, and they were obliged to consent. Napoleon hoped by this measure to silence the Chapter of Ghent. He only succeeded in making Mgr. de Broglie more prominent than he already was as the leader, in popular opinion, of opposition in the Council. The Minister of Police discovered at Beaune a merchant sent by the Chapter of Ghent to see Mgr. de Broglie. It served as a pretext for banishing the bishop outside the pale of human life to the lonely Isles of St. Margaret, where the mysterious state prisoner, the Man with the Iron Mask, had smouldered away his existence. With an ardent and highly strung nervous temperament, Mgr. de Broglie was thus condemned, at forty-five, to eat out his heart in absolute solitude in the terrible dungeon which had hidden a great and fearful state secret. A rocky, inaccessible fortress cut him off from human life and all that it holds dear, enriching him, however, with one of the divine secrets, forgiveness of Napoleon, his enemy.[1]

A magic sword and brilliant success will sometimes make the world temporarily forget the interests of

---

[1] *Lettre de Maurice de Broglie, ancien Évêque de Gand, à M. Bigot,* 11 décembre 1811.

truth and justice. But Napoleon's glory had reached its culminating point, and its waning awoke slumbering memories. On the 18th of December 1812, he returned a fugitive to his capital. Fire and ice were doing their work amongst his soldiers in Russia and Poland, and he himself came back alone. It was the beginning of the end.

CHAPTER XIV

THE CONCORDAT OF FONTAINEBLEAU

1813

THE hour-glass of Napoleon's glory was fast running down. The result of the Russian campaign produced both terror and relief. Those who had fancied Napoleon invincible awakened to the fact that their hero did not possess the magic sword Excalibur after all. The annexed provinces breathed a sigh of relief. Their different nationalities had been suddenly swallowed up, and they were added as French subjects to a new and huge empire in which they were simply units. A dark and heavy pall stretched from Fontainebleau over every member of the Catholic Church. Thirteen cardinals exiled to various provincial towns, under the supervision of the police, expiated their fidelity to Pius VII. Three bishops, who had been fathers of the Gallican Council, shared the same fate. A number of priests were detained in Fenestrello and other State prisons on similar pretences; and a great many dioceses languished for want of pastors, because Napoleon willed the evil and would not will the remedy. In Italy things looked even worse. Rome, the centre of the Catholic world, was reduced to the

rank of second city in the French Empire; the convents and monasteries were despoiled; a large proportion of bishops and ecclesiastics had been carried
off by violence to France, because they obeyed God
rather than man. Some of the number were silenced
by Fenestrello; others—and perhaps it was the majority—had been banished to Corsica.

Worldly prudence and interested motives of policy
had hitherto directed Napoleon's dealings with the
Church, and it was so to the end. He was not an
unbeliever in theory, but he was far from a Christian
in practice. The words *Providence, God*, did not
come to him naturally, because the thought of them
was absent.[1] The first touches of adversity showed
him the real worth of the men who surrounded him.
To be feared and to be obeyed he needed prosperity,
for his government was a despotism which required
success. Losses of men and disagreement between
generals and soldiers, which had followed upon
Napoleon's return to Paris, made him anxious to
secure at any price the almost indispensable mediation of Austria. At Dresden he had scouted the
feeble remonstrances of the Austrian Emperor as to
his unseemly proceedings against the Head of the
Church. The crisis, however, was too grave to be
disregarded. In order, therefore, to maintain the
alliance of the Emperor Francis, he judged it now
politically necessary to reopen negotiations himself
with the Holy Father. The year before, he had

---

[1] *Madame de Rémusat, Mémoires,* iii. p. 164.

fancied it even beneath his dignity to answer one of
Pius VIL's most paternal letters.

New Year's Day 1813 served as an excuse to
Napoleon for the renewal of intercourse with Pius
VII.   In the letter which he wrote on this occasion,
he begged the Pope to believe that his feelings of
respect and veneration were independent of any outward event or circumstance.   Mgr. Duvoisin was
charged to treat with Pius VIL The Concordat of
Fontainebleau in its original scheme was perhaps the
most audacious bit of diplomacy ever submitted to a
Sovereign Pontiff.   It is just what might have been
expected had Napoleon conquered Alexander, but his
glory was now on the decline: success was gradually,
yet perceptibly, deserting his banner.   The principal
features of the projected treaty presented by the
Bishop of Nantes were these: Before their coronation the Popes would be required to swear that
they would neither do nor command anything contrary to the Four Propositions of the Gallican Church.
They would nominate only one-third of the Sacred
College.   The nomination to the remaining two-
thirds would be the right and the privilege of
Catholic sovereigns.   Pius VIL was to condemn
solemnly by Brief the conduct of the cardinals who
had refused to assist at the Emperor's marriage with
Marie Louise; but by themselves signing the said
Brief, they might hope to be taken back into imperial
favour.   Cardinals di Pietro and Pacca, the author
and promoter of the Bull *Quum Memoranda*, were

alone to be excluded from the treaty, and as councillors to be banished for ever from the Holy Father's
side. The Papal residence was to be fixed in Paris,
with a revenue of two million francs raised on his
former territory. The Emperor reserved to himself
the exclusive nomination to bishoprics in the Roman
States, and in every case he stipulated that Papal
confirmation should be conferred within six months.
This period having expired, the Metropolitan would
have full right to confer it.[1]

The men who surrounded the Holy Father took
into account his weak state of body and agitated
mind only as far as they might further the Emperor's
pleasure. There was not one true councillor amongst
the five cardinals, the Archbishop of Tours, the
Bishops of Trèves and Evreux, and Mgr. Bertazzoli,
whilst all along Dr. Porta was continuing his paid
services. Probably they all shared Mgr. Duvoisin's
conviction that Pius VII. was physically unfit to
sustain much anxiety of mind, and yet that very
weakness constituted their best hope. They looked
anxiously for the moment when they might press
their sovereign's unlawful demands on the over-
strained Sovereign Pontiff. On January 13th, 1813,
the Bishop of Nantes wrote to M. Bigot: "The
Pope is in a very agitated state. He does not sleep.
His health is very much shaken. At present I
consider that he is not in a state to bear a discussion. He has very small confidence in those who

---

[1] *L'Église Romaine et le Premier Empire*, t. v. p. 216.

surround him. He persists in saying that he wishes
particularly to give satisfaction to the Emperor, but
that he cannot in conscience come to a decision alone
without counsel. However, I must have an answer.
I am watching for the moment when I can ask him
for it without affecting him too deeply." [1]

Mgr. Duvoisin hesitated to press for a reply, out
of a little remaining feeling of delicacy and consideration for the Holy Father's health. Napoleon did not
share his scruples. Instead of compassionating the
weakness he himself had produced, he laid hold of it,
and made it serve his own purposes. Pius VII.
afterwards admitted that if he had listened faithfully to the voice of his conscience, he would have
remained inflexible. The precise point of the question lies in the extent of the physical weakness
which, according to M. Duvoisin himself, incapacitated
the Pope for business.

A day or two after the reception of Mgr. Duvoisin's
letter, on January 18th, Napoleon was hunting in the
woods of Melun. Suddenly, in the middle of the day,
he announced his intention of visiting the Pope at
Fontainebleau, and ordered a post-chaise to be brought
for the purpose. He was aware of the charm that he
could exercise over Pius VII., and thought to surprise
him by another of those preconcerted scenes which
was to present the charm of spontaneity. He had
reflected sufficiently on the scheme to invite the Empress Marie Louise to go with him to Fontainebleau.

[1] *Lettre de l'Évêque de Nantes au Ministre des Cultes*, 13 janvier 1813.

R

Eight years before Napoleon had planned to encounter the Holy Father accidentally, as a huntsman, so now he carefully arranged all the details of a meeting which had the appearance of a resolution taken on the spur of the moment. When the Emperor, booted and spurred, entered the Papal apartment, night had overtaken the wintry day, and the Holy Father was talking, after his evening repast, with the cardinals and bishops who lodged in the palace. He was pleased to see Napoleon, who embraced him with every mark of affection. All serious discussion was postponed till the next day. The Holy Father made the most of the Emperor's outward demonstrations. He quite honestly imagined that the ill-treatment which had been inflicted upon him was in part the work of unprincipled subordinates. This accounts for the pleasure with which he spoke of Napoleon's greeting and embrace. He suspected no guile, and did not understand what the visit could mean.[1]

Serious business began the next day with the harassing private conferences to which Napoleon subjected him. During these interviews the original draft of the Concordat was considerably modified, in spite of the Emperor's want of courtesy. His tone was haughty and disdainful, and he was constantly reproaching the Sovereign Pontiff with his great ignorance on religious matters. Though little of what really passed during these five days of incessant private conference is known, the result has transpired,

[1] Artaud: *Histoire de Pie VII.*, ii. p. 320.

and it is called the fatal Concordat of Fontainebleau. The time that was not occupied by Napoleon's visits was employed by Cardinals Ruffo, Joseph Doria, Spina, Dugnami, de Bayane, as well as by Mgr. Bertazzoli, in urging Pius VII. to consent to the Emperor's demands. " If they were in his place," they were constantly remarking, " they would not hesitate for a moment to sign the document, and thus put an end to the troubles of the Church." No doubt this language produced an impression. The Pope's health was deplorable, and his very physical weakness served the designs of his enemies. Conscious of his weakness and prostration, he had repeatedly asked for disinterested counsel, and for the support of a true friend to stay him in his hour of need. He foresaw, perhaps, how Napoleon's persecution was to culminate, and the long chain of sufferings which would end by his fall. When his vital power had been weakened by long imprisonment and all that it entailed, his signature to the Concordat of Fontainebleau would be wrested from him in an hour of indecision. Did the Holy Father anticipate all this when he prayed that he might not be left alone in the fight ? His yearning to see his exiled friends once more, the modifications which Napoleon consented to make in the original treaty proposed by Mgr. Duvoisin, together with the understanding that the articles were the basis of a final settlement rather than that final settlement itself, and the entreaties of the Cardinals—all these things worked upon the sensibility of the Sovereign

Pontiff. After the event, Napoleon proved that, whatever he had previously proclaimed as his intentions, his sole aim in the matter was to secure the Papal signature. He consented, however, to repeal the stipulation concerning Gallican liberties, the intervention of Catholic sovereigns in the nomination of cardinals, and the censorious language used against Pacca and di Pietro. He left, too, the nomination to the six suburbicarian bishoprics in the Pope's hands. Thus modified, the text of the Concordat was as follows:—

"His Majesty the Emperor and King and his Holiness, wishing to put an end to the misunderstandings which have arisen between them, and to provide against various difficulties of ecclesiastical discipline, have agreed to the following articles as a basis of a final arrangement:—

"I. His Holiness will exercise the Pontificate in France and in the kingdom of Italy in the same way and external form as his predecessors.

"II. The ambassadors, ministers, and *chargés d'affaires* of different Powers at the Papal Court, and the ambassadors, ministers, and *chargés d'affaires* that the Pope may have with foreign Powers, shall enjoy the same immunities and privileges as the Diplomatic Body.

"III. The domains which the Holy Father possessed, and which are not alienated, shall be exempt from all taxes. Agents or *chargés d'affaires* shall administer them. Those which are alienated shall be made good by a revenue to the amount of two million francs.

"IV. Within the six months following upon the customary notification on the nomination of a bishop by the Emperor to the archbishoprics and bishoprics of the Empire and of the kingdom of Italy, the Pope shall confer canonical confirmation, according to the Concordats, and in virtue of these presents. The metropolitan shall proceed to the preliminary information. The six months having expired before the Pope confers confirmation, the metropolitan, or in his default, or in the case of the metropolitan himself, the bishop of the most ancient see in the province, shall proceed to confer confirmation on the bishop-elect, so that no see need remain vacant more than a year.

"V. Whether in France or in the kingdom of Italy, the Pope shall nominate to such sees as shall be subsequently established by mutual consent.

"VI. The six suburbicarian bishoprics shall be re-established. The Pope shall nominate to them. Possessions not alienated shall be restored, and measures shall be taken with regard to those that have been sold. On the death of the Bishops of Anagni and Rieti, their dioceses shall be united to the above sees, conformably to the agreement which shall take place to that effect between his Majesty and the Holy Father.

"VII. With regard to bishops of the Roman States who are absent *through circumstances from their dioceses*, the Holy Father shall be free to exercise in their favour his right of giving bishoprics *in partibus*.   A pension, equal to the revenues which they possessed, shall be given to them, and they may be nominated to vacant sees either of the Empire or of the kingdom of Italy.

"VIII. His Majesty and his Holiness shall opportunely concert together the reduction to be made, if necessary, in the bishoprics of Tuscany and the district of Genoa, as well as those that may have to be created in Holland and in the Hanseatic Departments.

"IX. The Tribunals of the Propaganda, the Penitentiary, and the Records shall be established wherever the Pope resides.

"X. His Majesty restores his favour to the cardinals, bishops, priests, and laymen who have incurred his displeasure in consequence of existing circumstances.

"XI. The Holy Father agrees to the above-stated articles out of consideration for the present state of the Church.   Moreover, he feels confident that his Majesty will grant his imperial protection to the numerous needs of religion in these our times."[1]

Napoleon here measured himself with the Church as if his dynasty had taken root after the fashion of those ancient oaks which flourish through centuries. "Only oaks and monks are eternal."[2]

[1] *Histoire de Pie VII.*, ii. p. 323.
[2] Lacordaire : *Conférences de Notre Dame.*

On the 25th of January 1813, the formality of
signing the Concordat took place in the presence of
the Cardinals. Their conscience and their honour
should have held them aloof from complicity with
the Emperor's designs. They, on the contrary, had
adopted Napoleon's views with an intensity of zeal
which could leave him nothing to desire, and they
did not scruple to overbear the Sovereign Pontiff's
manifest hesitation by assuring him that the treaty
was a mere preliminary, and that it would be kept
quite secret till the dispersed Cardinals could meet
and discuss the whole matter. They emulated the
sovereign under whose banner they had passed; after
deserting the cause of truth and justice, they cared
little what arguments they used, provided they reached
the end in view.

Before putting his signature to the document, Pius
VII. raised eyes full of yearning and entreaty towards
these wretched councillors. He looked for some one
to support and strengthen him, and found no one.
Napoleon had made these princes of the Church de-
serters to the kingdom of the world. The Cardinal
who stood nearest to the Holy Father, silently bent
his head; Pius VII. saw that his mute language had
been understood, and he, as silently, took the pen
from Cardinal Joseph Doria, and signed the Concordat
of Fontainebleau. Napoleon kept his eye fixed on the
Pope, as if he feared to let his prey out of his sight,
and Marie Louise also was present at the ceremony.
It was quite contrary to custom and etiquette that

the two negotiating sovereigns should sign the same
document. The possibility of the Pope's retractation
was even then in the Emperor's mind, and he did
what he could to forestall it by signing the Concordat
immediately after the Pope, and then publishing it,
almost before it was dry, as an important agreement
which had been effected between himself and the
Sovereign Pontiff. So much for its being only a
preliminary. The Austrian Emperor was apprised of
the fact in breathless haste, and the bishops received
orders from M. Bigot to have the *Te Deum* sung
solemnly in thanksgiving for the event.[1]

On the following day, Napoleon conferred upon
Cardinals Ruffo and Doria, as a public recognition
of their services, the decoration of the Legion of
Honour, and presented the other members of the
Sacred College, and Mgr. Bertazzoli, who had proved
useful, with a handsome snuff-box, ornamented with
his own portrait, and set in large brilliants. He thus
proclaimed officially the great importance he attached
to the Pope's signature.

Napoleon stayed on at Fontainebleau for three days
after January 25th, during which time the Holy
Father bore up against his emotion. But when other
engrossing affairs called the Emperor away, a deep
and settled melancholy took possession of Pius VII.
It was a return to the appalling sadness which M. de
Chabrol had noted at Savona. The imperially ordered

---

[1] *Instructions dictées au Ministre des Cultes*, 24 janvier 1813. *Not*
inserted in Napoleon's Correspondence.

Te Deum may have deceived some: the *Miserere* best expressed the Holy Father's attitude in its excessive anguish. The consequences of his act were constantly before him; but the new Concordat opened the gates of Fenestrello and Vincennes for the faithful cardinals, who hastened to the Sovereign Pontiff. After the burden of the day and of the heat he had sunk exhausted at the eleventh hour. Cardinals Gabrielli, di Pietro, and Litta were the first to arrive at Fontainebleau. Their confessorship lent strength to their remonstrances, and the reproaches which they ventured to address to the Pope fell as the voice of God on the expectant ear of Pius VII. What they said was an echo of his own conscience during the sleepless nights and anxious days he had passed since the 25th of January. He had lost in one moment the labours, the struggle, and the suffering of years. In his remorse the Pope judged himself unworthy to celebrate the Holy Sacrifice.

It is probable that the *Te Deum* expressed Napoleon's feelings, and Napoleon's alone. On his journey from Fenestrello to Fontainebleau Cardinal Pacca met with many tokens of sympathy and the public opinion of Catholics. Popular instinct suspected the truth; the Holy Father's hand had been forced to undue concession. Although the Cardinal was a State criminal, barely escaped from prison, to use his own words, he met with great enthusiasm. At Lyons the inhabitants would have wished to keep him longer in their midst, if it had not been for the Holy Father.

They urged him not to delay going to the Pope, who
was in a dangerous position, from which the Cardinal
might rescue him.   In a crowded church, a most
eloquent sermon was preached, in which Pacca was
addressed in these words: "We kiss your chains.
We look upon you as a confessor of the Faith, who
have suffered for the cause of Jesus Christ.   Let the
Head of the Church be told of our wish to be united
and obedient to him."   This, then, was the result of
Napoleon's efforts, *We kiss your chains*: the imperial
Te Deum with its fallacious cry of victory had deceived
only those who wished to be deceived.[1]

As Pacca approached Fontainebleau he was struck
by the silence and solitude of the place, which
seemed suggestive of another State prison.   In point
of fact it was nothing more.   Meeting nobody on the
way, he sent his servant on before him to try if any
information was to be drawn from this deserted
residence.   Pacca was invited to go in his travelling
dress to the Papal audience, and when at last he
reached the Pope's apartment, he was shocked to
find the change which had come over Pius VII.
Sorrow, rather than age, had broken him down:
energy and hope had departed from the sunken eyes.
Pacca received a formal embrace, accompanied by
the observation that he had not been expected so
soon.   The Cardinal replied that he had longed to
express his admiration for the Pope's heroic fortitude
under a long and severe imprisonment.

[1] *Memorie*, t. ii. pp. 185, 186.

"But at last we have sinned against our conscience," was the Holy Father's cry of grief. "Those Cardinals dragged me to the table, and forced me to sign the document."[1]

The audience ended by a cold intimation to Pacca that the French bishops were coming, and that he had better retire. He was taken to his room, and there his sorrowful thoughts nearly overpowered him. The silence of the place, the sad faces he had noticed, and the melancholy welcome he had received from Pius VII., all conspired to fill him with grief.[2] The long-desired concession had fallen as a heavy pall upon Catholic hearts. Outwardly things had assumed a more cheerful aspect. The Black Cardinals could now venture to visit the Holy Father. The palace was thronged with bishops of the courtier stamp. A certain pomp of ceremonial was visible in the household arrangements which bespoke a reigning prince as to magnificence. The want of independence was suggestive of no kingdom, and this was precisely the combination which suited Napoleon. Spies filled the splendid palace : its walls had eyes and ears. Before going to his second audience, Pacca was warned to be guarded in what he said. La Gorse, the under-gaoler at Savona, had followed the Holy Father to Fontainebleau, and could now do the honours of the imperial residence as governor

---

[1] "Ma ci siamo in fine sporcificati. Quei Cardinali . . . mi strascinarono al tavolino e mi fecero sottoscrivere."

[2] *Memorie*, ii. pp. 190, 196.

and chamberlain in one. Deeply as he felt the coldness of his greeting, Pacca's great anxiety was the Holy Father's state. The Cardinal feared for his life, and, still worse, for his reason. The conviction that he "would die mad, as Clement XIV. had died," took possession of Pius VII.

Sleepless nights and little or no food strengthened it. Continually as he was talking, the rigid look of fixity came into his face, and he would burst out into expressions of intense grief at the concessions wrung from his conscience as Sovereign Pontiff. At his second audience, Pacca found a little consolation for the Pope's troubled heart. In a few days all the Cardinals would gather together once more around him, and their disinterested counsels would see a way of escape from present evils. The mere thought seemed to give the Holy Father new life.

"Do you think a remedy is still in our power?" he asked.

"Most assuredly it is, Holy Father," answered Pacca. "Nearly everything can be put right with a good will"

On the evening of the same day Consalvi arrived at Fontainebleau. Once more the Sacred College was in its proper place, and the Holy Father could appeal to his natural councillors. Each Cardinal was required to give in writing his opinion of the Concordat, and under the special circumstances he had to be chiefly guided by his individual judgment. Theological books did not figure on the library shelves, neither could the Cardinals meet freely without falling under the suspicion of "intriguing." Consalvi and Pacca were the natural leaders of the Black Cardinals, but opinions were divided even in the faithful camp. Instead of pronouncing at once in favour of a retractation, some proposed that the treaty should be maintained, with the insertion of certain clauses more favourable to the Holy See and to the Pope. Whilst the Cardinals were discussing the question, Pius VII. practically took the matter into his own hands. He refused to touch the first payment of the imperial allowance, and to grant the Bulls of Confirmation. Napoleon's suspicions were aroused, and he resolved to publish the Concordat to the Senate, thus disregarding his promise of secrecy. Consalvi was quick to see the advantage which might be drawn from the Emperor's mistake. An entire retractation, he pointed out, was the only course open to the Holy Father; and he brought the thirteen to unanimity. The decision could only be executed by great ingenuity, as all proceedings of Pope and Cardinals were closely watched and supervised by the Minister of Police. It happened that Cardinal Pignatelli, who was old and infirm, was lodging in the town of Fontainebleau. His state made it difficult for him to leave his room, and partly on this account, partly to evade the police emissaries and spies, the Cardinals who were most interested in the retractation formed a habit of meeting at Pignatelli's lodgings. They agreed that the Pope should frankly disavow the Concordat, and immediately write his decision to the Emperor. To prevent his letter from being quietly ignored, the Pope was to present each cardinal with a copy of it, enjoining him to publish the retractation to the best of his power. It was necessary that Pius VII. should write the letter with his own hand, and here the Cardinals were met by a twofold difficulty. The Holy Father was almost too weak to hold a pen, and his writing-desk was no safe receptacle for a private document. Day after day during the Pope's Mass every bedroom was subjected to a thorough search. His desk and drawers were opened with false keys, and all his papers examined. Bodily infirmity and the Minister of Police had to be met and defied. Consalvi, Pacca, and di Pietro proved equal to the task. Immediately after Mass every morning Consalvi and di Pietro brought the Holy Father the letter already begun, to which he added a few lines. In the afternoon, about four o'clock, the same operation was repeated under the superintendence of Pacca, who folded away the Papal letter in his dress, and deposited it at Cardinal Pignatelli's lodgings. More than once Pius VII. was obliged to begin his letter afresh; and Pacca, in carrying it off, suffered a fever of anxiety, in spite of the bitter weather, lest he might be searched on the road.[1]

Whilst the Cardinals were thus negotiating with the utmost discretion and devotedness, the courtier bishops, who had participated, at Napoleon's bidding,

[1] *L'Église Romaine et le Premier Empire*, t. v. p. 252.

in the Concordat of Fontainebleau, had leisure for reflection. Mgr. Duvoisin, in particular, felt instinctively that something was taking place, and that he was excluded from the confidence of the Cardinals. No man can serve two masters: he had chosen correspondence with M. Bigot. On the 14th of March 1813, the Minister of Worship wrote to the Emperor that " all was as quiet as possible ; that there seemed to be no intention of interfering with the existing state of things by *any correspondence* ; that the Cardinals were divided amongst themselves, and those who lodged out of the palace showed no eagerness to pay their respects to the Pope." [1] So spoke and so thought M. Bigot. A few days later, Pius VII. asked for the chamberlain, la Gorse, and gave him the letter of retractation finally completed by prolonged courage and devotedness. It was the 24th of March 1813. The retractation was absolute, and ran thus :—

" SIRE,—However painful to us the avowal we are about to make to your Majesty, however painful to you, fear of God's judgments—our age and declining health are bringing us daily nearer to Him—should induce us to triumph over human considerations and forget the anguish which oppresses us. We declare to your Majesty, as in duty bound, as our dignity and position dictate, that since the 25th of January, when we appended our signature to articles that were to serve as a basis to a final treaty, we have felt the greatest remorse and the deepest contrition. We

---

[1] *Le Ministre des Cultes à l'Empereur*, 14 mars 1813.

immediately recognised our error. The more we reflect, the more we are convinced that the concession into which we allowed ourself to be drawn was evil. The hope of thus ending the troubles of the Church and the desire to please your Majesty moved us. The matter had only one ray of comfort for us. We thought our act of concession might counterbalance the harm to the Church of our signature. To our grief and surprise, in spite of your Majesty's pledged word, we found those articles, which were supposed to be the basis of a future treaty, published under the title of Concordat. Writing directly to your Majesty seems to us the most respectful form of remonstrance. In the presence of God, Who will soon require from us an account of the power delegated to us as Vicar of Christ, for the government of the Church, we declare, in all Apostolical sincerity, that our conscience is absolutely opposed to the articles contained in the document of January 25th. . . . With respect to it and to our signature, we repeat to your Majesty the words used by our predecessor, Pascal II., in a Brief to Henry V., in whose favour he also made a concession which justly caused remorse to his conscience. With him we say to you: As our conscience condemns the document, so do we; and, with God's help, we desire that it may be entirely annulled, so that no pernicious results may ensue for the Church and no prejudice for our own soul." [1]

---

[1] *Lettre du Pape Pie VII. à l'Empereur Napoléon*, Fontainebleau, 24 mars 1813.

On the same day the Holy Father delivered an Allocution to the Cardinals, in which they were all told the exact state of the case. "Blessed be God," were the Sovereign Pontiff's humble words in closing his address, "blessed be God, Who has not withheld His mercy from us. It is He Who chastises and Who quickens. He has willed to humble us by a salutary confusion, and at the same time has sustained us by His almighty hand, giving us the necessary assistance for the accomplishment of our duty in this trying circumstance. As far as we are concerned, we cheerfully accept this humiliation for the good of our soul. To Him be now and for ever all honour and glory." [1]

But Pius VII. clearly foresaw the possible consequences of an action which put an end to Napoleon's cherished dream. The Emperor, it is true, could no longer afford to treat with contempt that which did not suit his pretensions. He could not with any political wisdom ignore the Pope's letter of March 24th as he had affected to ignore the Bull *Quum Memoranda.*. Napoleon, however, maintained his habits of despotism, whilst the despotism itself was shaken on its basis. He answered the Sovereign Pontiff by inviting M. Bigot to impose secrecy and dishonesty on those French bishops who would still consent to receive their orders from Cæsar.

"The Minister of Worship," he wrote, "is to keep

---

[1] *Histoire de Pie VII.*, ii. p. 346.

the Pope's letter of March 24th absolutely secret, as I wish to be able to say either that I have or have not received it, according to the turn which circumstances may take. He must write to the bishops that on account of Holy Week, and their diocesan duties, they had best return to their dioceses, except the Bishops of Nantes and Trèves, who, as Councillors of State, are called to Paris. The Archbishops and Bishops must not know anything about the Pope's protest. They must be kept in complete ignorance of it, but they should have orders to go to Fontainebleau the day following this announcement, as if of their own accord. After presenting their address to the Pope, likewise as if from themselves, they are to set off at once for their dioceses. . . . The address might be worded somewhat in this strain: The undersigned Archbishops and Bishops of the Empire and of the kingdom of Italy, having complied with the orders of his Majesty to congratulate your Holiness on a Concordat which is to re-establish peace in the Church, see with grief that your Holiness has not yet executed any article of the treaty, and that the consequences are troubled minds and many vacant sees. They flatter themselves that your Holiness will come to their relief. The Concordat of Fontainebleau was an inspiration of the Holy Spirit to the Head of the Church, as a way of ending her troubles. Hence they are pained to think that, since the event, scruples have been suggested to him on the subject. As bishops and theologians they entirely accept the Concordat, and entreat His Holiness to come to terms with the head of the State, so that canonical confirmation may be conferred, &c."[1]

This time Napoleon looked in vain for compliant bishops. They refused to plead with the Pope that he would maintain the Concordat. Cardinal Maury alone consented to go to Fontainebleau, as if of his own accord, and to give at Napoleon's dictation a lesson of theology to Pius VII. When the Holy Father spoke confidentially of the letter and Allocution he had addressed to the Sacred College, Maury feigned ignorance. The matter called for a day's reflection, he said, whereas he had set out with a ready-made answer. It was delivered the following day, with a due regard to his personal reputation for eloquence. He won only a defeat, and severe words from the mild Sovereign Pontiff.[2]

Napoleon's mode of proceeding against opposition was uniform. First of all he ignored it. Then, when it would no longer be ignored, he called in the Minister of Police, and struck at the ringleaders with summary measures. After the failure of Maury's visit, Napoleon sent orders to M. Bigot that Fontainebleau should once more put on its prison attire. Access to the Pope was forbidden, and the Cardinals were to do no more than pay him mere visits of ceremony. La Gorse ceased to be Chamberlain, and became again a

---

[1] *Lettre de l'Empereur à M. Bigot de Préameneu,* 25 mars 1813. *Not* inserted in his Correspondence.

[2] *L'Église Romaine et le Premier Empire,* t. v. p. 274.

gaoler.   Cardinal di Pietro, twice a delinquent, was
seized in his bed during the night of April 5th, 1813,
and ordered to proceed at once to Auxonne.   He had
contributed both to the Bull *Quum Memoranda*, and
to the Pope's letter of retractation.   He was therefore
honoured by Napoleon's special vengeance.   The
Emperor, then, went on to act as if the Concordat
of Fontainebleau still existed.   By imperial decree
he gave it force of law for the hierarchy, and M.
Bigot, at his request, drew up a list of vacant sees,
with the names of different candidates for nomination.
Napoleon immediately nominated to twelve bishoprics,
amongst which were Tournai, Ghent, and Troyes, and
held out a delusive hope of pardon to "certain individuals in the departments of Rome and Thrasimene,
who had incurred penalties for refusing oaths which
had been required of them."

Few ecclesiastics suffering imprisonment for conscience' sake seemed anxious to profit by the proffered
amnesty.   Either they felt that it was a mock
pardon, or that prison walls were as good as a
dubious liberty.   At Troyes the Chapter refused to
acknowledge Napoleon's nominee.   A simple *curé*
had gone to Fontainebleau, foiled the police agents,
and learnt from the Holy Father's own lips that
Mgr. de Boulogne, and he alone, was the rightful
pastor.   At Tournai, Belgian dislike of French dominion may have added intensity to the opposition.
Some members of the Chapter resigned rather than
accept a schismatic bishop.   The Superiors of the

Tournai Seminary dismissed all the students before the end of the term, in order that they might not be called upon to recognise an unlawful administrator of the diocese. These doings particularly incensed the Emperor, probably on account of the political feeling which was associated with religious enthusiasm. The ephemeral success of Lützen prompted him to bring the rebellious Belgians to reason in his most arbitrary manner. He simply threatened to suppress the diocese of Tournai. "If," he wrote to M. Bigot, "I have the least indications of further rebellion from them (the canons and principal priests of Tournai), I shall suppress the bishopric, and Tournai shall forfeit its bishop. I shall unite it to another diocese, or transfer the see to a town in the vicinity of Ancient France."[1]

Again, Pius VII. was consulted when Napoleon nominated to the diocese of Ghent. The Holy Father replied that Mgr. de Broglie was its rightful bishop, absent or present. The Emperor's nominee had great difficulty in rallying thirty priests to his schismatic crozier. The only course open to the seminarists of Ghent was to choose the Conscription. "It was better," they exclaimed, in the warmth of their Catholic feelings, " to be good soldiers than schismatical priests."[2] Some were incapacitated by bad or weak health from adopting a military career. They were

---

[1] *Lettre de l'Empereur à M. le Cte. Bigot de Préameneu*, 14 août 1813. *Not* inserted in his Correspondence.

[2] *L'Église Romaine et le Premier Empire*, t. v. p. 285.

conveyed to Paris by an escort of police, and imprisoned at Ste. Pélagie, whilst priests who had preached against compliance with the imperial demands were also sent to languish in French prisons. These disturbances were visited upon the three bishops, whose rights had been trampled upon, whilst they themselves had suffered a cruel imprisonment. Mgr. de Boulogne had refused to disapprove of his resisting Chapter, and was taken back to Vincennes. Its walls seemed to gain in thickness with Napoleon's years of reign. Mgr. Hirn had agreed to sign the formula, but he could not materially influence the decisions of his canons. The health of Mgr. de Broglie was ruined in his terrible prison of the lonely Iles. His keepers had been forced to take him back to Beaune for fear he should die obstinate.[1]

Three dioceses were suffering persecution, and many others a hopeless vacancy through Napoleon's obstinacy. His imperial decree, therefore, had not succeeded in giving force of law to a Concordat rejected by the Holy Father. Napoleon had disturbed the peace and prosperity of Flanders. Bands of ex-seminarists were abroad, going, perhaps, to death on the battlefield, because they might not recognise their lawful bishop. Many confessors in French prisons might have envied the youthful soldiers marching to death. For them death would

---

[1] *Relation Latine adressée au Saint Père*, par Mgr. de Broglie, Évêque de Gand.

not come. Their lot was the privation of all that makes life pleasant or even tolerable, until God should be pleased to open their prison door.

Peter's chains pressed heavily on Mgr. Duvoisin as he lay on his death-bed in the half light of eternity. In July 1813 he wrote to Napoleon for the last time: "I entreat you to restore the Holy Father to liberty. His captivity troubles my last hours. The return of His Holiness to Rome is, I believe, necessary for your happiness."[1] The conviction of the dying Bishop of Nantes was silently shared by the whole body of the clergy. They quietly fixed their hopes on the only event which could restore ecclesiastical matters to their normal state—the fall of the Empire. A moment of gloom and crisis was at hand, after all the flimsy splendour of useless conquests. If Napoleon did not radically alter his policy, events would alter it for him, and the finger of God would be palpable in his defeat. Cardinal Fesch had said it already. For some time past the Primate had been in a kind of exile at Lyons. He had brought it upon himself by his fearless predictions of misfortune to the Emperor. From his retreat he contemplated with anxiety and alarm the increasing temerity of his nephew. "The Emperor is ruining himself, he is ruining us all," he would say to Mme. Bonaparte. "I foresee the moment when he will be borne down and annihilated.

[1] *Mémoires Historiques sur les Affaires Ecclésiastiques de France,* t. ii. p. 527.

All who touch the Holy Ark experience the same fate. . . . My nephew is lost, but the Church is saved; for if the Emperor had returned in triumph from Moscow, who knows what he would have done?"[1] This time Cardinal Fesch was a true prophet.

[1] *Vie du Cardinal Fesch* (Lyonnet), t. ii. pp. 379, 455.

CHAPTER XV

FALL AND RESTORATION

1814

THE year 1813 witnessed the rapid decline of Napoleon's power, which was too gigantic to last.   A sixth
coalition of Europe, headed by Russia, rose up against
him with that unity of purpose which seldom aims
in vain.   Never had his military genius asserted itself
more powerfully than at the moment when he was
unconsciously bidding " a long farewell to all his greatness."   Germany, the former theatre of his conquests,
was now the scene of defeat and disaster.   Gradually
deserted by those whom merely selfish considerations
had drawn into his alliance, he found himself alone to
meet his overwhelming ruin.   Russia, Prussia, England,
and Sweden bore down in the European balance the
feeble assistance of Denmark.   Lützen, Bautzen, and
Würschen were a brilliant gleam of success.   From
Dresden the French army penetrated as far as Breslau,
and made Napoleon temporarily master of Lusatia.
At this critical moment the support of Austria might
have turned the scale in his favour, but about August
1813, the Emperor Francis declared himself against
the son-in-law whose throne he had once been so

eager for his daughter to share. This determination
increased Napoleon's enemies by three hundred thousand men. His star was paling so rapidly that the
country which proved faithful to him the longest had
already paid the penalty of its generosity. Denmark
had lost Norway. The position of the French in
Germany was almost untenable through Austria's
change of policy, when the crushing defeat of Leipsic
came in October. Eighty thousand perished in the
fight. The Napoleonic yoke in Germany was loosened.
Nations threw off their surreptitious Bonapartist sovereigns, and returned to their hereditary princes, as
soon as they had made sure that Napoleon's luck was
exhausted.

Whilst the year 1813 was drawing its sombre
shadow over Napoleon's glory, Pius VII. calmly
awaited events, possessing his soul in patience. On
the success of Lützen, the Empress Marie Louise
immediately despatched a page to Fontainebleau with
the news. She knew His Holiness's affection for the
Emperor, she said, and was sure the Pope would
rejoice at the intelligence.[1] Napoleon's success meant
continued imprisonment for the Pope, so there was
irony in bidding him rejoice. In his reply to the
Empress, he expressed courtesy towards her personally,
and protested strongly against the treatment inflicted
on himself, and the arrest of Cardinal di Pietro.[2] At
the same time the Holy Father composed a vigorous

---

[1] *L'Église Romaine et le Premier Empire*, t. v. p. 302.
[2] *Lettre de Sa Sainteté Pie VII. à l'Impératrice Marie Louise.*

Allocution, nominally addressed to the cardinals at Fontainebleau, but practically intended for the Universal Church, against the insertion in the *Bulletin des Lois* of the Concordat of 1813. In virtue of its decrees episcopal confirmation might follow upon the Emperor's nominations, without the Holy See. In July 1813, the Congress of Prague furnished the Sovereign Pontiff with a plea for appealing officially to the Emperor of Austria for the restitution of the Temporal Power. Once more, however, Napoleon approached Pius VII. From a sure source he heard that the United Powers would infallibly require the restoration of the Papal States. He would negotiate whilst the Holy Father was still his prisoner, and he could thus save his pride a rude fall. Towards the end of 1813, a lady of the Empress's court, the Marquise de Brignole, was charged to feel her way, or rather Napoleon's way, in this delicate matter. Her mediation was courteously declined by Consalvi, on the ground that " neither time nor place were favourable for a new treaty."[1] Mme. de Brignole was followed by the Bishop of Piacenza, Mgr. Fallot de Beaumont. His orders were to give the Holy Father to understand that return to Rome was a possibility. The message was to be delivered as *if from himself.* The Bishop met with no better success than the Marquise. The Holy Father listened to him patiently, attaching no weight to his words. The Pope had forbidden even the Cardinals to mention the subject to him, and he knew

[1] *L'Église Romaine et le Premier Empire*, t. v. p. 307.

now how to value Napoleon's empty phrases. After
Mgr. de Beaumont's fruitless attempt, M. la Gorse
ventured to offer his services. In a letter to M.
Bigot, he expatiated on his singular aptitude for the
office of negotiator. Long and close observation, he
said, had made him thoroughly acquainted with the
character and habits of Pius VII., "who was more
anxious to be esteemed a martyr than a great prince.
It is easier to say prayers than to make treaties."[1]
These sentiments were worthy of the man, and of the
work he had done so efficiently at Napoleon's bidding.

Cardinals Pacca and Consalvi tried to enlighten
the ignorance of Mgr. de Beaumont. After mature
reflection, the Pope considered that no treaty made
under the circumstances could be permanent. He
was not in a position either to discuss spiritual
matters freely, or to come to a final understanding.
The first thing to be done was to put matters on
their proper footing. A fortnight later Murat's
designs on the Roman States altered Napoleon's mind
with regard to the Holy Father. Of two evils, he
preferred the Pope to Joachim Murat, a prince whose
dynasty he had founded.

The position of his army on the Rhine was also
seriously aggravated. Circumstances, therefore, dictated justice. Once more Mgr. de Beaumont was
despatched to Fontainebleau, bearing a letter dictated by M. Bassano at the Emperor's request. It
was in reality Napoleon who spoke, and what he said

---

[1] *Lettre de M. la Gorse au Ministre des Cultes*, décembre 1813.

was, that he begged the Pope to take back St. Peter's Patrimony, not because it was an act of justice, but because it suited his convenience.   The letter ran :—

" MOST HOLY FATHER,—I approach your Holiness to inform you that as the King of Naples has joined the coalition which apparently aims at ultimately reuniting Rome to his States, his Majesty the Emperor and King judges it expedient for the Empire and the Roman people to restore the Roman States to your Holiness.   He *prefers seeing them in your hands rather than in those of any other sovereign, whoever he may be.*   Consequently, I am authorised to sign a treaty by which peace would be re-established between the Emperor and the Pope.   Your Holiness would be recognised in your temporal sovereignty, and the Roman States, as incorporated in the French Empire, would be restored to your Holiness, or to your agents.   The fortresses would be included in the restoration.   This convention would be restricted to temporal matters, and would treat with the Pope as Sovereign of Rome."[1]

Pius VII. rejected these overtures of Napoleon. He replied that " the restitution of his States, being an act of justice, it did not enter into a treaty; that if he accomplished anything important, whilst an exile, it would seem to be the result of violence,

---

[1] *Projet de Lettre au Saint Père, remis le 18 janvier à Myr. de Beaumont.*

and would give scandal to the Catholic world. His one desire was to return to Rome, and that was in the hands of Providence." He added, "It is possible that my sins have made me unworthy of seeing Rome again, but be assured that my successors will entirely recover the States which belong to them." "Assure the Emperor that I am not his enemy," were his parting words to Mgr. de Beaumont. "Religion would not allow me to be so. I love France, and when I am in Rome again you will see that I shall not forget your country."

Napoleon still had it in his power to be generous to the Sovereign Pontiff, whom he had so grievously wronged. He preferred to think with la Gorse that it would be a "dangerous proof of magnanimity" to allow the Holy Father to regain Italy in freedom. After leaving the Pope, as Mgr. de Beaumont was walking through Fontainebleau, he saw three carriages driving towards the palace. They were to take the Sovereign Pontiff away before the allied forces approached to loosen his chains. He left, as he had come, a prisoner, with the same escort which had brought him nearly two years previously from Savona to Fontainebleau. It would have been easy to retrieve in some measure, though even at the eleventh hour, the ill-usage of so many years, by a final act of generosity. War was now brought into the heart of France, and Napoleon's mind was absorbed in the French campaign and its eventualities. His genius looked a long way ahead, and whilst ostensibly offering restitution to the Pope, he was in reality scheming how to retain his grasp on Pius VII., if fortune should be faithful to his banner. To all outward intents and purposes, M. la Gorse was accompanying the Pope to Rome. His secret orders, however, were to gain Savona by outlying roads. An account was opened with the officials of Montenotte for reorganising the Papal Household at the rate of twelve thousand francs a month. The Cardinals were not to accompany Pius VII. They were to leave Fontainebleau four days later for a destination best known to Napoleon, and they would be required to furnish their own expenses for the journey. Napoleon had thus provided for the decision of events: if fortune favoured him, the Pope would be taken to Savona; if, on the contrary, success deserted him, the Holy Father would be safely landed in Rome, and he, Napoleon, would have the merit before the public of a magnanimous deed. Napoleon's misfortune and failure alone led Pius VII. back to Rome.

The Pope saw his departure from Fontainebleau in its true light. He was exchanging one prison for another. In vain he asked la Gorse for the company of two or three cardinals. He was informed that Mgr. Bertazzoli would travel in his carriage, whilst la Gorse would follow with two valets. The serenity of Pius VII. was beyond the power of human vicissitudes. He calmly said his Mass on the morning of January 23rd, 1814, then called the Cardinals together

to give them a parting address, perhaps a farewell till
eternity.   In simple and touching words he told them
that he was setting out on an unknown journey, and
that he might never see them again : under all circumstances, and whatever might happen, he counted
upon their fidelity to the Church.   Her sufferings
should be reflected in their whole life, and they were
to be mindful of their Mother's tears.   He left written
directions in case of need with Cardinal Mattei; and
above all he enjoined them to reject any proposal
relating to a treaty, whether spiritual or temporal.
This, he said, "was positively his firm and steadfast
will."[1]   The Sacred College was much moved.   After
a short prayer in the chapel, and a last blessing for
the group of people gathered round the château, the
Holy Father entered the carriage.   A few days later,
war was raging at the very doors of the palace.   The
Apostolic pilgrim did not escape its eventualities.
Napoleon's gleam of success during February and
March made him reject disdainfully the proposal
that he should be contented with the France of
Louis XIV.   Far from accepting any conditions what-
soever, he suggested to la Gorse that the Pope should
be kept clear of Italy.   The Congress of Châtillon
expressed at least the sentiments of the Allied Powers
with regard to the Temporal Sovereignty.   They were
in favour of its restitution.   By the middle of March
Napoleon's ill-fortune had set in with a strong tide,

---

[1] *Allocution du Pope Pie VII. aux Cardinaux réunis au Palais de
Fontainebleau.*

and he became anxious that he, rather than events, should undo his own handiwork. On the 10th he published by decree the Pope's restoration. After all his resources were exhausted, he yielded grudgingly to a hated necessity. La Gorse had been ordered to avoid the large towns for fear, in reality, that the sight of Pius VII. should excite too great an enthusiasm. The battlefields of Champagne, as they strengthened Napoleon's ill-luck, relaxed the gaoler's arm. Gradually the Holy Father's progress assumed the appearance of an ovation. He had reached Savona when the Emperor's compulsory decree was made known to him, and for the first time since 1808 words of liberty were spoken to him: "Your Holiness is free, and can start for Rome to-morrow."

On the morrow the Sovereign Pontiff pontificated in the cathedral of Savona, his chains being now loosened. Cesena, Ancona, and Loretto formed the resting-places of his homeward way. During the Pope's stay at Cesena, Joachim Murat requested an audience of the Holy Father. He affected ignorance as to the Pope's destination. When told that it was Rome, he brought forward the ill-will of the Romans, and in proof of it produced a memorandum addressed by some Roman noblemen to the Allied Sovereigns.

It contained a request that in future they might be governed by a secular prince. The Holy Father quietly took the document, and threw it still unopened into the fire.

T

" Is there anything *now* to prevent us from returning to Rome ? "[1] he asked.

His troubles had begun by the occupation of Ancona, where he received a magnificent welcome. Salvos of artillery and the pealing of bells greeted the Papal carriage, which was drawn by the inhabitants. The next day Pius VII. crowned in the Cathedral a statue of Our Lady, under the title of *Regina sanctorum omnium*. Murat laid claim to the Marches of Ancona, and would still have retained them, had not the matter been referred to the Allied Sovereigns by Consalvi, at the Pope's desire. He, together with the other cardinals, had left Fontainebleau soon after Pius VII. On his arrival in Paris, he found that the plenipotentiaries had left for London. He followed them, settled his business with them, and saw the Prince Regent, afterwards George IV., who offered Pius VII. very material help —a blank exchequer bill, which he was to fill up according to his requirements.[2] The friendship of the Prince Regent was always gratefully remembered by a Sovereign Pontiff who had suffered in the cause of England.

Great as the humiliation had been was now the triumph. The 24th of May 1814, the feast of Our Lady *Auxilium Christianorum*, ushered in one of those days which make earth a foretaste of paradise. Charles IV. of Spain with his Queen and the Infante,

<hr>

[1] Weather's "Modern History," p. 384.
[2] Ibid. p. 385.

Don Francisco, the ex-King of Sardinia, the Queen
of Etruria, amongst others, swelled the procession
as it passed through the Eternal City. For the
Romans it contained only one figure, that of an old
man, with eyes dim from emotion, blessing his people
on their knees. A white-robed band of young men
and girls met him at the *Porta del Popolo*, bearing
palms, which looked golden in the glorious sun of
Rome. "Blessed is he who comes to us in the name
of the Lord," was the cry echoing from mouth to
mouth. At the Ponte Milvio, thirty young noblemen
of the first Roman houses replaced the horses, and
drew the Papal carriage to St. Peter's. When the
old man mounted at last the steps of the great
basilica, enthusiasm gave way to that silent emotion
which is deeper than all words.

The Holy Father in his exaltation was still humble.
The day after his return, a Roman noble, who had
signed the memorandum presented by Murat at
Cesena, sought an audience of Pius VII. to crave
forgiveness.

"Do you think that we are without reproach?" was
his answer. "Let us all forget what has passed."[1]

A short time before the palace of Fontainebleau
witnessed a scene strikingly different in all its details
from that which closed the month of May in the
Eternal City. On the 24th of January 1813, Pius
VII. had signed his forced abdication of his States.
On the 28th of April 1814, that is fifteen months

[1] *Histoire de Pie VII.*, t. ii. p. 381.

later almost to a day, at the same palace of Fontainebleau, and at the very same table, Napoleon put his
name to the decree which declared his Empire at an
end, and he himself to be a fallen sovereign.　It was
not enough to uncrown Napoleon ; it was necessary
to put the ocean between him and Europe, whose
peace he had shaken with its boundaries.　Only on
the lonely rock of St. Helena was there security
against the man who had gathered into his single
hands all the forces of the Revolution, and, true to his
parentage, had not respected the Rock of Peter.

CHAPTER XVI

THE WORKS OF PEACE

1814–1823

Pius VII. did not find all things as he had left them. Napoleon had made Rome the second city of his Empire, and filled the Quirinal with priceless objects of art, and a luxurious elegance hitherto unknown. This imperial magnificence fell to the lot of the Sovereign Pontiff, but did not extend to his own room, where, as if Radet had been mindful of his request, simplicity remained undisturbed.

The Holy Father's first use of his restored power was particularly significant. At Fontainebleau he had already contemplated this great work of his reign, to which Cardinal Pacca powerfully contributed. Pius VI. and Pius VII. suffered more than any other Popes from the assaults of Revolution. Pius VII. was now in a position to give back to the Church her standing army, whose services no one could appreciate better than himself. Amongst religious orders the Society of Jesus has the unique glory of following our Lord to death and resurrection. Persecuted to death, it has risen again without obeying the laws of human things.   There was neither weakness in death, nor corruption in coming forth from the tomb.   Both death and resurrection kept their likeness to our Lord in His strong passing away, and His vigorous Easter morn.   All through his pontificate Pius VII. had been more or less occupied with the Jesuits.   In 1801 he re-established the society in Russia; in 1805, at Naples;[1] finally, in 1814, he uttered the solemn "Come forth" in favour of the whole Church.[2]   A priest who visited him when at the Tuileries for the coronation in 1804, testified to the Holy Father's great appreciation of the society.   This priest, M. Proyart, was the biographer of both Mme. Louise de France and her royal nephew, Louis XVI.   Speaking to Pius VII. of his book on Louis XVI., he said—

"People have given me a scruple for speaking as I have done of Clement XIV., most Holy Father, yet God knows that it was not in the bad sense of philosophers, who have calumniated every Pope except the destroyer of the Jesuits."

"What you say of him is unfortunately only too true.   I heard the minutest details of the business from a prelate who was in Clement XIV.'s service, and then entered mine.   He was the very prelate who offered Pope Clement the Bull of Suppression to sign.   As soon as he had signed, he threw his

---

[1] Sanguineti: *La Compagnia di Gesù*, Appendice.   "See Briefs of Restoration," xxx.

[2] De Ravignan: *Clément XIII. et Clément XIV.*, p. 477.

pen on one side, the paper on the other, and seemed beside himself."

"It seems to me, most Holy Father," remarked the Abbé, " that if the Powers forced him to suppress their own staunchest auxiliary, the Pope should at least have avoided blaming those whom he was compelled to use unjustly. Still less should he have treated them as if they were criminals."

"Most certainly. Even supposing that the Church had been threatened by far greater evils than the suppression of this important Order, at the dictates of kings misled by their advisers, a Bull of three lines should have given this unhappy sentence : Yielding regretfully to the force of things, &c. &c."

"France then, Louis XV. at least, did not ask for the suppression ? "

" No, it was Spain that was absolutely bent upon it. The Pope unfortunately promised it to the Spanish Ministry (not, observe, before his election, but afterwards). From that moment he had not an instant's peace. The Spanish Cabinet bothered and worried him to keep his word until the fatal day when he yielded."

" And yet these enemies of kings are re-established, most Holy Father."

" Yes, and admire the ways of Providence. The apostles of the Catholic religion are re-established at the request of schismatical powers."

" In France we have a small society of picked

and most tried men, who flatter themselves that they are walking in the footsteps of the Jesuits."

" Yes, I know and esteem them very highly. The worst of it is, they are a body without a head : *deest caput*." [1]

Pius VII. therefore cherished the Society of Jesus in his faithful heart, and now that the hour of his power had struck, he proceeded to deeds.

A month after his return to Rome, towards the end of June 1814, Cardinal Pacca reminded him of their conversations at Fontainebleau about "the Order of Jesus," as he called it. " We can re-establish the Society at the approaching feast of St. Ignatius," was the Holy Father's reply. On the 7th of August 1814, the Bull of Restoration, *Sollicitudo Omnium Ecclesiarum*, was published. "The Catholic world," it said, " asks with one accord that the Society of Jesus should be re-established. Every day the most urgent requests to this end are made to us by our venerable brethren, the archbishops and bishops, and by persons of most distinguished rank, more especially now that the abundant fruits produced by this Society in Russia and Sicily [2] are generally known. Recent calamities, which it is wiser to deplore than to call to mind, have dispersed the very stones of the sanctuary ; the destruction, too, of religious orders, which are the support and glory

---

[1] *Clément XIII. et Clément XIV.*, Pièces Justificatives, No. xvii.

[2] Russia and the kingdom of the Two Sicilies maintained the Jesuit organisation, as mentioned above.

of the Catholic Church, make yielding to so just and widespread a desire our positive duty. We should esteem ourself most guilty before God, if in the crying needs of the Christian commonwealth, we neglected to offer it this powerful support which God by a special Providence puts within our reach. We should be most guilty if we refused to make use of vigorous and experienced rowers who voluntarily offer themselves to stem the tide which threatens us in St. Peter's bark, tossed by the waves, with shipwreck and constant destruction."[1]

Subsequent events have proved that the Holy Father did not overrate the services of the Society which rose from the tomb at his command. Since 1814, as before, it has sustained great and glorious wounds on every Catholic battlefield.

The first year after Pius VII.'s return to Rome was spent by Europe in recovering its equilibrium. The Congress and Treaty of Vienna, 1814–1815, restored its former national boundaries, and undid the displacements of revolution in the person of Napoleon. Consalvi represented the Pope at the Congress: At the time of his accession, Pius VII. had been no more than a nominal sovereign. The Treaty of Tolentino, enacted under his predecessor, Pius VI., had in reality despoiled the Church of her temporal possessions. The Congress of Vienna, at which Austria, England, France, Prussia, Russia, and the Sovereign Pontiff were represented, closed on June

[1] *Histoire de Pie VII.*, ii. p. 403.

9th, 1815. On that day a treaty composed of one hundred and twenty articles was signed by the assembled plenipotentiaries. The Marches of Ancona, Benevento, Ponto Corvo, and the Three Legations were restored to the Pope. Avignon, alone, was given up to France, and the Papal Nuncios recovered the right of general precedence in the Courts of Europe.

But before the happy termination of negotiations, the newly acquired European peace was seriously threatened by the invasion from Elba, called in history the *Cent Jours*. Napoleon left Elba on February 26th, 1815, gained France, and once more strove to rally Frenchmen to his magic flag. At the same moment Joachim Murat summoned the Pope to allow right of passage through his States to twelve thousand men. He tried to rally Neapolitans with the deceptive cry of Italian unity. The glimmering of success that befell his arms at Ferrara and Florence was soon frustrated by the Austrians and the co-operation of the English, who aimed at securing by treaty the deposition of Murat. Joachim's name and dynasty had not taken root in Neapolitan hearts: the Pope refused to temporise, preferring once more to follow the path of exile. At Genoa, his words to the French ambassador were prophetic. " Have no fears; *questo è un temporale che durerà tre mesi.*"[1] Louis XVIII., momentarily re-established on his throne, had fled to Ghent. Napoleon was issuing proclamations

---

[1] *Histoire de Pie VII.*, ii. p. 416.

from the Tuileries; and during the three months, which surely enough constituted the "*temporale*," he found time to write to the Pope. His letter never reached its destination, though probably the Pope was apprised of the step. Napoleon was no longer a sovereign *de facto*, and Pius VII. had ceased to count with him as a crowned head. Whilst Murat was Napoleon's sole ally on the Continent, Europe referred his fortunes to the battlefield. They were decided by the crushing defeat of Waterloo in June 1815. Napoleon cast himself upon the mercy of England, and was sentenced to a life-long imprisonment on a solitary island of the Atlantic. It was a question of setting the security of a whole continent against the comfort of one man, therefore of punishing a criminal against the public good of Europe. As long as Napoleon was at large he would have broken all bonds. The solitary rock of St. Helena was an absolute necessity, not however harshness in the execution of the sentence. Whatever may have been said of Sir Hudson Lowe's severity, he never equalled the gaolers of Savona and Fontainebleau.

Murat, who had retired to Corsica after the Battle of Waterloo, had feebly imitated the *Cent Jours* by making a descent on Naples in October 1815. He met with resistance, was arrested, tried, and shot on the 15th. So ended the Napoleonic dynasty in Italy.

Consalvi came back full of honours from the Treaty of Vienna to find Pius VII. installed for good in Rome. After a momentous interval of nine years, he resumed his post as Secretary of State. His administration aimed at producing unity in the Papal States, at introducing modern improvements, and at repairing the ravages of revolution under the triple head of the common weal, science, and the fine arts. Immense public works were planned and executed, amongst others important excavations at Ostia. A subterranean street, formerly inhabited by the goldsmiths of the place, was brought to light. In Rome itself the work of restoration was vigorously carried on. The monuments of the Eternal City could not be appreciated, surrounded as they were in many cases by dust and rubbish. The Roman Forum, the Piazza del Popolo, and the Piazza di San Pietro in particular, benefited by the general clearance, whilst the Forum of Trajan was rescued from its ruins, and the Ponte Molle considerably improved. Pius VII. added new rooms to the Vatican museum, and built the part which is called Braccio Nuovo. The learned labours of Mgr. Maï added a scientific glory to his reign, of which the Romans were not a little proud. Mgr. (afterwards Cardinal) Maï succeeded in discovering part of Cicero's *Republic*.

At the Congress of Vienna, Consalvi had pledged his word that an administrative reform should be carried out in the Papal States. Revolutions and change of masters do not come upon a people to no purpose, and for many years the government of the Popes had been most precarious. Their temporal throne had been undermined by the social storm of

1789. Other sceptres shake and quiver at the approach, and long after the departure of similar tempests, and the Temporal Power is affected by the vicissitudes attending all human government. The Pope's *motu proprio* of July 1816 notified administrative changes which received his entire approval. In the first place, the law was strengthened by five new codes. Napoleon himself had adopted many of the Roman laws, and the new civil code was the work of an ex-Councillor of State. The financial system was refounded on a stronger basis, and the department of inland receipts put on a better footing. The attributions of judiciary and administrative tribunals and the Court of Exchequer were clearly defined, and the price of salt and tobacco was made uniform in the Roman States.

Religious settlements were more important and more engrossing. France had set the example of Concordats, but that of 1801 was now found defective. It had been concluded at a moment of crisis, when building up the walls of the spiritual edifice, almost at any price, was a necessity. Under the Restoration, a fuller measure of light and air was wanted. The Holy Father, in a situation without precedent, had made sacrifices also without precedent, and now three classes of bishops opposed the conclusion of a further Concordat. There were former titular bishops of the *ancien régime* who had not obeyed the Holy Father's injunction to resign. A certain number of Constitutional bishops, after obtaining Papal confirmation, had reproduced errors which

unfitted them to be pastors. Finally, there were the
bishops of the Concordat, and perhaps the Council of
1811 represented their tone and feeling with sufficient
accuracy. They would have been true to Pius VII.
if they had dared, but in point of fact this courage
had been the exception. The limited number of sees
allowed in 1801 was also a further and a very serious
difficulty. On the 11th June 1817, an agreement,
known as the Concordat of 1817, was finally signed
between Consalvi, acting for Pius VII., and the Comte
de Blacas, for Louis XVIII. Its chief articles declared
that the Convention of 1801 had ceased to take effect,
and that the Organic Articles were repealed as prejudicial to religion. A certain number of suppressed
sees were restored, and his Christian Majesty pledged
himself to the further consideration of religious interests with the Holy Father.[1] Whatever may have
been the intentions of Louis XVIII., his ministers
were alarmed by the proposed treaty. The Restoration
had not produced piety around the throne, and the
prospect of new sees was viewed with disfavour by
men who inherited the Gallican traditions of the old
French magistracy. Although Pius VII. maintained
his part of the transaction, the Concordat of 1817
never took effect, and remained a dead letter. In
1822 negotiations were again opened, and a middle
course between the Concordats of 1801 and 1817 was
finally adopted, the number of sees, the chief point of
contention, being fixed at eighty.[2]

[1] *Historie de Pie VII.*, ii. p. 503.   [2] *Vie du Card. d'Astros*, 281.

Piedmont, Russia for Poland, Naples, and Prussia, also had their Concordats. When Ferdinand I., King of the Two Sicilies, as he was now styled, returned to his hereditary States, after the expulsion of Joachim Murat in 1815, he found the state of religion seriously affected by dearth of the monastic life. The spirit of an infidel minister rested as an evil inheritance on the scene of his iniquitous labours. Tanucci was no more, indeed, but Medici, Ferdinand's chief minister, perpetuated his influence. It was greatly to Ferdinand's credit that, in spite of the godless counsels which prevailed, he succeeded in concluding a Concordat in 1818. It built up again the Episcopate and the religious orders, and restored full working faculties to the Church. The majority of bishoprics were vacant. Henceforth, in virtue of the Concordat, one hundred and nine were to constitute the whole number; monastic vows were legally recognised, whilst intercourse with the Holy Father was possible for both flock and pastors. The King would nominate the bishops, and the Pope would bestow confirmation.[1] These conditions, with the necessary local variations, were those of the Concordats in general.

Pius VII. showed the world an example of vengeance after God's own Heart. It was a crowning " work of peace." He, who had been the chief sufferer from Napoleon, was alone mindful of the exile at St. Helena. On October 6th, 1817, he wrote to Consalvi :—

---

[1] Möhler : *Kirchengeschichte*, iii. pp. 372, 366.

"The Emperor Napoleon's family has approached us, through Cardinal Fesch, to inform us that the rock of St. Helena is killing him, and that a rapid decline is undermining his strength. It gave us great pain, and no doubt you will share it, for we must both remember that, under God, the re-establishment of religion in the great kingdom of France is principally due to him. The devoted and courageous initiative of 1801 makes us forgive and forget all subsequent wrongs. Savona and Fontainebleau were errors of judgment or dreams of ambition. The Concordat, as a heroic and Christian undertaking, saved society. The mother and family of Napoleon appeal to our generosity. We think that, in justice and gratitude, we ought to listen to them. We charge you, in all confidence, to write from us to the Allied Sovereigns, and especially to the Prince Regent,[1] who has given us so many tokens of esteem. He is a true friend of yours, and you must ask him to mitigate the sufferings of this dreary exile. It would be an unspeakable joy for us to soften Napoleon's pain. He can no longer wrong anybody: let him be a reproach to no man."[2]

Consalvi fully entered into the Pope's views, and shared the blessing of his vengeance. A few months later, Madame, as she was called, spoke her thanks from the fulness of her heart :—

---

[1] Later George IV.

[2] *Mémoires de Consalvi*, i. p. 78; *Lettre de Pie VII. au Cardinal Consalvi.*

" It is a pleasure as well as a duty for me to thank your Eminence for all that you have done for us since exile has fallen upon me and upon my children. My brother, Cardinal Fesch, has told me how generously you received the request of my great and unhappy proscript—that, upon the Emperor's just and Christian demand, you at once approached the English Government, and inquired for devoted and able priests. I am the most sorrowful of mothers. The one consolation I have is that the Holy Father consents to forget the past and to treat us with affection. . . . Under the Papal Government alone we find support and rest, and our gratitude is great in proportion. I ask your Eminence to lay it as a homage at the feet of the holy Pontiff, Pius VII. I speak in the name of all my proscripts, and especially in the name of him whose life is being slowly consumed on a deserted rock. No one, except His Holiness and your Eminence, tries to soften his sufferings or to shorten them. I thank you both, as a mother, from the bottom of my heart, and I beg to remain your gratefully devoted   MADAME." [1]

The same hospitality was extended to all Napoleon's relations. When Cardinal Fesch announced his intention of living in Rome, the Pope at once answered, " You are heartily welcome. I will do all I can to make it agreeable for you here. Rome has always

---

[1] *Lettre de Madame au Cardinal Consalvi,* 27 mai 1818 ; *Mémoires de Consalvi,* i. p. 102.

U

been the country of noble exiles. It will be doubly yours, both as a cardinal and as the Emperor's uncle."

Cardinal Fesch outlived Pius VII. by many years, but he did not outlive the Pope's hospitality. He survived till 1839, when the Eternal City was still the home of his exile.

Two priests were despatched by the Sovereign Pontiff to St. Helena,[1] and there is hope that Napoleon made his peace with God. However, the man had not changed. On his death-bed he added these words to his will: "I had the Duc d'Enghien arrested and condemned because the safety, interest, and honour of the French people required it at a time when the Comte d'Artois owned to keeping sixty assassins in Paris. Given the same circumstances, I should do it over again."[2]

Napoleon expired on the 5th of May 1821, and his captivity corresponded almost to a month with the imprisonment he had inflicted upon Pius VII., first at the Quirinal Palace, then at Savona and Fontainebleau. M. Vignali, one of the priests deputed by the Holy Father, gave him, it is to be gathered, the consolations of the Catholic faith, and prayed at his death-bed.

The Holy Father had sought to stay the hand of sickness and death at St. Helena. There was only one death-warrant which he would willingly have signed, that of the Revolution.

---

[1] Hergenröther : *Kirchengeschichte*, ii. p. 792.
[2] Montholon : *Captivité de Napoléon à Ste. Hélène*, ii. p. 105.

As time goes on, words change rather than things. The word *Revolution* then represented the most active efforts of diabolical power. Freemasonry and secret societies flourished in its lawlessness, and manufactured the terrible moral dynamite which then, as now, would undermine Church and State, government and society, if the world belonged to the devil and not to God. He "who keeps Israel neither slumbers nor sleeps." Against the upholders of the devil's device, *non serviam*, Pius VII. spoke his last protest from the chair of truth. On September 13th, 1821, a Bull was published against secret societies, exposing their deadly aim, and forbidding Catholics to take any part in their doings of destruction. "Let faithful children of the Church," were its words, "beware of those who did the devil's work, and profaned in their ceremonies the Passion of our Lord."[1]

The Church in England had a share in the gracious acts and words of Pius VII. It was in 1820, whilst Catholics still groaned under the whole weight of the Penal Laws. The present church at Moorfields was finished; and, although the Papal treasury and sacristy were very empty, the Holy Father ordered the most valuable object in church plate he possessed to be prepared for a present. Those about him were inclined to remonstrate. He silenced them by saying, "There is nothing too good for me to give the English Catholics."[2]

---

[1] *Histoire de Pie VII.*, ii. p. 587.
[2] "Position of the Catholic Church in England and Wales," p. 49. Edited for the Fifteen Club.

Pius VII. and his minister, Consalvi, were fast approaching harbour. The Secretary of State had an organic disease which gave him, he thought, a chance of not outliving the Holy Father, whom he eventually survived by a few months.

Consalvi was the only member in office of the Roman Court who made a real impression on Napoleon. In 1814, as the Emperor was on his way to Elba, he met Consalvi on the road. "That is a man," he remarked to his companion in the carriage, General Koller, "who does not wish to appear *cagot*, but who is, in fact, more *cagot* than anybody in the world." [1]

In his will Consalvi bequeathed his possessions, which comprised handsome presents from the majority of Europe's crowned heads, to the honour of God and the memory of his friend Pius VII. He left his money partly to the work of restoring the principal churches in Rome, partly to raising a monument to Pius VII. It is to Consalvi that St. Peter's owes the costly tomb which was executed by Thorwaldsen.

Little less than a month before the death of Pius VII., in July 1823, the church of St. Paul, beyond the walls, was destroyed by fire in one night. It was in the convent of St. Paul's that Dom Gregorio Chiaramonti had passed so many years as a Benedictine monk. The Holy Father had fallen, a few days previously, in trying without assistance to reach his bell, and, in consequence of the fall, had been

---

[1] Möhler : *Kirchengeschichte*, iii. p. 380.

obliged to take to his bed. The fire at St. Paul's, his old convent, probably added a further shock to his exhausted system. The doctors tried to keep from him the serious nature of his fall, but how could Pius VII. fear death? Of his own accord he asked for the Holy Viaticum, the stay of the Sovereign Pontiff as it is of the poorest and weakest Catholic. A few hours before the end, a priest addressed him as *your Holiness.* "How can you call me Holiness?" replied the dying Pope; "I am only a poor sinner." Almost the last words he was heard to murmur were, "Savona . . . Fontainebleau." They were a further cry of humility and contrition. He expired on the 20th of August 1823, aged eighty-one years and six days, after a pontificate of twenty-three years and five months.

He was brought to St. Peter's for his last rest, and in the great basilica his tomb, erected at the expense of Consalvi, is a well-known object. After a pontificate of almost unprecedented trial, Pius VII. had enjoyed many years of unbroken peace in his borders. Napoleon fell a victim to a cruel disease in the flower of his strength and age. He died in exile at fifty-two, and left behind him ruins and desolation: ruins in thousands of homes, robbed, by his selfish ambition, of their sons and bread-winners; desolation in his own family—a wife who did not mourn him, and a son he scarcely knew. The King of Rome, at least, died before dreams of human pride could make themselves heard. In the days of Savona and

Fontainebleau, Napoleon seemed to hold the life of the Sovereign Pontiff in his hands as by a slender thread. Pius VII. was never spared when it suited Napoleon's convenience, and yet he lived to see his lot reversed, and to be crowned afresh in a joyous return to his people. The persecutor also lived to see the proud edifice of all his hopes fall to the ground, and the crown, which he had set on his own head, snatched from him by a European coalition ; and, with humiliation written on his heart, he was called to the home of his eternity.

In the desert land of Savona and Fontainebleau Pius VII. had drawn honey from the rock and oil from a hard stone.[1] From the promised harbour of Rome, after accomplishing great works of peace, he bequeathed to the Church one more lesson of confidence in Divine power. The Kingdom of the Cross is ruled by supernatural wisdom. It draws strength from trouble, and is exalted by oppression.

[1] "Mel de petra oleumque de saxo durissimo."

AUTHORITIES CONSULTED

ALISON. European History. 10 vols.

ARTAUD DE MONTOR. Vie de Pie VII. 2 vols.

CANTÙ. Storia Universale.

CAPEFIGUE. L'Europe sous Napoléon. 2 vols.

Captivité de Ste. Hélène, d'après le Marquis de Montchenu. 1 vol.

CARRON. Confesseurs de la Foi dans l'Église Gallicane. 4 vols.

CASSE, Baron du. Les Rois Frères de Napoléon. 1 vol.

CAUSSETTE. Le Cardinal d'Astros. 1 vol.

CHOTARD. Pie VII. à Savone. 1 vol.

CONSALVI, Cardinal. Mémoires. 2 vols.

DUERM, Père C. van. Un peu plus de Lumière sur le Conclave de Venice.

FIFTEEN CLUB. Prize Essay on Position of the Church in England and Wales.

GOSSELIN. Vie de M. Emery.

HALLER. Histoire de la Révolution Religieuse en Suisse.

D'HAUSSONVILLE, Cte. de. L'Église Romaine et le Premier Empire. 5 vols.

HERGENRÖTHER, Cardinal. Kirchenlexicon ; Kirchengeschichte.

JEAN, Rev. Père A. Les Évêques et les Archevêques de France. 1 vol.

JOLY, J. CRÉTINEAU. L'Église Romaine en Face de la Révolution. 2 vols.

KLEINSCHMIDT, A. Die Eltern und Geschwister Napoleons I. 1 vol.

LACORDAIRE, H. D. Conférences de Notre Dame de Paris.

LANFREY. Napoléon I.

LAURENTIE. Histoire de France.

LYONNET. Vie du Cardinal Fesch. 2 vols.

MAISTRE, J. de.   Du Pape.

Mémoires Secrets sur Napoléon Bonaparte.

MÖHLER.   Symbolik ; Kirchengeschichte.

MONTHOLON, Cte. de.   Captivité de Napoléon à Ste. Hélène.
2 vols.

NAPOLÉON I., Correspondance de, publiée par ordre de Napoléon III.   32 vols.   Correspondance inédite de.   4 vols.

ONCKEN, Dr. W.   Zeitalter der Revolution.

PACCA, Cardinal.   Memorie Storiche.   2 vols.

PISTOLESI.   Vita del Papa Pio Settimo.   4 vols.

RAVIGNAN, X. DE.   Clément XIII. et Clément XIV.   1 vol.

RÉMUSAT, Mme. de.   Mémoires de.   2 vols.

SANGUINETI, Rev. Fr. S.   La Compagnia di Gesù e la sua legale
Esistenza nella Chiesa.   1 vol.

SOREL.   La Révolution Française.   4 vols.

THEINER, A.   Affaires Religieuses de la France.   2 vols.

THIERS.   Histoire du Consulat et de l'Empire.

VANDAL.   Alexandre I. et Napoléon.   2 vols.

WEATHERS, Dr.   Modern History.

WEISS.   Lehrbuch der Weltgeschichte.

WISEMAN, Cardinal.   Recollections of the Four Last Popes.

ZALENSKI, Rev. P. S.   Les Jésuites de la Russie Blanche.   Tra-
duit du Polonais, par le P. A. Vivier.   2 vols.

Zeitschrift für Katholische Theologie.   1888.   Innsbrück.

INDEX

THE END

SELECTION

FROM

BURNS & OATES'

Catalogue

OF

PUBLICATIONS.

LONDON: BURNS AND OATES, Ld.

28 ORCHARD ST., W.

1896.

SELECTION

FROM

BURNS AND OATES' CATALOGUE
OF PUBLICATIONS.

—————++++++————

ALLIES, T. W. (K.C. S.G.)
A Life's Decision. Second Edition. Crown 8vo, cloth. £0 5 0
The Formation of Christendom.
   Vol. I.—Popular Edition. Crown 8vo, cloth.   .   0 5 0
   Vols. II. and III. Demy 8vo, . . . each   0 10 0
The Throne of the Fisherman, built by the Carpenter's
   Son, the Root, the Bond, and the Crown of Christ-
   endom. Demy 8vo 0 10 6
The Holy See and the Wandering of the Nations.
   Demy 8vo 0 10 6
Peter's Rock in Mohammed's Flood. Demy 8vo   .   0 10 6

"It would be quite superfluous at this hour of the day to recommend
Mr. Allies' writings to English Catholics. Those of our readers who
remember the article on his writings in the *Katholik*, know that
he is esteemed in Germany as one of our foremost writers."—
Dublin Review.

ALLIES, MARY.
Leaves from St. John Chrysostom. With introduction
   by T. W. Allies, K.C.S.G. Crown 8vo, cloth.   .   0 6 0

"Miss Allies' 'Leaves' are delightful reading; the English is re-
markably pure and graceful; page after page reads as if it were
original. No commentator, Catholic or Protestant, has ever surpassed St. John Chrysostom in the knowledge of Holy Scripture,
and his learning was of a kind which is of service now as it was at
the time when the inhabitants of a great city hung on his words."—
Tablet.

History of the Church in England, from the begin-
   ning of the Christian Era to the accession of
   Henry VIII. Crown 8vo, cloth 0 6 0
The Second Part, to the End of Queen Elizabeth's
   Reign. Crown 8vo, cloth 0 3 6

"Miss Allies has in this volume admirably compressed the substance, or such as was necessary to her purpose, of a number of
authorities, judiciously selected. . . . As a narrative the volume is
capitally written, as a summary it is skilful, and not its least
excellence is its value as an index of the best available sources
which deal with the period it covers."—*Birmingham Daily Gazette.*

ANNUS SANCTUS:
Hymns of the Church for the Ecclesiastical Year.
   Translated from the Sacred Offices by various
   Authors, with Modern, Original, and other Hymns,
   and an Appendix of Earlier Versions. Selected and
   Arranged by ORBY SHIPLEY, M.A.
   Edition de luxe. Reduced to *net*.   .   .   0 5 0

ANSWERS TO ATHEISTS: OR NOTES ON
Ingersoll. By the Rev. L. A. Lambert (over 130,000
copies sold in America). Paper 0 0 6
   Cloth 0 1 0

BAKER, VEN. FATHER AUGUSTIN.

Holy Wisdom ; (Sancta Sophia). Directions for the Prayer of Contemplation, &c. By the Ven. Father F. Augustin Baker, O.S.B. Edited by Abbot Sweeney, D.D. Beautifully bound in half leather. £0 6 o

"We earnestly recommend this most beautiful work to all our readers. We are sure that every community will use it as a constant manual. If any persons have friends in convents, we cannot conceive a better present they can make them, or a better claim they can have on their prayers, than by providing them with a copy."—*Weekly Register*.

BELLASIS, EDWARD. (*Lancaster Herald*.)

Memorials of MR. SERJEANT BELLASIS New and cheaper Edition. 8vo. 250 pp., bound in cloth, with fifteen Portraits and Illustrations . . . . o 6 o

"A noteworthy contribution to the history of the Tractarian Movement."—*Times*.

BOWDEN, REV. H. S. (of the Oratory) Edited by.

Dante's Divina Commedia : Its scope and value. From the German of FRANCIS HETTINGER, D.D. With an engraving of Dante. 2nd Edition. . . o 10 6

"All that Venturi attempted to do has been now approached with far greater power and learning by Dr. Hettinger, who, as the author of the 'Apologie des Christenthums,' and as a great Catholic theologian, is eminently well qualified for the task he has undertaken."—*The Saturday Review*.

Natural Religion. Being Vol. I. of Dr. Hettinger's Evidences of Christianity. With an Introduction on Certainty. Second edition. Crown 8vo, cloth o 7 6·

"As an able statement of the Catholic Doctrine of Certitude, and a defence, from the Romanist point of view, of the truth of Christianity, it was well worth while translating Dr. Franz Hettinger's 'Apologie des Christenthums,' of which the first part is now published."—*Scotsman*.

Revealed Religion. Being the Second Volume of the above work. With an Introduction on the "Assent of Faith." Crown 8vo, cloth, ... o 5 o

"It is a book practically invaluable to the educated Catholic who is forced one way or another to read the flippant and most irreligious criticism of the hour, and who, unless supported by some antidote of this kind, must imbibe a good deal of that insidious poison." *Freeman's Journal*.

BRIDGETT, REV. T. E. (C.SS.R.)

Discipline of Drink, The. An Historical Inquiry into the Principles and Practice of the Catholic Church regarding the Use, Abuse, and Disuse of Alcoholic Liquors, especially in England, Ireland, and Scotland from the 6th to the 16th Century. By Rev. T. E. Bridgett, C.SS.R. With an Introductory Letter by H. E. Cardinal Manning. Fcap. 8vo, cloth. . . . . o 3 6

Our Lady's Dowry ; how England Won that Title. New and Enlarged Edition. . . . . o 5 o

"This book is the ablest vindication of Catholic devotion to Our Lady, drawn from tradition, that we know of in the English language."—*Tablet*.

BRIDGETT REV. T. E. (C.SS.R.)—*continued.*

Ritual of the New Testament. An essay on the principles and origin of Catholic Ritual in reference to the New Testament. Third edition . . . £0 5 0

The Life of the Blessed John Fisher. With a reproduction of the famous portrait of Blessed JOHN FISHER by HOLBEIN, and other Illustrations. 2nd Ed. 0 7 6

The True Story of the Catholic Hierarchy deposed by Queen Elizabeth, with fuller Memoirs of its Last Two Survivors. By the Rev. T. E. BRIDGETT, C.SS.R., and the late Rev. T. F. KNOX, D.D., of the London Oratory. Crown 8vo, cloth, 0 7 6

"We gladly acknowledge the value of this work on a subject which has been obscured by prejudice and carelessness."—*Saturday Review.*

The Life and Writings of Blessed Thomas More, Lord Chancellor of England and Martyr under Henry VIII. With Portrait of the Martyr taken from the Crayon Sketch made by Holbein in 1527. 2nd Ed. 0 7 6

The Wisdom and Wit of Blessed Thomas More. . 0 6 0

"It would be hard to find another such collection of true wisdom and keen, pungent, yet gentle wit and humour, as this volume contains."—*American Catholic Quarterly.*

BRIDGETT, REV. T. E. (C.SS.R.), Edited by.

Souls Departed: Being a defence and Declaration of the Catholic Church's Doctrine touching Purgatory and Prayers for the Dead. By Cardinal Allen. First published in 1565, and now edited in modern spelling. Black cloth, with a Portrait of Cardinal Allen 0 6 0

BROWNLOW, BISHOP.

A Memoir of the late Sir James Marshall, C.M.G., K.C.S.G., taken chiefly from his own letters. With Portrait. Crown 8vo, cloth . . 0 3 6
Lectures on Slavery and Serfdom in Europe. Cloth 0 3 6

"The general impression left by the perusal of this interesting book is one of great fairness and thorough grasp of the subject."—*Month.*

Memoir of Mother Rose Columba Adams, O.P., first Prioress of St. Dominic's Convent, and Foundress of the Perpetual Adoration at North Adelaide. Crown 8vo. cloth, with Portrait and Plates . . 0 6 6

"An edifying and touching biography of one who was both a charming woman and a saintly nun."—*Dublin Review.*

BUCKLER, REV. REGINALD, (O.P.)

The Perfection of Man by Charity. A Spiritual Treatise. Second edition. Crown 8vo, cloth 0 5 0
"The object of Father Buckler's useful and interesting book is to lay down the principles of the spiritual life for the benefit of Religious and Seculars. The book is written in an easy and effective style, and the apt citations with which he enriches his pages would of themselves make the treatise valuable."—*Dublin Review.*

BUTLER, REV. ALBAN.

People's Edition of the Lives of the Saints.   In twelve
volumes. Each volume containing the Saints of the
Month.   Superfine paper, cloth extra, each volume £0 1 6

Or the Complete set, in handsome cloth case to match   0 18 0

The lives of the principal Martyrs, Fathers, and other more illustrious Saints, whose memory is revered in the Catholic Church, are
here presented to the public. The whole work, comprising over six
thousand pages, well printed on good paper, and bound in an
attractive style, is by far the cheapest and best edition in the
market. Alban Butler's "Lives of the Saints" has long been
recognised as a standard work, and it is the most comprehensive
Series ever published in the English Language.

CATHOLIC BELIEF: OR, A SHORT AND

Simple Exposition of Catholic Doctrine. By the
Very Rev. Joseph Faà di Bruno, D.D.   Fifteenth
edition .   .   .   .   . Price 6d.; post free,   0 0 8½
     Cloth, lettered, .   .   .   10d.;   .   .   0 1 0½
Also an edition printed on better paper and strongly
bound in cloth. With Steel Frontispiece.   .   .   0 2 0

CHALLONER, BISHOP.

Meditations for every day in the year. Revised and
edited by the Right Rev. John Virtue, D.D., Bishop
of Portsmouth. 7th edition. 8vo   .   .   .   0 3 0
And in other bindings.

COLERIDGE, REV. H. J. (S.J.) *(See Quarterly Series.)*

DALE, REV. J. D. HILARIUS.

Ceremonial according to the Roman Rite. Translated
from the Italian of JOSEPH BALDESCHI, Master of
Ceremonies of the Basilica of St. Peter at Rome;
with the Pontifical Offices of a Bishop in his own
diocese, compiled from the "Cæremoniale Epis-
coporum"; to which are added various other Functions and copious explanatory Notes; the whole
harmonized with the latest Decrees of the Sacred Congregation of Rites. New and revised edition. Cloth,   0 6 6

The Sacristan's Manual; or, Handbook of Church
Furniture, Ornament, &c. Harmonized with the
most approved commentaries on the Roman Ceremonial and latest Decrees of the Sacred Congregation of Rites. New Edition with numerous additions.
Cloth 0 2 6

DEVAS, C. S.

Studies of Family Life: a contribution to Social
Science. Crown 8vo 0 5 0

"We recommend these pages and the remarkable evidence brought
together in them to the careful attention of all who are interested in
the well-being of our common humanity."—*Guardian.*

DRANE, AUGUSTA THEODOSIA, Edited by.

The Autobiography of Archbishop Ullathorne. Demy 8vo, cloth. Second edition £0 7 6

"As a plucky Yorkshireman, as a sailor, as a missionary, as a great traveller, as a ravenous reader, and as a great prelate, Dr. Ullathorne was able to write down most fascinating accounts of his experiences. The book is full of shrewd glimpses from a Roman point of view of the man himself, of the position of Roman Catholics in this country, of the condition of the country, of the Colonies, and of the Anglican Church in various parts of the world, in the earlier half of this century."—*Guardian*.

The Letters of Archbishop Ullathorne. (Sequel to the *Autobiography*.) 2nd Edit. Demy 8vo, cloth   0 9 0

" Compiled with admirable judgment for the purpose of displaying in a thousand various ways the real man who was Archbishop Ullathorne."—*Tablet*.

EYRE, MOST REV. CHARLES, (Abp. of Glasgow).

The History of St. Cuthbert : or, An Account of his Life, Decease, and Miracles. Third edition. With maps, charts, &c. handsomely bound in cloth. Royal 8vo 0 14 0

FABER, REV. FREDERICK WILLIAM, (D.D.)

All for Jesus : or the Easy Ways of Divine Love . 0 5 0
Bethlehem 0 7 0
Ethel's Book : or Tales of the Angels. . . . 0 2 6
Growth in Holiness : or the Progress of the Spiritual Life 0 6 0
Notes on Doctrinal and Spiritual Subjects, 2 vols. . 0 10 0
Hymns. Complete Edition 0 6 0
Poems. Complete Edition. 0 5 0
Sir Lancelot : A Legend of the Middle Ages . . 0 5 0
Spiritual Conferences 0 6 0
The Blessed Sacrament : or the Works and Ways of God 0 7 6
The Creator and the Creature : or the Wonders of Divine Love 0 6 0
The Foot of the Cross : or the Sorrows of Mary. . 0 6 0
The Precious Blood : or the Price of our Salvation . 0 5 0
The Easiness of Salvation. (Reprinted from "The Creator and the Creature.") Cloth, gilt. . . 0 1 0
Life and Letters of Frederick William Faber, D.D., Priest of the Oratory of St. Philip Neri. By JOHN EDWARD BOWDEN of the same Congregation. With Portrait 0 6 0
Father Faber's May Book. Compiled by an Oblate of Mary Immaculate. Arranged for daily reading, from the writings of Father Faber. 18mo, cloth, gilt edges, with steel Frontispiece . . . 0 2 0

FAWKES, REV. ALFRED.

The Sacred Heart, and other Sermons. Red buckram, gilt 0 2 6
" Bright, scholarly, thoughtful, and redolent of the modern spirit."—*Academy*.

FORMBY, REV. HENRY.

Monotheism: in the main derived from the Hebrew nation and the Law of Moses. The Primitive Religion of the City of Rome. An historical Investigation. Demy 8vo £0 5 0

FRANCIS DE SALES, ST.: THE WORKS OF.

Translated into the English Language by the Very Rev. Canon Mackey, O.S.B., under the direction of the Right Rev. Bishop Hedley, O.S.B.

Vol. I. Letters to Persons in the World. 3rd Ed. . 0 6 0

"The letters must be read in order to comprehend the charm and sweetness of their style."—*Tablet*.

Vol. II.—The Treatise on the Love of God. Father Carr's translation of 1630 has been taken as a basis, but it has been modernized and thoroughly revised and corrected. 2nd Edition 0 6 0

"To those who are seeking perfection by the path of contemplation this volume will be an armoury of help."—*Saturday Review*.

Vol. III. The Catholic Controversy. . . . 0 6 0

"No one who has not read it can conceive how clear, how convincing, and how well adapted to our present needs are these controversial leaves.'"—*Tablet*.

Vol. IV. Letters to Persons in Religion, with introduction by Bishop Hedley on "St. Francis de Sales and the Religious State." 2nd Edition . . . 0 6 0

"The sincere piety and goodness, the grave wisdom, the knowledge of human nature, the tenderness for its weakness, and the desire for its perfection that pervade the letters, make them pregnant of instruction for all serious persons.—*Scotsman*.

GALLWEY, REV. PETER, (S.J.)

Precious Pearl of Hope in the Mercy of God, The. Translated from the Italian. With Preface by the Rev. Father Gallwey. Cloth 0 4 6

Lectures on Ritualism and on the Anglican Orders. 2 vols. (Or may be had separately.) 0 8 0

Salvage from the Wreck. A few Memories of the Dead, preserved in Funeral Discourses. With Portraits. Crown 8vo 0 7 6

GIBSON, REV. H.

Catechism Made Easy. Being an Explanation of the Christian Doctrine. 10th Edition. 2 vols., cloth. . 0 7 6

"This work must be of priceless worth to any who are engaged in any form of catechetical instruction. It is the best book of the kind that we have seen in English."—*Irish Monthly*.

GILLOW, JOSEPH.

Literary and Biographical History, or, Bibliographical Dictionary of the English Catholics. From the Breach with Rome, in 1534, to the Present Time. *Vols. I., II. III. and IV. cloth, demy 8vo* . . *each* 0 15 0

5th, and concluding vol. in preparation.

"The patient research of Mr. Gillow, his conscientious record of minute particulars, and especially his exhaustive bibliographical information in connection with each name, are beyond praise."—*British Quarterly Review*.

The Haydock Papers. Illustrated. Demy 8vo . 0 7 6

"We commend this collection to the attention of every one that is interested in the records of the sufferings and struggles of our ancestors to hand down the faith to their children."—*Tablet*

GILLOW, JOSEPH.

St. Thomas's Priory; or, The Story of St. Austin's, Stafford. With Three Illustrations. Tastefully bound in half leather £0 5 0

" A moving record of the stormy times through which our fathers kept alive the torch of Faith. No one can read without emotion the toilsome apostolate, the capture, trial, and execution of the first pastors in Staffordshire. — *Weekly Register.*"

GLANCEY, REV. M. F.

Characteristics from the Writings of Archbishop Ulla-thorne, together with a Bibliographical Account of the Archbishop's Works. Crown 8vo, cloth . . 0 6 0

"The Archbishop's thoughts are expressed in choice, rich language. We have perused this book with interest, and have no hesitation in recommending our readers to possess themselves of it."—*Birmingham Weekly Mercury.*

GRADWELL, MONSIGNOR.

Succat, The Story of Sixty Years of the Life of St. Patrick. Crown 8vo, cloth 0 5 0

"A work at once bright, picturesque, and truthful."—*Tablet.*
"We most heartily commend this book to all lovers of St. Patrick."—*Irish Ecclesiastical Record.*

GROWTH IN THE KNOWLEDGE OF OUR LORD.

Meditations for every Day in the Year, exclusive of those for Festivals, Days of Retreat, &c. Adapted from the original of Abbé de Brandt, by Sister Mary Fidelis. A new and Improved Edition, in 3 Vols. Sold only in sets. Price per set, . . . 1 2 6

HEDLEY, BISHOP.

Our Divine Saviour, and other Discourses. Crown 8vo 0 6 0

"A distinct and noteworthy feature of these sermons is, we certainly think, their freshness—freshness of thought, treatment, and style; nowhere do we meet pulpit commonplace or hackneyed phrase —everywhere, on the contrary, it is the heart of the preacher pouring out to his flock his own deep convictions, enforcing them from the 'Treasures, old and new,' of a cultivated mind."—*Dublin Review.*

A Retreat: consisting of Thirty-three Discourses with Meditations, intended for the use of the Clergy, Religious, and others. Crown 8vo, half leather 0 6 0

"This 'Retreat,' which will remain as a treasure with Catholics of English speech, shows forth once more, and very attractively, his (Dr. Hedley's) qualifications as a preacher and a guide of souls. It gives amplest evidence of his piety and his literary gift, his keen insight into the motives and the weaknesses of the human heart, and withal such a winning humility as leaves the erring one unwounded, though he is enlightened and rebuked."—*Weekly Register.*

INNER LIFE OF FATHER THOMAS BURKE, O.P.

By a Dominican Friar of the English Province. Dark green buckram, gilt. 0 2 0

In this little work the writer has endeavoured to depict that side of Father Burke's character which if it is least known, gives the truer as well as the higher idea of the well-known preacher of fifteen years ago.

KING, FRANCIS.

The Church of my Baptism, and why I returned to it. Crown 8vo, cloth 0 2 6

"Altogether a book of an excellent spirit, written with freshness and distinction."—*Weekly Register.*

LEE, REV. F. G., D.D. (of All Saints, Lambeth.)
Edward the Sixth : Supreme Head.   Second edition.
Crown 8vo £0   6   0
"A curious and interesting addition to the accessible information
concerning the troublous times of King Edward VI. The style of lan-
guage, is keen, vigorous and telling.—*Oxford University Herald.*"

LIGUORI, ST. ALPHONSUS.
New and Improved Translation of the Complete Works
of St. Alphonsus, edited by the late Bishop Coffin : -
Vol. I. The Christian Virtues, and the Means for Obtaining them.   Cloth 0   3   0
Or separately :—
   1. The Love of our Lord Jesus Christ . . . 0   1   0
   2. Treatise on Prayer. *(In the ordinary editions a
       great part of this work is omitted)* . . . 0   1   0
   3. A Christian's rule of Life 0   1   0
Vol. II. The Mysteries of the Faith—The Incarnation ;
containing Meditations and Devotions on the Birth
and Infancy of Jesus Christ, &c., suited for Advent
and Christmas. 0   2   6
Vol. III. The Mysteries of the Faith—The Blessed
Sacrament 0   2   6
Vol. IV. Eternal Truths—Preparation for Death . 0   2   6
Vol. V. The Redemption—Meditations on the Passion. 0   2   6
Vol. VI. Glories of Mary. New edition . . . 0   3   6
Reflections on Spiritual Subjects 0   2   6

LIVIUS, REV. T. (M.A., C.SS.R.)
St. Peter, Bishop of Rome ; or, the Roman Episcopate
of the Prince of the Apostles, proved from the
Fathers, History and Chronology, and illustrated by
arguments from other sources.   Dedicated to his
Eminence Cardinal Newman.   Demy 8vo, cloth . 0 12   0
Explanation of the Psalms and Canticles in the Divine
Office. By ST. ALPHONSUS LIGUORI. Translated
from the Italian by THOMAS LIVIUS, C.SS.R.
With a Preface by his Eminence Cardinal MANNING.
Crown 8vo, cloth 0   7   6
"To nuns and others who know little or no Latin, the book will
be of immense importance."—*Dublin Review.*

"Father Livius has in our opinion even improved on the original,
so far as the arrangement of the book goes. New priests will find
it especially useful."—*Month.*

Mary in the Epistles ; or, The Implicit Teaching of
the Apostles concerning the Blessed Virgin. Crown
8vo, cloth 0   5   0
The Blessed Virgin in the Fathers of the First Six
Centuries. With a Preface by CARD. VAUGHAN.
Cloth 0 12   0
" Father Livius could hardly have laid at the feet of Our Blessed
Patroness a more fitting tribute than to have placed side by side
with the work of his fellow-Redemptorist on the ' Dowry of Mary,'
this volume, in which we hear the combined voices of the Fathers of
the first six centuries united in speaking the praise of the Mother of
God."—*Dublin Review.*

MANNING, CARDINAL. Popular Edition of the Works of

	£	s	d
Four Great Evils of the Day. 7th edition	£0	2	6
Fourfold Sovereignty of God. 4th edition	0	2	6
Glories of the Sacred Heart. 5th edition	0	4	0
Grounds of Faith. 10th edition	0	1	6
Independence of the Holy See. 2nd edition	0	2	6
Internal Mission of the Holy Ghost. 6th edition	0	5	0
Miscellanies. 2 vols. *each*	0	6	0
Pastime Papers. 2nd edition	0	2	6
Religio Viatoris. 5th edition	0	1	6
Sermons on Ecclesiastical Subjects.	0	6	0
Sin and its Consequences. 8th edition	0	4	0
Temporal Mission of the Holy Ghost. 4th edition	0	5	0
True Story of the Vatican Council. 2nd edition	0	2	6
The Eternal Priesthood. 11th edition	0	2	6
The Office of the Church in the Higher Catholic Education. A Pastoral Letter	0	0	6
Workings of the Holy Spirit in the Church of England.	0	1	6
Lost Sheep Found. A Sermon	0	0	6
Rights and Dignity of Labour	0	0	1

The Westminster Series

In handy pocket size. All bound in cloth.

	£	s	d
The Blessed Sacrament, the Centre of Immutable Truth	0	1	0
Confidence in God.	0	1	0
Love of Jesus to Penitents.	0	1	0
Office of the Holy Ghost under the Gospel	0	1	0
Holy Ghost the Sanctifier	0	2	0

MANNING, CARDINAL, Edited by.

	£	s	d
Life of the Curé d' Ars. From the French of the Abbé Monnin. Popular Edition. Fcap. 8vo, cloth	0	2	6

"The authorised translation of the work by the Abbe Monnin, the friend and fellow-labourer of the Curé written by command of the Bishop of Belley, and is the only authentic work published."

MEYNELL, ALICE.

	£	s	d
Lourdes : Yesterday, to-day, and to-morrow. Translated from the French of Daniel Barbé by Alice Meynell. With twelve full pages water colour drawings by Hoffbauer, reproduced in colours. Royal 8vo, blue buckram, gilt	0	6	0

MORRIS, REV. JOHN (S.J., F.S.A.)

	£	s	d
Letter Books of Sir Amias Poulet, keeper of Mary Queen of Scots. Demy 8vo *net*	0	3	6
Two Missionaries under Elizabeth	0	14	0
The Catholics under Elizabeth	0	14	0
The Life of Father John Gerard, S.J. Third edition, rewritten and enlarged	0	14	0

MORRIS, REV. JOHN—*continued.*

The Life and Martyrdom of St. Thomas Becket. Second and enlarged edition. In one volume, large post 8vo, cloth, pp. xxxvi., 632, ... £0 12 6
or bound in two parts, cloth 0 13 0

"Father Morris is one of the few living writers who have succeeded in greatly modifying certain views of English history, which had long been accepted as the only tenable ones. . . To have wrung an admission of this kind from a reluctant public, never too much inclined to surrender its traditional assumptions, is an achievement not to be underrated in importance."—*Rev. Dr. Augustus Jessopp, in the Academy.*

MORRIS, REV. W. B. (of the Oratory.)

The Life of St. Patrick, Apostle of Ireland. Fourth edition. Crown 8vo, cloth 0 5 0

"Promises to become the standard biography of Ireland's Apostle. For clear statement of facts, and calm judicious discussion of controverted points, it surpasses any work we know of in the literature of the subject."—*American Catholic Quarterly.*

Ireland and St. Patrick. A study of the Saint's character and of the results of his apostolate. Second edition. Crown 8vo, cloth. . . . 0 5 0

"We read with pleasure this volume of essays, which, though the Saint's name is taken by no means in vain, really contains a sort of discussion of current events and current English views of Irish character."—*Saturday Review.*

NEWMAN, CARDINAL.

Church of the Fathers. Fcap 8vo, cloth, 361 pp. . 0 4 0
Prices of other works by Cardinal Newman on application.

PAGANI, VERY REV. JOHN BAPTIST,

The Science of the Saints in Practice. Complete in three volumes. Vol. 1, January to April (out of print). Vol. 2, May to August. Vol. 3, September to December . . . . . each 0 5 0
"This work is eminently adapted for the use of ecclesiastics and of religious communities."—*Irish Ecclesiastical Record.*

PAYNE, JOHN ORLEBAR, (M.A.)

Records of the English Catholics of 1715. Demy 8vo. Half-bound, gilt top 0 15 0
"These simple records speak eloquently of the sufferings endured by our forefathers in the Faith, at a time when martyrdom was passed, and will remain as a memorial long prized, not only by the particular families whose names appear in it, but by the great family of Catholics in England.—*Weekly Register.*"

English Catholic Non-Jurors of 1715. Being a Summary of the Register of their Estates, with Genealogical and other Notes, and an Appendix of Unpublished Documents in the Public Record Office. In one volume. Demy 8vo . . 1 1 0
"Most carefully and creditably brought out . . . From first to last, full of social interest and biographical details, for which we may search in vain elsewhere."—*Antiquarian Magazine.*

Old English Catholic Missions. Demy 8vo, half-bound. 0 7 6

"These registers tell us in their too brief records, teeming with interest for all their scantiness, many a tale of patient heroism."—*Tablet.*

PAYNE, JOHN ORLEBAR,—*continued.*

St. Paul's Cathedral in the time of Edward VI.   Being a detailed Account of its Treasures from a Document in the Public Record Office.   Tastefully printed on imitation hand-made paper, and bound in cloth £0 2 6

PERRY, REV. JOHN,

Practical Sermons for all the Sundays of the year. First and Second Series. Sixth edition.   In two volumes. Cloth 0 7 0

"The price at which it is issued puts it within reach of the most moderate purse. It has been carefully edited, printed in clear type, and neatly bound. We trust its circulation may be so extensive as to verify in Father Perry's regard that which was written of another great servant of God : 'being dead he yet speaketh.' "—*Tablet.*

POPE, REV. T. A. (of the Oratory.)

Life of St. Philip Neri.   Translated from the Italian of Cardinal Capecelatro.   Second and revised edition. 2 vols, cloth 0 12 6

"Altogether this is a most fascinating work, full of spiritual lore and historic erudition, and with all the intense interest of a remarkable biography. Take it up where you will, it is hard to lay it down. We think it one of the most completely satisfactory lives of a Saint that has been written in modern times."—*Tablet.*

POUVILLON, E.

Bernadette of Lourdes.   Translated from the French. By Henry O'Shea.   Blue buckram, gilt,   .   . 0 2 6

"A very charming little miracle-play. It is in the form of prose-narrative, interspersed with dialogue and lyrical snatches ; simple, devout, and strewn with tender fancy."—*Weekly Register.*

QUARTERLY SERIES. Edited by the Rev. John

Gerard, S.J. 94 volumes published to date.
Selection.

The Life and Letters of St. Francis Xavier.   By the Rev. H. J. Coleridge, S.J.   2 vols.   .   .   . 0 10 6
The History of the Sacred Passion.   By Father Luis de la Palma, of the Society of Jesus.   Translated from the Spanish. 0 5 0
The Life and Letters of St. Teresa. 3 vols. By Rev. H. J. Coleridge, S.J.   .   .   .   .   . each 0 7 6
The Life of Mary Ward.   By Mary Catherine Elizabeth Chalmers, of the Institute of the Blessed Virgin. Edited by the Rev. H. J. Coleridge, S.J. 2 vols. 0 15 0
The Return of the King.   Discourses on the Latter Days. By the Rev. H. J. Coleridge, S.J. .   . 0 7 6
Pious Affections towards God and the Saints.   Meditations for every Day in the Year, and for the Principal Festivals. From the Latin of the Ven. Nicolas Lancicius, S.J. 0 7 6
The Life and Teaching of Jesus Christ in Meditations for Every Day in the Year.   By Fr. Nicolas Avancino, S.J. Two vols. 0 10 6

QUARTERLY SERIES—(*selection*) *continued*.

QUARTERLY SERIES—*(selection) continued.*

Jesus : His Life, in the very words of the Four Gospels. A Diatessaron by HENRY BEAUCLERK, S.J. Cloth £0 5 0

First Communion. A Book of Preparation for First Communion. Edited by Father THURSTON, S.J. With Nineteen Illustrations 0 6 6

VOLUMES ON THE LIFE OF OUR LORD.

The Holy Infancy.

The Preparation of the Incarnation 0 7 6
The Nine Months. The Life of our Lord in the Womb. 0 7 6
The Thirty Years. Our Lord's Infancy and Early Life. 0 7 6

The Public Life of Our Lord.

The Ministry of St. John Baptist . . . 0 6 6
The Preaching of the Beatitudes 0 6 6
The Sermon on the Mount. Continued. 2 Parts, each 0 6 6
The Training of the Apostles. Parts I., II., III., IV. each 0 6 6
The Preaching of the Cross. Part I. . . . 0 6 6
The Preaching of the Cross. Parts II., III. each 0 6 0
Passiontide. Parts I. II. and III., each . . . 0 6 6
Chapters on the Parables of Our Lord . . . 0 7 6

Introductory Volumes.

The Life of our Life. Harmony of the Life of Our Lord, with Introductory Chapters and Indices. Second edition. Two vols. 0 15 0
The Passage of our Lord to the Father. Conclusion of The Life of our Life. 0 7 6
The Works and Words of our Saviour, gathered from the Four Gospels 0 7 6
The Story of the Gospels. Harmonised for Meditation 0 7 6

RENDU, A. (LL.D.)

The Jewish Race in Ancient and Roman History. Translated from the eleventh corrected edition, by Theresa Crook. Crown 8vo, cloth . . . 0 6 0

" Wonderfully well executed."—*Tablet.*
" It has the merits of clearness and condensation."—*Scotsman.*

ROSE, STEWART.

St. Ignatius Loyola and The Early Jesuits, with more than 100 Illustrations by H. W. and H. C. Brewer and L. Wain. The whole produced under the immediate superintendence of the Rev. W. H. Eyre, S.J. Super Royal 8vo. Handsomely bound in cloth, extra gilt. . . . . . net. 0 15 0

"This magnificent volume is one of which Catholics have justly reason to be proud. Its historical as well as its literary value is very great, and the illustrations from the pencils of Mr. Louis Wain and Messrs. H. W. and H. C. Brewer are models of what the illustrations of such a book should be."—*Month.*

RYDER, REV. H. I. D. (of the Oratory.)

Catholic Controversy: A Reply to Dr. Littledale's "Plain Reasons." Seventh edition . . . 0 2 6

SCHOUPPE, REV. F. X. (S.J.)

Purgatory. Illustrated by the lives and legends of the Saints. Cloth 0 6 0

" We feel absolutely confident that Father Schouppe's work will soon become one of our most popular works on Purgatory, and that we shall ere long have to notice its second edition."—*Tablet.*

STANTON, REV. R. (of the Oratory.)
A Menology of England and Wales; or, Brief Memorials of the British and English Saints, arranged according to the Calendar. Together with the Martyrs of the 16th and 17th centuries. With Supplement, containing Notes, enlarged Appendices, and a new Index. Demy 8vo, cloth £0 16 0
The Supplement, separately 0 2 0

SWEENEY, RT. REV. ABBOT, (O.S.B.)
Sermons for all Sundays and Festivals of the Year. Fourth edition. Crown 8vo, handsomely bound in half leather 0 10 6

" For such priests as are in search of matter to aid them in their round of Sunday discourses, and have not read this volume, we can assure them that they will find in these 600 pages a mine of solid and simple Catholic teaching.'—*Tablet.*

THOMPSON, EDWARD HEALY, (M.A.)
The Life of Jean-Jacques Olier, Founder of the Seminary of St. Sulpice. New and enlarged edition. Post 8vo, cloth, pp. xxxvi. 628 . . . . 0 15 0
The Life and Glories of St. Joseph, Husband of Mary, Foster-Father of Jesus, and Patron of the Universal Church. Grounded on the Dissertations of Canon Antonio Vitalis, Father José Moreno, and other writers. Second edition. Crown 8vo, cloth . 0 6 0
Life of Marie Lataste. Cloth 0 5 0
Letters and Writings of Marie Lataste, with Critical and Expository Notes. By two Fathers of the Society of Jesus. Translated from the French. 3 vols . . . . each 0 5 0

ULLATHORNE ARCHBISHOP.
Autobiography of, (*see* Drane, A. T.) . . . 0 7 6
Letters of.   do.   ,, ... 0 9 0
Christian Patience: the Strength and Discipline of the Soul. Fifth and Cheaper Edition. Demy 8vo, cloth 0 7 0
The Endowments of Man, Considered in their Relations with his Final End. Fourth and Cheaper Edition. Demy 8vo. cloth 0 7 0
The Groundwork of the Christian Virtues. Fifth and Cheaper Edition. Demy 8vo, cloth . 0 7 0
Memoir of Bishop Willson, First Bishop of Hobart, Tasmania 0 2 6

WATERWORTH, REV. J.
The Canons and Decrees of the Sacred and Œcumenical Council of Trent, translated by the Rev. J. WATERWORTH. To which are prefixed Essays on the External and Internal History of the Council. A new edition. Demy 8vo, cloth. . . . 0 10 6

WISEMAN, CARDINAL.
Fabiola. A Tale of the Catacombs. New edition. Crown 8vo . . . . . 3s. 6d. and 0 4 0
Also a new and splendid edition printed on large quarto paper, embellished with thirty-one full-page illustrations, and a coloured portrait of St. Agnes. Handsomely bound 1 1 0